Mad wizards wrenc  ell
on Eotrus land. A to stay open. ed

What is the young knight, Claradon Eotrus, to do when he discovers that the man he recruited to help him close that gateway is either the greatest hero the world has ever known or the devil himself, thrown down from the heavens by the gods in olden days? Is he out to save Midgaard or destroy it? Does he serve the Norse gods: Odin, Thor, and the rest, or did he slay them? And if he's truly the harbinger of doom, how can Claradon stop him? How can he even survive him?

Claradon's Midgaard is a world filled of valiant knights, mysterious sorcerers, ruthless bounty hunters, complex political intrigues, monsters of myth and legend: the undead of this variety and that, gods and demons, and otherworldly evils so frightening you dare not read these books before sleep. But most of all, it's filled with stories that you will always remember, and characters that you will never forget.

PRAISE FOR GLENN G. THATER'S HARBINGER OF DOOM SAGA

"...a masterfully crafted epic fantasy about the ages old struggle between good and evil."
--- Carol Marrs Phipps, author of Elf Killers

"Thater is one of the most talented and exciting authors of our time. He is right up there with Tolkien, maybe even better. His unique writing technique leaves you pondering what is going to happen next and yearning for more." — a Google Play reviewer

"...a must read for all fans of classic sword and sorcery. A blend of Howard, Moorcock, Wagner, with a twist of Lovecraft. Well written and hugely entertaining."
--- An Amazon reviewer

"For a long time I have searched for a fantasy worthy of Lord of The Rings and I have found it!"
--- An Amazon Reviewer

"From page to page Thater weaves a tale so thoroughly explicit you feel like you're more than an observer." --- An Amazon Reviewer

"A fantastic mix of Norse and Middle eastern mythology held together by an epic tale."

"Absolutely the best action medieval books that I have read since the Lord of the Rings series..."

"Pulls no punches in describing the horror of war..."

"One of the best book series ever!!!"

HARBINGER OF DOOM
(VOLUMES 1 - 3)
BY
GLENN G. THATER
Tales from the Harbinger of Doom Saga

ISBN-13:9781717740663

Visit Glenn G. Thater's website at
http://www.glenngthater.com

July 2018 Print Edition

GATEWAY TO NIFLEHEIM

BY

GLENN G. THATER

Volume 1of the Harbinger of Doom Saga

"You will not thwart us again, Harbinger of Doom.
We will have this world this time.
What once was ours will be ours again."
—Bhaal, Lord of Nifleheim, to Angle Theta

PREFACE

Gateway to Nifleheim is the first story in a new collection of the adventures of the ancient warrior-hero most commonly called Angle Theta. Although the original, historical manuscripts that detail the life and times of this classic warrior remain unavailable to the general public, my contacts and travels have afforded me rare opportunities to study and duplicate some of the source material, which consists of more than ten thousand documents stored in protected archives at leading museums and universities scattered across seven countries.

Due to the inaccessibility of these documents, few modern scholars or authors are familiar with the "Thetian manuscripts." Consequently, the public knows little or nothing about this ancient hero, who some scholars believe helped shape much of the ancient world and perhaps was the historical inspiration for the legends of Beowulf, Gilgamesh, and others.

Until now, no scholar has attempted a detailed compilation of the entire Angle Theta saga, although several notable works that contain Thetian stories have been penned through the centuries. Grenville's work, *Ancient Warriors of Scandinavia* (1884), and Addleson's, *Lost Cities of Prehistoric Europe* (1921), each contain several stories of Theta's exploits. *The Warlords* (1408), by Chuan Chien contains two tales of Theta's adventures in Asia during the Neolithic Age. Although there is no complete English translation of Chien's text, the accounts contained therein provide independent evidence of the existence of Theta as a historical figure. The essay, *Forgotten Empires* by Charles Sawyer (1754), and Da Vinci's manuscript, *Of Prehistory* (1502), also contain story fragments and references to the *historical Theta*. The voluminous treatise, *Prehistoric* Cities of Europe and the Near East, by Cantor (1928), presents noteworthy, though inconclusive evidence of the historical existence of the city of Lomion in what is now southwestern England.

Despite the robust written record, some modern scholars dispute the historical accuracy of the Thetian manuscripts due to the limited corroborating archeological evidence for the ancient cities and cultures detailed therein. Thus, they relegate Theta to the realms of myth, legend, and allegory. Others maintain that the scholarly texts mentioned above, coupled with the original archived manuscripts, are sufficient evidence to verify the historical existence of Theta, the man. One can only hope that in time the archeological record will further reinforce this position.

Several years ago while researching Theta for a story that I planned to write, I had the good fortune to meet and begin a long-standing collaboration with several leading Thetian scholars, most notably, Professor Augustine DiPipcorno of the University of Padua, and Dr. Ann Lewis of Indiana University, who have for many years been actively translating the entire body of available original manuscripts. These professors lead a multidisciplinary team that is preparing a series of detailed scholarly texts that include all the original Thetian tales, supplemented with extensive commentary and a thorough critique of the corroborating scholarly, historical, literary, and archeological evidence.

Using the professors' translations as my primary source material, I re-envisioned the first volume of their work into modern prose and added additional dialogue and descriptive language to make the Thetian stories more accessible and entertaining to the typical reader. That resulted in a novella length work entitled, *The Gateway*, which was published in 2008.

In 2011, "Thetian" scholars were shocked to learn that the traditional Gateway story is actually a significantly shortened version of the complete tale, the only known copy of which was discovered in near pristine condition that year in the Ashmolean Museum archives in Oxford. The Ashmolean's thirteenth-century vellum copy, written in Old Norse, contains an impressive array of additional detail about Midgaard's Land of Lomion and augments the Gateway story with new action-packed battles and additional scenes that flesh out the backgrounds of some of the Saga's most beloved characters. The discovery and translation of the Ashmolean vellum inspired me to revise and expand The Gateway into the work you are now reading. To distinguish between the two versions of the tale, I chose to give the longer version a different title: hence, Gateway to Nifleheim was born.

Interestingly, the Ashmolean vellum doesn't contain the Gateway story's epilogue, further reinforcing the long held suspicion of the

the stump was strapped a metal and wooden contraption to which various attachments could be affixed. With practiced ease, he fitted it with a long dagger's blade pulled from its slot on his crowded belt where were hung myriad tools, gadgets, and weapons. His brow furrowed as he looked back and forth from his liege to the mist that lurked before them. "It must be trolls, down from the high mountains. First time in generations that we've seen them, but it has to be them. Nothing else wails like that."

"I should've heeded my instincts," said Eotrus, though he seemed to be speaking to himself; his voice, quiet; his eyes still upraised to the midnight sky. "I should never have ridden out here, not with so few, not at night. What a fool I am, and now we'll all suffer for it."

The distant wailing grew ever louder and more frantic.

"I don't know what's out there," said Talbon as he stared into the mist. "But it's not trolls, of that I'm certain. I've heard their calls a time or two, and they are nothing like this. Nothing I've ever heard is like this."

"Gabriel would know what's out there," said Donnelin. "Ob probably would too."

"Well, they're not here," said Talbon. "Gabe is probably off polishing his medals, and Ob is dead drunk by this hour, leaving us to sort out this mess, as is usual."

"If not trolls, then what?" said Donnelin, a sharpness to his voice.

Lord Eotrus turned back toward his men. "Nothing of Midgaard, my good priest," he said in

13

an even tone. "Nothing born of this world."

A hiss passed through Talbon's lips.

"What say you?" said Donnelin to Eotrus. "I miss your meaning."

"The icy cold, the lightheadedness and nausea that afflicts us since came the mist," said Talbon. "It's no coincidence that the wailing began soon after that started. This business stinks of sorcery, dark and deep. If my head wasn't spinning, and my stomach not churning, I would have seen it from the first. Maybe I did see it, and didn't want to believe it, but now I do. Aradon speaks the truth. It's chaos magic—the stuff of Nifleheim. A maelstrom of it, and we've stumbled into its maw."

"No," said Donnelin as he sharply shook his head. "I won't believe that. That's rubbish. This is just swamp gas, and out there are a band of trolls, or an animal pack down from the North, that's all. Who knows what lurks up in those mountains, way back deep, farther than we ever go. There could be anything in there. Lions, panthers, or who knows what. It's nothing more than that. It doesn't need to be something—unnatural. It can't be. Not again, for Odin's sake," he said, glancing down at his stump. "What you're spouting is nothing but rubbish."

"Then make ready your basket and broom," said Talbon, "for it sounds as if rubbish is headed this way."

Lord Eotrus's gaze drifted up again and lingered on the midnight sky until he let out an anguished sigh. When next he spoke, his voice was somber, his eyes clear and sound. "More than forty campaigns we've weathered together and never once tasted defeat, but this, my friends, be the last. This night marks the end of our long road. Ironic that after all our adventures, we meet our end on our own lands. But such, it seems, be our fate. Valhalla beckons. Our path is clear."

"What are you saying?" said Donnelin, surprise and worry filling his face. "We haven't even seen them yet, and you have us dead? We're not that old, you know. There is some fight yet left in us and swords aplenty to back us," he said, gesturing toward the troops.

"Do not lose heart, Aradon," said Talbon, "or in peril, we'll truly be. We will see this through, just as we always have. Chaos magic or not, I will send them screaming back down whatever hole they crawled up from."

"Not this time," said Eotrus. "Can't you see what is above us?" he said as he gestured toward the sky.

The priest and the wizard gazed upward. "I see naught but the heavens," said Donnelin, his hands tightly gripped around the holy symbol that hung about his neck, his knuckles white. "And barely that through the mist."

"An apt choice of words," said Eotrus, "for above us, the sword maidens gather. Our time on Midgaard has reached its end, old friend. Soon they will carry us home. We will drink tonight in Valhalla amongst the honored dead."

"Valkyries?" said Donnelin, a shocked expression on his face. "Is that of what you speak?"

"Aye."

"What madness has taken you, Aradon?" said Donnelin. "There are no Valkyries. They are but stories and legend. Nothing more."

"The pious priest to the end," said Talbon.

"I thought I would have more time," said Eotrus quietly. "Thank Odin the boys aren't here. Gabriel and Ob should be with us, here at the end, but perhaps it's best that they're not. My boys will be alone in the world now—except for them. The walls of the Dor are high and strong. They've never been breached. Our folk may yet have time to mount a defense. That will give my sons a chance. By Odin, they must have that chance; I must give them that at least. All may not yet be lost if the breach be small and if few make it through. Gabriel would know better what to do. He should have told me more; I pray that he told me enough. We must stem the tide and close the gap, though it cost us all our lives. What nobler purpose could any man aspire to? We will do our fathers proud before we breathe our last."

"I don't understand what you're saying," said Donnelin. "You're not making any sense, but Valhalla can wait. I say we stop them here, whatever they are, and drink tonight in Dor Eotrus as is our place."

"If this enemy be as deadly as you imply," said Talbon. "Let us flee while we yet can. They're still a ways off. We can make it back to the Dor and prepare the defenses. As you said, the walls are strong."

"We can't run fast enough," said Eotrus. "Not from what's coming."

"Not even on horse?" said Talbon.

the foul odor. To his right, he saw Talbon. He wasn't burned like the others, but he lay still, his eyes closed, his horse dead atop him, smoking and charred.

Donnelin swayed where he stood, unsteady on his feet. He prayed that he was trapped in a fevered nightmare—some figment of his imagination, or even the onset of madness. Anything that made it not real. He started and nearly fell over when Lord Eotrus shouted, "Get up!"

Donnelin turned and saw the old lord pull himself to his feet. Eotrus nearly dragged his stunned horse up with him. "Get up," he roared, "they're not done with us yet, nor we with them. Make ready, men."

Dazed as he was, those words pulled Donnelin back to reality. He knew where he was. He knew it was real, there was no escaping that, but he didn't grasp the meaning of Eotrus's words until he noted the sound. The wailing. It was still there. It had been all along, though somehow Donnelin hadn't noticed it. It was distant, as it had been minutes before, but with each passing moment, it grew louder, and they grew closer. Those things. Those things from the mist. "Dead gods," he said. "What in the nine worlds were they? There can't be more of them. There can't be."

Donnelin looked about in a panic and assessed the situation. The entire company had been thrown to the dirt, man and horse alike. Battered, bruised, and bleeding, all but one or two, not counting the wizards, still lived. The dead, taken by shrapnel lodged in their heads.

Could they ride out? Were the horses able? Did they have enough time? Yes, they could. He was certain of it, but they had little time to spare. He tried not to think of what had charged out of the mist, but the image of those things was burned forever into his mind's eye. He knew Talbon's magic had killed untold numbers of them. It had to have. The wizards' sacrifice had not won the day, but it bought the rest of the company time— the time they needed to withdraw, and to live to fight another day.

"Ready yourselves," boomed Lord Eotrus. "Get to your feet, men."

Those who could followed his commands.

"Aradon," shouted Donnelin. "We must flee. For Odin's sake, we cannot stop what is out there."

Eotrus turned his head toward his old friend. Blood streamed from his nose and from gashes in his cheek and forehead. "We will hold them here."

"That is madness," said Donnelin. "Our best magic is spent and swords will not win the day. Not against those things. We must flee."

"A man cannot outrun his fate," said Eotrus before he turned back toward the sounds. "Though I would think no less of any man that tried."

The soldiers formed up around their lord and pressed close into a tight wedge. Their faces carried a mixture of shock, fear, anger, pain, and disbelief.

"Eotrus!" burst from the old lord's throat as he spurred his horse and charged forward to meet his fate, his sword held out before him, his horse mad with fear. His soldiers followed him, as they always followed him, one last time, into the very mouth of hell.

Talbon's eyes opened and he shuddered as he regained consciousness. His skin felt afire from head to toe, muscles twitched and cramped up all over his body, and his hair stood on end. His legs were pinned beneath his horse. He could barely see, the smoke and mist so thick about him. His nose stung from a pungent, bestial odor like that of a slaughterhouse. His hand found his staff, which mercifully had fallen just beside him. He looked around and nearly panicked when he realized that he was alone but for two corpses. Two Eotrus soldiers, dead, who knows how, laid in the dirt not far away. Though he knew each man in the company, from his vantage point, he couldn't name them, nor did he have any idea what had befallen his apprentices, or the others. They were all gone. They had left him for dead. He needed to find them, but he knew better than to call out and give away his position. He squirmed and struggled, as quietly as he could, until he freed himself from the horse—his legs bruised and numb, but not broken.

The wailing had stopped sometime before he awoke, but an eerie sound persisted and frayed his nerves. Talbon's every instinct told him to flee as fast as he could and not look back. But which way to go? The low rumbling sound that assailed him came from all directions, and it was slowly getting louder, closer. Then he realized what it was he heard: breathing.

Dead gods, they were all around him, lurking in the dark just beyond his vision. He couldn't see them no matter how hard he strained, but they were there. He smelled them. He heard their breathing and their rustling about in the dark like giant rodents. By the gods, Aradon was right: this time, there would be no escape. There was no way out, no direction to run. This was the end. Why they hadn't finished him as he lay unconscious, he couldn't fathom, but he would make them regret that decision.

He pulled himself to his feet, his head pounding. He realized that the others must have charged unto their deaths. He was the last. "So a warrior's death it will be," he whispered. "So be it. I will make my father proud, in this at least. To victory and Valhalla." Then he spoke in his loudest voice. "You will not feast on the flesh of an archmage of Lomion today, creatures. Feel the wrath of Par Talbon, son of Mardack, of the ancient line of Montrose." The tip of the wizard's staff began to glow and a beacon of light burst forth from it in all directions. It drove back the smoke, mist, and the darkness, and revealed the unspeakable horde that encircled him not ten yards out.

As the beasts charged screeching and roaring, Talbon grinned, and spoke but one word in the old tongue as he used all his strength to break his arcane staff across his knee. The ancient staff exploded—a magical blast the likes of which Midgaard had not seen in an age. Leagues away, the mighty walls of Dor Eotrus shook.

II
THE OUTER DOR

A group of armed men on horseback slowly rode through the sprawling, moonlit streets of the Outer Dor—the town that surrounded the citadel called Dor Eotrus. Though bundled against the night air, their accoutrements and bearing marked them as more than mundane passersby to those few citizens out and about despite the late hour.

One of the lead riders was diminutive, the size of a young child, though his gravelly voice and wrinkled face marked him as the oldest of the group by many years. Beside him loomed a glinty-armored leviathan of a knight known as Angle Theta. Next came Sir Ector, a young knight of more pedestrian proportions, and Dolan Silk, a wiry man of sickly pallor and strange ears. Behind them rode several soldiers dressed in the blue and gold livery of House Eotrus.

"Like a good baker's belly, the Outer Dor grows a bit every year whether we like it or not," said Ob, the tiny man, to Theta. "For generations, the town got on fine with two walls, the inner being a good bit taller than the outer, as it should be—you'll see when we get there. Solid the walls are—granite and mortar, cut into blocks big as a wagon. Smooth and plumb even after all these years. You don't see that kind of workmanship anymore; almost certainly Gnomish." Ob uncorked his wineskin, lifted it to his lips, and took a generous drink.

"Ten years ago, we put up a third wall a good ways out. Not as stout and fancy as the old two, but solid enough to stop what don't belong. We figured that gave the folks room enough for growth, good pastry notwithstanding. But only three stinking years later, we were bursting at the seams with new folk, and they set to building outside the walls again."

Theta looked at the well-ordered rows of wooden buildings and gravel covered streets that extended well beyond the outermost wall. "They've been busy," he said in an accent that was difficult to place, save to say that it was foreign.

"Most show up on our doorstep and set straight away to building," said Ob. "At least they're not slackers, not most of them anyways, and they've kept our carpenters well fed these past few years."

"From where do they come?" said Theta. "And what attracts them?"

"Some come from the east, out towards Kern, but most are from down south around Lomion City."

"My father says most seek a quieter life away from the big cities," said Ector, "but some others want a bit of adventure."

"Which do they find here?" said Theta.

"It's not the quiet or the adventure," said Ob. "Freedom is why they come here. Some folks think the council has gone a bit oppressive these last years, so they set out chasing greener pastures, and some of them end up hereabouts. You see we got the freedom up here in the North, away from the big cities and the stinking bureaucrats. Here a man can live as he wants, so long as he leaves others to do the same. That's the way we like it. That's the way it has always been around here, and that's the way it's always going to be, as long as there's an Eotrus in charge."

"Freedom has ever been a magnet," said Theta. "But it's also a target."

"Well, freedom for these pilgrims means me and mine gotta ride through muck and mud every time we leave the Dor," said Ob. "Within the walls, there are cobblestones on every street—solid stuff, like any civilized place has. You can walk about and not get mud all over you—not like out here in this pigsty. The worst of it is, there are no sewers out here, so the whole place stinks and never stops stinking, not even in the deep winter. The lighting is spotty and the well water is suspect. The buildings are all wood, even the foundations, instead of honest stone like most everywhere within the walls. The whole place is just not civilized, if you ask me. Our own fault, I suppose, letting folks do as they will. But if they want to live like this, they should go live in the woods. At least out there it don't stink."

"The buildings look solid and well kept—permanent construction," said Theta. "This is no nomad camp or shantytown. The streets are straight and level. There's no garbage lying about. And no beggars. Most towns aren't half as good."

"Aye, that might be true enough," said Ob. "But it's not up to Eotrus standards all the same. We should've built another wall. My mistake it was. Aradon wanted to, but I talked him out of it.

I figured that rather than waste good stone and sweat and a heap of silver on more masonry, we would tell the folks that anyone what wants to build outside is on their own come trouble. I figured that would put the fear in them, since folks don't care to see to themselves, all lonesome like, when things go bad. But it didn't work. I'm not ashamed to admit when I'm wrong. That's the Gnome way, you know."

"Must not get much trouble around these parts," said Dolan, who also spoke with an accent, though different from Theta's, "or them folks would've heeded your warnings, they would have."

Ob looked over his shoulder at Dolan, eyebrows raised. "Dor Eotrus guards Lomion's northern border, sonny. We're on the edge of the wild out here, so believe me, we get our share of trouble, time and again. It comes down from the mountains, more often than not," he said, pointing at the white-capped peaks in the distance. "There's no civilization out that way, my friend. None at all. All a man will find in the deep mountains is death. Sometimes quick, sometimes slow. Whatever trouble what comes this way, whether from the mountains or not, it's we Eotrus that stop it cold, and protect the realm, as is our duty. Most of the time, it's Lugron, there's a mess of them up in the hills, in caves and such; bandits every once in a while; a man-eater: wolf, lion, or bear, now and again. In years past, we had trolls down on us too, but they've not been seen in numbers in a Gnome's age. Every once in a long while, something worse comes down from the north, with the cold and the dark and the mist; things held over from the old world, maybe even back to *The Dawn Age*; stuff best not spoken of, not even here, not even amongst men like us. And if you go up in them mountains, and none of them things kill you, the cold will. You've never felt cold, real cold, until you spend a night high up one of them peaks. First, it will freeze your bones solid so that you can hardly move. Then it will freeze the blood in your veins; no man survives that, tough or not."

"I guess we'll stay clear of the mountains," said Dolan. "With all those dangers that come down this way, why do folks build outside the walls?"

"Some folks' memories aren't long enough for their own good," said Ob. "Or else they're just stupid."

"Common afflictions, both," said Theta.

"Aye," said Ob. "Your manservant speaks his mind," he said, referring to Dolan.

"Every man should," said Theta. "Not that he has much to say."

"Not much at all," said Dolan. "I'm practically mute, I am."

"Sometimes them what says the least, says the most," said Ob."

Theta smiled. "Another truth."

"If the folks out hereabouts aren't afraid of much," said Dolan, "why do they flee us?"

"What do you mean?" said Ob.

"People have been blowing out their candles, pulling their curtains, and closing their shutters all up and down the street since we rode into sight,"

29

said Ector. "And those few folks still out, scampered inside at the first sight of us."

Ob stopped his horse and looked around for some moments. "Good eyes, lad. You're right. Something's not right here. It's too quiet. I should've been paying better heed. Let's make haste to the gate and see what's what."

The group rode at a trot to the raised portcullis that stood at an opening in the outer wall.

"The guard has been doubled," said Ector.

"Tripled," said Ob. "And there be crossbowmen up on the allures. There's been trouble for certain."

Apparently recognizing Ob, the guards moved aside, bowed respectfully, and waved them through. Ob pulled up his horse, stopping a few feet from the nearest guard. "What trouble?" he said.

The young blond-haired man looked uncertain and turned to his fellows for support, but they were busy staring at their boots.

"Speak, you dolt," said Ob. "What goes on here? Why have we got so many men on the wall?"

"A patrol has gone missing, Castellan," said the guard.

Theta raised an eyebrow at that.

Ob paused for a moment and stared at the guard, but the man offered nothing more. Ob turned toward his companions. "Let's get to the citadel. There is more to this than just some overdue patrol and I aim to get to the bottom of it, and quick."

"You didn't tell us that you were the governor

of this keep," said Theta.

"You didn't ask," said Ob. "But I'm no governor, anyhow. I'm the Castellan of Dor Eotrus, as that fool said—though I suppose, it is much the same thing."

"You had me fooled, you did," said Dolan. "I figured Mr. Ector was the captain of your patrol, and that you were his chief scout."

"That's what we wanted you to think," said Ob. "The roads can be dangerous these days, even for the likes of us, so we don't always reveal who is who when we come upon strangers on the road, especially if they're stinking foreigners. No offense. But since you've now taken an interest and we've made it safe and sound to the Dor, I'll tell you that Ector is Lord Eotrus's son. The gatemen were bowing to him, not me. I don't go in for that treatment and they know it. Now let's move."

III
THE WAILING

Angry wood screamed as the stairwell door burst open. Startled, Brother Claradon Eotrus's hand went to his sword hilt as several figures raced through the portal onto the tower's roof. Standing beside Claradon, Par Tanch spun toward the new arrivals in a panic. Death flared in his eyes and blue fire licked the apex of his staff, but the wizard's aspect softened and he lowered his ensorcelled weapon at the sight of Sir Ector Eotrus's haggard face. At the young nobleman's heels were Ob, Theta, and Dolan.

Ector, clad in a heavy cloak over combat armor, silver and polished, approached his older brother and Tanch, Ob following, while Theta strode past them to the crenellated parapet, and Dolan disappeared into the shadows by the stairwell's bulkhead. Enshrouded in a midnight blue cloak, Theta stood silent and transfixed, gazing westward through the starlight at the Vermion Forest, his hand curiously cupped behind his ear as if listening for something.

"Thank the gods you've returned," said Par Tanch, though his gaze was affixed on the mammoth figure at the parapet—a man heretofore unknown to him. "We were afraid you hadn't got our message."

"We got no message," said Ob. "What's going on? Your delicate back acting up again? Or did you lose your slippers?"

"We heard a patrol disappeared," said Ector.

"Tell me what has happened," said Ob. "And don't waste my time with any of your blubbering. I want the facts, plain and simple."

Tanch ignored them and continued to stare at Theta. Claradon, who was taller and broader than his brother, and in truth, looked little like him, avoided his gaze and looked at Tanch, apparently determined that the wizard should answer and not he.

"I'm talking to you man," shouted Ob. "Tanch!"

Tanch turned back toward them, an inscrutable expression on his face.

"Where is father?" said Ector. "Where are Sir Gabriel, Brother Donnelin, and the others?"

"Oh it's dreadful, Master Ector, just dreadful," said Tanch. "Your father has gone missing."

"They're all missing," blurted Claradon. "Father, Brother Donnelin, Par Talbon, and all the rangers rode into the Vermion on patrol two days ago and haven't returned. There's been no word, no word at all."

Ector's face blanched. His mouth agape—he was too stunned to speak.

"Stop shouting," said Theta, his eyes never straying from the distant wood as one hand gestured to quiet the others, the other remained cupped behind his ear.

"And Sir Gabriel is in the mountains somewhere," said Claradon more quietly this time as he glanced back toward Theta.

"A hunting trip," said Tanch. "Can you believe that? We're in the midst of a major crisis and he went off hunting."

"Master Ector, who in Odin's name is that?" said Tanch, pointing at Theta. "And where did the other one go?" he said, as he looked about for Dolan. "I'm sure that I saw someone else with you—some scrawny fellow."

"We've got to find out what happened to father," said Claradon. "Tanch and I have been debating all day about what to do and we've gotten nowhere."

"I'll certainly not stand here whilst my father lies dead or dying or worse," said Ector. "We must fly. We should scour the Vermion until we find him."

"Zounds," said Ob, "I'm with Ector on this. What are we waiting for? Let's move." Ob turned back toward the stairwell, then froze. He cocked his head to the side and his prodigious ears twitched up and down in strange fashion, as the pointy ears of Gnomes are sometimes wont to do. "What the heck is that racket? That don't sound right natural to me."

"Everyone stay silent," Ob said, as he gestured the same command, and moved toward the parapet. He planted himself at a spot a few feet from Theta, which happened to be the only place where he could see over the wall, for that spot, in what was otherwise a meticulously maintained structure, still bore the scars of a trebuchet shot that struck the tower some 400 years earlier.

Tanch turned toward the parapet and fixed his gaze on the distant wood. "Oh no, not again," he said. "For Odin's sake, please don't let it start again. I'll not be able to stand another night of it."

"Can you hear it?" said Ob to no one in

particular.

"Hear what?" said Ector as he looked around, confused.

"The wailing," said Claradon. "Please don't tell me that it started again."

"Can't you hear it?" said Ob. "It is getting louder by the moment."

"We don't all have Gnome ears, you know," said Claradon.

"You Volsungs are as deaf as doornails," said Ob. "Even so, you will hear it soon enough if it keeps getting louder. It's coming from the wood."

"Gods preserve us," said Tanch. "We're doomed."

IV
THE WAR ROOM

Frantic servants scrambled hither and fro, securing the war room's storm shutters, while others rushed in carrying thick draperies, pillows, and great tapestries. Some of the new arrivals looked confused as to what to do, still half asleep, having been roused from their beds when the wailing began.

"Stuff the pillows against the glass, you dolts," yelled Ob, "and get those draperies hung fast. Double them up—no, triple them. Cover every window, and seal them tight. We've got to block out that stinking noise."

A nervous servant's stray elbow dislodged one of the House pennants hung high on the wall. The old flag, stiffened with age, drifted slowly toward the floor. The offending servant, one Adolphus, newly appointed to House Eotrus's service, dived from his stepstool to catch it, for he knew that if it hit the floor it would be regarded as a grave insult to the House.

Adolphus nearly grabbed it in time, but one corner of the fabric brushed the floor's stone tile before he scooped it up. As he rose, he looked fearfully around to see if anyone had noticed. Several servants had, but pretended they hadn't. Ob, however, stared directly at him, a scowl on his face.

Adolphus froze and went white as a sheet. Of all people to see his misstep—the Dor's own

Castellan, second-in-command to the great Lord Aradon himself. Adolphus looked as if he might faint, or vomit, or both. The terror on his face was real and palpable for he knew that he would be whipped at the very least—15 lashes, no less, for that was the minimum penalty for such a slight. More likely, the Eotrus would throw him in a subterranean cell to rot—to waste away with little food or water and not a glimpse of sunlight for a year or more. They might even forget about him down there and he'd die of thirst. When you insult a noble house, that's what they do to you, and everyone knows it. A servant's life isn't worth much—they might even kill him outright to save the trouble and expense of dungeoning him. He prayed that they weren't the sort that would torture him first—but he had heard rumors about the Eotrus. Frightful rumors.

It wasn't fair or just, but it was the way of things. He'd seen it happen before at other Houses, and now it was his turn. His time had come. He thought of running, but knew there was no point. They would be on him in moments, and even if he escaped the keep, they would chase him down with horses and hounds. The noblemen were relentless in their vengeance. It was a sport to them. He was finished and he knew it. One tiny mistake, one momentary slip, and now his life was over. He would never see his family again, and they may never know the truth of what became of him. He closed his eyes and steeled himself to his fate. Maybe it would be quick.

"Don't just stand there," yelled Ob. "Put it back up, you fool."

Adolphus was numb with shock. For several moments, try as he might, he couldn't move, he couldn't even think. Was the Castellan going to let him live?

"We're the Eotrus, you moron, not the Alders, the Tavermains, or the Grondeers—there will be no floggings or flayings here. We have no racks or spikes or thumbscrews. Just put the pennant back and hang the darned curtains already. We don't have all stinking night. Now move it!"

Still in a daze, Adolphus scrambled up the stepstool, pennant in hand, and restored it to its rightful place.

The fact that only one of the walls' adornments fell, was a testament to the servants' care, despite the frantic speed at which they toiled, for the war room's stone walls were covered throughout, floor molding to crown, with historic pennants, banners, and flags, and battle tested shields, daggers, and swords, all handed down through the Eotrus line, and hung in places of honor, each with its own plaque or inscription memorializing its history and pedigree.

Ob drained the last swallow from his wineskin and tossed it down in frustration. "My head will explode if we don't keep that darned wailing out. Move it, you slackers. And somebody bring me wine, for Odin's sake," his voice growing louder with each remark. "Would you have me die of thirst? Then where would you fools be? In the deep stuff, I'll tell you—that's where. It's the cool head of a Gnome that you want in charge in times like these."

Ector stepped beside him, heavy cloth tightly

wrapped around his head, covering his ears. "Maybe we ought to hold our council in the Underhalls. Loud as it is, I doubt this noise will reach below ground."

"No," said Ob.

"But we may be wasting time here; if we're not able to block out enough of the sound, we'll have to move below anyway—maybe it's best we do so now."

"Never," said Ob through gritted teeth. "The Eotrus do our planning here—that's what the war room is for. That's why we built it. Your father and I plan whatever needs planning here, your grandfather before him, his father before that, and back for hundreds of years. We'll not be chased from here by some stinking noise." He turned toward two servants struggling with a heavy tapestry. "Get them up, you slackers. We'll quiet it down, you'll see—those old draperies will cut the sound by half at least. I knew we would find a use for them someday, that's why I had them stored. Throw nothing out, I always say, for you never know when you will need it. That's the Gnome way, you know."

"You're a hoarder Ob, and we all know it. You're not fooling anyone," said Ector, though Ob provided no reaction, but for some reason turned toward the door.

"Your brother is finally back," said Ob.

Moments later, Claradon dashed into the room and made his way over to Ob and Ector, his cloak's hood up and pulled tight around his face to dampen the sounds. "Everyone is taking refuge in the Underhalls, as we agreed," he said. "Why are

39

you still up here?"

"Because I said so, boy," said Ob. "And we're staying."

Claradon rolled his eyes.

"How fare our defenses?" said Ob.

"All the gates are secured, but only a handful of men are at their posts," said Claradon. "Most are holed up in whatever nearby rooms have no windows. The wax is on its way to all the guard posts and towers. In the meantime, the walls are thick enough to keep out the worst of the noise—it's the windows that are the real problem."

"We noticed," said Ector.

"So we're near deaf and blind with enemies afoot," said Ob. "Not good at all. We've got to get men back up on the walls."

"Within a half hour at most, they will all get the wax," said Claradon. "I sent it to the main gate first."

"You didn't leave it to servants, did you?" said Ob.

"I gave Artol, Marzdan, and Glimador the duty," said Claradon.

"Good man," said Ob, nodding. "Those three will get the walls manned as quick as can be. Knowing they're on it, makes me feel a good deal better, it does."

"What of the folks in the Outer Dor?" said Ector.

"Heading for their basements and root cellars, same as last night," said Claradon. "They should be alright, so long as the wailing doesn't get much louder."

"Good, but those fools out beyond the outer

wall have nowhere to hide," said Ob. "Their wood buildings got no basements. I told them not to build out there. Nobody ever listens. Serves them right, whatever happens."

"Hopefully, they will have sense enough to seek refuge within the walls," said Ector.

"Many of them already have," said Claradon. "Marzdan says they came in by droves as soon as the wailing started, some even before, as they expected the sounds to start up again tonight. We should have expected it too. We should have been better prepared. I'm sorry—I just didn't think things through."

"Don't worry, boy," said Ob. "You did just fine; nobody could have asked more of you."

Claradon nodded. "Is Lord Theta still on the roof?"

"Aye," said Ob. "And his servant too. Them two don't seem to mind the noise. They must be even deafer than the rest of you."

"And where's Tanch?" said Claradon as he glanced around the room.

"Last I saw, he was lying on the map closet's floor, moaning and whimpering, hands over his ears," said Ob. "You can barely hear the noise back there, and he's still out of commission. Useless, that one. Always has been. Don't know why you keep him underfoot," he said to Claradon, who ignored him.

"What do we do now?" said Claradon, wringing his hands, his nerves now catching up to him.

"We set a plan," said Ob, "and pray to Odin that they don't attack before we get the walls manned."

"The sounds are loud, but they're still far off," said Claradon. "Whatever they are, I think they're still deep in the Vermion somewhere."

"I agree," said Ob. "The Dor is safe for tonight, I think, but maybe not tomorrow. Either way, we've got to be ready for whatever comes."

"I can't believe this," said Claradon. "Father is missing and now we may find ourselves under siege. And by whom or what? What in Odin's name is out there?"

"I don't know, boy," said Ob as he gripped Claradon's arm. "We will deal with them, whatever they are. Don't lose heart."

Claradon began to pace back and forth, from one side of the war room to the other. A vacant expression filled his face and sweat beaded on his brow.

When the sound muffling operations were completed, the servants quickly cleaned up whatever detritus had fallen to the floor and prepared the room for its intended purpose. The hickory and applewood they fed the stone hearths at each end of the hall lent the war room its characteristic, pleasant, if smoky, scent and brought it up to a more comfortable temperature. Two servants dropped wax into an old cast-iron pot and placed it on an iron cooking rack in one of the hearths to soften.

The ponderous old oaken table that dominated the room was scarred, gouged, and infilled here and there with wood filler, yet it was waxed and polished to a shine, and clean enough to eat from. No one knew how long it resided in the Dor's war room, though its tenure was certainly measured in centuries, not decades. The heavy oaken chairs that surrounded it were equally worn and meticulously cared for. Their thick, leather-covered seat cushions were no contemporaries of the wood, having been replaced time and again over the years as the need arose. The Eotrus assembled around the table, each taking their customary seats, though most of the chairs stood vacant. Theta and Dolan joined them in council.

Ob climbed the short ladder affixed to the chair that Brother Donnelin had made for him and plopped down into the seat, his chainmail armor clanking against the hardwood. The finely crafted mahogany chair didn't quite match the rest of the set and was so tall that when the old Gnome sat in it, his head was nearly level with those of the others. A servant passed him a small bowl filled of the softened wax from which he plucked a finger full to stop up his ears. "Don't much need it now that the windows are covered, but it can't hurt." He rolled the warm wax into a shape that would fit his ears and pushed it in place. "That's much better," he said with a broad smile on his face. "Now I can think straight again. Claradon, me boy, it's time that you tell me all that you know of your father, and of this foul wailing, and pray speak quickly; far too much time has been wasted already. Gob up your ears with a slab of this stuff so your head will be on straight, then start your telling."

Claradon made use of the wax, but continued pacing behind his chair, ignoring Ob, who shook his head in frustration, but gave the lad some time, meanwhile, focusing on downing another

43

flagon of wine. Claradon paused his pacing only to doff his heavy cloak, which was no longer needed for warmth or to muffle the sounds. He hung it over the back of his chair, to the right of the table's head—the spot reserved for his father. Beneath his cloak, the white shirt that he wore was emblazoned with symbols of Odin, the father of the gods. The silver medallion that hung about his neck bore the same symbols etched into the base metal.

Dolan found a seat, promptly leaned back, and put his boots up on the table's edge, seemingly heedless of the skirling sounds that still found their way inside. He even waved the wax bowl away when a servant tried to pass it to him.

Ector and Tanch sat to Dolan's right, and made use of the wax in turn. Tanch alternated between laying his head on the table and moaning, and sitting up with his hands over his ears and his eyes tightly shut. Though Tanch was a wizard, he looked and acted little like those of song, story, and legend. He wore no pointy hat and carried no wand. He had no beard or rumpled robes like the charlatans of the bizarre. Instead, his clothes fit the style of a minor nobleman or merchant. He was well-groomed, but rather nondescript, save for his sandy blond hair, unusual for a northerner, and his height, which was a few inches more than average. Despite his complaints of this ailment or that, he was still well in his prime. The circlet he wore about his forehead was his one concession to his esoteric profession, and marked him as a wizard of the Tower of the Arcane to all but the most sheltered and naive.

Before taking the seat across from Dolan, Lord Theta propped his massive battle shield against the wall. The old shield was sorely battered from untold battles, yet so highly burnished was its surface, much to Dolan's credit, that one could clearly see their reflection within its depths.

A disheveled servant ran into the room. "Master Claradon, Sir Gabriel has returned. He's on his way up."

V
FRIEND OF OLD TIMES

Claradon sighed in relief, as if a great weight lifted from his shoulders. He found a seat near the table's head, and took a sip of wine as he fidgeted, first slouching back into his seat and then sitting upright and stiff. His breathing was quick; he was sweating and pale.

"Thank the gods," said Tanch, perking up. "Sir Gabriel will know what to do. He will clear up this troubling business. Then we can get things back to normal again. In a few days, we will be laughing about how silly we were to get so worried about this odd wailing—you mark my words."

Soon they heard Gabriel's strong, clear voice shouting from down the hallway.

"Can't I leave you people alone for even a few days without all hell breaking loose? My first darned hunting trip all season and now it's ruined. For what, I ask you? Did someone stub their big toe? Or did a bird fly down the chimney and send you all scurrying to the cupboards? Where are Aradon and the boys? What the heck is going on? And what is this cursed din? Someone answer me, for Odin's sake."

Guards and servants scattered before his wrath. One servant tripped and landed on his face as he passed the war room's door. The flustered retainer barely managed to scramble out of the way as Gabriel stormed up to the war room's entrance. The weapons master's unusual height and sinewy frame filled the doorway and captured the attention of all within.

Clean-shaven and handsome of face, his black hair was long and straight, and he wore it pulled back in a ponytail. His face was chiseled, lined, and careworn, but neither old nor gray. How many winters he had seen was hard to say, but often a topic of conjecture amongst the highborn ladies and the knights alike. As he entered, he rapidly scanned each face. He froze for a moment, and his blue eyes widened, when he spied Lord Theta, but his gaze lingered for only a moment before he turned his attention to the others.

"What is going on here?" he said. "What is this noise and who has gone missing?" He looked around, but no one was quick to answer. "Someone speak up," he said, his withering gaze clearly focused on Claradon.

The room was silent for a few moments before Claradon was able to speak.

"Father is missing. So are Brother Donnelin, Par Talbon and his apprentices, and all the rangers. It's a long story. We had scouts out searching all day with no luck. And we have no idea what the wailing is."

"Thor's blood," said Gabriel. "This is what I get for taking a holiday."

"The garrison is gearing up in case of an attack," said Claradon, "and we have tripled the guard in the Outer Dor. We sent softened wax around to the guardsmen so they can plug up their ears enough to tolerate the noise and still stand their watch."

"Where was your father's patrol heading and

47

how long overdue are they?" said Gabriel.

"They were only planning to go a few miles into the Vermion," said Claradon. "They're a full day past due. We are planning another patrol to leave at dawn."

Gabriel's aspect softened as he moved to Claradon's side. "You have done well." They clasped arms in a firm embrace. "You took sound measures and kept your wits. Your father would be proud, as am I. Take comfort that Aradon is in good hands—Par Talbon is most capable and Stern and his rangers are the best woodsmen north of Doriath."

"Pardon my interruption, good sirs," said Tanch, "but protocol requires that I introduce a visiting dignitary."

Gabriel's eyes flashed to Theta.

At this, Theta rose and confidently strode toward the new arrival. Theta's face was clean shaven and as chiseled as Gabriel's; his hair, blond and cropped short. His blue eyes stood out amongst his rugged, weathered features. His highly ornate plate armor, which bore the dents and gouges of untold battles, was enameled deep blue and damasked with a proud and noble standard on its breastplate. His long, stylish cloak, although open at the front, partially obscured the two exotic curved swords sheathed at his waist— one slim, the other unusually broad at its tip. Dolan scrambled to his feet and followed his master.

"Sir Gabriel Garn, this is Lord Angle Theta, a renowned knight-errant from a far-off land across the sea. Attending him is his manservant, Dolan

Buttermilk."

"Silk," said Dolan, though no one seemed to hear him.

"Lord Theta," said Tanch. "Sir Gabriel is House Eotrus's weapons master."

"When I heard your name and reputation," said Theta, "I wondered if you might be the Gabriel I knew of old. Now I see that I was correct, though I have feared you dead these many years."

"Death hasn't caught me yet, my Lord, though it pursues me relentlessly. It's good to see you again, friend of old times," said Gabriel as they firmly clasped hands.

Standing face to face, the affinity between the two could not be missed. They could easily be mistaken for cousins or even brothers, yet in many ways, they were wildly different. Theta was the taller and, by a good deal, the broader and more heavily muscled. Where Gabriel's garb and gear were modest, minimalist, and utilitarian, Theta's were ornate to a point some would call garish, and he carried more gear stuffed in pouches, packs, and pockets than ten knights needed, yet he moved with such agility that he seemed unencumbered.

In addition to the belt from which hung his warrior wares, Theta wore a second belt inscribed with olden runes and studded with what looked like emeralds. This one was fastened about his waist but also featured straps that ran over his torso and shoulders like suspenders. To this belt was attached an impressive war hammer, though it was mostly hidden beneath his cloak. Several wicked-looking daggers were strapped in various places to his armor and boots. In all, the man was a walking arsenal—a veritable harbinger of doom.

"Friend of old times," responded Theta. "It has been far too long."

"Aye, it has," said Gabriel. "What brings you to Dor Eotrus?"

Theta smiled. "I go where I am needed, just as I have always done. Now it seems I may be needed here."

"How is it you know this here fellow, Gabe?" said Ob. "We just met up with him on the road the other day and he tells of how he never set foot in Lomion afore, though he has told us almost nothing else. Besides, in all the years I've known you, I have never heard tell of his name."

"Gabriel was never a teller of tales," said Theta.

Gabriel frowned, paused a moment, and locked his gaze on Ob before responding. "We served together many years ago, but those are stories for another time as we have more pressing matters at hand. Now, who can tell me the details of what has happened here? Aradon doesn't often ride out on patrols himself. There must be more to it than what Claradon just explained."

"There is, of course," said Tanch. "Everything Brother Claradon said was quite true and precise, of course, but there are details that he left out for the sake of brevity. I shall be happy to expound."

"In fact, the timing of your arrival is most fortuitous for Brother Claradon and I were about to relate the full tale to Lord Theta, Ob, and young Master Ector, who only recently arrived themselves. If you gentlemen would be so kind as to take your seats," said Tanch in his most deferential tone, "perhaps Brother Claradon will begin the tale."

"Start talking, boy," said Ob. "Where are your father and the others?"

"Claradon," said Gabriel as a servant passed him the wax bowl, "start at the beginning, take it slow and clear, and leave nothing out. Good thinking about the wax, by the way."

"The wizard's idea," said Ob. "Nobody better at avoiding pain or work."

"Harrumph," went Tanch.

Claradon somberly related the mysterious events of the prior few days. He told of how several nights previous, horrible, guttural sounds began to emanate from the Vermion Forest to the west of Dor Eotrus, the magnificent fortress in whose central tower they were now gathered. The patrician diction in which he spoke marked him as having studied under some of Lomion's finest scholars. Similarly schooled, his brother Ector's coloring and slightly ill-favored features branded him as one of Lord Aradon Eotrus's sons. Happily, Claradon was said to somewhat resemble his mother, a renowned beauty, gone these last years.

"The sounds began around midnight four nights ago, and continued unabated until dawn," said Claradon. "That first night, it wasn't loud like it is tonight—we barely heard it while outside, and not at all indoors, but it was eerie all the same, and caused quite a stir amongst the people. Rumors of everything from Lugron invasion, to dragons, trolls, and more, ran wild through the citadel and the Outer Dor by breakfast.

That morning, father organized a patrol to investigate. Deep in the wood, they discovered a strange area that we have never seen before. It was completely desolate and devoid of life. The place was flat, circular in shape, and some fifty yards in diameter. The ground within consisted only of hardened gray soil and dust, featureless save for some scattered pebbles pressed into the dirt. They found no invading army, and no strange animal or troll spoor; no clues whatsoever as to the origins of the sounds or the circle. The patrol withdrew and returned without incident to the Dor. Later, we learned that residents of the outlying farms had heard similar sounds the night before we first heard them at the Dor."

"The following night, the strange sounds resumed. As before, they commenced around midnight and continued until dawn."

"That wretched wailing kept the whole Dor up all night," said Tanch. "Without the wax it was unbearable. My poor ears were—"

"It really wasn't that loud that night, or the next," said Claradon. "Just an annoyance, nothing more, although, each night, it has grown progressively louder. On the second night, from atop the Dor's towers, the moonlight revealed a dense fogbank over the wood. We think it was centered on the desolate zone, or at least, very close to it. The next morning, father sent out another patrol to investigate."

"We never get fog this time of year," said Tanch. "It's not natural; in fact, it's quite unnatural, if you follow me." Tanch looked furtively about, as if some unseen spirit were about to pounce on him.

"When the patrol got back, late in the day, they reported that the diameter of the desolate area was now over one hundred yards. Trees that were there the day before were inexplicably gone—no trace of their existence remained."

"So the barren area got larger?" said Gabriel.

"Aye, and we have no idea how or why," said Claradon, "so father decided we should investigate the area at night. He felt whomever or whatever was causing these strange goings-on was hiding amidst the fog."

"Quite sensible," said Tanch. "I would have advised the same but, of course, I wasn't consulted. Most folk hold the advice of wizards in high regard, but—"

"The next patrol left at dusk. Father led it himself." Looking toward Theta, he continued. "With him was House Eotrus's high cleric, Brother Donnelin; Par Talbon, our House Wizard, and his apprentices—five or six of them, I think, though I'm not really certain, as they are a mysterious lot. With them was Captain Stern and our other three rangers, eight knights, a dozen men-at-arms, and a half squadron of archers. Before he left, father ordered that in the event . . ." Claradon paused and looked as if he were about to vomit or break down. He took a breath and then continued, his voice unsteady at first. "In the event that he didn't return, I was to await the return of Sir Gabriel or Ob before taking further action. Father had sent scouts to locate you," he said gesturing toward Gabriel and Ob, "the same day that the circle was first discovered, and he sent more the next, so we hoped you would be back soon."

"Get to the point, boy," said Ob, "What became of the patrol?"

"I am getting there," said Claradon, his voice strained. "Sir Gabriel said to leave nothing out, so I'm not."

"Fine," said Ob. "Just talk quicker."

"Alright," he said, and took a deep breath. "Very late in the evening of the third day, shortly before midnight, the guards atop the battlements spotted the fog. It had expanded further from its extent the previous evening. Shortly thereafter, the horrid sounds began anew and were louder than before. Then we saw several bright flashes of light and heard two thunderous explosions that shook the keep. Par Tanch and I were atop the central tower, watching."

"Tanch—what do you make of them flashes and explosions?" said Ob. "Was it a storm over the wood, or something else?"

Tanch hesitated, and glanced over at Theta and Dolan. "I'm not sure that—"

"Do you think the arcane arts were invoked?" asked Gabriel.

"I—well, I wouldn't—"

"It's alright," said Gabriel. "Such things are known to our guests. Speak freely."

"Very well then. Yes. I have no doubt that the explosions were magical discharges and that the fog itself has a sorcerous nature. Lord Eotrus's party engaged some enemy force within the fogbank, and one side or both threw powerful spells—very powerful spells. The last blast before the wood went silent held a sorcery greater than any I have felt before. The blast before that was near as strong. Something frightful happened out there. Something beyond my ken, I freely admit."

"My apologies, Lord Theta, but I didn't think it appropriate to mention things arcane. Besides, this is all so hard to imagine. A lord of a noble house attacked on his own lands by sorcery. Such things just don't happen—not in Lomion. Not in modern times. It's unfathomable. The nerve, the audacity, the—"

"The sounds," said Claradon, "stopped for some time after the second explosion, but then they began anew and continued until first light. Father's patrol failed to return; their fate unknown. A full day and this much of the night has passed since their disappearance, and the fog and the sounds have continued in the same pattern. Most of us saw the fog from the high tower not long ago."

"Tonight marks the fifth night since the sounds were first heard. The rumors making their way through the Dor have grown worse, and taken on a life of their own," said Claradon. "People are saying that father is dead—killed by whatever is making that cursed noise. They say the Dor is next; that we're all doomed. The people are beginning to panic."

"Bah," spouted Ob as he rose. He stood on his chair's high footrest and pounded his small fist on the table. "Who cares what them folks say; they don't know nothing from nothing. Your father is alive," he said, his voice wavering and his face contorting as he tried to stay his emotions, "until

I say he's not. Do you hear me, boy? We will be going to them woods and we will be bringing him back, I say. Him and Donnelin, Stern, Talbon, and the rest." Quaking, he sat back down, and loudly blew his bulbous nose into his handkerchief.

"The circle," said Gabriel. "Where in the forest is it?"

"Two hours ride through the wood, nearly due west," said Claradon.

"Near the old stone ruins?" said Gabriel.

"It must be close, but the men say they didn't come across them."

"Those ruins," said Tanch, "There's nothing there but a few scattered pillars of some peculiar black stone, and one crumbling building that looks like an old temple. To what forsaken gods, though, who knows? Sir Gabriel, you'll remember, we rode out there together once—must have been six or seven years ago. You spent half the day studying the ruins."

"He rides out that way all the time," said Ob. "Odin knows why."

"The woods are quiet," said Gabriel. "Helps me think straight, which I need to do to keep you lot out of trouble."

"That one time was enough for me," said Tanch. "That wretched place made my skin crawl. And it wasn't just me; we had a terrible time keeping the horses calm near there. I can't imagine why you would go back. As I recall, there is no game to be found within a mile or more of the ruins, which is why we never hunt out that way. The whole time we were there, I felt as if we were being watched by someone or something unseen, something sinister—as if the place was haunted."

"Bah," said Ob. "Don't start spouting fairy stories, Magic Boy. I have no interest in hearing about boggles, sprites, bugbears, and such. We get enough of those from Donnelin. Ain't no such thing as hauntings or forest faeries. Spirits and such are nothing but bunk, bother, and bad digestion."

"I'm not saying it was haunted, Ob. I'm just saying that's what it felt like when I was there."

"How would you know what a haunting felt like, when there's no such thing?" said Ob. "It makes no sense. Pluck the wax back out of your ears and I bet I can see clear through to the other side."

"So who is doing the wailing?" said Dolan before Tanch could fire back.

No one responded; no one had an answer.

Theta leaned forward and spoke in a strong, measured voice. "Speak more of these ruins, Gabriel."

All eyes turned to the foreigner and then to Gabriel.

Gabriel hesitated for some moments before responding. "Par Tanch is correct," he said. "It is a dark and evil place. The ruins are ancient." He stared across the table at Theta for several seconds, seemingly considering whether to continue. "I believe they were not Volsung made."

Theta nodded.

"I'm doubting that, Gabe," said Ob. "Dwarves and Gnomes don't build in the woods. Elves and smallfolk don't work much in stone, and Lugron and their kin don't have the brains. It's you Volsungs—your ancestors anyway—that had to make it; there is nobody else it could've been."

"What about the Svart?" said Tanch.

Ob's eyes narrowed to slits and his next words came through clenched teeth. "Best not to speak of that lot, especially around me."

Tanch rolled his eyes and shook his head.

Theta glanced down at the war hammer that hung from his belt.

"Who cares about the darned ruins anyways?" said Ob. "All I care about is what happened to our people. Let's keep our focus on that. They must've been ambushed. That's the only way that patrol could've been defeated or captured to a man."

Tanch shook his head. "Between the wizards and Brother Donnelin we had a formidable magical force in the field that night. Such men cannot easily be overcome."

"Maybe some force fell on them quickly, before they were able to mount a defense," said Ector. "Maybe a whole horde of Lugron came down from the north looking for plunder and prisoners to ransom."

"Doubtful," said Ob.

"Lugron don't make sounds like we've heard," said Gabriel. "And Stern and his rangers would not easily be taken unawares. There is more to this than a simple ambush, and we've seen no evidence of an invasion."

"Is it possible that those flashes and explosions were spells thrown by the enemy, against our patrol?" said Claradon.

"Aye, maybe that could be," said Ob. "That

would mean a magical ambush. But Aradon is no fool; I doubt he would walk into such a thing, and Talbon would have smelled it coming from a league away."

"Who would have the power to mount such a magical attack?" said Claradon.

"Not many," said Tanch, "but the mystic arts are so hidden these days, it's hard to say who and how many know its secrets—and of those few, how many have real power."

"We have our share of enemies, same as any noble House," said Ob. "It's doubtful any of them would act against us directly, but there are rogue wizards and mercenary companies for hire for the right price. Anyone could be behind it."

"Are you saying that there are mercenary companies that have wizards in their employ; true wizards?" said Tanch.

"Aye, there are a few," said Ob.

"Scandalous," said Tanch. "Shocking. Our members would never work for mercenary companies—I can't believe this."

"Not every wizard got their training at your pretty tower, you know," said Ob. "There are other sources of such knowledge."

Tanch looked surprised.

"We will not find any answers sitting here," said Ob. "None at all. We need to get our behinds out there." He looked over at Gabriel. "Only question is—who and how many is to go?"

Gabriel paused for a few moments, gathering his thoughts. He turned toward the younger Eotrus. "Ector," he said, "you are needed here."

Ector grumbled and clenched his jaw, but

offered no protestations.

"You must take command of the Dor, and try to quell the panic of the people," said Gabriel. "They need to see your face and hear directly from you that everything is under control. They need to know that the Eotrus family is with them and that they've not been abandoned." He shifted his gaze to Claradon. "Claradon, in your father's absence, you are the acting Lord of the Dor. The expedition is yours to command."

Claradon's mouth dropped open and his eyes went wide. "But I thought since you are here—"

"Unless he defers command to the Dor's Castellan," said Ob. "Which he does, and I hereby pass it to you, weapons master—and there will be no more debating about it. We can't fool around with this one, it's too darned important. In a standup battle, either Claradon or I could lead, but that's not what we have. There's something odd about this whole business, what with the wailing and the circle and such. It's just not natural at all. I hate to admit it, but it does stink of sorcery, top to bottom." Ob turned to Claradon. "In this, the only man amongst us that has the right experience to lead is Gabriel. He must take command."

"I agree," said Claradon quickly. "Sir Gabriel, you can handle this much better than I. You must lead us. I don't have the experience."

Gabriel stared down at the table for several seconds. "For good or ill, it is your place to lead us, Claradon, not mine. But Ob's points are well taken. Aradon's life and that of every man on his patrol, and perhaps more than that, may well depend on our course. For that reason only will I agree to this."

He stood up. "We will take two squadrons of knights equipped with full battle gear and heavy horse. Ob, you will choose them and captain the squadrons. Be sure to include Glimador and Indigo—as they're among my best students. And Artol and my squire, of course, will accompany us. The rest of the garrison will remain to defend the Dor. Par Tanch, since matters arcane are involved, you will come with us as well."

Tanch's face blanched.

"Ob—you will need to choose your squadrons quickly, because we're gathering in the Odinhome in an hour to vow our paths. Make certain that the men you select are there—every one. Claradon— in Brother Donnelin's absence, I trust that you will lead us in prayer."

"I will; I can do that."

"Good," said Gabriel. He turned to the group. "Have your gear ready—we will leave at dawn. I know it won't be easy, but once we're done at the Odinhome, do your best to get some sleep, as much as you can before dawn, for tomorrow will be a long day."

"Should we leave sooner?" said Claradon. "Tonight, I mean?"

"The Vermion is too thick and the footing too treacherous to venture through in the black," said Gabriel. "Ector—if there is no word from us by midday, the day after tomorrow, send word to Lomion, Kern, and Doriath Forest, beseeching them each for aid. You will also send scouts and ravens to each manor, keep, town, and hamlet within our demesne, instructing them to prepare for battle or to flee to Lomion City or to the Dor. Understood?"

"Understood," said Ector.

"Perhaps I should stay behind and assist young Master Ector," said Tanch. "What with my delicate back and such I may not be of much—"

"We need your skills, wizard," said Gabriel. "You're going."

Tanch slumped back in defeat.

Gabriel's gaze, and then everyone else's, shifted to the two foreigners.

"I will accompany you," said Theta before any could address him, "and Dolan as well."

"I thank you, sir," said Claradon, "but you are a guest here, this isn't your fight. Don't feel obligated."

Theta cut Claradon off with a wave of his hand and a shake of his head. "I will accompany you."

"Then you have my gratitude."

Theta nodded.

VI
ON MAGIC AND MUMMERY

As the men filed from the room, Theta motioned to Claradon to remain. He walked over as Theta gathered up his equipment.

"That's quite a shield," said Claradon as he moved in to get a better look. Theta held it out for inspection.

"Nearly all steel and a heavy gauge," said Claradon as he looked it over, a surprised look on his face. "Very heavy gauge," he said, running his fingers along its length. "I've never seen a large shield made entirely of metal. Even a man your size can't hold such a thing for long—it must weigh at least fifty pounds. No offense, but it just doesn't seem practical."

"Try it," said Theta, passing it to him.

Claradon grasped it, his eyebrows rose, and he smiled. "What a wonder. It's so light. What kind of steel is this?" he said, as he maneuvered it around. "It's not even half the weight of mine."

"The plates are three times as thick as those commonly used in shield work," said Theta. "They are made from a rare alloy that is five times as strong as standard steel, but only a fraction of the weight."

"You could win wars with an army equipped with these," said Claradon, a look of wonder lingering on his face.

"I have," said Theta with a smile. "Your wizard was reluctant to speak of magic," said Theta. "Tell me why that is."

"In Lomion, it's considered improper to speak of things arcane."

"That much is clear," said Theta. "My question is why?"

"One reason being, most folks believe magic is no more than mummery. The greater reason being, it's illegal to publicly practice the true arcane arts. The Crown and the council take a hard stance on this, even more so in recent years. Those who violate the edicts face ostracism at best, or imprisonment or exile if things go against them. I gather that in your lands such is not the case."

Theta nodded. "Why do your rulers fear magic so?"

"A good question, often asked in private by those of us who know the truth of things—but one never adequately answered. Perhaps it's because they can't fully control magic or those who weave it, so instead they suppress it and seek to deny its very existence."

"With your laws as they are, how is it that you have a House Wizard?"

"Ah, well—being a wizard, or rather, proclaiming yourself a wizard is not illegal and never has been. On every street corner in the great cities of the realm, there are those who call themselves wizards, sorcerers, or seers, but they are charlatans all. They trick the unwary and unwise with sleight of hand, and fool the foolish with palm readings, astrology, and other such bunk. As far as the common people know, that's all there is to magic and wizards."

"So your government has done its job well."

"They have, and have been doing so for generations. All that the common people know of true magic comes only from legend and superstition. We Lomerians are a superstitious people you see, so many fear those tales, and the olden magic and those who weave it. It's better to believe only in the card tricksters and their ilk, or so they think."

"So they think your House Wizards are no more than well-dressed street hawkers?"

"Aye."

"And I gather that that isn't the case."

"Indeed, it is not—at least not amongst the great Houses. Our House Wizards are chosen from those most singular few that belong to the Order of the Arcane. They are learned in the true mysteries of the magical arts of thaumaturgy, divination, sorcery, necromancy, and other such esoteric fields of study. Many of their members can command fantastic magics and enchantments to accomplish all manner of wondrous deeds. Par Talbon, our House Wizard, is such a man, as is Par Tanch."

"The wizards are sworn to never publicly use their skills, save in the defense of their master's life, or by order of the Crown. They may not even cast their magic in self-defense. Even in defense of their lord there can be repercussions, if the need for its use be not so great. Rare it is that such oaths are broken, and on those occasions when magic is used, the authorities quickly cover up the incidents and remove the evidence, the government long ago having decided that the common people must never know of such things. For good or ill, that is the way of things."

"And which is it, good or ill?"

"Ill, I would say."

Theta nodded. "Magic is a dangerous thing. There is wisdom in limiting its use."

"A sword is a dangerous thing too," said Claradon. "Yet used wisely, it's a valuable tool."

"True enough," said Theta. "Can only those Lomerians in the Order command the magical arts?"

"Some few members of certain militant orders are trained in the ways of magic, but their command of the arts is typically far more limited than members of the Arcane Order."

"I take it that these knights are under the same restrictions regarding using their arcane skills."

"They are."

"You have such skills," he said in a manner that could easily have been mistaken as a question, though it most certainly was a statement.

"I do," said Claradon, not quite holding back a grin at Theta's insight. "As you've no doubt already discerned, my brother and I are knights of the realm of Lomion, each holding membership in one of the militant orders. I serve the Caradonian Order of the Knights of Odin, and they afford me the title of 'Brother'. We are a religious order and perform various duties typically carried out by monks and priests. Ector and my brother Jude are members of the Tyrian Order, whose patron is Tyr, god of justice."

"I have not met Jude," said Theta.

"No, he and Malcolm, my youngest brother, are in Lomion City, our capital, on House business.

VII
THE ODINHOME

Ob carried a small lantern to guide their way, as he, Theta, and Dolan quickly walked toward the octagonal building the Eotrus called the Odinhome. In many ways, the Odinhome was the heart of life at Dor Eotrus. By design, it was a spiritual place of worship, but in practice, it was also a hall for fellowship, storytelling, and debate, and often, for feasting and drinking. It connected one to the past, through traditions and ritual, through ancestors and the gods.

"We don't got no grand cathedral as do some Dors and them big cities, but our worship hall is better than most by a good stretch," shouted Ob so that he would be heard over the wailing. "And that's no accident. Like most folk in the provinces, we respect the old ways and take our religion seriously. Not like them fancy city folk what lost their way and don't believe in nothing anymore."

"The Odinhome is the only big building we got what is mostly made of wood. The rest are stone, slab to peak, but don't let that fool you. We build them all to last up here in the North. Storm or siege, fire or axe, it don't matter none, what we build endures whatever needs enduring."

"You see them fancy double doors?" he said as they approached the Odinhome's entrance. "Stout oak, six inches thick and banded in cold-forged iron. Take an army to pound them doors down while we rained death on them from on high," he said, pointing at the battlements more than 25 feet up. "There be seven sets of doors just like these spaced around the building—one for each of the gods."

"Aren't there more than seven gods?" said Dolan.

"You ask a lot of questions, fella," said Ob as he gave Dolan the eye. "I can hardly get a word in with you jabbering all the time. Don't know how you tolerate this fellow, Theta."

"He can cook," said Theta.

Ob nodded. "That explains it. Half the servants we got burn the water and boil the toast. Stinking bumpkins," he said as he lifted his wineskin to his lips for a goodly swallow.

"Anyhow, in addition to Odin, there's seven gods what we northerners fancy a bit more than the rest," said Ob. "Inside, we got statues and such to each of the others, so as not to leave anyone out. Never a good idea to offend a god, so we make certain each one is held high and touted in some way or another somewhere in the 'home. Some in the South got other godly preferences, mind you, but we don't much care what them folks think. We do things our own way up here. Always have."

Ob approached the entry doors and pulled on a large iron rung that served as a door handle. "This here is Tyr's gate," he said as he strained to swing the massive door open. The smell of firewood, hickory and birch, wafted toward them as the door opened, along with the welcome scent of roasting meat.

They stepped through the entrance onto the

grand arcade that encircled the interior perimeter of the building. The place was mostly one huge open room. The covered arcade opened to a sunken seating area with a very high domed ceiling. Sturdy looking men with somber expressions walked purposely along the arcade while the subdued and mirthless voices of others rose up from the seating area beyond. When Tyr's gate closed behind the group, the wailing sounds almost entirely disappeared and they breathed the easier.

"This is one of my favorite places in the Dor," said Ob to Theta. "As long as at least two of the doors are propped open, there is always a nice breeze in here, so the air is fresh, unless the priests have the incense burning, and even that stuff don't smell half bad. It never gets too hot in here, and rarely gets too cold. It's a good place to sit, talk, and think and whatnot."

"Look around—we don't build random in these parts. Everything we put together has got its proper function and place, or else some symbolic meaning that's important to us. Them stairs, for instance," he said, pointing across the arcade, "they're aligned with the doors, so that when you stroll in, you cross the arcade and head straight down to grab a seat in Tyr's section, no fuss or wandering about required. Seven steps there are, each seven feet wide. They take you down to the central dais where abides the All-Father's altar and other sacred thingamabobs. And between each set of stairs, there is a long narrow table and bench what sits seven at least on each and every step. Seven's got some religious meaning what escapes me at the moment, but it's something important, I'm sure. Donnelin would know—he prattles on about it during one of the high holy days every year." Ob scrunched up his face and shook his head. "Anyway, if you can cypher good and proper, you'll come up with seats for 350 warriors, battle clad and blood ready. We can squeeze in twice that many folks all casually dressed and sitting cozy. Not to mention the hundreds what can stand around up here on the arcade bleating like sheep and picking their noses instead of paying attention to the service, just so they can say they were here."

"Ole Brother Donnelin is many things, but an inspiring orator, he is not. So the place don't get crowded much, especially since them weaselly prelates from the Outer Dor's temples have siphoned off most of his flock and their tithes with them. I get stuck having to dip into the House treasury to pay the upkeep on this place—there are just not enough donations to keep the roof tight and the paint on the walls, and there hasn't been for years," he said as they walked across the arcade. They warmed their hands at one of the long, rectangular, iron fire pits arranged at the inner edge of the arcade, just behind the top row of benches. The pits were topped with iron gratings, and here and there, a slab of meat roasted over a crackling fire.

"The hour is late for supper," said Theta.

"I won't say no to a nibble, if asked," said Dolan.

"We always feast before going to war," said Ob. "It's tradition. We're big on that in these parts.

Tradition, that is. It grounds us. It reminds us of who we are and where we come from, and that's important. Fiercely important to us northerners, especially to the Eotrus. The family line hails all the way back to Odin himself—a direct bloodline to the gods, or so goes the tale."

"Tradition is why each of them seating sections," he said pointing, "is dedicated to one of the big seven: Thor, Heimdall, Balder, Tyr, and the rest. Them friezes along the walls behind us feature each god's deeds, even the ones what make little sense to us mere mortals. There's also a statue, big as life, of each god at the top of their stairs," he said pointing. "Some of them are near as tall as Artol. I suppose that's to be expected, them being gods and all."

"We got stained glass in the windows way above us—hard to see right now owing to the dark, but trust me, it's there, and it's not just colored glass, mind you, them windows tell tales: prayers, stories, and such. That glass goes back hundreds of years, salvaged by the Eotrus from some forgotten temple in the mountains. Tradition. It means something."

"Impressive workmanship," said Theta as he looked around.

"Don't see no workman's ship," mumbled Dolan as he turned this way and that. "Not even any water in here. Dry as a bone, it is."

Ob beamed. "The stonework is Gnomish, of course, made way back in olden days, except for a few recent additions whittled by Dwarves out of Tarrows Hold. The best of them was carved by me ole buddy McDuff—that granite statue of Heimdall at the top of yonder stair. We had to replace the original about ten years back—it got busted up during some unfortunate fisticuffs. I still say it wasn't his fault, but Aradon told McDuff he had to replace it or else. So he did—carved it by his own hands. Took him nearly a month working night and day. I have to admit, he did his penance right and proper, as his work is a sight better than the original. More lifelike and bigger muscles. A statue of a god ought to have some muscles, don't you think? But I always pictured Heimdall shorter."

"That section over there is reserved for Odin, the All-Father," said Ob pointing to the northernmost portion of the building. He held off describing what they saw in that direction, and instead turned to study his guests' reactions.

Across the seating area, on the far side of the building was an enormous granite statue of Odin seated on a polished, white marble throne. If the statue could have stood, it would have surpassed thirty feet in height. The All-Father leaned forward, hand to his chin, horned helmet atop his head, a long spear in hand, and gazed down on his followers with his one wise eye. A stone wolf stood on either side of him, and a raven perched on each of his shoulders.

Dolan's eyes went wide, but Theta gave nothing away—as if he had seen such sights a thousand times.

"No grand cathedrals, but we got that," said Ob pointing to the statue. "And nobody else has got nothing like it. We figure the Eotrus of olden days built the Odinhome around it, because there's no way they could've hauled it in here."

"Is it one piece of stone?" said Theta.

"Aye," said Ob.

"Then it is a wonder," said Theta. "Such things are rarely seen these days—the skills of the old world, long lost."

"Long lost, they are," said Dolan.

"And look up there," said Ob, pointing to the ceiling.

At the inner edge of the arcade, the building transitioned from its octagonal shaped base into a grand ribbed dome of heavy timbers that rose up some 75 feet above the altar at the building's center. The dome's apex was open to the sky. A huge mural of Odin riding a chariot pulled by an eight-legged horse dominated most of the dome's inner surface, its once vibrant colors muted by long years of exposure to smoke and to the elements. Below the mural was Ob's line of stained-glass windows, inset between each of the dome's timber ribs.

"They always put a beard on him," said Theta under his breath.

"Of course they do," said Ob, hearing the remark where a Volsung's ears would not have. "Everybody knows Odin has got a beard, long and white, and such. In times past, most every man in Lomion wore a beard, not like today, though they're still common enough here in the North, especially after winter sets in."

A knight walked to a lectern on the dais at the hall's center and shouted to all to find their seats and quiet down.

"Glimador is calling things to order," said Ob. "Claradon must have finally got his butt over here.

Let's grab some seats. Who are your patrons?"

"What?" said Dolan, confused.

"I have no patron," said Theta rather abruptly. "I need no patron."

Ob looked more confused than Dolan. "I'm asking, because by tradition each warrior sits in the section marked for his patron god, or in any section he likes, if his patron is Odin. Don't your people follow the Aesir?"

"Most do," said Theta, "but I'm not much of a follower."

"I can respect that, I suppose. Not every man goes in much for religion nowadays. The thing is, Claradon don't got the loudest voice—you'll hear next to nothing back here. Best pick a god, whichever one you followed back before you stopped following."

Theta sighed. "Odin."

Ob's eyes narrowed. "Good choice, same as mine, but why him? I mean, if you sit somewhere you shouldn't, the gods may take offense. I can't have that. This mission is too important." Ob stared up at the big knight demanding an answer.

"Let's just say that Odin and I are old friends. I doubt he would mind me sitting in one of his pews."

"You speak as if you know him," said Claradon, as he stepped up beside them wearing a clerical vestment. "As if he were no more than a man."

"Some say that he was," said Theta. "A man, that is."

"Heresy, my lord?" said Claradon.

"What's that mean?" mumbled Dolan.

"Not if it's true," said Theta.

75

"Truth is in the perception more than the fact," said Claradon.

"Who taught you that?" said Theta.

"An observation of my own, but I believe it to be correct more often than not."

"Then you are a man of wisdom, Eotrus. Midgaard needs men with like that to balance out the abundant stupidity," said Theta, as he glanced sidelong at Dolan, who in turn, stared at Ob, who huffed and took another large gulp from his wineskin.

"Enough chatter," said Ob. "Get down there, boy, and lead us in the oath. We need to get this done and get a bit of sleep before comes the dawn."

***

Rising up more than eight feet in height at each point of the octagonal dais at the building's center was a cylindrical plinth intricately carved with runes and religious imagery. The great altar loomed at the dais's center; the lectern off to the side. Two white-robed pages stood near Claradon, one held a smoldering, perforated iron box of incense, the other, a golden holy symbol.

"Hear me my brothers," said Claradon as he stood behind the Odinhome's lectern clad in the priestly vestments, robe, and sash of the revered order of Caradonian Knights, their sigil prominently displayed at his breast. His hooded robe resembled that worn by priests and monks, though it was tailored to accommodate the long sword that he wore at his hip and contained myriad pockets for carrying and concealing gear, large and small.

A thick leatherbound tome lay before him. He reverently opened it to a bookmarked page, though he barely glanced at the words, so familiar to him were they. "The Warrior's Oath, from the *Book of the Aesir*," he said in a bold, strong voice, enunciating each word. "Now gather close and harken to my words, for they are passed down to us from the *Age of Heroes*."

"Good, he's speaking the modern version of the oath," whispered Ob to Theta. "We get nothing but the old one from Donnelin and nobody understands a word of it since it's in Old High Lomerian. Who the heck speaks that nowadays? Nobody, I'll tell you, so what's the point?"

The page passed Claradon the chain by which he held the smoldering incense box. Claradon took it and slowly walked to each point of the dais while mumbling some religious words no one could make out. He paused at the corners and swung the box several times, which caused the incense to waft about, its gray smoke billowing up around him. The odor, not unpleasant, soon filled the hall.

"I say that the old version is good for the high holidays only, if even then," whispered Ob. "But Donnelin will hear nothing of it. He just won't get with the times."

"Ain't he supposed to speak from behind the altar?" whispered Dolan.

"More questions, Mister Chatterbox?" said Ob.

"Only the House Cleric speaks from the altar. Anyone what else got reason to speak, stands tall at the lectern. It's tradition."

As Claradon recited the first verse, the knights each dropped to one knee and bowed their heads. The sun still several hours from rising, near seventy men were gathered in the Odinhome to hear his words, though that number sparsely populated the great hall. Dolan respectfully lowered his eyes, while Theta looked around, studying the gathered men, taking their measure. Gabriel, Artol, and Paldor (Gabriel's squire) sat in the front row of Heimdall's section. Sir Glimador, Sir Indigo, and Sir Bilson sat in Thor's area, and Tanch lounged in the last row of Frey's section looking tired and gloomy. The rest of the knights each sat in their chosen place. As Claradon recited the prayer, a page turned a handled wheel beside one of the plinths, which caused the plinth to rotate. Carvings on the plinth's surface depicted images or symbols evoked by each line of the prayer.

"Look unto the north and behold the Bifrost and beyond—ancient Asgard, shining and bright, though hard and cold as the stone, the ice, and the sea," said Claradon.

"To the north lies Asgard," said the men in unison.

"Now look unto the east and behold thy brothers, thy sons, and thy comrades."

"Now look unto the west and behold thy sisters, thy wives, thy mothers, and thy daughters."

"Around us are our kinsmen, always," said the

men.

"Now think not again of them until we march on the homeward road."

"Not until the homeward road," said the men.

"Now look unto the south and behold thy father, and thy father's father, and all thy line afore thee, back unto the beginning."

"Unto the beginning," said the men.

"Now look forward and behold thy fate. Before thee lay the paths to victory and glory, and the paths to defeat and disgrace. Intersecting these paths are the road to tomorrow, the road to Valhalla, and the road to darkness."

"Beware the dark road," said the men.

"Now look above thee and behold the All-Father. He beckons us forth to meet our fate. He tells us that the path we choose is of our own making."

"Our path is our own," said the men.

"Now my brothers, vow thy path."

"To victory and tomorrow if we can, to victory and Valhalla if we must," said the men. "This we vow."

"We will bring Lord Eotrus home, or take vengeance on his slayers if he has fallen," said Claradon. "This we vow."

"This we vow," said the men.

"Rise now my brothers," said Claradon, "and go to thy fate with Odin's blessing."

The men arose and stood silently for several moments. Sir Gabriel left his seat and quickly walked down to the dais, his squire and sergeant following. He turned and faced the men. "I've some gear to distribute to you before you leave," he said loud enough for all to hear. "Everyone wait here."

"What's this?" said Ob.

Gabriel walked around the central dais, and entered the northernmost section of the hall. He and his men passed the statue of Odin, turned, and disappeared from view.

"That is an odd thing," said Ob. "Gabe is up to something. I didn't even think he had a key for that door. By rights, he shouldn't. A weapons master has got no business back there, no business at all, but there he goes, all la dee da and casual, as if he had been in there a hundred times, and them two with him. I'll have words with Artol about this, I will."

"What is back there?" said Theta.

"The ossuary."

"What's that—some kind of outhouse?" said Dolan.

"It's the House crypts," said Theta.

"The place of the dead," said Ob. "What gear does he have stowed back there? Old great-grandpap Eotrus's rusty sword? Makes no sense."

"No sense at all," said Dolan.

Claradon was puzzled when he saw Sir Gabriel, Artol, and Paldor enter the ossuary. He thought that only his father, Jude, Ob, Brother Donnelin, and he were permitted entry, except during burials. Only the five of them knew that there were secret ways through the ossuary's warren of deep tunnels. Ways that led under the wall, to emerge well into the northern hills—an escape route, should the family ever need it. That use aside, he hated the place, but when his attention was drawn to it, he found it hard to turn away. Its very look frightened him—it had since he was a little boy.

Bleached bones were affixed to the door frame, the wall, and the door itself, and countless more were piled in great heaps on either side of the entry. Claradon knew that the bones were merely symbolic—they were not the bones of men, for such a display would be barbaric. Instead, they were bones of horses, deer, elk, mountain lion, bear, and mammoth killed during hunts over the years. He had contributed his share to the pile. Those on display were mostly ribs and leg bones, which were more easily mistaken for those of men, which was the intent. The place was supposed to repulse common folk. And it did.

Claradon hadn't ventured inside since they laid his mother to rest there. Lifting her frail body into the stone coffin and closing the lid had been the hardest things he had ever done. It was the only time he'd seen his father weep. Even years later, Claradon could barely think of that day without his eyes growing wet. He remembered that when she died, the masons labored nonstop for three days to ready the coffin for her funeral. Teams of them worked in shifts to carve it from a single block of black granite hefted down from the hills.

What ghosts and spirits dwelled beyond the ossuary's door, and worse, in the crypt's lower levels, he shuddered to think, though his rational mind told him there were no such things as spectres. Dead was dead. No one in the Dor was more superstitious than Ob, yet he never feared going in there, at least not that he let on, so Claradon shouldn't fear it either, but he did. It was a fear he couldn't shake.

He dreaded the thought of carrying his father down there—of leaving him alone, in the cold dark, to rot. His mother was taken far too young. It wasn't fair. His father was still in his prime. The norns wouldn't dare take him too, would they? If he were gone, he wouldn't put him down there, tradition or not. The old way of placing a chieftain aboard a boat and burning it was better somehow, cleaner. But his father would want to lie next to his mother. They had to find him. He just wasn't ready to lose him. Not yet. Not for long years. Claradon snapped himself out of his daze. He took off his priestly vestment, sent the pages off to their beds, and walked up the steps to where Ob, Theta, and Dolan still sat.

"You know what Gabe is up to?" said Ob.

"No idea," said Claradon. "But he's taking his time about it, whatever it is. Lord Theta, I hope that our rite did not offend or make you uncomfortable."

"Not at all," said Theta.

"The Warrior's Oath," said Claradon, "is an ancient prayer amongst our people. We wouldn't embark on a quest or go off to battle without speaking it."

"We speak a similar prayer in our lands," said Theta.

"I hope that you don't mind my saying this, but I noticed you didn't join us in reaffirming your path."

"I chose my path long ago, Eotrus. I know its every crag and crevice. I could no more divert from it, than could the sun choose not to rise in the morn."

"Then I'm glad that we will face this road together, since you know it so well."

Theta stared off into the distance. "Mine is a perilous road; those that walk it with me are seldom long for Valhalla."

Dolan raised an eyebrow at that; Ob just shook his head.

"Ominous words, my Lord," said Claradon. "I would gladly end the day in Valhalla, if before I drew my last breath I avenged my father."

"Be not so quick to fly to Valhalla, young Eotrus, it will still be there however long your journey. It is—eternal."

"And don't be so quick to assume Aradon needs avenging," said Ob. "We are going to find him out there, I'm sure of it."

"Here they come," said Ob, as Gabriel and his men appeared. Each dragged a large, ironbound chest behind them. Artol and Paldor looked spent from the effort—even Gabriel was sweating. They heaved the chests up on the edge of the dais, and Gabriel unlocked one of them.

"Gather around," said Gabriel, and all the men did. Hinges creaked when he lifted open the lid and an unnatural glow crept from within. The open chest smelled of wood and oiled leather. Gabriel reached in and pulled forth a long dagger housed in a bejeweled, leather sheath. When he bared the silvered blade, it glowed with a soft white light.

Similar blades filled the chest—all well-kept and shining, without a hint of rust or decay.

The men gasped at the sight of that eldritch blade, ensorcelled as it was with some forgotten magic of bygone days to luminesce so.

"Sorcery," shouted one knight as he drew his sword.

"Witchcraft," cried another, backing up. Most of the others did much the same.

"Hold," boomed Gabriel. "There is no danger here. This blade and its kin are weapons for us to gird, not foes for us to fight. Cover your blades. Now."

Fear and doubt filled many a face, but the men complied.

"What's this humbug, Gabe?" said Ob. "We've no need of fairy magics; we have honest steel to gird us," he said, patting the hilt of the sword that hung at his hip.

"And honest steel is all one needs when facing mortal man or beast," said Gabriel. "But today I fear we face something more."

"Bah," said Ob. "Don't spout me children's stories of monsters. That be all bunk and bother. If there are enemies skulking about out there, they are made of flesh and blood, same as us, so our weapons will work just fine."

"You've never known me to meddle with magic, and normally I don't," said Gabriel to the men, "but sometimes, it's a tool that must be used, just like an axe or a hammer. So long as we're mindful that it can cut us just as quick and deep as our enemies, we can make good use of it if it's needed, and if Ob's right, we won't need to use it at all."

"Sir Gabriel speaks wisely, as always," said Par Tanch. "We're facing something whose howls carry for miles, that spouts evil fog, and waylays our finest men. To face such an enemy, we need a bit of the arcane, I think."

"Well, I will have none of it," said Ob, waving his hand before him. "Nothing but rubbish."

"I will not touch those things," said one knight.

"Nor will I," said another.

"I will take one," said Claradon, as he and Theta moved toward Gabriel. The knights looked surprised and made way for Claradon. Claradon reached for the glowing blade.

"Dargus dal is mine," said Gabriel as he sheathed it and reached down into the chest. "But you may have its twin." Gabriel pulled another wondrous blade from the chest and handed it to Claradon. "It is called Worfin dal," he said, pointing to the runes inscribed on the side of the blade, "which means the lord's dagger in the old tongue."

"Asgardian daggers," said Theta. "I thought them all lost long ago."

"Not all, my Lord," said Gabriel. "Some few remain. I regret that I cannot offer you one, for of them I possess only two."

"What makes them things special, besides the weird glow?" said Ob.

"Legend says they were forged by Heimdall himself during *The Dawn Age*," said Gabriel. "And ensorcelled by Tyr."

"Daggers of the gods?" said Claradon.

"Oh boy," said Ob, shaking his head. "That is a

tall one, if I've ever heard."

Gabriel reached into the chest and withdrew another dagger. This one was longer and thinner than the first two. Its scabbard and pommel were less ornate, and although it glowed, its luminescence paled in comparison to the first two. He presented it to Theta.

"This one, and all the rest in these trunks are of the finest Dyvers steel and ensorcelled by the archmages of the Order of the Arcane. No finer blades are forged in Midgaard today."

Theta nodded his thanks.

"These blades will protect us from the fog and blind our enemies with the light of Tyr," said Gabriel. "There are enough for each of you. Each man will take one, like it as not. That includes you, good Castellan."

Ob narrowed his eyes, set his jaw, and glowered at Gabriel.

The men grumbled and grunted in protest, but in the end, each dutifully girded one of the daggers about their waist or leg.

"You should've come to me when you wanted these made," said Ob. "I could've fixed you up with my cousin Bork—best smith this side of Heimdall. So who made these?"

"McDuff forged the steel," said Gabriel, "and a tower wizard ensorcelled them."

"Good ole McDuff," said Ob. "Wears a lot of hats, he does. That old Dwarf has some skills, there is no doubt, but genuine Gnomish blades are better than anything Dwarvish by a good stretch. It's all in the heat, you know. You've got to get the blade hot enough, but not too hot, and then fold the metal enough—a hundred times or more for a blade of quality. Dwarves don't understand that— they're all about sticking jewels in the pommel, getting some wizard to magic them up so that they glow in the dark, and smearing silver pigment on them so they can tell folks they're made of mithril or some other mythical gunk. No real talent in that, if you ask me. Bunch of frauds and cheats, they are. Stinking Dwarves." Ob looked down at the blades and shook his head. "Well, I suppose, these will have to suffice."

"I look forward to hearing the tale of how you acquired the Asgardian blades," said Claradon.

"And I will gladly tell it to you and Aradon both, on our return," said Gabriel.

"I'll be hearing that tale too," said Ob, "as long as it comes with mead or good Gnomish ale—the best that Portland Vale has to offer."

"I will need an entire keg, no doubt," said Gabriel.

"Only one, assuming it will be just us four," said Ob. "Any more than that, and you had best get two."

VIII
SHADES

To be ready to leave for the Vermion at dawn, Claradon needed to retrieve armor and gear from his chambers before retiring for the night to the makeshift accommodations that the servants prepared in the citadel's Underhalls. He could have sent his manservant, Humphrey. Humph always knew what to pack, and with the help of another servant or two, he could have hauled down everything Claradon needed. But Claradon wanted to go himself. There were one or two things he wouldn't trust to anyone else, not even Humph. Besides, he was too worked up to sleep just yet. Perhaps the long walk up the stair would tire him enough to get a couple of hours sleep before dawn. At least he hoped it would.

Humphrey and a House guard called Gorned silently shadowed Claradon as he trudged up the stairs, lanterns in hand. Normally, he wouldn't task a House guard with porter duties, but Ob insisted that Claradon take a guardsman with him, "just in case". Ob feared that the Dor might come under attack at any moment, and he wasn't taking any chances, even within the citadel.

Rare it was that Claradon walked through the Dor's halls and found them empty and silent. There was always some family member or retainer going about their business, and servants cleaning, scrubbing, and polishing everything in sight, and guards guarding whatever Ob or his father thought needed guarding. But not that night. That night the halls of Dor Eotrus were deserted, everyone having fled to the Underhalls to escape the bizarre wailing sounds that demanded entry through every window, crack, crevice, and door, and even through the stout walls themselves. The emptiness and noise made the place feel odd in a way that Claradon couldn't explain, except to say that it just didn't feel like home. Not any longer. Not until he found his father and things returned to normal.

He walked slowly up the long flights of stairs, much more slowly than was his custom. Tapestries lined the walls and regal carpet runners woven in far-off places called Ferd, Bourntown, Dyvers, and Lent were perfectly aligned down the center of the stairs and the connecting halls; they minimized the hollow echoing sounds that plagued most keeps.

For 1200 years, the Eotrus called the Dor home, but over the centuries, the core bloodline dwindled. The last three generations saw no more than one son born to the lord of the House, despite some reportedly vigorous efforts by Claradon's great-grandfather, a man of wide wanderings but otherwise sound reputation. Claradon's father rejuvenated the Eotrus line at long last, begetting four sons, and thus ensuring the continuation of the ruling family. Only a very few of the various and sundry Eotrus cousins that ruled manor houses, estates, and stout keeps in the countryside and the surrounding villages and smalls towns were disappointed by those births, their lofty dreams of lordship crushed.

While the long years threatened the Eotrus bloodline, they also conspired to accumulate untold treasures that filled the Dor, most purchased with silver, some with blood, but the most prized heirlooms were crafted by family members, noble allies, or loyal retainers. Claradon passed those antiques every day of his life, but he rarely saw them, his thoughts focused either on his duties and obligations or on far off places, wild adventures, or a certain young lady. Amongst other things, he took the antiques for granted, especially the artwork, but that night was different—he needed to look at them, to study them. He needed to appreciate them and to carve their likenesses into his memory, "just in case".

Each piece of art he passed had a plaque affixed nearby it that described its creation, history, and subject matter. The plaque below one marble bust that caught his eye read:

Lord August Eotrus, the seventh of his name, sculpted by Lady Sirear Eotrus, first daughter, in the year 651 by Lomerian reckoning.

Claradon's companions patiently waited behind him as he read the plaque and studied his ancestor's face for some moments before moving on.

A striking painting entitled, *The Dor in Winter*, resided at the top of the stair landing at the same floor as Claradon's chambers. It depicted a happy scene of children frolicking in the courtyard's snow and reminded Claradon of many similar times he shared with his brothers.

Humphrey and Gorned exchanged concerned looks as Claradon lingered before the painting. "Brother Claradon?" said Humphrey. "The hour is late, we should—"

Claradon raised a hand in a gesture that called for silence and Humphrey complied, though he looked taken aback. "This may be my last chance to see these," said Claradon softly. He knew that whatever waylaid his father's patrol might well do the same to his. If that happened, he might not live to return to the Dor. And if Eotrus lands were being invaded, the Dor itself might be sacked before his return. As hard to believe as it was, his whole world might be on the verge of crumbling. Or, his father might be found safe and sound, and all would go back to normal, and like Tanch said, they would all laugh about how afraid they were and about how they overreacted to some weird sounds in the night.

A sketch drawn in charcoal hung just beside the door to Claradon's chambers, its canvas protected by clear glass and a stout oak frame. The drawing was a near perfect likeness of him as a child of three or four. He felt his eyes begin to grow wet when he read its inscription and he felt ashamed that he hadn't read it in years.

Master Claradon Eotrus, first of his name, drawn by his mother, Lady Eleanor Malvegil Eotrus. Year 1246 of the fourth age of Midgaard, year 832 by Lomerian reckoning.

Claradon ran his hand along the words and paused when his fingers brushed his mother's name. Her loss terribly plagued him, and he still thought of her every day. He couldn't imagine not thinking of her. Recent events aside, the Dor was a happy place, but not like it was when his mother graced its halls. Her energy was electric and contagious. Her support, comfort, and unconditional love could never be replaced, and were sorely missed by every member of the House.

Humphrey stepped past him, unlocked and opened his door. "Brother Claradon, I'll get your clothes and armor, but I'll need Gorned's help to carry it."

His words snapped Claradon back to the present. "Fine, Humph. I'll get the rest," said Claradon as he stepped into the modest anteroom that served as both coatroom and Humphrey's duty station. Through another door, he entered the large sitting room where Claradon entertained guests. It had a water closet, which was large by most any standard, and featured: a huge griffin's foot tub, a granite basin with a pump handle and spout beside it to bring up water from the Dor's aquifer, a small wood burning stove to heat the room and the bathwater, a toilet carved from a block of white marble, and various accouterments, both rich and functional. He grabbed what he needed from there and headed through the lounge to his bedroom, dodging Humphrey who shuffled awkwardly out, a teetering pile of clothes in hand.

The cavernous bedchamber's walls were paneled in dark wood, and the granite floor tiles were softened by area rugs and animal furs. Two wood-burning stoves, one at each end of the chamber, kept the room as warm as he liked, unlike the Dor's halls, which were always a bit too cold and leaned toward frigid at winter's peak.

Claradon tried not to look at the sketch he had left half-finished on the writing table beside the window as he strapped on his sword and dagger belts. He only glanced at it for a moment, just to be certain it was still there and undisturbed. Satisfied, he scooped up the gear he needed, and crammed it with some difficulty into his bulging pack. He liked to be prepared, which resulted in a tendency to carry too much.

When he was done, he turned his attention to the sketch. It was a drawing of a girl that he fancied and that his mother had wanted him to marry. Retrieving it was much of the reason that he had walked up there, of that, there was no denying any longer, at least not to himself. He needed to look at her face one more time, just in case. As his eyes lingered on her lovely features, he decided to take the sketch with him. At least she would be near him, in a way. The sketch might get damaged, maybe ruined, but he could always redraw it. He had the skills for that—his mother had taught him well.

Marissa Harringgold was the second daughter of Harper Harringgold, the Archduke of Lomion City, a lifelong friend of his father's, and arguably the most powerful man in the realm, save for the king and perhaps the chancellor. While her pedigree lent an air of excitement, it had little to do with his feelings. Those took root for other reasons.

Usually, Claradon had trouble speaking to women. He would get nervous and clam up, and inevitably, they would think him dense or odd or just not interested. He had no such trouble with Marissa. They used to speak for hours on end about every topic imaginable and he never grew tired of it. They never fought or argued—not once in all the years they knew each other. He was drawn to her and couldn't take his eyes off her whenever she was in sight. It's not that she was a great beauty—while she was certainly pretty by most men's standards, she was not unusually so. There was just something about her. He couldn't define it and it didn't matter. He wanted her and that was that. But as far as he could ever tell, she didn't want him as any more than a friend, or at least not enough to ever let on, despite both their mothers' meddlings. Beyond being friends, he never knew where he stood with her, and that was vexing.

He wanted to tell her how he felt, and often thought about how and when and what he'd say. The planning was an utter waste of time and he knew it, since he knew he would never go through with it. *She knows, she has to know*, he would assure himself. *She just doesn't care*. If he told her directly, she would likely say nothing, leaving him hanging, or else tell him she felt nothing for him. Either way, the discomfort between them would damage and perhaps even end their friendship. Then he wouldn't even have that. And that is all he had of her. He didn't want to give that up.

His hopes and his mother's plans ended when

the Caradonians accepted his application and called him up for training. They didn't strictly forbid their members from marrying, but seriously frowned upon it. It was well known amongst their ranks that if you took a wife you would never advance to a leadership position in the order, because the leadership believed it demonstrated a lack of devotion and focus. If he would never advance, why join at all?

But he had wanted to be a Caradonian Knight for years, despite Sir Gabriel's urgings that he petition a secular order—one of the rare issues about which he and Gabriel failed to agree regardless of how much they talked it out. Gabriel encouraged him to let Marissa know how he felt and even offered to intercede on his behalf, but Claradon would have none of it. Curiously, when he failed to progress his relationship with Marissa, Gabriel was quick to point out other eligible young ladies, quite a number of them in fact, but not one could compare to Marissa and so Claradon paid them no heed. No doubt, Gabriel assumed once one of them got their claws into Claradon he would have to put aside his plans with the Caradonians and follow Gabriel's advice into a secular order.

All that notwithstanding, Claradon knew the religious knights were his calling: the sword and the staff, the scepter and the shield, warrior and priest; that duality was his destiny. He felt it in his bones. He would follow that dream and no one would dissuade him. Not Sir Gabriel and not even his mother.

He often wondered what he would have done

if Marissa had pleaded with him not to join the Caradonians. In his heart, he knew he would have done anything for her, to be with her—dreams and destiny be damned. To have her would have been worth more—more than anything. But she didn't plead; she didn't even ask. She didn't speak out against or in support of the idea. She offered no opinion at all. She just didn't seem to care. After he announced his plans, if anything, she withdrew from him, which made Claradon question her friendship. Perhaps he didn't even have that. Perhaps even that was just in his head—a pathetic delusion of a lonely young man too long under the protection of his parents' roof. Perhaps Marissa only spent time with him out of some sense of obligation to her mother's wishes. Maybe she didn't even like him. He just didn't know. He just wasn't sure.

So after much thought, he decided to end things with her, not that there was anything to end—mostly just hopes, plans, and desires in his head. And ending it turned out to be easy. He just stopped calling on her, and she never called on him; she never had; he always had to initiate things—so that was the end of it. He hoped that she would show up one day, even if in anger—at least then he would know she cared, at least a little. But she didn't. That hurt him badly, but it made him feel as if he had made the right decision, to move on. And so they lost touch, as simple as that. No battle, no harsh words, and no goodbyes.

He never told her how he felt. How could he have the courage to face death in battle, but not to face rejection by a girl not yet twenty? He didn't understand it, but that was the way it was. Maybe that failing meant he wasn't worthy of her. Sad, because if so, then he wasn't worthy of any girl, for he would be no braver with any other, probably less so. In any case, it was far too late to change things. He would have to learn to live with his regrets, but he never stopped thinking of her.

He made it a point not to know how she fared in life these past few years. He didn't want to hear that she had married another and started a family. It was better not to know. The problem with that approach, of course, was that if the archduke's daughter became engaged, everyone would know. It would be a social event amongst the nobles, a highlight of the year, just as it was when her older sister got married a few years earlier. The Eotrus would all be invited, of course, and he would be obligated to attend. The horror of that was something he didn't want to think of in the best of times, and certainly not with his father missing. If his mother were alive, she would find a way to get him out of it, but his father would have no such sympathy. But no invitations ever came. She must still be a maiden.

She had probably long forgotten him, not that he ever really mattered to her anyway. He didn't even want to see her again—it would be too painful. Maybe just from afar, such that she couldn't see him, but he could see her. It would be easier that way. He'd like that, to see her face again, her smile, and the way she walked, and the smell of her perfume. Best not to think of such things he told himself.

The clanking of his armor as Humphrey and Gorned carried it from the storage closet drew him from thoughts of Marissa. Before he turned to leave, he carefully folded up the sketch and placed it in his shirt pocket. He stepped up to the window to gaze one last time at the spectacular view of the Dor and its surrounding environs that his chamber's position in the high tower afforded. But it was to no avail. It was too dark to see much of anything, the moons hidden behind clouds. Unlike most nights, nearly all the Dor's lanterns and sconces were out—only a few at ground level still burned. In fact, as far as he could tell, his was the only window in the citadel or in any of the towers that was lit.

When he heard a light footstep behind him, he turned, expecting to see Humphrey, one of his impatient looks plastered to his face. But no one was there.

"Claradon," came a whisper—a man's voice— but so slight that he wasn't certain whether he had really heard it and he had no idea from what direction it had come. If it were Humph, he would call out again if he had something useful to say, so Claradon ignored it and continued about his business. He had just grabbed his gear bag when the window rattled behind him—a strange sound, different from when the wind shook it. He spun around and stepped back from the glass, but there was nothing there, just the darkness. He felt a sudden chill, and the candles and lantern noticeably dimmed.

Then he sensed something off to his left. Something in the bedchamber's sitting area, which was full in shadow since Humph hadn't lit any candles in that part of the large room. Claradon didn't hear it. He hadn't caught even a glimpse of movement out of the corner of his eye, but somehow, he knew someone or some thing was there. He spun toward it, dropped his bag, and pulled his sword free of its sheath. He raised it to the ready.

He saw nothing there, but it was dark. More than dark enough for someone to lurk unseen in the shadows. But nothing moved. Nothing made a sound.

He stood there tensed and stared into the shadows for several moments as his eyes adjusted to the darkness. Where were Humph and Gorned—were they playing a joke on him? He was in no mood for that. After a while, he imagined he saw the outline of a figure sitting in the old leather chair in the far back corner of the room—the chair his father had gifted him and that he often sat in when he called on Claradon.

"Who is there?" said Claradon, his voice sharp. Strangely, his breath misted before him, and the room grew colder by the second. And then he was sure—a large man sat back there in the shadows: silent and still.

"Beware the scion of Azathoth," came a breathy whisper, much louder than before; a man's voice for certain, strangely familiar, though whether from the shadows or some other direction, Claradon could not be certain. Then it spoke again. "For he will call down death on us all."

"Show yourself," said Claradon loudly, hoping

Humph and Gorned would hear and back him up.

"Step away from the window," whispered the shadows, its voice quickening.

Claradon started to back toward the bedchamber's exit, sword at the ready, when the window exploded inward and a large shape vaulted in. Glass shards pelted Claradon, head to foot, and he went down on his rump, his sword fallen from his grasp.

Before him was a creature the like of which he had never seen except in darkest nightmare. It was a monster. A six-legged beast the size of a full-grown mountain lion, pitch black in color, with a scaly, hairless hide, and long, clawed feet. Its head was twice as large as it should be and somewhat ursine in appearance, though it was no bear. Its teeth were as black as its hide and several were as long as a sabertooth's.

Claradon's sword had fallen between him and the beast. There was no possibility to retrieve it before the creature would be on him. He scrambled back, grabbed his pack, and held it before him as a shield. The creature roared and pounced on him, Claradon, still on the floor. Its claws raked into the large pack that shielded his torso.

Claradon couldn't believe his ears when the creature spoke. "Give up your soul, human," whispered the beast in a thick accent, its voice ragged, its breath foul and fast. "It belongs to us and will be ours in the end anyway." Claradon twisted his shoulders and dodged his head to the side as the beast's jaws snapped shut where his face had just been. The thing was powerful, but

Claradon used its momentum to push it off him, and scrambled to his feet. He brought the pack up to shield himself and realized there was little left of it but tatters. Acrid smoke and a burning scent rose from it, as if the beast's very touch had scorched it. His sword still out of reach, from his belt he drew Worfin Dal, the Asgardian dagger that Sir Gabriel had lately gifted him.

The beast should have been on him in an instant, but it hesitated, eyeing the dagger, somehow repelled by it. Claradon saw that the thing was horribly wounded. At least two of its legs were blackened and charred and dragged behind it. Even worse, much of one side of its torso was ripped open, its bones exposed to the air, and the black ichor that was its blood smeared the floor and Claradon's garments. How it still lived at all was a wonder.

Gorned and Humph rushed into the room.

"Dead gods," shrieked Humphrey, drawing the beast's attention.

Gorned's sword was out in an instant, his eyes wide with alarm. He grabbed Humph by the collar and pulled him back, behind him. In that moment of distraction, Claradon lunged. The beast reared back, but it was too slow. Claradon's dagger thrust caught it in the neck and sunk deep before he jumped back and pulled the blade out.

The beast fell over onto its back, its legs flailing wildly as ichor gushed from its neck.

Claradon grabbed a lantern from the sideboard and threw it at the beast. The glass housing shattered and doused the creature with burning oil: its shrieks were deafening. Claradon dashed to his cupboard and threw open the doors. He reached in and grabbed a battle hammer and a two-handed axe. He tossed the axe to Gorned and the two set upon the beast. They hacked and cut and smashed it until it moved no more. The flames persisted and they doused it with water to keep it from spreading.

Humph sat in the corner shaking.

Gorned kicked the beast to make certain it was dead. Claradon had already mashed its head to pulp with his hammer and it had long since stopped moving, but Gorned slammed it once more with the axe for good measure. "Best to be sure," said Gorned. "That some kind of a troll, you think?"

Claradon shook his head. "As far as I know, trolls have two legs, not six. I don't know what that thing is."

"Ob will want to see it," said Gorned. "And probably won't believe us until he does."

"Sir Gabriel as well," said Claradon. "Humph, I need you to head down to the Underhalls, find Ob, and tell him what happened. We will wait here."

"What if there are more?" cried Humphrey.

Claradon looked surprised. "I don't know," he said. "I doubt there are more of them."

"You don't know that," said Humphrey. "There could be army of them attacking the Dor even now, and we're up here all alone. I'm not going down those halls by myself. What if they are waiting down there, in the dark? What if they came in through other windows? I'm not going— no way, no how."

Claradon turned to Gorned.

"He might be right," said Gorned. "Ob would have my head if I left you alone up here. You can order me to go if you want, but I won't."

"Then we will all go together," said Claradon. "But first, we need more water to douse what's left of these flames. We can't have the tower burning down on us."

While Humph and Gorned dealt with what remained of the creature's smoking carcass, Claradon took a lantern and walked to the far end of the room where something had lately lurked and spoken to him. There was nothing there. No one in the shadows, and the chilling cold he felt when whatever it was had spoken to him was no more. He stood before the old leather chair that had once belonged to his father. That old friend had sat in his father's study for as long as he could remember—wrinkled, bursting at the seams, and patched over and over again. His mother had nagged his father for years to get rid of it. It wasn't until after her death that he finally broke down and decided to replace it. To his father's surprise, Claradon rescued it from its destiny as kindling and placed it in his own chambers.

There was no evidence that anyone had recently sat in that seat. It looked undisturbed and the cushion wasn't warm, but as Claradon bent to check it, he smelled pipe smoke—the very blend his father smoked on those rare occasions that he lit his pipe. It was gone as fast as it appeared. Claradon stepped away, quicker than his courage wanted, and rejoined the others, but said nothing of the shade that had spoken to him or its ominous warning.

* * *

"**N**ot much left of it," said Ob as he, Claradon, Dolan, Gabriel, and Theta studied the scene. Several knights and guardsmen searched the other rooms and patrolled the hallway. A haze of smoke still filled the room, which smelled strongly of burned and putrid meat.

"You overcooked it quite a bit, you did, Mister Claradon," said Dolan.

"Lots of legs, like you said," said Ob as he nudged the smoldering heap with the toe of his boot. "You sure there ain't two or three of them piled atop one another?"

"I'm sure," said Claradon.

"Well, you earned your pay for the day, soldier," said Ob. "You killed it right and proper. Would've been nice if you left it in fewer pieces and didn't burn it to cinders so we could figure out what the heck it was. From what is here, I just can't tell."

"It was wounded, badly, even before it smashed through the window," said Claradon. "Charred and busted up more than enough to kill a man."

"Yet it climbed up near two hundred feet," said Gabriel from where he stood by the window, holding a lantern over the sill to light up the outer face of the wall. "I see a blood trail down the facade. It must have seen your light, and climbed all the way up from the courtyard. That's determination."

"That stone is sheer and smooth as a baby's

104

bottom," said Ob. "Even a Hand assassin couldn't scale it on his best day."

"Well that thing did," said Gabriel.

"Let's get that window plugged up," said Ob. "My head is starting to spin from the darned wailing again."

"It spoke," said Claradon.

"Who?" said Ob.

"That thing," he said, pointing to the remains. "It said something about giving up my soul."

"Your soul?" said Ob. "It's just an animal, boy. How could it talk? And even if it could, what would it know of souls? You sure your head's on straight? Did Gorned hear it too, or Humph?"

"They weren't in the room yet."

Ob pulled out his sword and poked its tip around in the remains. "Maybe it was no beast at all. Maybe it was a man—all dressed up in a costume, trying to look like some kind of monster. If it spoke, that has to be it. Dagnabbit, maybe I spoke too soon before. Maybe the Black Hand is involved. That's all we need. We might be better off with an invasion. I'll take a stand-up fight any day over stinking assassins."

"It's too charred to tell for certain one way or the other," said Gabriel.

"This was no man," said Theta.

"Then it must be some creature what come out of the caves up in the hills," said Ob. "Some holdover from olden days. But such a thing couldn't talk—it would be just an animal. What say you, Gabe?"

"I say we had better search the grounds and the Outer Dor in case there are more of them. To climb up the tower wall in the condition it was in, and to put up the fight that it did, tells me all I need to know. It's dangerous, and if there are more, we need to root them out and put them down. The quicker the better."

"Maybe this here fellow and his kin are what jumped your patrol," said Dolan. "Maybe that is why it was wounded, maybe."

"Maybe so," said Ob nodding his head. "Maybe so."

"Do you know what it is?" said Gabriel to Theta.

"As you said, there is not enough left to tell for certain," said Theta, "but more than likely, it's a reskalan."

"What is a reskalan?" said Dolan.

"They're foot soldiers out of Nifleheim," said Gabriel.

"A what out of Nifleheim?" said Ob. "You are joking, right?"

"He doesn't joke," said Dolan.

"Then you're daft," said Ob. "Nifleheim and everything about it is a fairy story handed down through the ages. Me grandpop used to tell me tales of Nifleheim when I misbehaved. Them monsters are nothing but figments and bunk, dreamed up to scare the whelps, nothing more. The only ones what believe different, is some religious weirdos, and country bumpkins. This thing is an animal—a strange one, I'll admit, but an animal just the same, and now it is dead and that's the end of it."

"How would it have gotten here?" said Claradon to Theta, "If you're right about what it is?"

"A wizard would have conjured it up," said Theta.

"From Nifleheim?" said Claradon.

"Aye," said Theta.

"Oh boy," said Ob. "Now we've got magic and monsters. Next you will have giant bunnies attacking us and maybe a unicorn or two. You people are loons."

***

Two small Lomerian longboats drifted down a river whose water was as red as blood and plagued by jagged rocks and treacherous currents. Mist limited one's vision in all directions, though it was thinnest behind and thickest ahead. The lead boat flew the black; the trailing boat flew a white sail, though otherwise, the boats were as twins.

A lonely figure manned the tiller at each boat's stern, no rowers or crewmen in sight. Amidships of each was a small wooden platform upon which rested a body, richly dressed: garment, armor, and arms. Funeral boats were these, sailing into the afterlife, bearing the honored dead to Valhalla, though no pyre yet burned on either vessel.

Claradon looked up and saw, amidst the clouds, Valkyries astride their winged steeds, circling overhead, their gazes fixed on the doomed boats below. Claradon strained to see the faces of the pilots and of the dead, and moved closer to get a better look.

The armor of the dead man in the lead boat gleamed and sparkled so brightly that even in the diffuse light he had to squint to look at it, but he recognized the olden craftsmanship at once. The fallen warrior was his beloved father, his rugged face pale and sallow, hands crossed at his breast gripping his sword. Claradon's worst fears had come to pass. His eyes filled with tears and his throat tightened; he could barely breathe. The man at the tiller turned toward Claradon. It was Sir Gabriel, tall and strong as ever, his eyes sad, his face forlorn. His sure and steady hand guided the boat past the rocks and through the rapids, safeguarding it along its journey.

Claradon looked again at his father and realized his mistake. It was not Aradon Eotrus at all. It was Claradon's brother, Jude. His father and Jude looked much alike, despite Jude's youth and clean-shaven face. But how could this be? Jude was off in Lomion City, safe and sound at the Tyrian Chapterhouse. Dear gods, how could he be dead? His little brother, dead? Claradon's heart wrenched in his chest. It cannot be. When he looked again at Sir Gabriel, Gabriel had changed. His eyes were all wrong. They gleamed with a golden tint; no, more than that, they were completely golden—no whites to them at all. His expression was uncharacteristic, as was his stance, and he kept looking over his shoulder at the trailing ship, as if it were chasing him. As if he feared it. Now his steering was chaotic and bold as he pulled the vessel in one direction and then the other. Up ahead, the river split—quiet and calm water to one side, and rapids leading to great falls to the other. Strangely, it seemed that Gabriel maneuvered the ship toward the falls and certain disaster, or was the second ship forcing him in that direction? It wasn't clear. Confused, Claradon shook his head in dismay and forced himself to look away.

Claradon looked back at the second boat. The boatman was wrapped in a dark cloak with a deep hood. He looked up at Claradon and there was no mistaking who it was. Lord Angle Theta guided the boat, subtlely nudging it this way and that as it made its way through the mist. Claradon looked down at that boat's fallen warrior and recognized the dress garment and armor at once. It was he— Claradon, dead atop the pyre. But how? When? It made no sense. Claradon made to call out to Theta, but the man at the tiller wasn't Theta after all. It was Claradon himself; he steered the boat, standing at the rear, yet he also lay on the pyre. He was at once in both positions, both alive and dead. It made no sense.

Claradon felt himself falling.

He opened his eyes to the dim light of the Dor's Underhall. He heard the men stirring from sleep outside his makeshift bedchamber.

IX
DOR EOTRUS

A squad of guardsmen set out at dawn to reconnoiter, but the main group's departure was postponed due to the night's events. At midmorning, the expedition assembled in the shadow of the curtain wall near the inner bailey's gates. The night's chill was still in the air, though mercifully, the wretched wailing was hours gone. A throng of family, friends, and looky-loos gathered to see the expedition off and wish them well. Claradon stood by the portcullis, Ob, Gabriel, and Ector at his side, while the men adjusted their gear and said their goodbyes. Each knight was clad in battle armor polished to a sheen and impregnated with pigments: gold, silver, blue, or gray. Theirs wasn't the old-style armor of link and chain that was long the staple in Midgaard, nor was it the newer, fashionable and lightweight plate armor churned out by Lomerian smiths for the kingdom's guardsmen and the private soldiery of the nobility and prominent guildsmen. This was armor designed for the professional soldier—built for war, not pomp, pageantry, or tourney, though it was as ornate as any tooled for those tasks. It was frighteningly thick and strong, thorough in its coverage, and custom crafted to suit each man's shape by master smiths in Dor Eotrus's own forges. Few noble Houses boasted armor that could begin to compare. Heavy as it was, the knights moved freely in it. That was in some part due to their size and strength, characteristic of men of the northlands, as well as the ingenious design of the armor's joints, which provided robust protection while barely limiting one's reach and agility. The main reason, though, was that the Eotrus knights wore their armor daily as part of their ongoing training. For them, it was almost a second skin.

Atop their armor, each man proudly wore the House colors on tabard, cloak, and cape, and the Eotrus sigil was prominently displayed across their tabards. Similarly, each man was equipped with a shield of oak and iron, emblazoned in blue and gold, with their own family's sigil adorning the front. The matching armor, shields, and colors united them and identified them as a single force—as Eotrus men. Their weapons, however, held no such uniformity. Each man carried an array of death dealers of his own choosing that suited his skills, style, and tastes. Some favored lances, spears, or halberds; others, swords of one type or another; war hammers, great and small; one and two-handed axes; and crossbows of local make. And as instructed, each man girded one of Gabriel's daggers to belt, ankle, or shoulder.

The knights' warhorses were tall and strong and of shaggy coats common to the large northern breeds, with colors ranging from chestnut to maroon. The grooms brought them out from the stables fully accoutered—their barding and colors matching their masters' armor and garb.

"If the kin of that creature—the reskalan or whatever Theta named it —is what hit our patrol, we've no more time to waste," said Claradon. "We need to get out there and help them. Don't you think we should call the men to order? We've got to get moving."

"Not just yet," said Ob.

Gabriel noticed the furrow that grew along Claradon's brow as he stared at Ob, expecting some further word from him that did not come. "I know how you feel," said Gabriel. "You want to rush out those gates and find your father as fast as can be, and you want to tear apart anyone or anything that has hurt him. I feel the same, and so do those knights, every last one of them. But they have loved ones too. We need to give them some time to say their goodbyes. We've got to respect that."

"Sending men off to battle is not the same as moving pieces on a gameboard, my boy," said Ob. "Not by any stretch. Game tokens stand all lonesome, with no history, no future, and no connection to anyone or anything else. It's not that way with real soldiers. A good leader must never forget that."

"Do you understand?" said Gabriel, looking to Claradon and Ector, in turn.

They both nodded and said that they did.

Sir Bilson's wife and triplet daughters were all hugs and kisses and tears. Sir Erendin of Forndin Manor and his brothers, Sir Miden, and Sir Talbot were each embraced by their ladies fair. Sir Bareddal of Hanok Keep hugged his daughter of two, his wife sadly passed from the fever during the previous winter. Artol's entire brood came out to see him off—his petite wife, not five feet tall, and nearly a score of children ranging in age from two to twenty. Artol took the time for a hug and kiss or a handshake for each son and daughter. He looked each one in the eye and offered them his toothy smile and a brief word.

"Artol's two eldest boys petitioned me to take them along," said Ob. "They made it hard to say no."

"They are both of age and skilled with a sword," said Ector. "Why did you deny them?"

"Ours is a job for veterans," said Ob, "not eager boys."

"All the same," said Gabriel to Ector, "they will serve you well while we're gone, if it comes to it."

Sir Glimador Malvegil's lady was there and did not go unnoticed by the men. "She must have gotten up at dawn to get all fancied up like that," said Ob. "And what for, I ask you? The girl is as beautiful as Sif or Freya themselves and with curves like an Elven lass. What she needs with face paint and fancy gowns, I will never know."

"It's part of her style," said Claradon.

"A merchant's daughter doesn't get betrothed to the heir of House Malvegil unless she is something special," said Gabriel. "The Malvegils have only married other nobility as far back as anyone can remember."

"It's her style and personality as much as her looks that won my uncle's approval," said Claradon.

"Can't fault Torbin for that," said Ob. "I would not turn her away, I'm not ashamed to admit. But look at stinking Indigo. That boy has got no shame," he said as they watched the young knight get swarmed by several maidens that nearly came to blows vying for his attentions. Indigo's chiseled features, ready smile, extreme height and muscled build had ever made him the favorite of the ladies and he was never one to squander the opportunities so provided. "If he is fool enough to have more than one at once, he should at least keep them apart and secret like. Don't you think?"

"I think he likes to watch them fight," said Ector.

Ob considered that for a moment. "Might be something to that," he said scratching his chin.

A richly dressed middle-aged lady scowled at Indigo's girls as she stood beside Sir Paldor and another man whose rumpled clothes indicated he had hastily been pulled from bed. "Paldor's parents," said Ob. "Didn't know they were here."

"They arrived the day before yesterday," said Claradon. "Up from Lomion City on one of their quarterly visits. Sire Brondel would come with us if I let him—a good man."

"He is a good friend to your father, but a bit past his fighting days," said Ob.

"Out of practice," said Gabriel, "if not too old."

"He knows it," said Claradon, "and didn't press me when I turned him down. He would have gone though, all the same. Brave man and a loyal friend."

"His wife dotes on Paldor as if he were the prized turkey at midsummer's feast," said Ob. "Makes me want to puke."

"She's proud her son is squire to Sir Gabriel," said Ector. "What parent wouldn't be?"

"Old Sire Brondel," said Gabriel. "He never

114

approved of the assignment. Tried several times to convince Aradon and me to put an end to it, but I resisted. The boy has potential and he stands to gain more from the training I'm giving him. But Brondel says he is too old to be a squire. He says that a man full grown should stand on his own feet, and not serve another."

"There is a point there, on both sides, I suppose," said Ob. "In any case, we best bring his boy back safe or his wife will have our heads."

"And what do I do if you don't come back?" said Ector to Claradon, his voice sharp.

Claradon sighed. "You prepare for a siege. You know how to do that."

"And you fight, if there's fighting to do," said Ob. "Sarbek will be at your side, along with a garrison of other good men like Marzdan and Balfin. You will not be on your own here."

"Sarbek is down with a fever," said Ector. "Or else he would be riding out with you and you know it."

"He will recover, soon enough," said Ob. "He's as strong as an ox, that one, despite his years. He will give you good council, should you need it."

"We should send a raven to the Tyrian Chapterhouse," said Ector. "We've got to tell Jude and Malcolm what is going on."

"If you do that," said Ob, "them two hotheads will fly all the way back here from Lomion City without taking a breath. They probably won't even stop to pack or pee, or bring along anybody with them what can hold a sword. If we're being invaded, they're liable to run smack into the enemy. Then they will get themselves captured or killed dead. I will not have that, boy—not on my watch. There will be no ravens for them until we know what's what."

"I agree," said Gabriel.

"They have a right to know what is going on," said Ector.

"Right now we don't know much of anything," said Ob.

"We know that father is missing," said Ector. "That is what we need to tell them."

"You're getting more willful by the day, sonny," said Ob. "Maybe I should put you over my knee, as I did when you was a whelp. Maybe that will keep you in line and all respectful like."

"It didn't work back then," said Gabriel.

Ob nodded. "As I recall it didn't. We will tell your brothers what is going on just as soon as we know, and not before. Don't even think about sending a raven to them after we're gone—because I will have your hide if you do."

A little ways away across the courtyard, Theta and Dolan conversed quietly astride their horses. Dolan now looked little like a simple retainer, his aspect more akin to a veteran soldier or mercenary—donned as he was in a battered cuirass of brown and black-hued leather and equipped with a small arsenal of weaponry. He girded the well-oiled longsword sheathed at his side in the manner of a professional soldier, and the longbow engraved with strange pictograms that he carried over his shoulder was clearly often used. The hafts of several daggers protruded from sheaths at his boots and his shoulder.

"After we've seen this business through, will

we head back home?" said Dolan.

Theta grunted, his meaning unclear.

"We must be here for some reason, something big, more than just strange goings-on in some woods. We're not halfway around the world from home for just that."

Theta offered no response.

"What do you expect we will find here?" said Dolan.

Expressionless and even-toned, Theta replied, "Perhaps some world-eating monster or demon lord or ancient wyrm, but probably more reskalan or things akin to them, a lot more. It matters not, for I will put down whatever it be."

"I thought we took care of the last of them things already?"

Theta ignored him.

"Guess there are some more lurking about. Never liked lurkers."

"When we get going, ride up ahead and join the Gnome," said Theta. "Make sure he doesn't stumble us into an ambush."

"Aye, boss, that I will."

"All right, you slackers," bellowed Ob, "enough standing around. Check your weapons and secure your packs. We're heading out forthwith."

***

Despite the circumstances, riding toward the main gates, which led to the Outer Dor, Claradon couldn't help but be impressed by the strength and majesty of the Dor itself. The twenty-foot thick outer and inner walls of the noble castle, crafted by master stonemasons, stood forty and sixty feet in height, respectively. Mammoth towers flanked the main gate and additional towers were situated at the four corners of both the outer and inner baileys. The towers' crenellated parapets partially obscured an array of large catapults and ballistae that fortified the roofs. Looking back, whence they came, he saw the enormous cylindrical tower in which his family resided. It was a magnificent work of engineering that approached two hundred fifty feet in height and included several majestic turrets and minarets that branched off from the primary tower.

Claradon had ordered the Dor's forces to prepare to defend against a possible attack, and as they approached the main gate he saw that the preparations were well underway. Squads of men-at-arms guarded the entranceway and the barbican area beyond. Soldiers on the allures heated iron vats filled with oil, and squads of crossbowmen stalked the battlements—all under the watchful eye of Sir Marzdan, a steely-eyed veteran and Watch Captain of the citadel's outer gate.

There was an unmistakable and pervading sense of doom that plagued the keep. Dor Eotrus had ever been a place of strength, peace, and security. Now all that had changed. Citizens dashed about, frightened looks etched on their faces. Many carried bundles of food or other supplies, stocking up for a feared siege; some loaded wagons with all their worldly belongings, apparently preparing to flee the Dor for safer environs. Though where that could be, save for Lomion City herself, was not clear. Conversely, nearly all the residents from beyond the town walls had either taken refuge within the Outer Dor or were lined up outside the main gate to petition for sanctuary within the citadel. Claradon gave the gatemen leave to let in any and all that asked for refuge, for the Eotrus took care of their own. More than a few citizens noticed the heavily armed troop of knights and surmised their mission. Calls of support and "bring them back safe," rang out from all around the citadel and throughout the Outer Dor as the knights rode by.

The Outer Dor bustled with activity. Citizens scrambled to bar storm shutters, reinforce doors, and nail wood planks over the windows. The buildings were built of brick or stone, with walls at least double the thickness needed for stout defense against the northland's punishing winters. Northerners had long memories. In the tradition of their ancestors who suffered through Lugron raids, they built their buildings strong.

"We're not properly provisioned for a siege," said Ob. "Not when we've so many mouths to feed."

"Let's hope it doesn't come to that," said Claradon. "This may all blow over yet. It may be nothing."

"By Asgard, I hope you're right," said Ob.

Just after they passed through the Outer Dor's second gate, several riders in Eotrus livery approached at a canter from beyond the wall.

Their leader, a grayed veteran, pulled up alongside Gabriel and Ob.

"What news, Baret?" said Ob.

Baret's face was grave. "We found no sign of his Lordship's patrol, Castellan. We rode as far as five leagues into the wood. We found the circle, but there was no sign or trace within it and not much without. It's hard to explain . . ." Baret looked warily about, leaned toward Ob, and lowered his voice. "Near the circle, the wood is dead. Lifeless. Unnatural like. The rest of the wood don't feel right, neither. It stinks of sorcery to me."

"What do you mean, dead?" said Ob. "Speak plain, man."

"There weren't any animals about. That is as plain as I can put it. Not one squirrel or possum. Not a bird in sky, tree, or bush. Not even sight or sound of insects. Not a chirp, hoot, or howl. All life has fled the deep wood."

"I have never seen its like," said Baret. He lowered his voice further. "It must be sorcery. Dark and evil and on our doorstep. I don't envy you heading out there with night coming."

"Was there any sign of an enemy force?" said Gabriel.

"None," said Baret. "Whatever is out there comes in the night, I expect. In the deep black, with the mist," he said as he made a protective gesture across his chest.

X
THE CIRCLE OF DESOLATION

The expedition passed through the last street beyond the Outer Dor's walls, an unseasonable chill in the morning air, and headed down the main road, a wide cobblestone lane that led south toward Riker's Crossroads, and then on to Lomion City, Kern, or Doriath Forest, depending on which way one went. Soon, both sides of the road were lined with fields of vegetables and grains, and groves of fruit trees of many types, all well-ordered and closely fenced or walled. Farmhouses, some small and quaint, others akin to sprawling and impressive manors, some few, more castle than house, lay at the end of cobblestoned lanes that sprang from the main track. In the distance could be seen cattle and goat, sheep, pigs, and chickens. Here and there, guardsmen from the various manors and keeps patrolled the ways on horseback and with dogs, wary and nervous owing to recent events.

Two miles or so down the way, the expedition turned off the main road and headed west along a well-used dirt track, a hunter's trail that passed through fields of short grass and low rolling hills before reaching the Vermion Forest. Gabriel rode at the vanguard of the main group, followed by his picked men, Artol, Paldor, Glimador, and Indigo. Behind them were Theta, Dolan, Par Tanch, Ob, and Claradon. The rest of the expedition closely followed, save for the outriders

Gabriel deployed to cover their flanks.

The fields were unusually thick with pestering mosquitos and other flying insects, which made what was normally a pleasant, scenic ride an annoying ordeal. All along the way they spotted deer and elk running through the fields—odd for that time of the morning. In the distance to the north they spied several bears, and to the south, a roaming pack of wolves.

"Never seen game this thick hereabouts," said Ob as he uncorked his wineskin.

"They've been driven from the forest," said Gabriel. "No doubt by whatever created the circle."

"Maybe there is a pack of those reskalan things rampaging about the wood, putting the animals to flight," said Tanch. "I have no wish to come face to face with even one of them, little less a pack. Are we certain that we have enough men?"

No one answered him.

The edge of the Vermion Forest was only a few miles away—well within sight from atop Dor Eotrus's walls. The forest's border was abruptly defined, its trees cut back years before when many acres were harvested for firewood and building materials. Lately such was taken from far to the north to preserve the Vermion for hunting and as a buffer against the region's punishing winter winds.

The leaves were still on the forest's trees; those at its border grew tall and majestic, but the rest, the ones deep in the heart of the old wood grew twisted and gnarled—like giants warped and frozen in time. It was an eerie place in the best of times, but one they were all well accustomed to.

A flattened track took the expedition to the edge of the woods where they halted. "That is a racket," said Ob as hooting sounds filled the air.

"I've never seen so many owls," said Claradon. "And in the daytime, no less."

"Hawks gather in the upper branches," said Gabriel. "Ravens and eagles beside them. A strange thing."

The birds screeched and hooted louder and louder as the men resumed their approach.

"Are they going to attack us?" said Tanch. "I've heard that large birds can be quite dangerous when provoked or frightened. Perhaps we should take cover," though the only cover lay before them in the forest.

"They're warning us away," said Theta.

"You are joking," said Ob. "The man is a jokester. Birds warning us, he says. Ha, ha."

"Then you explain it," said Theta.

"They're only birds," said Ob. "Maybe they got some fancy birds back in your lands what talk and sing and dance the jig. Maybe they'd ask us over to sit a spell and have a smoke and a game of spottle, but hereabouts, they're just birds. They got no brains to speak of, so they couldn't warn nobody about nothing."

Theta offered no response.

"It's a strange thing," said Gabriel, "whatever it means."

As they moved into the wood, the trail narrowed and the forest slowly grew denser, the air closer, thicker, and stiller, and eventually, the sounds of the birds died away. Ob and Dolan struck out ahead of the others to scout.

"Bear sign," said Ob, as he studied the ground. "Boar, deer, elk, and rabbit too."

"And wolf," said Dolan as he crouched down beside Ob.

Ob raised an eyebrow and looked at Dolan. "Good eye, sonny," he said. "You know your tracks. Maybe there is more to you than you let on."

"Not so much. Lord Angle has schooled me up on a few things, but I still don't know much."

"All the signs are fresh," said Ob as he turned his attention back to the tracks. "And they're all heading east, out of the forest, which makes sense considering the game we saw on the way here. They're running from something, but what?"

"Something hungry, I expect," said Dolan.

"Aye," said Ob. "Something hungry. Keep your eyes peeled, sonny. If Wizard Boy is right, and there are a pack of them six-legs hereabouts, we best spot them afore they spot us."

"Aye, we best," said Dolan.

A league into the forest, the trees grew unusually tall and dense, twisted, and intertwined, many covered in moss. The thick canopy overhead blocked out most of the light and all of the breeze. The place was silent and still, and colder owing to the dim light. Branches hung low, and the footing grew treacherous with slick leaves and moss, holes and loose rocks, and fallen trees and broken branches everywhere. In some places the undergrowth grew so tall, thick, and uneven as to be impassable by the horses. More than once, the men were forced to dismount and walk the horses through or around the various obstructions. All of that was normal for the Vermion, except for the silence. In the heart of the forest, not a sound was there—not of bird or beast. No insect chirped, or called, or buzzed. Not one bee, fly, or mosquito to be found. Save for the trees and plants, the forest was dead, a graveyard of old tree falls and decaying leaves.

"There are things what chase animals from a wood," said Ob. "Fires, weather, huntsmen, and such. But what chases out the bugs?"

Nothing that I've ever seen," said Dolan, "except the coldest days of winter, and even they're not as silent as this. It's not natural, it's not."

Deep into the wood they caught a glimpse of a flattened, open area through the trees. They stopped their horses and went quiet.

"That is it," whispered Dolan, pointing. "Just like they said: a big circle of nothing." He paused and looked around for some moments and Ob did the same. "There is a strange feeling hereabouts, Mister Ob. My skin is beginning to crawl, it is."

"I feel it too," whispered Ob. "It's like Wizard Boy said—it feels like something is watching us, something unseen, out there, somewhere in the trees. It's giving me the creeps. The stinking hair is standing up on me arms."

"Mine too," said Dolan.

"Dolan me boy, ride back to the others, slow and quiet-like, but don't waste no time about it. Tell them we found it, the circle. Tell Gabe that you and me are gonna reconnoiter a bit by our lonesomes to scope things out good and proper. We will rejoin the group when we're done nosing about. Tell him to have his lot hold back a good ways and for Odin's sake, keep good and quiet. I will wait for you here. Hurry back straightaway after you've delivered the message—and if I'm not here, in this very spot, you run for it. You got me?"

"Aye, Mister Ob, I got you, I do."

When Dolan returned, Ob was waiting for him in the appointed place, no worse for wear but looking a bit pale.

"Anything?" said Dolan.

"Not a peep," said Ob. "There is nothing moving out there that I can see or hear or smell. But that feeling of being watched—I can't shake it. I'll tell you sonny, that has got me worried. Whatever is going on out here is outside what I know, and I've been around a long while."

"I expect Lord Angle will sort it out directly, he will," said Dolan. "He's good at that, he is."

"I don't know about that," said Ob, "but I expect we will see what your boss is made of before this adventure is done."

They tied their horses to trees, and slowly stalked forward, crouched over. Ob moved fluidly—he kicked up no rocks, rustled no bushes or leaves, and snapped no twigs. His passage made less noise than that of a squirrel or rabbit— his skills, the envy of hunter, ranger, or sneak thief alike. Dolan, however, was utterly silent, passing between the trees like a ghost. Ob was shocked when he noticed Dolan's stealth, but made no comment on it. They crawled the last twenty yards toward the circle on their bellies, pausing every few feet to look and listen.

"It is a circle alright, a big one," whispered Ob, breathing heavy as he peeked out from a bush some twenty feet from the circle's edge. Sweat dripped from his forehead and matted his hair despite the cool air. "Flat, almost smooth; the dirt looks packed down tight. Not a bush or even a leaf in sight. Never seen nothing like this. How big do you figure it is?"

"I'm not much for measuring," said Dolan, wrinkling his nose. Unlike Ob, Dolan was not winded from the crawl, and his forehead was dry; his face, its usual pale.

"Four hundred yards across, give or take, I would mark it," said Ob. "Took a bit of work to make this, I would say. Rain didn't make it. Nor did wind, bird, bug, or bush."

"Do you smell it?" said Dolan.

"For a while now," said Ob. "Was wondering if you would notice it. It is faint, but it's there. Smells like what was left of that six-leg Claradon killed in the tower."

Dolan took a deep breath. "Yup. Burned and dead mixed together, it is. You think it was magic that made this circle? Black sorcery, was it?"

"Bah," spat Ob. "I don't put much stock in that bunk. Bunch of crazy cultists with shovels and sweat done made this. Most things can get built with a shovel or two and a barrel of sweat. I'll bet a keg of Portland Vale's best that is what went on here. Why they built it and what it's for is what I want to know."

"Cultists with shovels," said Dolan nodding. "Look at the edge, it's sunk, it is," he said, pointing to the circle's rim.

"Aye," said Ob. "The circle is a good few inches down from the surrounding soil. I wonder whether they hauled away the topsoil or just packed it down somehow. A bit of both, probably."

"Hauled and packed it they did, them crazies," said Dolan as he looked warily over one shoulder and then the next.

A short while later, Ob and Dolan made their way back to their horses as silently as they had come, walked them back to the main group, and made their report to Sir Gabriel.

"Take a full squadron and scour the woods around the circle in all directions," said Gabriel to Ob, "but stay close together in case there are enemies about. Find me some sign of our patrol and of whatever enemy force waylaid them, but do not set foot within the circle until I give you leave. Not one step within."

As Ob's squadron went about their business, the others examined the perimeter of the circle itself, none daring to venture beyond the rim after Gabriel's orders. Gabriel and Claradon eyed the strange construction.

"We will find him," said Gabriel. "Ob can track a mouse through a haystack."

Claradon nodded.

"You think it's safe?" said Claradon as his eyes drifted in Tanch's direction.

"If it's not magical, yes," said Gabriel. "If there is sorcery involved, who can say. To be safe, we need to check it out before we step within."

"I can find out," said Par Tanch. "I believe the Arcane Order would approve the use of the sorcerous arts in this circumstance. So with your permission, Sir Gabriel, I will call on my humble powers to divine if fell sorcery is at work here."

"That is what I was counting on," said Gabriel. "Have at it."

Par Tanch began his divination by chanting in a strange, guttural tongue. He soon coupled his rather oppressive intonations with strange arm and hand movements, akin to a bizarre, primitive, and awkward dance. He tossed various sparkling powders about that gave off small bursts of light and puffs of smoke that smelled like rotten eggs. Such antics were mere mummery, and though wholly superfluous, the members of the Arcane Order seemed to think such things expected of them, so they carried on thus. The knights looked on, amazed, as true sorcery was so seldom seen.

As Par Tanch put on his performance, Theta quietly approached the circle's rim several yards to the backs of the rest of the company. From a belt pouch he produced an amulet inset with an oblong, azure-hued gemstone that had the look of a sapphire, though it was actually something much rarer. With that ancient charm, Theta could detect the presence or residues of all manner of arcane magics and mark them as either beneficent or fell. As he held it aloft and moved it toward the rim, the gem emitted a soft, flickering glow. The color of the stone quickly changed to a fiery red. As he passed his hand beyond the rim, the glow faded but did not extinguish.

Theta quickly replaced the amulet whence it came, and pulled from beneath his breastplate a strangely twisted ankh that hung from a leather

129

cord about his neck. The ankh was stained and battered, and whether it was made of wood, or stone, or metal was impossible to say, but it was clearly no mere accouterment. It was an ancient holy symbol preserved from some bygone age. One who grasped its deepest secrets could use it to detect the presence of certain maleficent creatures, beasts, or men. In its ear, Theta whispered words from ages past, forbidden words of power in a language long since lost to the world. He tightly gripped the relic and surveyed the barren landscape before him. His eyes scoured the circle for several seconds, devouring every inch of it. Finally, he released the ankh, allowing it to fall against his chest. He then tucked it back beneath his armor, safely out of sight.

He passed the tip of his lance across the rim of the circle and thrust it, gently at first, then more forcefully against the bleak soil within, testing it as one might use a pole to probe the firmness of the ground when traveling through swamp or bog.

"Oh my," said Par Tanch as he completed his ritual. "There is dark sorcery at work here. Fearful, insidious magic of a kind quite alien to me. I would say that—"

"Chaos sorcery lingers along the rim," said Theta, as he moved to stand beside Tanch. "The stuff of Nifleheim. It emanates from something buried below the surface, but its power is waning."

Tanch raised an eyebrow at Theta's proclamations and looks of surprise and suspicion contested for control of his face. The knights looked to Tanch, apparently skeptical of the conclusions of the foreign soldier.

"I agree with Lord Theta's most astute assessment," said Tanch in slow, measured tones as he studied Theta. "I had no idea that you were so well versed in the arcane arts, my Lord. May I ask your method?"

"No," said Theta. There would be no further explanation.

Tanch raised his eyebrows and looked taken aback. "Very well then. To your assessment, I would add that we can safely pass the threshold and enter the circle."

"I concur," said Theta. He stepped across the rim and walked about to no ill effect.

"You men," said Gabriel, pointing to several of the knights. "Break out the tools and uncover whatever is buried below the rim. Whatever you find, for Odin's sake, don't touch it—call Tanch and me over to examine it."

XI
CHAOS, COINS, AND CULTS

"**H**ow goes the work?" said Tanch.

"Mr. Artol has broken three shovels so far, he has," said Dolan. "Mr. Paldor has only broken one. Not that he isn't trying as hard; it's just that he's a lot smaller."

"This bloody ground is like frozen dirt in the dead of winter," said Paldor.

"More like the packed dirt of an old road . . . in the frozen dead of winter," said Artol as he wiped his brow with the back of his hand.

"Not easy work," said Dolan.

"That much is clear," said Tanch. "I do wish I could assist you in your labors, but with my delicate back, I'm afraid such work is quite beyond me. Perhaps after I've rested a bit under yonder tree, I will feel strong enough to heft a shovel for a time." He turned and walked away mumbling to himself.

"All work is beyond him, I hear," said Artol.

"Hold on, look at what we got here," said Dolan as he lifted a shiny, metallic object from the soil. "A coin, it is."

"Wait," said Paldor. "Sir Gabriel said not to touch whatever we found."

Dolan brushed the dirt off the coin and polished it with his fingers. "It's just a coin," he said. "What's the harm?"

"Best put it down," said Artol as he made a sign of protection across his chest and waved

Tanch over. "It might be cursed or something." The wizard quickly realized what was happening and trotted back, out of breath from the effort.

"Found something, have we?" said Tanch.

"It's gold," said Dolan. "And it's got strange markings on it that I can't read." Dolan passed the coin to Tanch. "There could be more," he said before he returned to his digging.

Theta, Gabriel, Claradon, and many of the other knights gathered around while Tanch studied the coin, turning it over and around multiple times as he scrutinized its every feature.

"There is no doubt," said Tanch, "some strange arcane signature emanates from this coin." He offered it to Theta. "Would you care to examine it?"

Theta waved Tanch's hand away. He wouldn't touch the thing. Tanch rolled his eyes and shook his head, for the superstitious nature of knights always vexed him. He was confident that Claradon and Gabriel would be above such things and held the coin out toward them. "Master Claradon? Sir Gabriel?"

"The symbols are most interesting in that—" said Tanch.

Claradon reached for the coin.

"No," shouted Gabriel as he swatted at Claradon's hand. The coin went flying.

"Ow!" cried Claradon, when his finger brushed the coin even as Gabriel knocked it away. His face contorted in pain and revulsion. He gripped his injured hand with his other and doubled over, wincing in pain.

"It doesn't seem to like you, Eotrus," said

Theta chuckling.

"How bad is it?" said Gabriel, trying to see.

"It burned me. How could it do that?"

Gabriel grasped Claradon's arm. "Show me."

"I'm alright," he said, his hand shaking. "It's not too bad, I think, just the tip of one finger is a bit singed."

"A burn?" said Tanch. "That coin has been sitting in the cold ground—how could it burn you?"

"Was it covered in acid?" said Artol.

"It is dry," said Dolan, leaning over the coin where it had fallen. "And it didn't burn me or Mister Tanch."

"Oh my, oh dear," said Tanch as he hopped from one leg to the next. He wrung his hands and checked them several times for damage, his face contorted in panic. "I beg your pardon, Brother Claradon," he said, his voice wavering. "How could I know it would harm you? It didn't feel hot to me; not hot at all. I never would've offered it to you if I ever dreamed it would harm you. Please accept my deepest apologies. I didn't know. Truly, I had no idea that—"

"It felt—evil," said Claradon.

"It is not my fault," said Tanch. "I will not be blamed this time." Tanch's face drained of color, his forehead beaded with sweat. "Oh my, my head is spinning." Tanch's eyes fluttered, closed, and he toppled over in a faint.

"Someone douse the wizard with water," said Gabriel, "and get him to his feet. We need his expertise. There will be no lying down on the job today. Cursed coins; I thought I had seen it all, but that is a new one. Paldor—break out some

134

burn salve from the supplies and wrap up Claradon's hand."

"Dolan," said Gabriel. "You seem immune to the coin's effects. Pick it up and place it on that boulder so that the rest of us can examine it without having to touch it."

"Just the same, I think I'll use the shovel," said Dolan as he scooped up the coin.

Artol poured water onto Tanch's face. The wizard sat up and spewed what could only have been curses in some strange language the others didn't know.

"It has a bunch of strange markings on it, it does," said Dolan as he set the coin down and then returned to his digging. The others gathered around the boulder.

Gabriel leaned in to get a good look at the markings. "Mystical glyphs and symbols," he said. He used a small twig to flip the coin over to view its obverse side.

"Mortach," said Theta.

"You've got the eyes of a hawk to name that symbol from where you stand," said Tanch as he wiped dry his face with a handkerchief, though he still looked unsteady. "But you are correct. The symbol embossed on the surface is indeed the mark of Mortach. The glyphs on the other side are used by Mortach's priests and followers for their vile rituals."

"Who is this Mortach fellow?" said Dolan. "One of your enemies? A rival lord, is he?"

"A Lord of Nifleheim," said Claradon.

"And what is a Lord of Nifle—Nifle—whatever you said?" said Dolan.

135

"Nifleheim," said Tanch. "The Lords of Nifleheim are vile, maleficent, completely inhuman, otherworldly creatures."

Artol spat on the ground, a look of disgust on his face.

"Once they were men," said Theta.

"No longer," said Gabriel. "Now they are patrons of death, destruction, and all that is unholy and corrupt."

"Sorry I asked," said Dolan.

Gabriel looked around to make certain that he had the men's attention before he continued. "The Lords of Nifleheim are few in number, but said to have lived since the dawn of time. They possess superhuman powers and wield incredible magics beyond the ken of even the greatest mortal wizards. They reside in Nifleheim, the very hell of myth and legend. A place of fire, ice, madness, and chaos. There they command vast armies of lesser fiends, devils, demons, call them what you will."

"Their followers call Nifleheim, heaven," said Tanch, shaking his head. "A vast, timeless land of love and happiness where they bask in the glory of their one true god, Azathoth, curse his name. It is their paradise, where they hope to go when they pass from this life."

"Legend has it," said Tanch, "that the Nifleheim lords are the sworn enemies of our lord, Odin, and the rest of the beneficent gods of Asgard," the Aesir. "The old stories tell that long ago they walked freely on Midgaard, but were driven off— back to their Halls of Chaos, by the great heroes of yore."

"What man could stand against such things?" said Artol.

"A bit of luck can see a man through many things, if his courage holds," said Theta.

"Oh, now I get it, I do," said Dolan. "We call them fellows "Old Ones" back home. Lord Angle and I don't get on well with them, we don't. Best we steer clear of them folks, no? You have a lot of them around here, do you?"

"No, of course not," said Claradon. "If they were ever truly on Midgaard, and I'm not convinced that they were, they are long since gone."

"But they are not forgotten," said Gabriel. "Even now, they are worshipped as gods by practitioners of the black arts—those schooled in necromancy, demonology, chaos sorcery, and the like, and by other base individuals. These followers are a morbid collection of murderers, lunatics, and fanatics. They sacrifice innocents on unholy altars dedicated to their foul lords, in return for promised power, wealth, or more base desires. Their cults are scattered here and there throughout all the known lands."

"There is even a secret temple in Lomion City dedicated to one of their number—Hecate, or so I've heard," said Tanch.

"Here's another one," said Dolan as he shoveled a second golden coin out of the dense soil a few feet from where he found the first. He passed it to Tanch who placed it on the stone beside the first. Soon Dolan and the others unearthed several more golden coins. They were spaced every six feet around the perimeter of the

137

circle, buried some six inches down. Each bore the symbols of one Nifleheim lord or another—some Mortach, some Hecate, still others were of Bhaal.

"It seems likely that these coins were enchanted by the followers of the Lords of Nifleheim and placed here by them for some as yet undetermined purpose," said Claradon as they stood about the boulder and studied the coins. Some few of the knights crowded in, eager to get a look at the coins and interested in hearing all that was discussed. Most of the knights, however, paid little or no attention to the whole business. Men of action cared naught for such discussions. Instead, they checked their gear and stood the watch.

"I cannot explain it otherwise," said Gabriel. "We will be going up against the followers of Nifleheim, or some fell sorcery or fiends or beasts that they have conjured up." He paused for a few moments and then turned to the rest of the group. "I will tell you that although it's not widely known, the Nifleites have caused much suffering throughout Lomion over the years. The Crown and the Churches don't want such news causing panic so they've suppressed it. Few even know of the existence of these heathen cults. But various covert military groups in Lomion, like the Rangers Guild and some of the Church Knights, have battled the cults a number of times. Ob, Artol, and I have even had our troubles with them over the years. They're not to be trifled with. I'm sorry to say that unless they have taken our men prisoner in hopes of extorting a ransom, their involvement does not bode well for Lord Eotrus's safe return."

"Oh my, oh dear," said Par Tanch. "We of the Order of the Arcane know of these fearsome cults as well. Going up against the followers of Bhaal or Mortach or Hecate is a serious thing. Facing all three cults is tantamount to suicide. Their assassins have slaughtered many in their beds; still others have gone missing, never to be seen or heard from again. Perhaps we should reconsider this venture and return to the Dor to get more men, or better yet, send for help from Lomion City. This is clearly a job for the Lomerian army or the rangers of Doriath Hall—much too perilous for our small band. My delicate back just can't take the stress and exertion and—"

A wave of Gabriel's hand cut Tanch off. "Have you forgotten the nature of this mission, wizard? We are here to aid Lord Eotrus if we can, or to avenge his death if he has fallen. There is no reconsidering; we will do this thing."

Tanch's face reddened. "Of course, of course, we must press on for Lord Eotrus," he said.

"Yes, we must," said Claradon, glaring at the wizard. "And two squadrons of Eotrus knights are no small band. Woe to any cultists that linger here—for we will ride them down and make them pay."

"Please forgive my insensitivity, Brother Claradon. I just meant to say that if there is fighting to be done, I might not be able to help due to my injured back. A man of lesser constitution than I wouldn't even be able to walk suffering the pain that I wrestle with daily." He put his arm behind his back and winced in pain to demonstrate his plight. "Walk all day for you I will,

139

but fighting is another story. I just don't have it in me, not with my back the way it is. I did mention that I may have been more useful if left at the Dor with Sir Ector. But we must press on. Indeed, we must, we must."

XII
WORDS OF POWER

"**I** found tracks of Aradon's patrol," said Ob, pointing to the ground before him. Ob and Indigo were crouched at a spot past the eastern edge of the circle's rim, and had just waved over their companions. Claradon, Gabriel, and Theta all crouched down beside Ob to get a close look at the tracks.

"Their number and age matches Aradon's patrol," said Ob, "but here is the clincher: these shoe prints are from Aradon's horse. It's a distinctive shoe; no other horse from the Dor wears it."

"How do you know that?" said Tanch.

"Because I'm the stinking castellan, Wizard Boy. It's my job to know everything what goes on. Besides, I was master scout for years–I know horse tracks as good as anybody."

Claradon bent low to study the print. "I'm no expert with tracks, but I recognize that shoe too— it is from father's horse, for certain. He and his whole patrol were here; now there's no doubt."

"They came in from the east," said Ob, from the direction of the Dor, "but the tracks get cut off right at the rim. There's no evidence that the patrol stopped at this spot or turned around and headed back east. So for certain they entered the circle right here, but there's no tracks within the circle showing their passage."

"Then someone blotted out the tracks for

some reason," said Gabriel.

"Aye," said Ob. "That is what it looks like."

"The other patrols reported that the circle grew in size each night," said Gabriel. "That means that when Aradon's patrol was here, the circle was smaller. Since then, it must've gotten larger and blotted out the tracks."

"But we still don't know how and why it's expanding," said Claradon.

"There's no shovel marks, I can tell you that," said Ob. "I don't know how they made it, and I'm not sure that I care so long as we find our people. I found tracks from each of the other patrols too. They all end at the edge of the circle, same as these, but I found tracks from them others leading away from the area, returning back toward the Dor, which makes sense, since the other patrols made it home. I've found no evidence of Aradon's patrol ever leaving this place. It's as if this stinking circle swallowed them up."

"Oh dear gods," said Tanch.

"Have you checked along the entire perimeter?" said Gabriel. "Could you have missed anything?"

"I scoured the whole rim except for this area and a short stretch on the south side before Indigo called me over to look at these tracks. I left Glimador to finish up on the south end, but I doubt he'll find anything worth finding."

"If they didn't walk out, then they're still here," said Gabriel.

"Where?" said Ob. "It's wide open, do you see them?"

"Down," said Gabriel. "Have you checked?"

"Buried?" said Tanch.

Gabriel shook his head. "Maybe there is a tunnel."

"It's the only explanation other than magic," said Claradon.

"That was my first thought," said Ob, "but there's no tunnel. I checked thorough for that. The ground is solid and almost as hard as stone."

"I hate to say it," said Tanch, "but it is a good deal easier to dig a hole and put folks in it, even in dirt as hard as this, than to make them disappear using magic."

"Then they're buried," said Claradon. "Dead and buried. All of them. Dead gods, I can't believe this. We've got to find them. We need to start digging."

"There would be evidence of such a hole," said Ob. "But there's not. It would have to be huge to bury all those men and horses."

"I heard there's flying horses, with wings and such, out this way," said Dolan. "Maybe they flew out of here."

"Nope, that is wrong," said Ob.

"Why?" said Claradon.

"Why?" said Dolan.

"Besides there not being any evidence of a hole, somebody would have had to bury them—and there's no tracks of anybody leaving the circle except our earlier patrols. The enemies didn't bury themselves, and neither did our men."

"So we're back to a tunnel?" said Claradon.

"Like I said, there is none, I'm sure of it," said Ob.

"Then could we be misreading the tracks?"

said Claradon. "What if they stepped in the tracks of the earlier patrols, to disguise their passage out and away?"

"That's an old Lugron trick," said Ob. "I checked for that too. The tracks leaving the circle are clean."

"Spic-and-span," said Dolan.

"So it's magic," said Claradon. "There's just no other explanation."

Ob spat at the ground. "I always hated sorcery," he said, glaring at Tanch. "But if there's no other answer, maybe that's what it is."

"Must be," said Dolan, "or else flying horses."

"What do we do?" said Claradon.

"I don't rightly know, boy," said Ob. "I ain't ever seen the like of this. There is more to tell, though."

"We found us a couple of black pillars a ways out over that way," pointing off to the west. "They're part of them ruins you talked of earlier, Gabe."

"I knew we had to be close to that fell place," said Gabriel.

"I remember two pillars being about a quarter mile west from the old temple," said Ob. "Them pillars we found are the same two. I'm certain of it."

"But that would put the main ruins—" said Claradon.

"Right smack in the middle of this darned circle of nothing," said Ob.

"What?" said Gabriel, a shocked look on his face.

They all turned and looked toward the circle's

center, which remained as flat and featureless as the rest of that barren place. Gabriel quickly walked out to the center of the circle, the others following. He paced back and forth mumbling to himself and looking about at the surrounding landscape, as if trying to confirm their location. He was more agitated than Claradon had ever seen him. Worse than that, he seemed worried, or perhaps, even afraid. And Sir Gabriel feared nothing.

"Did you search the wood out far enough?" said Gabriel. "We have to be at the wrong spot."

"Our outriders went a mile out," said Ob. "This is the spot. I've no doubt."

Gabriel shook his head; his face gone pale. "That temple stood here for ages beyond count," he said. "And now it's gone, foundation and all? Just like that? That is hard to believe, and it can't be good."

"The cultists must've been using the old temple for some unholy rite of black magery," said Claradon. "But that doesn't explain what happened to the temple ruins, or what this strange circle is about. Like Sir Gabriel said, stone temples, even ruined ones, don't just disappear. Even masters of the arcane arts cannot easily accomplish such feats, I think."

"Perhaps the cultists' magic went awry, and the temple was somehow destroyed," said Tanch.

"Blown to pieces," said Dolan. "Up in smoke."

"Destroyed?" said Gabriel. "No, I doubt that. Besides, there are no big chunks of stone lying around that I've seen. No debris of any kind."

"Could a magical explosion have completely

pulverized the stone down to nothing?" said Claradon, looking to Tanch.

Tanch shook his head. "I don't know. This is all beyond me."

"Could the circle of coins be used to conjure up something, wizard?" said Theta. "Something from another world; something from the very realm of Nifleheim itself?"

Tanch looked shocked and stared at Theta for a moment before responding. "Perhaps, but I cannot be certain. The most powerful chaos sorcerers may possess the skills required to summon fiends from the beyond to do their bidding. But this circle, it's so vast, so enormous— far larger than needed for calling up some fiend or familiar. It must have some other purpose."

"Maybe they were magicking up something really big," said Dolan.

"I shudder to think of what such a thing could be," said Tanch. "No, I'm quite sure that their magic must have gone awry and caused the destruction of the temple and the formation of the circle."

"What if they put the come hither on one of them Nifle fellows you told of, Mister Claradon, sir?" said Dolan.

"It's hard to imagine such a thing being possible," said Claradon. "Even if it were, the cultists would have to be mad to attempt it."

"Nevertheless, the circle is here," said Theta.

"The cultists see the Lords of Nifleheim as saviors, as blessed minions of their god," said Gabriel in a slow deliberate voice. "They would have little fear in conjuring them up, if they had the means to do so. Dead gods, maybe that is what they tried. Maybe that is what happened here."

"So they need not be crazy to want to bring them over," said Ob. "They just have to be stupid."

"All of this is academic," said Tanch, "for despite the colorful myths, my friends, the Lords of Nifleheim aren't men at all. They are more akin to forces of nature. The scholarly texts imply that they are beings of energy and thought, not mortal flesh."

"Scholarly texts," mumbled Theta as he shook his head.

"They couldn't really walk our world," said Tanch. "No, the circle must be here for some other purpose."

"They can enter Midgaard given the right conditions," said Theta.

"Respectfully, sir, I don't think such a thing is possible," said Par Tanch.

"I wonder," said Claradon, "if perhaps they can change their form and take on a shape akin to a mortal body, becoming some type of avatar. Perhaps, in such a guise, they can enter Midgaard through some mystical portal or gateway."

"Such a theory would reconcile the ancient texts with the folk stories we have all heard," said Tanch, "but—"

"Those are nothing but fairy stories, told to scare wet-eared whelps," said Ob. "There is no truth to them. Them Nifleheim bumpkins are nothing but figments."

"Let's pray that is the case," said Tanch. "For if a Lord of Nifleheim did cross over to Midgaard, the

147

entire world would be at utmost peril. Such a fiend would rampage across the land and leave nothing but death and destruction in its wake. No mortal man, be he archwizard or knight champion, could defeat such a beast. I doubt that even the full might of the Lomerian army could put it down."

"I would defeat it," said Theta in an even tone, almost, but not quite under his breath.

"Bah!" spouted Ob. "You pompous tin can."

Theta glared at the Gnome, but did not respond. "This is not what you expected," said Theta to Gabriel.

"No," said Gabriel. "I expected no Lords of Nifleheim."

Glimador trotted up, an anxious expression on his face. He leapt off his horse and landed lightly despite his heavy armor.

"What did you find?" said Ob as he pushed past the others to get closer to Glimador.

"A blood trail," said Glimador. "Right at the circle's rim."

"Show us," said Ob.

***

Brother Donnelin's horse's eyes were mad with fear, and foam flew from its mouth and nose as it galloped for its life. Donnelin's knees pressed its flanks with all his strength to keep him in his seat as he twisted around, his staff in his right hand pointed toward his pursuers. The priest's eyes were wide and his mouth hung open, his cheeks numb from a frigid cold that appeared from nowhere, and his nose burned from the acrid stink of the things behind him—a seemingly endless horde of nightmarish creatures that descended on him from all directions but the front.

Through the darkness and the wild chase he couldn't see them clearly. He only caught fleeting glimpses of fangs and claws and drooling maws when the moonlight peeked through some break in the mist. But he heard them. Their wild caterwauling. Their pounding feet that shook the very earth beneath him as they charged. Horrors to break any man's courage and shatter the most stolid man's sanity.

They would be on him in a moment—just as Aradon had warned, there was no outrunning them. His only chance was to make it to the circle's rim and hope that it proved a boundary that they could not cross—otherwise, he was a dead man for certain, bound for Valhalla, if Odin's favor fell full on him. If not, who knows?

But Brother Donnelin was not ready to yield. He was not just a priest. He was a warrior, a northman, born and bred to battle. He would make the creatures pay dearly for his life. He readied his words of power—holy words, mystical words preserved down through the ages by Odin's priests. Words capable of sending many of his foes to the void—of that he was certain.

Even as several creatures closed the last few yards between them and leapt, he leveled his staff and shouted a single word of Old High Lomerian. That word reached out across the worlds and tapped the wellspring of magic in the very heart of eternal Asgard. From the magical weave's source it drew forces beyond the ken of man and pulled them at lightning speed through the shadowy ether, across time and space, to Midgaard, to heed Donnelin's call.

A pulsing sound issued from the tip of Donnelin's staff, though it went unheard in the riotous din. With it, a shockwave sprang from the staff's tip and shot outward, expanding in a conical shape, its structure barely visible as a strange distortion in the night air. It collided with the creatures directly behind him, catching some midleap.

It was as if they'd run headlong into a solid wall, or rather, a solid wall that plowed forward and expanded on its way. They crashed against Donnelin's magic in a crunching of bones and a tangle of fractured limbs. The beasts' charge was shattered as those behind sought to leap over the fallen, but crashed as well, as did the next wave, and the next, and the next, all swept away as the magic thundered on before its power finally waned.

When Donnelin's horse leaped over a bush, the priest realized he had passed beyond the circle's rim and into the trees. The eerie fog however still surrounded him, and dear gods, the creatures still came on—the rim proving no barrier to them, at least no longer. As quickly as he could, Donnelin rotated his staff to his right and called down Odin's wrath again. The creatures that came from that direction broke against his mystical blast just as did the others, and tumbled and splattered against it as it roared on through their ranks, for it was a force beyond them, if all too fleeting for Donnelin's good.

Still galloping wildly, Donnelin pointed the staff to his left and spoke his word of power for the third and final time. As the wave of sorcerous energy formed and crushed his attackers, one snuck beneath its reach. It flung itself at Donnelin's horse, a low leap, parallel to the ground. The creature's claws latched onto the horse's rear leg. It stumbled and went down, slamming to its belly. Its momentum carried it forward for several yards along the grassy ground.

Donnelin's legs were torn and pinned beneath his fallen steed. His right arm was pinned as well. Its legs broken, the horse could not rise. The beast that had taken it down leapt at Donnelin's throat, but in midair it struck an unseen barrier with a dull echoing thump. The air shimmered about the point of impact, as if a transparent wall stood there; a wall that welcomed Donnelin through, but that would suffer no creature of Nifleheim to pass. With a quick glance to the left and to the right, Donnelin realized that that very spot marked the new edge or boundary of the fog and that that boundary extended far into the distance in both directions, no doubt carving out a broad circle as had the desolate zone's rim. The fog billowed up against it, but could not pass.

The creature could not reach him—he had escaped. Praise the gods. He was safe.

Donnelin's joy lasted but a moment before he saw that his horse's hindquarters lay on the wrong side of the boundary, amidst the fog. That horse, a friend that had served him well the previous ten years, not only was broken and doomed: it would be eaten too.

He saw the thing's eyes first. They were red, brick red. And not just the pupils—there were no whites to the eyes at all. They never blinked—they just stared at Donnelin, boring into his soul.

Bruised and bloodied, the creature slowly rose from where it had fallen, its eyes never drifting from Donnelin, its demeanor strangely calm, though its breathing was heavy. The face and body of the thing were too horrific to describe. It was no man, but far more manlike than the creature that had attacked Claradon in the tower. Call it a goblin if you want, just to give it a name. But it was no silly thing from some children's tales. No, call it a demon, for that olden term better describes its nature—a creature out of nightmare called up from hell by forbidden magics. A monster, a true monster.

It reached out a clawed hand and placed it slowly, purposefully on the horse's hind leg. The horse screamed and tried to kick as the demon closed its fist and the razored claws dug deep into its flesh, but that grip was too powerful for even a horse to overcome.

All the while, Donnelin struggled to pull himself free, but the weight of the horse was too much. He was held fast.

The creature began to pull the horse across the barrier, and dear gods, it grinned when it saw that Donnelin was being dragged along with it. Donnelin turned, twisted, and pulled as hard as he could, desperate to free himself, though his efforts were ineffective.

The horse thrashed, still desperate to get away, its nose filled with the pungent odor of the creature that held it. The creature reached over with another clawed hand and with barely a glance at the horse, sliced deep into its leg; a precise, straight cut that severed an artery and sent blood pulsing into the air. It sprayed onto Donnelin, ran down his cheek, and across the top of his head. The horse thrashed and struggled but soon moved no more.

Donnelin heard more creatures coming, many more.

"Tsk, tsk, so close," said the demon in a deep clear voice, its wicked smile growing broader. "So close were you, so close; oh, what a pity; how sad for you that Zymog has caught you, and caught you good we have."

Donnelin's face contorted in shock. He had thought what fronted him was no more than a beast, an animal, and yet it spoke like a man, though its voice carried a haunting reverberation.

"The turns of fate are ever fickle, priest," it said as saliva dripped down its maw. "Fickle, fickle, fickle," it shouted in a voice altogether different in tone and pitch from its voice a moment before: as if a different creature had spoken, though the sounds all spewed from the same beast's mouth.

When next it spoke, it repeated certain phrases. This time, in myriad voices, some deep and booming, others shrill. All wholly different from the first. They were not clownish voices, nor were they the rantings of some mad thing. They were eerie and frightful and grating to the ears.

Donnelin shuddered at the sounds and his hair stood on end.

"If your magic had been a second sooner (*a second sooner*), or your horse a stride faster, you would be off and away (*off and away!*), clear and free at least until the morrow. But now here you lie before us, and we with such a hunger we can't describe (*a hunger, a hunger, a hunger!*)."

Donnelin shuddered and fumbled with the holy symbol that hung from a silver chain about his neck. He steadied it and held it out before him. "Back demon, back to whatever pit you crawled from. In the name of Odin, the All-Father, lord of the mighty Aesir, I cast you out. Begone. Begone from here."

A hideous parody of a laugh escaped the creature's lips. "Odin holds no power over us, mortal (*no power, no power, no power!*). Give up your soul freely, and Zymog will end your suffering quickly. Make your choice (*make your choice, make your choice*)."

"*No, make him suffer, suffer, suffer!*"

"Never," said Donnelin. "Go back to hell and plague me no more."

"What know you of hell, mortal? (*What know you?*)" said the creature. "More than we, perhaps, for we come not from there, but from paradise (*paradise!*)." The creature pulled on the horse's leg again and Donnelin was dragged nearer to the edge of the fog bank.

Donnelin eyed his staff, which had fallen some yards away. There was no hope to retrieve it.

"Your token of power is far from your grasp, priest (*far from your grasp*). You'll not hold it again, not in this life. Now you've only mortal flesh to fight with, and that can do us little harm. Fled from your friends, did you? (*you fled, you fled, you fled!*)" said the creature in a voice gone almost soft. "Left them to fight without you? Left them to die? Coward (*coward!*) they'll call you. Traitor (*traitor!*) they'll mark you. No place with them will you now have. (*traitor, traitor, coward and traitor!*) Forsake that fraud Odin and give up your soul freely, priest. Pledge it to the one true god, Azathoth the almighty, and all will yet be forgiven. A place of honor in the paradise of Nifleheim can still be yours. (*Join us, join us, join us in paradise!*)"

"Odin," yelled Donnelin, as loud as his lungs allowed. "Odin!"

"He cannot hear you, priest," said the creature. "He's long since dead and gone to dust (*dust, dust*), and was nothing more than a mortal man even when he lived."

The creature's grin grew wider and eyes wilder as Donnelin slid within its reach. It loomed over Donnelin, ichor dripping onto his face. The creature brushed Donnelin's protective hand aside and pinned it to the ground. It pressed closer, nose-to-nose. Donnelin turned away; he couldn't bear to look at it.

"Not a man of courage, you are, yet you do not yield. You mortals are ever the enigmas. (*Join us. Join us while you still can*)."

With a groan, Donnelin wrenched his arm free from beneath the horse, arced his head forward, and slammed it into the creature as hard as he could. The headbutt pushed the creature back and gave Donnelin the moment he needed to move his arm into position and thrust the short sword it held into the creature's breast with all his strength. It sank deep.

The sword stuck fast on the creature's breastbone and when it reared back, howling, it pulled Donnelin forward and his legs slipped free from beneath the horse. The creature looked down in shock as the thick black blood spurted from its chest. "Aargh!" screamed the creature, over and again, its many voices now blended into one.

It opened its maw, hatred burning in its eyes, and clamped down on Donnelin's arm with its dagger-like teeth. It ripped and tore and severed the limb at the wrist. But the bite caught only the false arm that Donnelin wore affixed to his stump. The priest scrambled back, kicking and flailing. The heel of his boot caught the thing square amidst its forehead as it lunged in, and knocked it back. Donnelin rolled and spun and found himself on the good side of the fog's edge.

The creature threw itself once and then again with terrific force at the unseen barrier, but rebounded off, for the mystical boundary would not yield. The creature slumped against it, holding its chest, its lifeblood drenching the ground. "Your wicked blade has killed Zymog," bespoke a chorus of voices. "We who've lived for a thousand centuries should not die at the hand of a pitiful mortal wretch. This evil deed will be revenged (*revenged, revenged, revenged!*)."

Even as the light of the creature's eyes grew dim another beast as horrid as the first but of a different type slammed into the unseen barrier, rebounded back, and fell to the ground. Then another of its kind slammed into the boundary, and then another, and then a score of creatures of myriad types, all monstrous and demonic in appearance, did the same. In moments, there were hundreds of wailing, screaming, screeching things, all fighting amongst themselves to be the first to breach the boundary. They jumped, some 10 feet high, others jumped 20 feet or more, but the boundary was still higher, if it had any top at all. After but a few moments, they scrambled atop one another, and formed a monstrous living ladder that grew higher by the second. Donnelin pulled himself to his feet, terror on his face, and limped into the trees as fast as his numb and throbbing legs would carry him.

Donnelin had not gone far when he tripped and fell flat on his belly. Before he could rise, a boot pressed down on the back of his neck and he saw the tip of a sword blade positioned just in front of his face.

"Do not move, priest," said a deep voice, though not belonging to the one who held him down.

"Want me kill him?" said the booted man.

"No, he's a priest," said the first voice. "What a lucky chance this is. The fates smile on us this night, for I have an important use for him."

***

"What do you make of it?" said Claradon, as the men gathered where Glimador had led them.

"It is blood, no doubt, but whether that of man or beast I cannot be certain," said Ob. "A horse fell here—of that I have no doubt. It landed partly within the circle and partly without, though whatever impression it left on the inside has been blotted out. A man lay beside it. There was some thrashing about, and the horse was dragged back within the circle. There are no prints visible of whoever did the dragging.

"What of the man?" said Claradon. "Is there any way to tell who it was?"

Ob studied the ground for some time. "I think he ran for it," said Ob, his voice brightening. "He may have got clear."

"Let's follow," said Claradon. They all turned to follow the meager trail that only Ob seemed able to see. Theta stood nearly fifty yards away, just where the trees started to grow thick and he was staring down at the ground. The others rushed over.

"Did you find something?" said Claradon to Theta.

"Tracks."

"Move aside, Mr. Fancy Pants," said Ob. "I need to have a gander."

"Two large men dragged another to a wagon back there," said Theta. "They took him. The tracks head south."

"Toward Lomion City," said Claradon.

"You are daft, man," said Ob. "These are Eotrus lands, no one gets taken by nobody around

158

here."

"Must have been the cultists," said Tanch as he looked all around. "They could be watching us even now, waiting to pick us off one by one when we're unaware. Oh, dear."

"Dagnabbit, he's right," said Ob as he stared down at the tracks. "They took him. They dragged him off. Stinking cultists. Let me see them wagon tracks."

They all followed.

"The wagon was a big one," said Ob, "and heavily laden with something or other, because it sunk deep into the sod. They must be dumb as rocks to take a wagon in here. Nobody like that could've outsmarted Aradon."

"Maybe them folks with the wagon needed some stones, so they hauled the ruins away," said Dolan."

"Maybe it wasn't the cultists that took our man," said Claradon. "Maybe some passersby stopped to help him."

"There was a struggle for certain," said Ob. "They took him. I'm sorry boy, but I can't tell who it was by the tracks. The boots are large, but a lot of the men on your father's patrol got big boots."

"There were eight to ten horses with the wagon," said Theta.

"What do we do?" said Claradon, looking to Gabriel.

"We have three choices," said Gabriel. "Stay here the night as planned to see what the fog brings; or leave now and follow the tracks to rescue our man and deal with those who took him; or split our force to do both."

"Ten horses and a wagon," said Ob, shaking his head. "There could be 15 of them scum all told, maybe even more if they're piled high and deep in the wagon. We would need to send half our force to deal with them hard and fast. That don't leave us near enough to deal with whoever battled our patrol, assuming it wasn't them with the wagon."

"I'll go," said Sir Bareddal. "Give me four men only. I'll track the wagon, but keep my distance, and I'll send back reports of what we see."

"We can catch up to Bareddal tomorrow evening or the next day at the latest, if things work out well here tonight," said Claradon.

"It's settled then," said Gabriel.

"What if its Lord Eotrus that they kidnapped?" said Bareddal. "Do I move in to free him if I see the chance or do I wait for you?"

"It is not him that they have," said Theta. "Unless your lord wields powerful magics."

"How do you know who they got?" said Ob. "Explain yourself."

"The man that fell at the rim threw powerful magics—that spot reeks of it," said Theta.

"How do you know that?" said Ob.

"I have my ways and they're none of your concern."

"What?" said Ob. "Who do you think you are, talking to me like that? This is Eotrus land, Mr. Stinking Foreigner, and you will explain yourself good and proper or I'll be knocking you on your behind and beating the answers out of you." Ob marched toward Theta, fists clenched and fight in his eyes. Gabriel grabbed Ob by the collar and stopped him in his tracks.

"If Lord Theta says the captured man used magic," said Gabriel. "Then you can be certain that he did. Leave it at that."

Ob's face was beet red. He narrowed his eyes and glared at Theta and Gabriel both.

"That means the kidnapped man was Par Talbon or one of his apprentices," said Claradon.

"Or Donnelin," said Gabriel as he turned to Bareddal.

"Pick your men and head out forthwith. Go light and go quick, but most of all, go quiet. Do not let them detect you."

"Aye. You can count on me."

XIII
MISTER KNOW-IT-ALL

Claradon, Ob, Dolan, Artol, Par Tanch, and Glimador sat around a campfire over which was hung a good-sized cook pot that Artol attended to. Groups of five to ten men sat around similar fires nearby, all positioned close to the circle of desolation.

"We're a bunch of idiots to be sitting around a fire when there are enemies in the wood," said Ob. "The fires foul our night vision and give away our position and numbers to anyone within a league what ain't blind. Half our men got their backs to the woods and their guards down. The stinking cultists are liable to skulk out of the underbrush and stab half of us all good and proper, our hot dinners spilling out holes in our guts, before we know what's what. What we should have done was lie here in the dark, all quiet as we can be, and wait on them to show their faces. Then it would be them what gets jumped, not us. But no, old Mr. Fancy Pants says—Artol, what did he say exactly?"

"The danger won't be coming from the wood," said Artol, doing an exaggerated and stilted impression of Theta. "It will come from the circle."

"Come from the circle, he says," said Ob. "Conjured up from the beyond, I guess that means. Insanity, I tell you, but Gabe went along with it. I never seen him take on a stupid idea before, but Mr. Know-it-All comes along and everything changes. What is that about? Can anyone tell me?"

"I don't understand it," said Artol. "Gabe has never taken advice from anybody in all the years I've known him. Even Aradon doesn't bother to try."

"Sir Gabriel positioned ten guards in the woods," said Claradon. "We're well protected."

"Not well enough," said Ob, as he took a draught from his wineskin. "Not near as well as we could be, and there is no good reason for it. Reckless and stupid, I say."

"But we needed to set a civilized camp," said Tanch. "The men need rest—maybe even to grab a few hours sleep before the fog comes, assuming that it comes, and assuming any of us could sleep knowing what's coming, not that we know, but you know what I mean. And all of us needed a hot meal—you can't begrudge us that, can you? It is only soup after all."

"Yeah, only soup," said Ob. "Just don't eat too much—it will slow you down and unsettle your stomach. You don't want that going into battle. But I bet if Mr. Fancy Pants had his way, we would all be roasting chestnuts and singing cheery songs. Then when the cultists happen by, he would have us ask them to dance a bit and share our suppers."

"Alright, Ob. Enough," said Claradon.

Ob grumbled a bit and then turned his attention back to his jerky.

"Mr. Claradon," said Dolan, "Mr. Ob is right about eating too much, but it's just as bad to eat too little. It's still a few hours until we expect the fog. Best to keep up your strength, it is. You should try to choke down a bit more than just bread."

"I can barely manage the bread. I chew it and chew it, but without the water I can't get it down."

"Nerves is normal, boy," said Ob as he chewed on a piece of jerky. "I'm worried about your father too, but we need to be at our best when we face whatever is to come."

"I know. You're right. I'm just afraid if I eat more, I'll end up spewing it back up."

"Spew on them Nifleheimers," said Dolan. "That will teach them, it will."

The men shared a chuckle.

"Claradon, me boy, I have known your father all his life, and his father afore him. He is as tough as nails, and a right fine swordsman—one of the best. He'll be alright, I'm sure."

"I wish I could believe that, I'm trying to," said Claradon. "It just doesn't look good."

"You need to understand that he and his guard aren't no common soldiers," said Ob. "You've known them all your life, but you haven't seen them in action in the field, or out in the wild, or at war. I'm not talking the small skirmishes against bandits and such that you've been part of. I'm talking the real deal—blood and gore. Death on a scale to make your heart break and your courage shrivel to nothing.

"Your father, Talbon, Stern, Donnelin, and half the knights and soldiers on that patrol are veterans of Karthune Gorge—one of the bloodiest battles of our age. We Eotrus stood that line. They came at us all day and half the night, no respite or reprieve. Bodies piled as high as a horse around us, and still we didn't yield. We didn't break. We stood tall and laid them low, though the price was sore and steep. Gabe was there, and Artol, and me too.

"And all of us fought the Lugron out East in the mountains—that campaign lasted near two years and cost us half our number, good friends and family amongst the fallen.

"And we was the ones what repelled them things that came out of the White Wood years back. It wasn't the Lomerian regulars like the stories say, and it sure wasn't the stinking Chancellor's men. It was us, the Eotrus. Your father led us on those campaigns and dozens more throughout the northlands and beyond.

"You haven't even heard half the stories—nowhere near half. You and your brothers were too young; we couldn't tell you of such things. The things we did for our country, for our king, to keep our people safe. But we always did the right thing—never forget that, not ever. Your father and Gabe made sure of that. We kept our honor clean.

"I've been with him through it all and I can tell you that near every man on that patrol is as good as five of Lomion City's best and that ain't no exaggeration. And that ain't the half of it. Talbon has got powers beyond anything you've seen or even dreamed about. You know I don't put no stock in magic, but he's the real deal—not no hedge wizard like your boy Tanch, no offense. Talbon can put down a battalion by his lonesome if you get his hackles up. When it comes to it, Donnelin isn't too far behind him. Sword to sword, Stern can even stand against Gabe for a time, when he puts his mind to it. There's not much in this world that can best that group in battle. So keep up your spirits for we may yet find them hereabouts, all good and proper and ready to head home with us. We have to believe that. That's all we can do for now."

Claradon nodded in response as he looked over toward the edge of the circle. "I want to know everything; to hear all those stories."

"It will take more than a few sittings to tell it all," said Ob. "We can start just as soon as we find your father and get our behinds home."

"You and father should have told me these things before," said Claradon. "I'm no child and haven't been for goodly years."

Ob acknowledged Claradon's words with a nod, and then his eyes drifted to the fire.

Dolan pulled out a piece of wax and placed it in a metal cup beside the fire.

"You didn't use the wax back at the Dor," said Ob. "Thought you was deaf."

"The noise didn't bother me so much back there," said Dolan. "We're a lot closer now, we are. Lord Angle says it's best to be prepared, so I'm preparing."

"You always do what he says?" said Ob.

"If I didn't, I would have been killed dead long ago," said Dolan. "He's not often wrong."

"Huh, well, getting that wax ready is smart," said Ob. "Smarter than some of our boys are being. A good half a dozen won't use it, I'm certain, orders or not. Stubborn they are. Stinking blockheads."

"Sir Miden was saying the wax made him dizzy

166

and gave him a headache," said Tanch.

"Better dizzy than deaf," said Ob, "as any fool can tell."

"Such a little thing—putting wax in our ears," said Claradon. "Strange to think that it could turn the tide of a battle, or make the difference between life and death."

"It's often the littlest things that make the most difference," said Ob.

"Lord Angle says that survival is the art of being prepared," said Dolan. "So I expect that he's more prepared than anybody, he is."

Claradon continued to stare off into the distance and said nothing for a time.

"What are you looking at?" Ob turned around to see. Gabriel and Theta stood the watch together at the circle's rim.

"They've been standing there a long time," said Claradon. "I was wondering what they're talking about. Lord Theta doesn't say much, but has much to say. Dolan—is he always like that?"

"Mostly," said Dolan as he pulled some carefully packaged salted pork from his pack. "They also say he's an enigma. I don't rightly know what that means, but they don't say it to his face, so it must be something bad, it must."

"There's worse things to be, I expect," said Ob as he too fixed his gaze on Theta. "That's some suit of armor your boss has, sonny," he said. "Why, it's as fancy as the ceremonial armor of old King Tenzivel himself."

"It should be. I keep it polished and bang out all the dents, I do. There always seems to be more dents."

"Hmm. It sure is mighty pretty, but I'm a wondering if it can stand up to cold hard steel, or beasties' claws. Myself, I wouldn't wear no fairy armor like that in any case. No offense."

"None taken," said Dolan as he finished off a piece of pork. "But I wouldn't say that to Lord Angle, if I were you. He has a high opinion of it, as he made it himself way back when, he did."

"I'm doubting he forged his own armor," said Ob. "To forge that fancy suit would take a skill maybe only three or four smiths in all of Lomion possess and we have the best smiths in Midgaard no matter what the Dwarves say. There's no way some dandy knight has that kind of skill. Besides, what lord makes his own armor?"

"Heimdall made his own and he's a god," said Dolan. "But if you think Lord Angle's armor is fancy, you should see his castle—what with the weapon and trophy collections, the paintings, and all those old wines. It would take a hundred years to drink all them bottles. A sight to see, it is."

"Has his own castle does he?" said Ob. "He must be some important fellow over there across the sea where you hail from."

"That he is. He's a brave hero, he is," said Dolan matter-of-factly.

"You don't say," said Ob. "Now sonny, tell us— just what has that fellow done that makes him a hero? Does he help old ladies cross the street? Or does he just tell folks he's a hero enough times until they start to believe it?"

Dolan narrowed his eyes. "He's a real hero, Mr. Ob, he is. The kind that slays dragons, giants, monsters, and such. Saved the world—all of

Midgaard—several times since I've been with him. They say he even fought the old gods back in olden days, but I wasn't around then."

"Ho, ho. So you are a teller of tales, Dolan me boy," said Ob, chuckling. "Killing dragons, fighting gods, ho ho. I bet them's some goodly yarns to pass a cold night on the trail."

Dolan furrowed his brow and shook his head as he stared at another piece of pork.

"He seems a man of courage and strength," said Claradon.

"He's stronger than any man I've ever seen," said Dolan. "There was that time that—"

"Bah," said Ob. "My boy Gabriel there," gesturing toward him, "smashes beasties afore breakfast. He be a true hero, not some fancy-dressed dandy wearing a tin can and having a pole up his behind. He got his reputation on the battlefield, not in some children's tales."

"That's true enough," said Claradon, as he looked toward Dolan. "Sir Gabriel served as the Preceptor of the Order of the Knights of Tyr for several years before he took up service with my father."

"Them's one of the toughest outfits of knights in all Midgaard," said Ob, "and Gabe was the best of them."

"Many consider him the finest swordsman and weapons master in all Lomion," said Claradon.

"And the only ones what don't think Gabe is the best is dumb or dead or both," said Ob. "Tell him about the dragon. The short version, we'll save the whole tale for when we've more time."

"More than twenty years ago," said Claradon,

"Sir Gabriel slew the old fire wyrm that plagued the villages of the Kronar Mountains."

"Plagued them?" said Ob, his voice growing sharper. "It took at least one of their folk each month and some of their livestock nearly every day for years—years. They couldn't stop it, no matter what they tried. Even a battalion of Lomerian Regulars that ole King Tenzivel sent up there couldn't take it down. Half of them ended up dead, the rest ran for it, the cowards."

"But Gabe smote it good," said Ob. "Can you imagine that—a man killing a fire wyrm—a full grown one, a hundred feet long or more, teeth the size of spears. A mouth what spits acid and breathes fire out 50 yards or more. A body wide around as a mammoth. And Gabe killed it—on his lonesome."

"Hey—I was there," said Artol. "And I still have a scar or two to remember it."

"Me too, but we didn't do much," said Ob. "It takes an army to bring one of them things down. An army—and Gabe did it practically alone: sword and muscle against a monster. That's what a hero is boys. That's what courage is and true mettle. And as for strong, just look at him," he said, pointing toward Gabriel. "He could squash that Mister Foreign Fancy Pants like a bug."

"I doubt that, I do," said Dolan, scowling at the crusty Gnome.

"Bah," spouted Ob before taking a long swill from his wineskin. "I would fancy a taste of them wines you mentioned though. I suppose if he likes a good bottle, he can't be all bad."

"I thank the gods that Sir Gabriel is with us in

this," said Claradon. "If he hadn't returned from hunting, if we had to do this without him . . ." Claradon shook his head, and tightly closed his eyes for a moment. Then he tried to down a spoonful of the soup.

Though Gabriel only served House Eotrus for the previous dozen years or so, he had made his mark on Claradon's upbringing and his life. Of all the great men that Claradon knew, Gabriel was the one he yearned most to be like, the one whom he endeavored to model himself after. Where Aradon was his beloved father, Ob his friend, mentor, and lore master, Sir Gabriel was his hero. Where his father's book learning and Ob's vast experience about the realms had brought them great knowledge and wisdom, Gabriel far surpassed them. There seemed to be nothing he didn't know, nowhere he hadn't been. Where his father was a great swordsman with few peers in all the land, even his skills paled in comparison with Gabriel's. Verily, Gabriel could best any five knights of the Dor at once in mock combat—such was his skill. When Sir Gabriel spoke to a group of men, even those that didn't know him, he had no need to shout above them to gather their attention. The moment he uttered a word, they all went silent; everyone wanted to hear his words. Perhaps it was the stories about him—his slaying of the fire wyrm, his defeat of the barrow-wight, his routing of the Lugron horde, or any of the myriad tales that abounded of him, or perhaps it was merely his regal bearing and commanding presence. Why a man such as he, who had the strength, skills, and knowledge to carve out an empire for himself would be content to serve as Weapons Master of a border fortress, Claradon could never fathom. When he asked him one day, Gabriel said that he had his reasons, but would speak no more about it. He was secretive about some things, which was odd because he was so generous in gifting knowledge to others, whether it be in the form of martial training or most any subject you could name."

Claradon looked at his friends and then at the knights who huddled around the other fires. How many of them will be alive in the morning, he wondered. How many will return to the joyful embraces of their family and friends? How many—and which ones—will never see home again?

Claradon dreaded the thought of seeing the faces of the grieving families: the wives, the children, the crying, the wailing, the pain that they would all feel—that same terrible pain he struggled with every day since his mother's passing. They would blame him, and rightly so. For the first time, he understood the weighty burden his father bore every day. Claradon wasn't certain he was strong enough to bear it—and, at any rate, he knew he wasn't ready to do so.

After a time, Ob grew curious, as Gnomes are often wont to do. "Come on boy. Let's go and see what them two is up to." Ob, Dolan, and Claradon rose and walked toward the two knights at the rim. Theta and Gabriel glanced at the three as they approached, hesitating only a moment before they continued their conversation.

"Do you sense it?" said Gabriel.

"I do," said Theta, "I thought you might as

well."

"The weave of magic is strong here—stronger than it has been in ages, and it's more than just this magical circle," said Gabriel. "There was great evil here of late; it comes with the mist, I suspect."

"When the mist returns, creatures of Nifleheim will return with it," said Theta.

"Gabe and me have fought such beasties a time or two over the years," said Ob. "Once over in the Dead Fens, another time in Southeast. I expect you have also, you being such a big hero and all."

"I have fought their kind, many times," said Theta as he peered down at the bellicose Gnome.

"But the others have not," said Gabriel, gesturing toward the encampment. "They are fine soldiers, but they have no idea what terrors await them here this eve."

"They will learn, or they will die," said Theta. "Such is the way of things."

"A regular ray of sunshine, aren't you, Theta?" said Ob.

"Put your teeth together, Gnome, and open your ears," said Theta. "This place, it is even more sinister than I think you realize. It is becoming a gateway, a portal, to a place more horrific than any mortal can imagine—a place of incomprehensible evil, of mind-shattering, idiotic chaos, of pure insanity. Those who dwell there, would make Midgaard like that. This is what we must prevent. This is why we are here. We must seal this gateway, forever. This is our true quest."

Ob's mouth dropped open and he stared at

Theta in disbelief. Gabriel merely stoically nodded his agreement. Theta's words so shocked Claradon he could say nothing.

"What are you about, Theta?" said Ob. "Portal to another world? What madness are you spewing? Listen, young fellow—I know you wouldn't guess it from looking at me pretty face, but I'm three hundred and sixteen years old and have been from one side of this continent to the other more times than you've had birthdays, and I have never seen, nor heard tell of such a thing. Sure, there be some crazed sorcerers what can conjure up a strange beastie or two from who knows where, but nothing more. Gateway to another world, bah."

Theta responded in a smooth and level tone. "Nevertheless, what I have said is true." Just a hint of anger showed in the set of his jaw and slight furl of his brow. "I will prevent the gateway from opening or close it once it does. You men can assist or not—it matters little to me. I will do what needs to be done."

"Bah! Mister Know-it-All," said Ob. "You are nothing but a boaster and a braggart with no true mettle. Theta, if some creature from another world be coming at you, I bet you would soil that fancy armor of yours in a heartbeat. Hell, you would be down on your knees begging for mercy, pleading for your life, or running away with your tail between your legs."

"Enough!" said Gabriel. "Lord Theta is here to help us, not to be insulted by a loudmouthed Gnome. I will hear no more of it."

"I think what I think, and I'll say what I say,

and if anybody don't like it, they can stuff it," spat the Gnome.

"Lord Theta," said Claradon, "perhaps you could explain your reasoning regarding this gateway you mentioned? What is it that you think is going on out here?"

Theta paused and took a slow, deep breath before responding. "It's what we discussed afore. I believe followers of the Nifleheim lords are using the arcane properties of this eldritch place, the ancient temple and the other ruins that were here, and their own fell sorceries, to open a gateway to the realm of Nifleheim. When that happens, all hell will come through—literally. It will mean the end of civilization. The end of everything we all hold dear. They will pour through by the hundreds, then the thousands, and tens of thousands: an army of madness and monsters without end. There will be no mercy or quarter given: they will kill everyone."

"But why do you think that? All we've seen here is an empty field, a few golden coins, and some tracks, nothing more. It doesn't—"

"In part, because I have seen such things afore, in times past, but mostly because of the demon spoor and stink that pollutes this place." He pointed to the smooth, stony soil. "The tracks in the circle."

"You are daft, man," said Ob. "I told you, there be no tracks there. The only tracks we've seen are outside the circle, and they're just tracks of men and horses. You're just spouting more of your fairy stories and they don't impress us. We're not country bumpkins out here, mister. We're soldiers, we're Northerens, born and bred. Bumps in the night don't scare us." He took a swig from his wineskin.

"Look again, Gnome," said Theta in an even tone as he pointed at the ground within the circle. "Perhaps you were blinded by the forest and failed to see the trees."

"What?" said Ob, turning toward Claradon with a bewildered expression. "I don't understand this fellow. He talks all funny."

"Maybe you should have another look," said Claradon. "Maybe there is something there, something that you missed."

"I was Master Scout of the Dor since before you were born," said Ob sternly. "Nobody can read tracks better than me—not rangers, not stinking elves, and certainly not no tin cans. But I'll have another gander, just to settle this business once and for all." Ob got down on his hands and knees at the rim of the circle, torch in hand, peered down and carefully studied the ground.

Theta squatted next to him. "There, and there," he said, as he gestured toward some small features on the surface of the hardened soil. "And there and there." Ob studied the ground, moved about over a small area, and poked at the soil. This went on for some time. When he finally stood up and turned towards the others, his face was ashen and contorted in a look of shock and bewilderment.

"I cannot hardly believe what I've seen. I missed it afore; I missed it entirely," he said as he shook his head in disgust.

"What did you miss?" said Claradon. "Are there

tracks there or not?"

"Theta spoke the truth, about the tracks at least. There be tracks all right. There be nothing but tracks, which is why I missed them. That ground—it has been stamped down and compressed by a thousand, thousand feet that walked over and over it. The tracks are so overlapped that they obscure each other almost completely, making them appear not to be tracks at all. But they are—I'm sure of it now. And they're not people tracks or the tracks of some animal neither. They're from some type of beasties—monsters the like of which I've never seen afore."

"How do you know that?" said Claradon.

Ob held out his palm and displayed an object that he pulled from the soil. It was a claw—pitch-black, more than nine inches long and nearly three inches wide, and strangely twisted.

Blood dripped from Ob's hand. "It's razor sharp," he said. "It was embedded deep in the soil—only the back edge stuck out just a hair. And look at the size of it. No natural beast has such a claw."

"Dead gods," said Claradon. "It must've broken off some creature; some thing from the hell Lord Theta spoke of."

"It looks scorched," said Gabriel. "Almost charred, as if it has been through a fire."

"It's more than charred," said Claradon. "It is melted."

"All right, Theta," said Ob. "So how do we seal this gateway?"

"When the mist returns, we will find a way,"

said Theta. "There is always a way."

"Find a way? What the heck kind of plan is that?" said Ob. "And what—and what of Aradon and the others?"

Theta looked toward Claradon before responding.

"Besides the one man that was taken away in the wagon, they are dead. Of this, I have little doubt."

Claradon's throat tightened up and his hands grew icy cold when he realized the truth of Theta's words. Time seemed to slow down and the world closed in around him. Gabriel put an arm around his shoulders. "We'll get through this," he said softly.

"How do you know all these things?" said Ob. "You're not just some knight on holiday. Who are you, Theta? Who are you really?"

Theta turned and began to walk away. "Perhaps tonight you will find out."

Ob's weathered visage blanched at Theta's ominous words. Gabriel, Ob, Dolan, and Claradon watched the mysterious knight walk back to the makeshift encampment.

"Should we tell the men?" said Claradon.

"What would you have me tell them?" said Gabriel. "That the world is ending?"

Claradon shrugged.

"That we have a madman amongst us?" said Ob. "Mark my words, he will be the doom of us all. Stinking foreigners."

"You're the stinky one," said Dolan wrinkling his nose before he set off after Theta.

XIV
THE FOG

"There," said Claradon, pointing. "The mist forms at the circle's center." He turned to Ob. "What is the hour?"

Ob looked up at the night sky. "Less than one bell to midnight. Right on time."

"It's forming too fast to be natural," said Claradon.

"So now you're an expert on mist formation?" said Ob.

"It's sorcery," said Tanch. "I warned you," he said glancing about furtively. "We don't have enough men."

"Black magic, it is," whispered Dolan.

"Mount up and form around me," shouted Sir Gabriel.

The knights scrambled to their feet.

"Stop up your ears with the wax, bare your weapons, and stand ready," boomed Ob.

The men rushed to their horses and aligned them shoulder to shoulder in expert fashion, four rows deep. In moments, they were ready; a bastion of solid steel and grim resolve. The knights in the front row held gleaming pole arms honed to a fine edge. Those of the second and third rows held shorter weapons. The fourth row was mostly crossbows.

An unnatural wind sprang up and the fog rapidly expanded radially outward from the circle's center and rolled toward them like a giant wave, gathering speed as it went.

"This is it," said Dolan, a smile on his face.

The men struggled to keep the horses calm and in formation as the mist wave came on; they braced themselves against it.

In moments, the eerie cloud engulfed the entire circle and blasted into an unseen barrier at the circle's rim with a dull, echoing thud. The fog crashed against the invisible barrier, but could not pass. The air about the men grew cold, and their steamy breath rose from their faces.

Standing just beyond the rim, the expedition was untouched by the foul vapors. No one dared move; they barely breathed. Moments passed that seemed like hours while they looked and listened for some sign of their enemies. But there was nothing. Nothing but silence. Nothing but the roiling mist before them. It billowed against the unseen barrier as if to topple it with a fierce pressure, as if it had a will of its own. It was like a wave that crested but could not fall.

"What's holding it back?" said Ob. "Wizard—is it you? You up to your tricks?"

"Not I," said Tanch. "This is quite beyond me. Perhaps the buried coins somehow hold it back."

"Or attract it," said Dolan.

They heard a rumbling sound, though from where it came they could not tell, and then a second gust of wind sprang up. Claradon saw Theta lower his visor and signal something to Dolan, who ducked and covered his eyes. Theta bent low in the saddle and leaned forward.

"Turn your horses," shouted Gabriel. "Put your backs to the fog. Now!"

The unseen barrier abruptly dropped. The fogbank blasted outward and swallowed the whole of the expedition within its maw. With the fog came a thunderous wind and a fierce cold that blasted through the expedition's ranks and momentarily blinded them all. The temperature instantly plunged to well below freezing. Horses panicked and screamed, snorted, reared, stumbled and went down. Helmets blew off. Shields went flying. Weapons were dropped. Men yelled and cursed and fell and were stepped on.

As his horse reared, Claradon was able to slip off its back and land lightly on his feet, but he was knocked over when another horse careened into him. Claradon looked up and saw Theta's horse rearing, but Theta was secure in the saddle, his lance pointed to the sky. Claradon watched as Theta looked toward the men and saw that most were down, along with their horses, the rest, scattered. He turned back toward the circle's center and boldly advanced alone into the preternatural mist. Dolan scrambled to pull his horse up, then vaulted into the saddle and followed his master.

"The fog stings my skin and my head spins," said one knight, before being overcome by a fit of coughing as he tried to rise.

"I can't see," said another man. "It's burning my eyes."

"And my throat," said another, coughing. "This mist is poison; we've got to get clear."

"It is troll's breath," said another knight. "They'll be on us in a moment. Stand fast."

"It's dark sorcery," said another man, who

promptly bent over and vomited his dinner.

"Troll's breath," repeated several others.

"Devil's work," said another. "It's devil's work."

There was coughing and wheezing and vomiting all around as the diabolical fog settled around them and the last of the wind died away. The fog clung to their flesh and threatened to rend it from their very bones. The frigid temperatures it brought with it chilled the men to the core and sapped their strength. A strange bestial odor filled the air and grew stronger by the moment.

"Steady men," shouted Ob. "It's not stinking troll's breath, you idiots. Hold your ground and remember your training."

"Get back in formation," boomed Sir Gabriel. "Get on your horses and reform the line, now."

"My horse ran off," said one man. Several others said the same.

"Forget them," said Gabriel. "Now you're footmen. Get back on the line."

The men scrambled to comply.

"What of the mist?" said Ob to Gabriel. "It could be some kind of poison gas; maybe deadly."

"We've already breathed it deep," said Gabriel. "If it is deadly, we're done for; we might as well hurry on and take some of them with us."

"Aye," said Ob. "Assuming that there's anyone in there," which was impossible to tell for the thick, clinging mist darkened the area and limited their vision to little more than ten feet.

Soon, they were ready, though down more than a dozen horses, and several of the men were battered, bruised, and bleeding. Serious injury amongst the knights was staved off only by the quality of their armor and their training. The effects of the mist diminished with time, but the nausea and lightheadedness remained, as did the frigid cold.

"Where is Mr. Fancy Pants?" said Ob as he looked around. "Hiding in the back somewhere or has he run off?"

"He went on ahead," said Claradon. "And Dolan with him."

"Went on ahead?" said Ob. "Are you serious? What does the fool think he's doing? We've no idea what lurks in there."

"Dear gods," said Tanch. "We can't just go blundering into that fog. It's chaos sorcery; I can sense it. It is powerful and it could harbor anything. It would have taken a cadre of archmages to conjure this up. For Odin's sake, Sir Gabriel, I implore you not to lead us in there. It will be the death of us all."

"Pipe down, Magic Boy," said Ob. "Or I'll take a switch to you."

"We're heading in," shouted Sir Gabriel, his eyes boring into Tanch. "Keep the daggers I gave you near at hand."

"Steady boys and forward," shouted Ob. "Eyes open and mouths shut, and for Tyr's sake, stay together. I will not search the fog for any slackers."

The warriors caught up to Theta and Dolan about a hundred yards into the fogbank. They stood amidst a killing field, but remounted their horses as the others rode up. The mutilated corpses of more than a dozen men and horses littered the ground where minutes before there was nothing. Gabriel ordered the knights to form a perimeter around the area. Ob and Tanch dismounted to get a closer look at the bodies. Gabriel grabbed the reins of Claradon's horse and they rode to Theta's side.

"Ob will check things out," said Gabriel to Claradon. "You just stay with me. The men are watching, so we must keep our wits, no matter what Ob finds."

"There was nothing here minutes ago, just empty dirt," said Gabriel to Theta. "What did you see when you got here?"

"The same as what you see now."

"Is it our patrol?" said Claradon.

"Probably, but I can't say for certain," said Theta.

Claradon didn't know why, but he looked to Theta's sword, to see if blood dripped from it, but his swords were in their sheaths and his lance looked clean and unbloodied.

"**D**ear gods," whispered Tanch as his face contorted in revulsion. "What could do that to a man?"

"I don't rightly know," whispered Ob, cringing as he surveyed the remains.

"They're torn to bits," said Tanch. "Odin protect us—they look chewed: eaten. How will we ever tell who they are? Is it even them?"

"It's them," said Ob. "Some of them anyway. There's a bit of a tabard over there," he said,

184

pointing. "I can see our sigil on it, and over there is part of a shield. I think it has got Worten's coat-of-arms on it."

"What is that smeared all over the remains?" said Tanch. "Mud? The ground is dry."

"Droppings," said Ob.

"What?"

"Their corpses have been desecrated," said Ob, "in unspeakable ways, more than just what you've noticed. There will be hell to pay for this."

"Dear gods, dear gods," said Tanch. "I can't believe this; I can't look any longer. Is Lord Aradon amongst them? By Odin, please tell me he's not."

Ob held up the battered hilt of a sword that he had pulled from the debris. Only a fragment of the steel blade remained. The hilt's leather was torn and the wood slashed, but the design was unmistakable.

"That's his?" said Tanch. "For certain?"

"Aye."

"Where are the rest of them?" said Tanch. "There aren't enough remains here for all those men, are there?"

"Killed elsewhere, or eaten," said Ob.

"Dear gods."

Ob walked over to the others. His jaw was set and his eyes were watery.

"Is it them?" said Claradon. "Is he there?"

Ob held up the sword hilt for Claradon and Gabriel to see. "We're going to find them, what did this," he said, "and we're going to kill them all.

We're going to stick their stinking heads on pikes for Odin and all to see. We're going to kill them all."

Claradon slipped off his horse before Gabriel could restrain him and loped towards the fallen.

"Get back boy" shouted Ob, as he interposed himself between the young knight and the grisly remains. "You don't want to see this." Ob grabbed Claradon's arm to hold him back.

"Stand aside. I have to see. I have to know. If he's dead, I have to know."

"No, you don't," said Ob. "You don't want to remember him this way."

Claradon shoved Ob aside, knocking him to the ground, and moved forward. "Dead gods," he said when he drew close. That was all he could utter. His eyes welled with tears, try as he could to prevent it. His face twisted in horror and revulsion. He fell to his knees and put his hands over his eyes. Gabriel was at his side in but a moment.

"Stay strong, Claradon," said Gabriel. "No matter how hard it is, now is not the time for grieving. You must—"

Gabriel's words caught in his throat when his eyes fell on the remains. His jaw dropped open; he froze, staring for several seconds before he turned away. "You must stand up," he said to Claradon. "You must be an example for the men." He grabbed Claradon by the arm and pulled him to his feet.

"We can't even bury him," said Claradon as tears streamed down his face, which was filled at once with rage, anguish, and disbelief. "There's nothing left. He won't be able to rest beside mother."

Gabriel's mouth opened as if to speak, but no words came.

"We need to say a prayer over them," said Claradon.

"We cannot linger here," said Gabriel. "Or we may share their fate."

"I'll be quick. Gather the men."

In a few moments, Gabriel had the men assembled around Claradon. More than one vomited when they saw what was left of their comrades. The others stared at their feet or off into the darkness, not daring to more than glance at the bodies. They bowed their heads respectfully when Claradon spoke in shaky voice.

"Odin—we beseech you to welcome our brave fallen into Valhalla, so that they may serve at your side in the great battle of Ragnarok whence comes the end of days. So say the knights of House Eotrus."

"Aye," said the men.

"Each of you is to look at what they did to your lord and his guard," said Claradon. "Look close. Let this horror burn into your heart and steel you for what is to come. This will be a night of blood and vengeance. To victory and tomorrow."

"To victory and tomorrow," shouted the men.

"Mount up and let's move," said Claradon.

Claradon's jaw was set; his eyes wild. He started off and then his head shook with rage. "Vengeance," he yelled. "Retribution."

"Vengeance," shouted the men, raising their weapons aloft.

"We will find whoever did this," said Claradon. "For them, there will be no escape."

Claradon picked up his shield, adjusted his helm, and wondered whether they would all end up dead or worse before the night was done. But Sir Gabriel was with him, thank the gods. He would stay at Gabriel's side and he would make it through.

"The boy is taking charge," said Ob to Gabriel.

"That he is. The hardest times have a way of bringing out the best leaders."

"Let's just make sure he doesn't send us headlong into anything stupid," said Ob.

"I'll stay close to him," said Gabriel.

Gabriel joined Claradon at the group's vanguard. Theta, Ob, Tanch, and Dolan behind them, with the balance of expedition closely following. Claradon was fuming. His eyes raged with hatred and his breathing was heavy.

As they rode along, Tanch studied an object that he held in his hand.

"What is that you carry, wizard?" said Theta.

"A piece of Par Talbon's staff," said Tanch. "I couldn't look at the bodies any longer and so I ended up walking off a ways and there it was, just lying on the ground. I practically tripped over it. There's not much left, and what there is, is charred, but it is his staff—I would know it anywhere. He's dead. Talbon of Montrose, dead. I can't believe it. I have said it before, and I'll say it again. We don't have enough men for this. Not for whatever brought down these heroes. I want vengeance as much as any man here, but we'll not achieve it with two squadrons of knights. All we'll get is dead."

"If you think you can get the boy to turn around, then ride up and ask him," said Ob. "I'll bet a silver star he knocks you off your horse."

Tanch shook his head in frustration. "There are things out here best left hidden. I can sense it. If left alone, they may let leave us in peace, and depart as suddenly as they've appeared."

"Many fools and many cowards throughout history have uttered such words," said Theta. "Take a lesson from them and don't repeat their mistakes."

"What do you think is out there, really?" said Ob.

"Pure evil," said Theta.

"If so, then maybe the wizard is right," said Ob. "Maybe we don't have enough men."

XV
THE TEMPLE OF GUYMAOG

"**D**o you see it?" said Claradon through clenched teeth. "Straight ahead, in the mist."

"The ruins have reappeared," said Gabriel. "And they're ruins no longer," he said as they drew closer.

The mammoth building that fronted them was located directly in the center of the fogbank, where nothing had been only minutes before. Its stone walls were blacker than the night and its upper reaches and extents were lost in the mist. They rode slowly around the building, and found no door or window or sign of life—nothing but solid walls—until they reached the northern side. There, at what was the front of the structure, two sets of tall steps, one to each side, led up to a raised landing. Atop it stood six massive stone columns shrouded in mist.

"Do you see any movement?" said Gabriel.

"I would be charging them down if I did," said Claradon as he stared at the temple, breathing heavily, his face red, his jaw set.

Gabriel looked to him, concern on his face. "We will have our revenge, but we need to keep our heads clear, our minds calm. Sound tactical decisions may be the difference tonight between victory and death. The men will look to you for guidance, for leadership."

"What are you saying?" said Claradon. "You're in command of this mission—that is what we agreed. They'll look to you and to Ob. Not to me. I've never been in command, nor do I want to be."

"Despite what we agreed," said Gabriel, "you are our leader. Every man back there knows that, whether you realize it or not. You're an Eotrus, not I, not Ob. You are the acting Lord and Master of the House until we find your father—so the men will look to you. You must keep a cool head no matter what happens, no matter what we find. The men will remember the actions you take here tonight. They will remember your words and the deeds you do long after they've forgotten most else that goes on here. You must set the example that your father would if he were here. You must not fail in this."

"I'll—I'll do my best," said Claradon, his voice wavering but harboring a bit less tension. "There must be a door somewhere on that landing."

"Aye," said Gabriel. "And to enter it, we'll need to walk south."

Claradon looked puzzled. "What does that matter?"

"Away from the north," said Gabriel.

Claradon nodded. "Away from the north—farther from Asgard and Odin. Makes sense, for a Nifleite Temple."

"What's the game plan?" said Ob as he marched up beside them. "Creep in first and see what's what, all stealthy like, or bash their heads in with a frontal assault?"

"It will be the hammer and the axe," said Gabriel loudly so that the others could hear.

Ob smiled and there were nods of approval all around.

"The men-at-arms will stay with the horses," said Gabriel. "Back in the wood, beyond the fog. They'll bolt if we try to hold them here."

Ob turned toward the wood; there was no sign of it through the fog. "It'll be a long run if we have to flee."

"I will not flee tonight," said Gabriel. "I will see this done. The gateway will be closed. Choose a few knights that will remain on the landing to cover our rear while the rest of us go in."

"I'll make it so," said Ob.

The men marched forward in rows of four: Gabriel, Claradon, Ob, and Theta at the van. Six wide steps of black stone, polished smooth, led up to the landing. The stone was so dark and so flat it felt as if each tread was a hole above a bottomless pit rather than a solid slab of granite.

Just as the men mounted the steps, they shuddered as they heard a deep moaning on the wind—a sound akin to a voice—though no human throat could emit sounds of such anguish, such pain.

"Oh, dead gods, what be that now?" said Tanch as he turned toward their left flank.

"It came from the front," said Claradon. "Not from over there."

"No, it came from behind," said Ob.

"I heard from our right," said Gabriel.

"That makes no sense," said Ob. "More stinking sorcery to confound us."

"That voice was no creature of Nifleheim, nor any mortal man or beast," said Theta.

"Then what?" said Ob.

"Midgaard weeps at this affront," said Theta. "What goes on here this night, this place, is not natural. It is abhorrent to nature."

Blacker than anything natural, the structure around them absorbed nearly all light, even that of Gabriel's mystical daggers. That and the dense fog prevented the men from discerning the true shape and full extent of the sinister edifice even as they mounted its steps. The tops of the columns, lost in the fog, presumably supported some canopy far above.

Climbing the steps, the feelings of lightheadedness and nausea that began when the mist appeared, returned, more powerfully this time. Claradon forced himself onward despite his swimming head and churning stomach. With each step, the air grew colder and thicker.

When he reached the top of the landing, he turned and faced the men. Through the fog, he gazed upon a sea of shining helmets lined up four abreast, awash in Eotrus colors of silver and blue, gray and gold, and coats-of-arms of ornate and noble design. The scene was surreal, for as the fog billowed about the company and steam rose from their breath, it appeared as if they floated amongst dark clouds or bobbed on the waves of an icy black sea. The biting cold of the place assaulted Claradon, though it failed to dampen the steely resolve on his face or that of his men. Despite his confident facade, Claradon was at war inside himself—fighting to banish the fear and uncertainty that welled within him and threatened to send him fleeing for his life. He remembered

Gabriel's words about leadership, gathered his courage, still emboldened by his anger, and through chattering teeth, he shouted to the troops. "Tyr's guiding light will preserve us, and we will have our rightful vengeance."

"For House Eotrus," shouted the men.

Claradon realized his mistake after catching Theta's withering glare and hearing the growls from Ob and Gabriel behind him.

"Let's pipe down and keep moving men," said Ob. "There may still be some beasties way in the back what haven't heard us coming yet—maybe we should take up a tune, so we won't startle them."

They proceeded across the wide landing, the mist thickening and swirling about them as they made their way. Their steps loudly echoed on the night air as they passed first one and then a second great column.

Claradon tried with little success to fan the mist from his face. "It's like the stuff is alive, and wants to blind us, and stop us from going on."

"Ignore it," said Ob. "It's just stinking fog."

"Draw the daggers I gave you," said Gabriel, "and we shall see."

Claradon pulled Worfin Dal from its scabbard and the fog immediately fled from him. Gabriel's dagger had the same affect. The lesser blades of the other men didn't work as well, but acting together, they quickly cleared the fog from the landing, though it gathered all the thicker just beyond. As the moments went by, the glow from the daggers began to fade (assailed no doubt on some magical plane by the strange sorcery that permeated the place), and as it did, the fog crept ever closer.

"Stinking sorcery," said Ob. "And what's the point of it anyways?"

"How's your stomach?" said Gabriel. "Still churning or has it settled?"

"Mine is a bit better," said Tanch, "now that you ask."

Ob paused a moment and then nodded his head. "Better since we pulled the daggers and the fog fled. That's it then, the stinking stuff was put hereabouts to weaken us. They are using the mist as a weapon, the cowards. It's softening us up for something. But what?"

"Something they don't want us to face until we're softened up," said Gabriel. "That means they fear us, and that means they know they can be defeated."

"That logic has a trail that I can't argue with," said Ob, "but it may just be wishful thinking all the same—there's our way in," he said, pointing at two enormous black stone doors that became visible at the rear of the landing when the fog dispersed, each one with a large circular bronze handle. Beside the doors, affixed to the wall, was a great bronze plaque inscribed with strange runes.

"Where's the wizard?" said Ob. "Someone wake him up and drag him over here."

"I'm right behind you," said Tanch, "and have been all the while, since you didn't notice."

"Well, you tall folk all look alike," said Ob.

"Move aside so I can get a look," said Tanch as he brushed past Ob and Gabriel and planted himself directly in front of the plaque, which was set high in the wall, its bottom no less than six feet above the landing's pavement. "It's an ancient form of runic script similar to that used by the Throng-Baz back in—"

"Can you read it?" said Ob.

"I was just trying to explain that—"

"We've no time for history lessons by babbling bumpkins," said Ob. "Tell us what it says and be quick about it."

Tanch shook his head in frustration and stepped closer to get a better look at the writing.

"Don't touch it," said Theta as Tanch raised his hand toward the plaque.

Tanch froze for a moment, no doubt remembering what happened with the golden coins. He lowered his hand, inched back from the wall, and squinted from where he stood, eyeing the runes. "*Temple of Guymaog* is what it says, whatever that means."

"Who or what is Guymaog?" said Claradon. "Does anyone know?"

"I bet Dolan will tell us he's some pagan god from the old world what Theta killed off once upon a time," said Ob, chuckling, as he turned to look at Dolan.

"It is an ancient evil from *The Dawn Age*," said Theta.

"Of course it is," said Ob sardonically. "What else could it be?"

"Is it some obscure Lord of Nifleheim?" said Claradon.

"No," said Theta.

Claradon didn't dare inquire further.

"No matter," said Gabriel. "Whatever it is, if it's in there, we'll deal with it."

"But how do we get in?" said Ob. "I doubt they left the doors unlocked."

Theta stepped forward, gripped the bronze handles, and pulled. Though there was no visible lock or bar, the doors didn't budge.

"We'll need a battering ram to get through those," said Ob. "They're probably a foot thick, maybe more."

Theta braced himself and prepared to pull again. Gabriel and Claradon moved to assist him.

"No," said Theta, waving them off. "Best stay back; all of you stand clear." He stared them down until everyone moved well away. Ob paid him no heed; he stood his ground.

Theta pulled on the handles again; this time, straining with the effort: veins on his forehead and neck sticking out.

"Give it up, Mister Fancy Pants," said Ob. "Muscle won't get us through them doors. It'll take brains to—"

As Theta continued to pull, thundering crunching and cracking sounds erupted from the doors and the entire landing vibrated and threatened to collapse around them. When stone shards fell from above, the men scattered. Ob tripped, went down on his face, and was stepped on. Some of the men jumped from the landing for fear that the canopy above might come down on them.

Theta stood his ground and continued to pull on the doors. Huge cracks appeared in the stone, and with a loud bang, the doors shattered and crumbled: Theta's mighty grip having literally torn them asunder. The stony remains collapsed in heaps about the entranceway. Ob rolled to the side just in time as a huge piece of stone struck the landing just where he'd lain. Theta stood amidst the wreckage as the dust settled about him—the two bronze handles remaining in his iron grip.

"Stinking show-off," said Ob as he struggled to his feet. "They was probably about to fall apart on their own, anyways. Bad workmanship; probably elvish."

Theta tossed the handles over the edge of the landing. "Put them in my saddlebag," he said to one of the men.

No sounds came from within the temple. It exhibited no signs of life—though it was far too dark to see in more than a few feet.

"Light some torches, men," said Ob. "We need more light than these faery knives will give us. And make certain your ears are well stuffed with wax—that stinking wailing could start up at any time. We need your heads on straight, so put it in good, so it won't fall out when things get nasty."

The men assembled on either side of the doorway and crouched behind the rubble: Theta and Ob at the van on one side, Gabriel and Claradon on the other. The balance of the company lined up behind them.

Theta removed his shield from its shoulder strap and readied it before him, his movements crisp, precise, and practiced, with no wasted motion.

"You're not going to step out there, are you?"

said Ob. "Because that would be a stupid thing. We should wait and see—"

Ignoring Ob, Theta stood tall and stepped forward into the doorway, his shield protecting his torso, but no weapon in his hand. Instead, in his left hand he gripped that curious ankh that he wore beneath his shirt.

"Fool," spat Ob.

"Or madman," said Artol, from over Ob's shoulder. "I'm not sure which yet."

"Both, probably," said Ob.

Theta stood there, braced and ready, but no battle cry rang out from within, no arrows flew, no monsters charged.

"Looky there, what's that?" whispered Ob when he noticed the ankh in Theta's hand.

"Oh, now that's an odd thing," whispered Artol.

"It's near a twin to that old relic what Gabe carries," said Ob.

"No coincidence is that, I'll bet you," said Artol. "What do you figure it means?"

"Don't know," said Ob.

Theta peered inside, looking this way and that, and even up toward the ceiling. He removed one small object and then another from a belt pouch and tossed one to each side of the darkened hall. When they struck the floor, the objects shattered as if made of glass, and then somehow illuminated a portion of the infernal place, flooding it with light that centered on the remnants of the objects, whatever they were. The mist fled from that light, just as it did the light from the glowing daggers. Moreover, the darkness itself fled from that light. It wasn't just extinguished by it, it actually moved away, as if the shadows in the temple were alive and feared it. After but a few moments, the foul blackness of the place returned and swirled about the light as if to smother it. The lights didn't wane entirely, despite all the shadows' efforts; enough remained for the men to see the way ahead.

The knights gasped at this bizarre phenomenon, never having seen such magic before.

"Theta's a sorcerer," said one knight. "He throws foreign magic."

"Don't trust him," said another.

"Witchcraft," said a third.

Several others muttered much the same sentiments.

"Clam up you dimwits," said Ob. "Lots of holier than thou tin cans can toss a cantrip or two. No need to go dampening your drawers about it. Besides, he's on our side, you fools. Raise a hand against him, and I'll cut it off myself."

There was grumbling and murmuring in the ranks but nothing more was said about it.

Theta paid them no heed. He slowly drew his falchion from its sheath as the men looked on. After a few moments, he stepped carefully over the rubble, and cautiously stalked into the malevolent edifice. Dolan followed close at his back, holding Theta's silver lance.

The others followed, weapons bared. (Ob took a long drink from his wineskin before he entered). Some of the men still held their mystical daggers, but others sheathed them in favor of longer weapons or a burning torch.

An unnatural malaise came over them the

moment each man's feet passed the threshold. Feelings of dread and hopelessness assailed them. They were torn between a desire to flee and one to lie down and give up, to surrender to the oppressive, ancient darkness that lingered there, to yield to the temple's alien will. Where common men would have faltered, these did not. Honor bound and anger brimming, they pushed back their feelings and soldiered on.

Strangely, it was even colder inside the temple than without, and the mist was there too—how it got inside, none could say. It was thinner, but clung about their legs. The air, oddly thick and heavy, had a curious, acrid taste. The same bestial odor resided there, as outside, only stronger.

The building's interior was a most singular hall, some hundred feet in width; it stretched back into the darkness beyond the limits of the men's vision. The size and scale, and the details of construction of the place were all wrong. It was too massive, too ponderous, and too meticulous to have been man-made in the days of yore. It featured two rows of immense, ornate, obsidian columns set forty feet apart. They formed a wide corridor that extended from the entranceway to the rear of the foreboding structure. The ceiling, lost in the darkness, surely resided more than fifty feet above. The flagstones were ground perfectly smooth; the joints between them so flawlessly cut and fitted as to require no mortar. Expert craftsmen that possessed skills far beyond those of the most renowned of modern masons and artisans had built that place. Surely, the Old Ones or their minions—those ancient fiends that walked

Midgaard before the dawn of man—had constructed it. Somehow, the fell sorcery at work had restored the antediluvian temple, which had only lately been no more than a crumbling ruin, to all its former majesty and frightful glory.

The men stalked into the sinister structure, their way illuminated: by Theta's magic, by the soft white light emitted by their mystical daggers, and by the torches that many of them carried. From the moment they entered that place, it seemed to Claradon that everything moved in slow motion. Perhaps it was the dizziness and nausea that afflicted him, or some byproduct of the feelings of dread that oppressed him, or maybe something more. Even his boots made ominous, echoing sounds as he crossed the black stones. Unnaturally loud were they—the mystical nature of the edifice somehow served to amplify the sound tenfold.

At Gabriel's direction, they fanned out and moved deeper into the black hall. As they did so, a bizarre, inhuman wailing sprang up all around them, emanating from the very walls themselves. The men halted, weapons held at the ready.

"What madness is this?" said one knight. Several others said much the same.

"It's the wailing," said Ob. "Sounds different up close."

"Where is it coming from?" shouted someone. "I can't see them."

The men turned this way and that, up towards the ceiling, and down at their feet, but they couldn't find the source of the sounds. It was everywhere at once—from all sides, but from no particular place.

"Steady boys," said Ob as he warily looked around. "Ignore the wailing and keep moving forward, the sounds can't hurt you."

But as they went, the shrill wailing increased. Growling, malefic intonations began: roaring and barking, howling, chattering, and gibbering. No throat of man or beast could produce the bizarre cacophony that filled that evil place. It surely sprang from the demonic tongues of a thousand wretched fiends reveling in the very pits of hell itself.

The faces of the soldiers blanched as the skirling sounds oppressed them and the bitter cold within the place took hold. They were knights, schooled in battle and tactics, the scions of noble families and olden northern bloodlines. They knew how to fight as a unit and were experts in single combat. But this was altogether different. An unseen enemy whose caterwauling deafened and disorientated—that was beyond their experience, beyond their training. All they could do was flee or follow their officers' orders and move forward against the din. Though their resolve was dampened and their wills were breaking, still they followed orders as their duty and honor required. They moved forward.

When they approached the first line of obsidian columns, the grotesque, painted bas-reliefs that adorned their surfaces came into view. Every manner of horrific, depraved, obscene, and unspeakable activity was prominently depicted on the pillars' gruesome faces. Such was the horror of those images, the men surely would have lost their sanity, if not their very souls, had they gazed on them for more than mere moments.

The hellish din intensified but did not prepare them for what came next. Beyond all reason and logic, beyond sanity itself, the walls of the temple and the surfaces of the black pillars soon began to move and wriggle as if alive. Hideous pseudopods shaped like malformed hands, claws, and demonic arms pushed against and protruded from within the black stone. The obsidian surfaces seemingly transformed to nothing more than thin, opaque, elastic veils. The horrid appendages writhed, flailed about, and sought to ensnare the men when they moved past.

For a moment Claradon questioned the reality of what he saw. Was he asleep? Was this naught but a fevered nightmare? If only it was. But it wasn't: he was wide-awake. Then he thought it must be some poison that hung in the mist. Some noxious weed or decaying fungus that clouded the mind and brought on hallucinations and visions of horror. But he knew it wasn't. His head pounded from the din, but his thoughts were clear enough. He was himself. He was there and it was real. Dead gods, they were real: monsters. True monsters surrounded them—the gathered hordes of hell, the spawn of Nifleheim. He shuddered and cringed as he saw them struggle to burst through the flowing stone and enter Midgaard from somewhere beyond sanity—just as they had done two nights previous. The night they killed his father.

The dim light and eerie shadows that filled the place only served to enhance the horror of the surreal scene and unnerve even the bravest of the company. Looking around at his comrades, Claradon saw stony resolve on the faces of some, stark terror marred the aspects of others. Steamy breath rose from all, as did the soft glow of the ensorcelled daggers, which leaked out even from those covered in their sheaths.

Gabriel and Ob shouted for the men to keep well away from the demonic arms and to keep moving forward. Through the din, most surely couldn't hear them. Lord Theta pressed on at the van. He cautiously stalked forward while he evaded the writhing things that protruded from the columns and sought to grab him.

One of the knights was not so careful. He strayed too close. A snakelike appendage darted out from a column and wrapped about his waist, pinioning his arms. It effortlessly lifted him into the air and pulled him toward the column as he cried for help and struggled to pull his arms free. Ob, Claradon, and others raced toward the struggling knight. It was Sir Erendin of Forndin Manor—a sparring partner of Claradon's who had near his skill with a sword. Erendin's eyes locked briefly on Claradon; Claradon saw his lips move, but couldn't hear his words. He knew that his friend pleaded for help. Before Claradon could reach him, another tentacle appeared from above and looped about Erendin's neck. The otherworldly limbs pulled in opposite directions and tore the knight's head from his shoulders. Blood spurted in all directions and washed over Ob and Claradon who gasped in horror at the monstrous sight. Erendin's head fell to the floor, but the creature's vile tentacles still gripped his body as they shot back whence they came. The body crashed into the column with a sickening crunch. The tentacles repeatedly smashed it against the stone until it was an unrecognizable heap of ruined metal and flesh. Ob and Claradon moved toward the column with swords raised, to deal out whatever vengeance they could.

"Stop," shouted Par Tanch as he ran to intercept them. "For Thor's sake, don't strike the things. You might break the seal and give them entry—then we would surely be doomed." Tanch grabbed Claradon's arm and pulled him away from the column. "You can't fight it," he said.

"Look at what they did," said Claradon.

"We have to back away," said Tanch.

And they did, though Tanch had to pull Claradon along, and Ob followed. Mindful of the wizard's words, Claradon took care to remain beyond the range of the writhing things that haunted the other columns. Adrenaline rushed through Claradon's system, but he still struggled with the thought that it must all be a nightmare. He had seen men die before, but never by magic or monster.

"This is it; it's the end of us and maybe of all Midgaard," said Tanch. "You think you're so smart," he shouted at Ob and Claradon. "I told you we should've sent for the army. You people never listen to me. You think I'm a fool, but it's you who are the fools, and now we are doomed. We'll all die here; mark my words. No doubt, they'll blame me. The wizard should have known better, they'll say. It'll be all my fault."

"Stow that talk, you sniveling turd, or I'll bash your knees in," said Ob. The Gnome raised his wineskin to his lips and took a long draught as he pressed forward.

Claradon's vision clouded and his stomach churned as the waves of nausea and lightheadedness flooded over him with renewed vigor. He couldn't believe what he had just seen. How would he face Rachel, Erendin's fiance? He couldn't tell her the truth of what happened, of how he fell. Not ever. He would never plant that image in her head; he could never be that cruel. He'd have to make up a story—the truth, too painful to hear.

The abominable clangor around him increased more and more to near deafening levels and threatened to implode his very skull. Time and space became increasingly distorted; everything moved slower and slower.

Blood streamed from the men's noses and ears as the pressure and maddening cacophony intensified. Several knights doubled over and vomited great gobs of putrescent green ichor as the sinister forces of the place assailed their mortal bodies. Others heaved and spat, but little came out. Some simply collapsed unconscious to the ebony slab.

Claradon watched in horror as a claw-like pseudopod pushed out from a column and ensnared the ankle of one of the fallen knights, Sir Zaren. The man screamed in terror as it dragged him to his doom; Claradon, too far away to come to his aid. Those who were closer were too dazed from the madness about them, or too shocked to spring to his rescue. The knight's magical dagger sent sparks flying everywhere as he repeatedly but ineffectually struck it against the obsidian slab, trying to slow his slide. Within seconds of reaching the pillar, other demonic pseudopods and misshapen hands fell upon him and rent him limb from limb. He never had a chance. (Another friend dead). Claradon shuddered with the thought that that could just as easily have been him.

"I can't take this noise—it's maddening," shouted one knight. "If we can't attack these things, we must flee before we're all torn to pieces."

Ob grabbed the man and pulled him forward. "You're a knight of House Eotrus, boy, and you'll not flee while I yet live, that's for certain. We face this together. Come on," he shouted as he steadied the knight and pressed forward. "For House Eotrus," he shouted. "To victory and tomorrow."

Tanch mashed his hands to his ears and desperately struggled to keep the maddening noise from reaching him. He must have tried to recall some bit of magic, some arcane spell or charm that would safeguard him from the din. But he failed—for how could any man focus his thoughts through that insane clamor? Blood streamed from his nose and his eyes were unfocused. His strength sapped, he collapsed to his knees.

The din grew worse, and soon even Ob staggered and fell, spitting curses all the while—his sensitive Gnomish ears being particularly susceptible to the horrid sounds despite two earfuls of wax.

Claradon focused his concentration as best he could, and through chattering teeth bespoke mystical words—words taught him by the lore masters of the Caradonian Knights—words that called forth the power of Odin. A brilliant white light appeared and encompassed him. What generated the light could not be seen—it simply manifested all around him. It bathed him in its glow and made his clothing and armor appear pure white in hue, though strangely, it had no effect on the look of his skin. This mantle of holy light diminished the deafening sounds and the spatial distortions that occurred directly around him, and safeguarded him from the claws and fangs of any creature of Nifleheim that appeared. Alas, his power was not nearly great enough to encompass and aid his comrades. If he had only practiced more, he might have been able to cloak a few others as well—but only a few. Even the grandmaster of the Caradonians didn't have the power to cloak the entire company. Already weakened, he could do little more than hold his ground. He flexed his fingers repeatedly, trying to shake off the sharp, stinging sensation that always came with the magic. It took a few minutes to wear off in the best of times, but flexing his fingers tended to help. Why it affected his hands he never understood, as the magic he had thrown was powered only by words and not by esoteric gestures. Regardless, his hands always stung after throwing magic—that was just the way of things.

At the far end of the hall, Claradon spied the temple's adytum—a black stone table, an unholy altar, no doubt, to the foulest fiends of Nifleheim. Its surface was covered in deep, reddish stains; the dried blood of untold innocents, spilled to sate the unquenchable thirsts of unspeakable, outré beings.

Behind the altar, the rear wall of the temple was embossed with a strange pattern of circles within circles. At the pattern's center was a gaping black hole of nothingness: a void. To where it led, man was surely not meant to fathom. The radius of each circle was twice that of the circle within it. The lines that formed the five innermost circles were blackened and charred, as if they had burned away; only moldering gray ash remained. Within these circles, inscribed in a dark-red pigment—which surely was human blood—were all manner of arcane runes and eldritch symbols from the bizarre lexicon of otherworldly fiends, forgotten gods, or mad archmages.

The sixth or outermost circle glowed and burned a fiery red; the very flames of hell danced and writhed on its unholy surface. Evenly spaced between the fifth and sixth circles were golden coins that looked like those they found buried at the desolate zone's rim. Surely, when the sixth circle burned away, there would be no holding back the infernal tide that was to come—the very armies of insanity and chaos, the maleficent denizens of the pit: the spawn of Nifleheim.

Even now, the rear wall, etched with the unholy pattern, bulged and flexed and flowed, ready to burst from the pressure of some massive monstrosities that strained against its far side. In moments, they would burst through, and the beasts from beyond would roam Midgaard once again and usher in mankind's doom.

Sir Gabriel pressed on toward the black altar. Artol soldiered through the maddening chaos, perhaps somewhat protected by his earplugs and thickly padded steel helm, if not his thick skull, but blood flowed freely from his nose, mouth, and even his eyes. Sir Miden staggered just behind them and valiantly tried to press forward, though blood gushed from his nose and mouth and ears. He hadn't stuffed his ears with wax like most of the others, and now it was too late. Overcome by the pain, Miden dropped his sword and shield, ripped off his helm, and pressed his hands to his ears to stave off the intolerable sounds and pressure. Just as he seemed to recover and bent over to retrieve his sword, his entire head erupted in fountains of blood that spouted from his ears and nose. His body swayed for a moment and then collapsed in a lifeless heap.

Claradon forced himself to look away and tapped his reserves of strength—that well of mystical energy from which sprang his magics. He couldn't imagine any way to survive that place, but he had to try, and so he threw more energy into the mystical mantle that shielded him. He felt all his power surging through it, shielding him better than wood or metal ever could. Yet it felt a puny defense. He felt vulnerable and weak, more so than he ever had in all his life.

Witnessing Sir Miden's fate, several knights turned and fled the temple in terror. Their loyalty to House Eotrus was without question, but that madness was too much. There were no enemies to smite there, no honor or glory to be gained, no vengeance to be had, only mindless suffering and senseless death. They'd had enough. They fled. A few even dropped their weapons or shields in their haste to escape. Ob's shouted commands and curses went unheard and unheeded in the chaotic din.

Claradon watched them flee. He wasn't angry with them. How could he be? He wanted to flee too, but he wouldn't. He looked at the others struggle forward, pushing on with all their strength. He hoped they would all turn and run so that he could too. No one could fault him for running if everyone else ran first. But Gabriel would never run. He didn't think Theta would either, though he wasn't certain why, since he barely knew the man. But if they didn't, he couldn't. He wouldn't. He could never live with the shame of it-with the dishonor that it would bring to his House and to his father's memory. He would stay and fight. He would seek his rightful vengeance, though he felt that Tanch was right-that place would be the death of him, the death of them all.

Theta seemed less affected by the evil phenomenon than were the others. No blood flowed from him and his eyes remained focused. How and why that was, Claradon couldn't imagine. Theta's face, however, turned bright red and his stride slowed nearly to a crawl. He trudged forward in slow motion, several yards ahead of Gabriel, laboring as if he dragged a great weight behind him or something powerful but unseen sought to hold him back. This went on for some time, until at last he reached the altar and the source of the temple's power.

A small orb of utter blackness and purest evil lurked atop the altar's ebony slab. You couldn't so much as see it, as see the absence of it-a sphere of nothingness. What that thing was and where it came from: unknown. Theta must have known it was the foul emanations of that unholy artifact that fueled the chaos about him. It was its power that threatened to open the gateway to the unspeakable outré realms-the very Halls of Nifleheim.

Theta pulled from his belt a war hammer that had been concealed behind his cloak-and no common hammer was it. It had a large head of gray steel and an ornate handle inscribed with archaic runes and studded with jewels. How a man even Theta's size could wield such a thing, Claradon couldn't grasp-it was a battle hammer fit for Thor himself. Theta gripped the haft with both hands and raised the hammer high. Strangely, the hammer's head seemed to grow to more than double its normal size and mass as he lifted it up. He swung it down at the orb with all his might, and as he did, several things happened, nearly at once, in what order, none could ever say.

The hammer struck with a booming sound akin to a thunderclap, which was immediately followed by an eerie, otherworldly groaning that heralded the orb's destruction.

Just before-or perhaps just after-the hammer hit home, the temple's rear wall exploded outward and a massive blast of air and heat roared into the place. Theta turned as if to run, but the blast crashed into him and hurtled him some forty feet before it slammed him to the unyielding stone slab. Momentum propelled him several yards farther before it mercifully released him. Though Theta surely took the brunt of the force, the blast knocked the entire expedition from its feet.

Atop the altar, the orb was no more: Theta's blow had pulverized it. The altar itself was cracked (broken by Theta's blow), and a large chunk of its top was gone-pulverized along with the orb.

Claradon looked over in shock at Theta's still form. Then he saw the six-foot wide rift in the temple's rear wall-a rift opened by the explosion that they had just weathered. Beyond the rift was utter blackness, a portal to some other place, some other dimension-some foul bastion of chaos. The portal's rim was aglow with wisps of yellow fire, their origin unknown. On the wall nearby, the arcane pattern's outermost circle was gone-its crimson border now nothing more than blackened and charred ash. The eldritch coins had melted and their remnants trickled down the shattered wall in golden rivulets.

XVI
THE BOGEYMEN

From out of that ominous hole in the temple's back wall, which proved indeed to be a gateway, vaulted a monster the like of which Claradon had never seen before, and until that very moment did not truly believe existed. It was an otherworldly creature of nightmare, of folklore; the very bogeyman of the children's tales come to life. A horrid caricature of a man: no flesh covered any part of the seven-foot tall creature's oversized skull. Its large, gold, glowing eyes and long, forked tongue were alight with demonic flame. It wore strange black armor that clung tightly to its muscular torso. In its right hand it held a six-foot long, white sword whose blade danced with red and yellow hellfire. On its massive breastplate was damasked the unmistakable symbol of Mortach, Lord of Nifleheim and mythical patron of death and destruction. Surely, any mortal who stood against that fiend would be tossed aside like so much chaff. Before Claradon or his men gained their feet, the creature sped through the hall, fiendishly laughing, and bounded out the entry—out into the world of man.

The unnatural pressure was gone and the earsplitting cacophony subsided. The writhing pseudopods and tentacles retreated, and the walls and columns returned to their normal, stony aspects. Waves of heat and the noxious scent of brimstone filled the air. It came from the abyss beyond the breach and pulsed into the temple in waves—as if the portal breathed. With those waves wafted a strong putrescence mixed with the bestial odor detected before, only it was stronger now, but still unidentifiable.

While those knights who were conscious staggered to their feet, coughing and gasping, Claradon gazed in disbelief as more unspeakable horrors manifested at the gateway. They rose through the rarefied ether of the abyss beyond the portal by some bizarre means of locomotion incomprehensible to man. Several nightmarish creatures more than six feet tall and roughly human shaped vaulted through the breach and entered the unholy temple. Their appearance was too monstrous, too ghastly to describe or even contemplate. No mortal creature ever possessed an aspect of such indescribable horror, such loathsome, abominable evil. Claradon shuddered as he looked upon faces of pure chaos—the putrid spawn of cursed Nifleheim. As horrific as they were, they were beings of flesh and blood and sinew; Claradon and his comrades knew how to deal with such things.

Claradon, Sir Conrad, and Sir Martin were the first to rush forward, yelling battle cries in honor of their patron gods: Odin, Tyr, and Heimdall. By the time they approached the gateway, an even more formidable being had pushed the ghastly fiends aside. It was nearly eight feet tall and covered from head to toe with sharpened, metallic spikes, though the spikes were no suit of armor: they grew from its thick leathery hide. It was brick-red in color throughout, except for its large eyes, which glowed a brilliant gold.

Claradon saw many more loathsome beasts behind the spiked giant, including many kin of the reskalan. They pushed forward and strove to gain entry to the world of man, though none dared touch their leader. Verily, a veritable horde of hell spewed forth from that malefic gateway to Abaddon. The spiked giant brandished a huge black sword and pointed it at the three knights.

"Bow down," it roared in the common speech of man, in a deep voice with a harsh accent. Its words dropped in spurts from its tongue—as if it struggled to form them with parts not meant for mortal speech.

"Bow down, petty creatures, and pledge allegiance to Lord Gallis Korrgonn, Prince of Nifleheim and son of almighty Azathoth. Bow down and swear fealty to me, and I may yet spare your pathetic lives."

Claradon's whole body shuddered and quaked at the sight and sound of that unspeakable nightmarish thing. He felt puny and naked. A paralysis washed over him and rooted him in place. He knew he was about to die. A Lord of Nifleheim was about to annihilate him.

He wanted to run. He wanted to hide. He wanted to scream. If he just bowed down, perhaps he might yet live. Such a little thing it would be, just to bow down. He could do that, couldn't he, to save his life? What harm would it do?

He remembered his father. He remembered what those monsters did to him. He remembered his burning need for vengeance.

He did not bow down—he would never bow down before any creature of Nifleheim or any servant of evil. That would go against all he stood for and everything it meant to be an Eotrus. He would have his vengeance.

"I am Brother Claradon Eotrus, Lord of Dor Eotrus," he shouted. "You killed my father: for this you die."

Claradon charged forward. From the corners of his eyes, he saw that his two comrades were still with him. The smaller fiends sprang forward and interposed themselves between their dark lord and the knights.

"Very well, petty creatures," shouted Korrgonn. "Tonight, we feast on your souls. This world is ours now."

The knights engaged the fiends and fought with incredible ferocity—their swords and strength against the claws and fangs of the hellish spawn of Nifleheim. Outnumbered, the fiends pressed them back, away from the gateway and away from Korrgonn. The fiends' attacks were poorly coordinated—chaotic and wild—but these were no mere beasts, they were creatures of intelligence and self-awareness.

Through the whirl of battle, Claradon was cut off from his comrades and fought on alone. The mantle of holy light that enshrouded him, blinded the fiends and they shrank from it, wailing. It burned them—their very flesh smoking and charring as they drew near him. Many turned from him and sought easier prey. That gave him a singular advantage in the wild melee and perhaps was all that preserved his life. It also allowed him brief moments of respite during which he caught glimpses of the deadly struggles that unfolded around him.

Numerous devils attacked his still dazed or unconscious comrades and others fought duels to the death with the knights that still stood.

He saw Sir Bilson's throat ripped out by one fiend—dear gods, how would he tell his wife, his poor children?

Young Sir Paldor's chest was slashed by another. A terrible, metallic rending sound rang out as the creature's claws raked across and shredded his breastplate, though the brave knight fought on.

Two fiends decapitated another knight and feasted on his corpse—ripping off large chunks of flesh with their bare teeth. Thank the gods, Claradon couldn't tell who it was—he didn't want to know; he couldn't bear it.

Through the dim light, Claradon spied Sirs Conrad and Martin, awash with blood and gore, pulled down and torn limb from limb by a group of bloodthirsty, reskalan fiends.

Then he saw Ob, fighting alone, darting here and there, evading the claws of the beasts, and no doubt cursing all the while as several fiends stalked his heels. It pained Claradon that he could do nothing to aid his comrades. It was all he could do just to stay alive in the wild melee.

Tanch opened his eyes and, before he had time to think better of it, pulled himself to a sitting position. The battle raged on all around him. Blood dripped from his nose and his vision was blurred. The bloody corpse of a fiend lay across his legs—how it got there, he never knew. It was drenched in putrid ichor that soaked through his pants and stung his legs, burning like acid. The smell of it was so foul; it was all he could do not to retch.

Just to his left lay the body of one of Dor Eotrus's knights, his ribcage splayed open, heart torn from his chest. Tanch forced himself to look away. He dared not look at the dead man's face. He knew these men, every one. Some more than others. Some few were close friends, or at least he considered them so, though they might not have said the same. If it were one of those—one of his friends—he knew he would break down; he would lose focus, and that would be his doom. But then he looked anyway. He couldn't stop himself. He had to know who it was.

He cringed in horror at what he saw—the man's nose and at least one of his eyes was gone. All the flesh was gone from his cheeks and chin. His teeth broken or missing. A red mess of bone and ruin. There was no hope to recognize him, to know who he was, but at that moment, Tanch thanked the gods for that. It was easier not knowing.

A few feet away, Ob desperately fought against two fiends; several others lay dead at his feet. Ob held a sword in one hand (long for him, but a short sword for a man of mundane stature), a glowing dagger in the other. How small he was compared to the fiends, yet it didn't seem to matter—their lower quarters being that much easier for him to attack. He spun a wild dance of death. He whirled, weaved, and darted to and fro in a manner impossible to believe for one of his age and stature. Tanch was shocked to see that the Gnome's prowess was not exaggerated after all—as he had always presumed.

Tanch looked on as Ob thrust his sword through the breast of a fiend, but the blade held fast when he tried to pull it out. As he struggled to free it, he buried his short blade in the second fiend's breast. It screamed as the glowing dagger entered its body; its flesh smoked and sizzled as if set afire. From out of nowhere, a third fiend appeared and clamped its devilish jaws deep into Ob's forearm, and bit through chainmail, shirt, and flesh with dagger-like teeth.

Ob wailed in agony but managed to stab the thing in the throat with his dagger. The beast fell back, shrieking and spouted steaming black ichor from its neck. Ob slumped back against one of the pillars and struggled to wrap a cloth about his injured arm, to stem the flow of his lifeblood. While Tanch watched in horror, a six-legged fiend with a vaguely batrachian aspect pounced on the tiny man. Par Tanch had only a moment to act.

"By the Shards of Pythagoras, *gek paipcm ficcg*," said Par Tanch in an accent that made his voice sound foreign, almost unrecognizable. Six fist-sized spheres of blue fire appeared in the wizard's hand, one after another, and shot at the vile demon in rapid succession—all too fast for the beast to react. The first bored into its left shoulder and exploded; the second detonated a few inches lower and blasted off the limb entirely. The third, fourth, and fifth spheres punctured the creature's side and chest; the last blew a large chunk out of its bulbous head. Its corpse collapsed at Ob's feet even as more fiends moved toward him.

Sirs Paldor, Glimador, and Indigo sprang to Ob's aid—each battered, bruised, and bleeding from their own wounds. The three stalwart soldiers interposed themselves between the devils and their wounded Castellan and held the fiends at bay.

XVII
THE HERO'S PATH

The monstrous fiend, Korrgonn, strode up the hall toward the temple's entrance. It stepped on as often as over the still unconscious knights strewn about the chamber, and tossed aside any of its minions that got in its way. A tall knight that brandished a bastard sword blocked its path. The demon threw back its head and laughed at the petty creature that opposed it. But its laugh was stifled when the cold steel of the warrior's holy blade sliced through its nigh impenetrable exoskeleton and punctured its innards—a blow that would have killed a mortal. The beast howled in shock; its golden eyes threatened to fly from their sockets; smoke and wisps of flame surged from its maw.

Sir Gabriel Garn withdrew his war blade and slashed it—once, and then again—across the demon's chest and shoulder. Each blow bit deep into the living armor and black blood surged from the jagged wounds as Korrgonn roared in anger and agony. Despite its grievous wounds, the creature raised its blade to parry Gabriel's next strike.

Gabriel swung his blade in a mighty, sweeping arc, employing a fencing maneuver used only by the Picts of the Gray Waste, but Korrgonn countered it. Gabriel tried the spinning thrust maneuver taught him by the Emerald Elves, but Korrgonn effortlessly deflected it, already seeming to regain its strength. The two squared off against each other and exchanged blow for blow. Gabriel expertly executed the infamous Dyvers thrusting maneuvers, the Dwarvish overhand strikes, the Cernian technique, the Sarnack maneuvers, and the Lengian cut and thrust style, but all were equally ineffective: Korrgonn countered them all. All the while, Gabriel dodged blow after titanic blow, and parried others with the flat of his blade. Although he countered every swing of Korrgonn's sword, the creature also made deft use of its spiked exoskeleton. With it, Korrgonn slashed Gabriel several times, shredded his thick plate armor, and sliced into his flesh. Though Gabriel had perhaps never faced an opponent with such strength and resilience, he would not allow the fiend to defeat him. He had fought too many wars and too many duels over the ages to allow even one such Korrgonn to best him.

A spray of black blood and foul smelling ichor washed over Gabriel, and a fiend's dismembered head struck his leg. A shout of "Doom" came from nearby. Lord Angle Theta was alive and had joined the fray.

Five fiends—long fanged, hairy, and apelike—stalked Theta, who stood beside the corpse of one of their fellows, his silver-hued falchion dripping with ichor. When they met his steely gaze, the devils froze in their tracks and looks of terror formed on their grotesque visages.

"No," bellowed one fiend. "It's the ancient enemy, the traitor."

"We are betrayed; the Volsungs knew of our

coming," cried another. "Spare us, lord, and we will serve you," implored the fiend as it fell to its knees and whimpered.

Theta's sword slashed by twice—almost faster than the eye could follow—and both fiends' heads tumbled to the floor. The other three overcame whatever fear they harbored and sprang toward him.

Theta worked sword and shield to masterful perfection. He wasted no movement; every thrust and slash and shield bash was precisely timed. He dodged, and parried, and cut, and dealt out death and destruction as only he could. Moments later, he stood alone; his opponents' dismembered, twitching corpses littered the floor, and green ichor pooled about his boots.

As Theta moved to assist Gabriel, another thunderous roar emanated from the breach; this time, much louder and deeper than before. More than a score of fiends of myriad types scampered through the black hole, followed by a beast of incredible proportions. That creature struggled to expand the breach—its bulk far too large to fit through the six-foot wide portal.

Theta didn't even glance at his old friend Gabriel before he turned to face that new threat. Theta charged toward the gateway and engaged the horde. He never looked back.

Claradon stood alone against a trio of multiarmed fiends of wicked fangs and barbed tails. Three others of their ilk lay in a heap about him, victims of his desperate swordplay. He bashed one attacker back with his battered shield as he deflected and blocked blow after draining blow with his long sword. His strength was quickly ebbing; soon he would have only his magic to sustain him.

Through Odin's grace, his protective magic still encircled him—that veil of diffuse light hovered about his shoulders like a broad cloak—and it moved with him. As he extended his arm to attack or parry, so went the magic, protecting the full length of his sword and the entirety of his shield. Each time a creature drew near, struck a blow that hit his sword, shield, or armor, or received the same from Claradon, the spell's magic took effect—and its effects were devastating. The creatures' flesh burned on contact with the mantle of light, sizzling and blackening as if it had been thrown on a fire. Even when only the creatures' weapons touched the light, the magic somehow burned their hands—their weapons falling useless to the floor as often as not. So as they fought, the creatures let out a chorus of screams and howls, and smoke rose about them; the scent of burned flesh filled the air. But still they came on, slavering and bloodthirsty—relentless in their pursuit of Claradon's life.

Claradon managed a series of furious counterstrikes that drove the devils back long enough for him to again tap the sorcerous arts he had honed as a Caradonian Knight. His powers called down a roaring column of white flame from on-high that engulfed one of the fiends. The blast instantly incinerated it and its ashes crumbled to the stone floor from the bottom up.

The remaining fiends had had enough. They turned and fled, seeking easier prey. Though calling down such power had terribly drained him, to Sir Gabriel's side he sprang, to aid him as best he could, for he caught a glimpse of the desperate battle his hero fought.

Sir Gabriel never needed aid before—but now he did. Claradon could see that clear enough, even with only a moment's glance at their titanic struggle. Though Sir Gabriel was the greatest swordsman—no, the greatest hero in all Midgaard, he was but a mortal man, and what he fought was not. If even half the legends were true, that monster that battled him had lived for ages beyond count and wielded godlike powers. What could Claradon do against something like that? What if Gabriel fell and he had to face it alone? Dead gods, he would flee—he would have to.

Claradon pushed his fears aside. Death didn't matter; he had his duty to do and he would do it. He would never abandon a friend. He would never dishonor the Eotrus name. He would help Gabriel as best he could, even if it cost him his life.

Before he reached Gabriel, more fiends appeared between them, six or eight at least: horned and scaled and reptilian of face, hairy and brutish of body. Each one taller than Claradon and broader too.

They charged. With no time to lose, he spoke more words of the *Militus Mysterious*, that olden language of warrior magic, passed down to man by the Aesir in time immemorial. Owing to those few words, high in the air above them, a tiny vortex materialized and a grand column of coruscating blue and yellow flame came with it. It shot down and enveloped the cadre of fiends: it burnt them all to cinders in but the blink of an eye. Claradon was shocked when he saw them crumble to ash, for he had no idea such power dwelled within him, never having used that spell in battle before. He was surprised he even remembered the words, for the spell was most effective against creatures of Nifleheim—and before that day, he wasn't certain that such things even existed.

No sooner was the magic spent, then Claradon collapsed to the ground, all his muscles aquiver and unresponsive to his call. He could have lain there for hours, and would have, but for his duty and the heat of battle. He gritted his teeth and steeled his jaw against the burning in his hands that now extended up to his elbows. He used every ounce of his strength to regain control of his muscles and pull himself to his feet. He was not done yet, but he knew he had not the strength to throw that spell again, not even to save his own life.

As Korrgonn and Sir Gabriel dueled before him, Claradon summoned all remaining mystical strength from deep within his very core and empowered one last sorcery. He unleashed his oldest and most forbidden words of arcane power—words he never dared utter before. With a grunt, he discharged a screeching blast of fiery death from the tip of his blade—a crackling azure bolt with the numinous energy to vaporize any mortal man or beast. It struck Korrgonn unawares, and enveloped its entire form in ravenous flame.

Claradon harbored no illusion that his magics were powerful enough to kill a Lord of Nifleheim, but he was certain that it would sap the fiend's strength and cause it to fall. That would provide Gabriel the opportunity he needed to finish it. But after only a moment, the spell's power waned, its flames sputtered, then vanished—consumed by the demon's stony soul. Claradon couldn't believe it, but the creature barely noticed the attack, and it fought on: unharmed.

Claradon's muscles burned from the tips of his fingers all the way up to his shoulders, but for some reason, perhaps the adrenaline rushing through his system, or some boon of the gods, his final sorcery did not further drain his physical strength. His magic, however, was entirely spent, though that mattered little since he commanded no words that could fell that abomination; that much was clear. But he had other tools.

His Dyvers blade was in his hand and he was swinging it at the creature. He didn't know how he got there, but there he was, in the thick of the melee with Korrgonn and Gabriel. He swung his sword with all his strength, again and again, but its finely wrought steel merely bounced off Korrgonn's exoskeleton and sent sparks flying. The creature ignored his ineffectual attacks, putting up no defense to them at all, and continued to parry Gabriel's deadly blows.

Undeterred, Claradon pounded on Korrgonn over and again with his heavy blade. Sweat poured down his face and he breathed so hard he thought he would drop. His nose and throat burned from the brimstone that wafted from the gateway and the heady musk of the creature—akin to the stink of the great jungle beasts. His sword arm was at once numb and yet on fire; his legs, rubbery and unsteady; his head, clouded. He felt as if he moved within a dream.

At last, after one tremendous blow, Claradon's sword—the blade his father gifted him when he came of age—fractured against Korrgonn's armor. He looked down at the shards in disbelief as they tumbled to the ground, seeming to move in slow motion.

They took his father and now they took the sword his father gave him. He couldn't even have that? Not even that? The anger welled anew within him, and it was all that kept him going. He drew forth Worfin Dal, lunged in, and thrust the dagger's point at the fiend's back. To his surprise, the blade sliced through—barely meeting any resistance—and punctured its exoskeleton near where a man's kidney would be. As the blade sunk in, for Claradon, things again moved in slow motion. Claradon knew at once that it was the alien metal and mysterious properties of the dagger that made the difference. He was back in the fight.

Korrgonn reeled, howled in pain and rage, spun around, and slammed the back of its spiked fist and forearm down on Claradon's helm. That blow crushed him to the floor. He lay there bloodied and stunned.

As Korrgonn loomed above him, Gabriel's blade pierced its back and the sword's tip erupted out its belly. A spray of putrid, black ichor lashed Claradon's tabard. Claradon heard a sizzling sound, felt his chest suddenly grow hot, and looked down through blurred eyes to see his tabard afire. The fabric of his shirt was already gone, and the creature's blood boiled atop his breastplate, as if it were some powerful acid.

He rolled to his side—Korrgonn and Gabriel battling above him—in hopes the vile stuff would spill off to the ground. Most of it did, but what remained continued to eat through the breastplate. He had no time to doff his gauntlets and undo the armor's straps, so instead, he scrambled to cut them with Worfin Dal before the vile stuff burned through to his flesh. As he sliced the straps, the fumes from the dissolving metal oppressed his lungs and assaulted his eyes; stinging and tearing, he had to turn away and work by feel. He got the breastplate off just in time, and thanked the gods he had worn so much extra padding below it, or else his flesh would have been sorely burned from the heat alone.

Still dazed, barely able to see, and coughing from the fumes, he looked up to witness Korrgonn roar and land a terrible forearm blow to the side of Gabriel's head. Somehow Gabriel kept his feet, still held his blade, and came in again. Korrgonn maneuvered to the side and caught Gabriel's next thrust with its sword's crossguard. It kicked Gabriel in the gut, which sent him reeling backward and caused him to trip over and fall beyond Claradon. The beast stepped forward, loomed large over Claradon once again, and raised its red blade high to finish him.

"No," cried Gabriel, as he bounded up and forward over Claradon's prone form with blinding speed and executed the reckless Valusian thrust maneuver. Gabriel's war blade arced upward as he lunged. The ensorcelled blade pierced Korrgonn's black heart and black ichor spurted everywhere. With all the knight's strength behind the blow, the wide blade sank halfway to the hilt. Completing the vicious maneuver, Gabriel pulled the sword back, nearly out the wound, before he plunged it back in and sharply turned the blade as it entered. This merciless attack was designed to eviscerate an opponent and instantly sap his strength, but it left much of the attacker's head and torso exposed. The Nifleheim blade dropped from the beast's grasp and its massive body sank to its knees. It roared in anguish as its lifeblood—putrid and black with the look and consistency of tar—showered the floor.

"I will have your soul yet," spat Korrgonn as it threw an uppercut toward the knight's chest. Gabriel, in the midst of wrenching his sword free, moved to catch the blow in his gauntleted hand. But from Korrgonn's gnarled fist sprang a twelve-inch long, barbed spike that glistened with black blood, though the spike itself was gray. The spike was limp and slithered and wiggled as it emerged from Korrgonn's fist, but then snapped taut as it struck.

Powered by Korrgonn's punch, the spike pierced Gabriel's steel gauntlet and sliced clear through his hand. It slammed his hand back against his chest and continued to punch on through Gabriel's steel breastplate and into his sternum—deep into his chest, through flesh and bone. So powerful was the blow, it lifted him into the air and held him aloft for several seconds. Gabriel stiffened and tried to pull away, but Korrgonn twisted the blade and jabbed it in ever deeper.

"You're finished," it spat as ichor dribbled down its chin.

The blow shocked Gabriel, but at first he felt little pain. He dropped his sword, for he was too close to use it, pulled his Asgardian dagger from his belt, and slashed it across Korrgonn's throat—once, twice, and a third time, slicing it from ear to ear. Blood and bile surged from both opponents' mouths. Still the beast held him fast.

Then the excruciating, indescribable pain washed over Gabriel and blasted him to his knees; Claradon's legs pinned beneath him.

From where he laid dazed, Claradon attempted to let fly another magical blast—to come to his hero's aid—but his strength was spent. He couldn't even pull himself out from under Gabriel. He could do no more than watch in dazed horror as the ghastly scene unfolded before him. For him, the battle was over.

Strangely, Korrgonn's arm began to glow a fiery red, first at the shoulder, but soon the glow extended down toward his fist. Gabriel continued to struggle to pull away, but the wicked spike would not release him. He felt it boring deep within his chest. It was moving, growing larger and penetrating deeper, twisting, probing. Probing for something. His heart? Dead gods, how had it come to this? He knew not how to get away.

The hellish glow that permeated Korrgonn's body reached Gabriel, and caused his chest to begin to glow as well. He coughed up blood and tried in vain again to get free.

"No," he gasped as he realized the fiend's plan. "No," he said, again and again. It was consuming his very body, devouring his immortal soul, assailing his mind, taking over his very being. He looked down and saw the blood that poured from his chest. He couldn't believe that it was happening, that it was real: that he was defeated.

Fleeting, ephemeral memories passed instantly before Gabriel's eyes and assailed his senses. A momentary image of smiting the fire wyrm of the Kronar Mountains; a mere wisp of the fetid stench of the barrow-wight who had killed those poor children. His duel with Valas Tearn, the assassin who had slain a thousand men; his conquest of the city of Saridden and of freeing its slaves; the great battle of Minoc-by-the-Sea; his victories over the demon-queen Krisona, and the blood-lord Jaros—and that unbelievable folly with the crazed master of the Dead Fens. A glimpse of that far-off, fateful day at R'lyeh when he and Theta banished the last of the great fiends whence they came, back unto the void, and extracted a small measure of vengeance for the abominable plague that the beasts had unleashed upon mankind. That victory had freed all Midgaard from the yoke of Nifleheim and bore witness to the dawning of a new age of freedom and hope. Gabriel would survive this battle, just as he had that day at R'lyeh. There could be no other outcome.

In desperation, he plunged Dargus Dal into Korrgonn's right eye and sunk it to the hilt. Still the spike held him fast.

His vision began to cloud; the sounds around him dimmed. He thought of the thousands of lives he had saved down through the years, of all those he had protected, of the uncountable mighty deeds he had done.

He withdrew his dagger and plunged it into the beast's left eye. "Around me are my kinsmen, always," he said, and then pounded down on the hilt again, and again, and again as faces from long ago flooded his mind's eye: Mikel, Arioch, Azrael, Thetan, Mithron, and more.

He could see little by then, and the sounds of the battle drifted away. He heard his heart beating and the rushing of blood at his temples, but nothing else. He wondered if it could be the end. Everything moved in slow motion, the merest moments extended to long minutes. He thought of all the things important to him, all the places and the people he had known, all the lands he had visited, all that he would never do again.

"To the south, my father, my father's father, and all my line before them, back unto the beginning," he said, though only Claradon was close enough to hear him.

The otherworldly glow covered nearly all his body, but Gabriel fought on and pounded down on the dagger's hilt again, and again, and again, and again.

"To the north, is Odin . . ."

Visions of fire, floods, and terror flashed before his eyes; visions of Azrael dying in his arms and a guilt beyond all guilt weighing on him like nothing else.

He pounded down on the hilt again, and again, and again, and again, and again.

The world went dark. The pain was less. He saw no more.

"The hero's path," he said, his commanding voice now barely a whisper.

Gabriel convulsed as the evil glow consumed him. He was alone. He would die alone.

Korrgonn's body stopped glowing and went limp.

Gabriel thought of the woman he had loved and lost and forever longed for. If only he had another chance, if only he could do things over, if only he could be with her again . . .

His eyes closed and his head rolled to the side.

"The homeward road . . ."

He thought of his mother's face and her undying and unconditional love. If he could only see her one more time. If only he had more time . . .

"Valhalla."

Then he thought no more. And Sir Gabriel Garn—greatest hero of Lomion—passed into legend.

At last, Claradon's head cleared and he pulled free from beneath Gabriel. Still dazed, he scrambled up, dived into Korrgonn, and ripped the beast away from Gabriel. Claradon pounded his gauntleted fists into Korrgonn's unmoving head, over and over, Gabriel's dagger still protruding from its eye, and mashed it to pieces. As he pummeled away, smoke rose from his gauntlets and they began to sizzle and melt. The acidic blood of the otherworldly beast ravaged the gauntlets' steel and leather, eating through them, just as they had his breastplate; he shed them before his flesh was sorely beset.

Claradon turned toward Gabriel; tears streamed down his face.

Moments later, when Gabriel's eyes opened, they glowed a brilliant gold instead of their natural blue. Claradon immediately surmised what that meant. He cried out for aid, but the din of the general melee drowned him out. Those terrible orbs were not Sir Gabriel's eyes at all; they were the eyes of the Son of Azathoth, the Prince of Demons and Lord of Nifleheim—he whose purpose was to herald in our doom. Claradon was so stunned that he couldn't move.

Gabriel's mouth opened and it spewed out a gory glob of blood. The wound on his chest glowed for a moment and then rapidly closed of its own accord, and defying all natural laws, healed itself. After but a few moments, all signs of his wounds were gone. The creature grinned an evil, unholy grin, picked up Korrgonn's sword as it stood up, turned, and fled the building.

XVIII
YOUR TIME HAS COME AND GONE

The enormous monstrosity at the breach—its aspect too horrific to describe, save to say that it had massive claws, curved horns, and cloven hooves—lashed out at the gateway, pounding the sides of the opening over and again, seeking entry. It could not hope to fit through the breach, large though it was, so it fought to make the opening the larger. Its blows struck like thunder and stone shards flew in all directions as the ancient masonry slowly succumbed to its fury. Dissatisfied with its progress, the thing rammed its body against the gateway, filling the entirety of the hole with its bulk, and strained against the stone, which bulged and cracked from the force. At last, the breach widened enough, just enough, and it forced its way through. It was here. On Midgaard. With us.

As it stepped through, its bestial form shrank and transformed into the likeness of a huge knight that held a crimson sword. That manly shape may have been naught but an illusion—some alien sorcery conjured up to deceive the gullible eyes of men—or perhaps, some force of nature prevented its transformation until it stood upon Midgaard's soil. Real or illusioned, no one could mistake its dark, unholy visage—so alike was it to the blasphemous idols and paintings that all had seen at one time or another. Its face was handsome and its frame, broad and muscled. Its armor, the envy of kings and emperors alike. Its name was Bhaal. It was known as the lord of death and chaos—one of the greatest and most feared of the legendary archdukes of Nifleheim.

However its transformation came about, Bhaal now held the shape it wanted as it walked among us. A shape pleasing in its way. A shape men would look upon in awe rather than horror. An aspect and a booming voice that some men would follow. That some men would bow down to and worship. That some men would call god.

Bhaal paused at the hell-mouth for several moments and surveyed the carnage taking place in the ancient temple.

It laughed.

Not a laugh of mirth; not the laugh of a man. It was a maniacal, inhuman cackling such as had not been inflicted on the ears of man or the air of Midgaard for untold epochs. The beast was here now, on our world—its long held desire at last fulfilled; its exile, at an end. It would make Midgaard his again. It had won.

As a multitude of smaller fiends leaped through the gateway, scurried past Bhaal, and moved to engage Theta who barred the path ahead, Dolan, Artol, and Sirs Glimron, Talbot, and Dalken closed with the transformed fiend from its flanks. With blinding speed, Bhaal struck a brutal overhand blow at Artol, who swiftly raised his battle-axe to parry, but the powerful hack sheared the axe haft in two. Bhaal's red sword rotated with the impact and the flat of the blade struck Artol squarely atop his helm and rebounded. Artol's eyes rolled back in his head and he crumpled to the floor. As quick as that, one of Midgaard's greatest soldiers was out of the fight.

Dolan charged Bhaal from the opposite side. He sprang into the air, his glowing dagger outstretched before him—that leap, beyond the skills of the most famed acrobats of the bazaar. Bhaal somehow sensed him and pivoted toward him, but its parry was too slow to stave off the dagger, which Dolan buried deep in Bhaal's sternum. Dolan crashed against Bhaal and landed at its feet.

Bhaal roared, grabbed Dolan by the throat, and lifted him high. As Talbot charged, Bhaal threw Dolan into him, which sent them both cascading across the ebony slab. Bhaal gripped the glowing dagger's hilt and pulled the blade from its chest, howling with pain. Smoke rose from its hand for its flesh burned on contact with the dagger. It threw the blade to the floor.

Glimron and Dalken simultaneously struck at Bhaal's legs. Their steel blades loudly clanged and sparked when they struck the Nifleheim-wrought armor, but did no damage, for that otherworldly metal was too thick and too strong for common steel to breach.

Bhaal's next cut entered Glimron's right shoulder. The massive blow cleaved clean through him and came out his left side. His body tumbled to the ground, twitching and spouting blood. Then Bhaal grabbed Dalken by the throat and lifted him up. The fiend opened its mouth, wide like a serpent, and a two-pronged, pincer-like object darted out and plunged into Dalken's eyes. The pincers retracted, and ripped the knight's eyes from their sockets.

Bhaal held Dalken aloft for several seconds, staring at him, seemingly admiring his handiwork while the knight screamed in agony. Then Bhaal tightened its grip and crushed Dalken's throat. It flung the corpse away as if it weighed nary a pound.

Nearby, Lord Theta's whirling blade sliced off fiendish arms and legs with abandon. No fiend could stand against him for more than moments. Even the press of numbers could not turn the tide against him. The demon corpses piled high about him in gruesome heaps. He was an unstoppable juggernaut. He was death incarnate. The last thing each of his foes heard was his booming mantra, "Doom". Ichor covered him and dripped from his blade. He finished off the last of the demons and leaped over the pile of corpses to engage Bhaal.

"You have slain my minions, mortal," said Bhaal (his voice a rich baritone) to the bloody knight that stood before him. "Impressive. But against a Lord of Nifleheim you cannot stand."

Theta sheathed his sword and picked up his lance, which still lay at the base of the altar, and brandished it as a spear. That weapon was of stout oak and tempered steel, filigreed in silver and bronze and inscribed with esoteric runes of a style seldom remembered. It was old and gouged and battered, and it was thick and heavy—weighing more than three common spears—yet Theta hefted it with ease. Its runes bespoke of Odin and the Aesir, Asgard and the Bifrost, Yggdrasill and the Nine Worlds. And if you drew close enough, you could hear it hum—not a tune, but a dull, low vibration, its origin, unknown.

"Do you not know me, Bhaal?" said Theta as he pointed the lance's tip at the fiend. "Has it been so long?"

Bhaal studied Theta for a moment and then its mouth dropped open. "You?" it shouted. "You will not thwart us again, traitor. Not again. We will have this world back. We will cleanse it of traitors, unbelievers, and blasphemers by fire and sword and you will not stop us. Never again will you stop us. What once was ours will be ours again."

"This be no place for you, Bhaal," shouted Theta. "Not anymore. You don't belong here. Your time has come and gone. Crawl back to Nifleheim and writhe in everlasting flames." Theta cautiously stalked toward the beast and looked for an opening to use his lance.

"Fool," shouted Bhaal. "Nifleheim is paradise— more so even than Vaedon ever was. You misguided fool."

Theta shook his head, a look of disgust on his face. "I will put you down as I have your brethren. You will sleep with them in the void."

Bhaal sneered. "It is you who are doomed, deceiver. At long last I will slay you and feast on your black soul. I will lay your severed head at the feet of the lord's altar as an offering. Bhaal advanced, and as he did so, a large, glowing, floating mace suddenly materialized in front of it, and struck it.

The mace pummeled Bhaal about the head

and chest and forced it backward, each blow striking with a dull thud and eliciting a groan or roar of pain. Bhaal wildly swung its sword as it attempted to dodge the mace, but its strikes met no resistance, for there was no foe for it to smite. The sword passed through the spectral mace and did it no harm. One wild swing caught the edge of the stone altar and sheared off a large chunk, though the impact barely slowed the mammoth blade. No swords of bronze, iron, or even the hardest steel could ever hope to cleave through a block of stone, yet Bhaal's Nifleheim blade not only did, but survived the blow intact. What strange metal it was made of was beyond the ken of men.

As he mouthed ancient words of power, Theta pointed the tip of his lance at Bhaal and the lance's hum grew louder. A sparkling arc of electricity, blue and white and blinding, rocketed from the lance, crashed into the beast's chest, and pushed it back. Where the arc struck, Bhaal's breastplate blackened, charred, crackled and sizzled, and fell off, which exposed the reddish leather-like flesh beneath. The armor shattered when it hit the floor, as if the attack somehow embrittled it. The beast roared in pain but continued to frantically swing its sword, though each blow cleaved nothing but air.

Par Tanch's magical orbs roared by Theta, humming as they went, and blasted into Bhaal—each one exploding upon impact. One struck its exposed chest, tore into the beast, and caused some damage, but the others struck Bhaal's Nifleheim-wrought armor and were completely

243

ineffective. Bhaal's black blood dripped from its chest wound and sizzled and smoked when it stuck the stone floor; a pungent, sulfurous odor wafted in its wake.

The enchanted mace, also controlled by Par Tanch's arcane arts, continued to pummel Bhaal and caused him to stagger farther backward—toward the breach—one hand clutching at its wounded chest.

Dolan skulked on hands and knees behind Bhaal who was oblivious of his presence. Dolan saw Theta advancing, lance in hand, and carefully positioned himself just in front of the breach, and directly behind Bhaal. Distracted by the array of magical attacks that assailed it, Bhaal did not react in time to counter Theta's lance. Theta lunged forward and buried its sharpened tip deep into the breast of the Nifleheim lord. Thick black blood sprayed from the wound, and some of it splashed across Theta's breastplate; the vile stuff smoked and burned gouges into the ancient metal. A look of shock and agony formed on Bhaal's face as the lance sunk in and pushed it backward.

Bhaal dropped its sword and roared in anger, as it struggled against Theta, who used the lance to push it inexorably backward.

"Give my regards to Arioch," shouted Theta. "Tell him, I haven't forgotten his black deeds, and I will yet have my revenge."

Bhaal stared down at the lance that protruded from its chest. "Curse you, traitor," spat Bhaal. "You will pay for this threefold; three evils to you I promise. So do I curse you."

As Theta pushed the beast back, it tripped over Dolan, just as Dolan had planned, and tumbled backward through the gateway, whence it came. As it fell, it grabbed Theta's lance— gripping it with all its strength—and somehow wrenched it from Theta's grasp.

Theta lunged through the air, grasping for the lance. He got a hold of it just as the lance passed through the gateway. Theta's grip was iron, but Bhaal's momentum was too much. Theta slid partway through the breach, but managed to hook his foot on the temple's crumbling back wall. Dolan dove onto Theta's other leg to stay his slide but his weight was far too little to matter. Theta had no choice but to let go of the lance or fall through the breach himself, and like as not, Dolan with him.

Bhaal fell out of sight, into the utter blackness beyond the breach and roared more curses at Theta as it fell—the lance still buried in its chest.

"Dagnabbit," yelled Theta, his hand still outstretched toward the lance that rapidly fell from his sight. And so that relic passed from the world, never to be seen in Midgaard again.

XIX
THE LORD OF THE LAND

Soon only the moans and wails of the wounded filled the air.

"We killed them all, boss," said Dolan. "All except the skull-faced one what came out first. But we lost a lot of the shiny men, we did."

"It is not over yet. We must close the gateway or all of Nifleheim will come through. If that happens, Midgaard will be lost."

"Let them come," said Artol as he pulled himself to his feet beside the altar. A thin stream of blood trickled down the side of his head. He looked confused and unsteady. "We can take them."

Ignoring the overconfident sergeant, Theta scanned the floor around the altar. "Find the shards of the black orb; they must be holding the gateway open."

"Black stone chips against a black stone floor: in the dark?" said Dolan, shaking his head.

Theta spied Bhaal's sword where it laid and reached for it. When his hand grasped the hilt, the sword flashed white hot for a moment and then disintegrated before his eyes.

Roars, howls, and maddening gibbering began anew from somewhere beyond the breach, although no new fiends could yet be seen.

"Another wave comes," Theta shouted to whoever could hear him over the increasing din. "I will hold fast the portal. You must find and destroy the shards. Shatter them. But if you value your souls, don't touch them with your flesh."

"There's not going to be enough time," shouted Dolan. "Wait—here it is; a big piece," he said, pointing to a faintly glowing chunk of obsidian on the floor.

Claradon stepped up next to Dolan, a battle hammer held over his head. "For my father," he shouted. Dolan sprang out of the way just as Claradon slammed the hammer onto the shard, smashing it to bits. The gateway instantly disappeared and the chaotic din abruptly stopped. Where the gateway once was, now remained only the crumbled back wall of the temple. The hole in the wall opened to the outside air; the circle and forest beyond were both visible—the fog, gone.

Before the men rejoiced in their victory, a loud rumbling began. Within moments, the ground beneath their feet began to shake. They heard roaring and rumbling sounds like those produced by a herd of large beasts, and then chunks of stone fell from the ceiling.

"The place is collapsing," said Dolan.

"Get the wounded out of here," shouted Theta.

"Get them out," echoed Dolan.

They did so, but in no good order. A stumbling, bloody panic would better describe it. The men's former poise, gone. They fled as the otherworldly structure collapsed around them. Two minutes after the ground began to shake, the Temple of Guymaog was no more—only a high mound of stony rubble and a cloud of dust remained. Those men that made it out lay strewn about the circle of desolation. Some staggered around, dazed;

others collapsed from blood loss or other injury. Strangely, the sun was beginning to rise. It was dawn. Somehow, the bizarre atmosphere within the temple's depths had distorted the flow of time itself, and turned what seemed like no more than minutes into more than six hours.

As soon as the dust from the temple's collapse began to disperse, all the men that were able, poured over the ruins, searching for survivors trapped in the rubble: none were found.

Young Sir Paldor was sent ahead to Dor Eotrus to summon aid, pausing for only a few minutes to examine and bandage his chest wound, which mercifully was not deep, thanks to his stout armor. Tanch and Claradon set about to aid the wounded in the party. Theta and Dolan searched for sign of the skull-faced fiend that had fled the temple. They found no trail, no spoor of the beast. It had vanished, but they found the corpses of nine men near the edge of the circle. Apparently, several knights had fled the temple and they and the soldiers that were guarding the horses were killed by the skull-faced fiend or some other horror that had also escaped. Two of the bodies lay just beyond the circle's rim. Strangely, they were cold and rigid, as if they had laid there for hours. The other bodies were within the circle and appeared as if they had been killed only minutes before. Even though those knights had fled the temple, they had stood their ground against the fiends outside and fought to the end. They could have run. Some would surely have escaped. But they didn't run. They were northmen, Eotrus men, and when an enemy stood before them they would not yield, even unto death. Heroes, even them.

After a short while, the survivors gathered about and Sir Glimador reported the casualty list. Some three dozen knights were confirmed dead and another two dozen were missing and presumed buried in the collapsed temple.

The only men of Dor Eotrus that still lived were Ob, Glimador, Artol, Indigo, Paldor, Par Tanch, and Claradon.

To everyone's astonishment, Sir Gabriel was amongst the missing. Nearly all the survivors were wounded to varying degrees, although most not seriously.

Theta was a bloody mess, covered in gore and ichor from head to toe, though little, if any, of the blood seemed to be his.

Once the men had caught their breaths, and seen to the worst of their wounds, Claradon recounted the battle between Korrgonn and Sir Gabriel—even Theta listened intently and asked more questions than anyone else. All were shocked by Gabriel's gruesome fate.

"The skalds will tell of that battle for ages to come," said Artol as tears streamed down his face.

"For ages, they will," said Dolan.

"Perhaps Sir Gabriel still lives," Claradon said as he rechecked Ob's wounded arm, though he only half believed there was any hope. "Perhaps we can free him of the influence of the monster."

"Aradon is gone," said Ob weakly, his eyes only half open. "I just can't believe it. Donnelin, Talbon, Stern, and now Gabriel. Gabriel for Odin's sake. How could this happen? Nobody could beat

Gabriel. Nobody. Dead gods, let me wake from this nightmare." His hand reached for his wineskin, but it was lost.

"A nightmare," said Dolan.

"It's the end of the world," said Tanch. "I told you it was coming; no one wanted to listen, but I foretold it. These are the end times."

"The end times," said Dolan.

"Perhaps, no longer," said Claradon. "We may have just staved off the end of the world."

"The cultists will try again," said Theta. "To open another gateway. This is not over yet."

Overcome by all that had happened, Claradon dropped to both knees and wept. His father and his mentor both dead at the hands of creatures of Nifleheim, and so many other friends and comrades as well. It was all too much; his head swam. He gripped Ob's shoulder, closed his eyes, and recited a prayer to Odin.

"Steady boy," said Ob, his voice unsteady. He pulled Claradon close. "You're the patriarch of House Eotrus now. That makes you the lord of the land and vassal to ole King Tenzivel. Show no weakness to the troops." Due to his wounds, Ob didn't realize that nearly all the troops were dead.

"Perhaps, we can cast out the monster from Sir Gabriel," said Tanch. "Perhaps he can be as he was. There may still be time. We must find him."

"I'm doubting it, pal," said Ob. "Gabe's the toughest warrior this side of Odin. Ain't nothing, not even some stinking Lord of Nifleheim as can take him over if he's alive. He's dead and it took his corpse, I say. And that's the end of him. It stinks, but that's the way it is."

"It's the end of him, it is," said Dolan.

"Oh my, don't say such things. I can't accept that. We have to try the save him."

"The Gnome speaks the truth," said Theta. "Gabriel is lost to us and to Midgaard—and the world will suffer for that loss. There is nothing we can do for him, save to avenge him and vanquish the creature that defiles his body."

Theta pulled a metallic flask from his belt, uncorked the top and carefully poured a single drop into a small cup. He filled the cup with water and put it to Ob's lips. "You fought bravely, Gnome," said Theta. "Drink this; it will strengthen you."

"Is it wine or mead?" said Ob.

"Neither," said Theta.

"Then I don't want it."

"Drink it. It will help."

"It will help?" said Ob. Tanch moved close to them to get a good view.

"It will," said Theta. "Drink it."

His mouth tightly shut, Ob stared into the cup for some moments, considering before he drank it. As he swallowed, his face scrunched up in disgust. "That's a foul brew, Theta," he said. "Not even fit for a stinking goblin."

"The dregs from some witch's cauldron, by the look of it," said Tanch.

"Dregs," said Dolan, mimicking Ob's expression.

Almost at once, the flow of blood from Ob's wound stopped and color returned to his face.

"Yet it has a potency, I see," said Tanch. "A wondrous thing, that. What is it?"

"Wondrous, it is," said Dolan.

"A healing draught," said Theta.

"Yes, but of what is it made?" said Tanch.

Theta offered no answer.

"It's a draught, it is," said Dolan, as if that was all the answer needed.

"You are full of surprises, sir," said Tanch.

"Many folks are more than they seem," said Theta as he looked pointedly at Tanch.

"No doubt, no doubt," said the wizard.

"The fallen," said Ob, as he clutched Claradon's arm.

Claradon looked around at the bodies of his men. "We've got to take them home."

Artol stepped forward. "We should burn them," he said.

"What?" said Claradon. "They're our men—our friends. We don't burn our dead. What are you saying?"

"They're tainted," said Artol. "Killed by a demon, come back as one. We've all heard that saying. We've got to burn them.

"I agree," said Glimador. "Best not to take any chances."

Claradon looked at the bodies, indecision on his face. He looked to Ob for support, but the Gnome was barely conscious—Theta's potion had eased him into a sleep. "These are our men," said Claradon. "We're going to bring them home to their families for a proper burial. I'll not dishonor their memories for fear of superstitious bunk. Wrap them in their blankets, and put them on their horses."

"Aye, my lord," said the men. Carrying out that

order though was no easy task, considering the number of casualties, the fatigue and injuries of the few survivors, and that the horses were scattered about the wood. In the end, they were unable to collect the remains of Lord Eotrus's patrol, for their bodies were dismembered and scattered, and the horror of that scene was too much for the men to bear after what they had been through. Of Lord Eotrus, all else that was found was his shield, bent nearly in half, and his helm, which was bloodied and crushed. These bits they reverently placed on the back of Sir Gabriel's horse. Patrols would return to recover the bodies of those missing in the rubble.

They were an eerie sight as they rode slowly through the wood, gloomy and foreboding even in the light of day. A mist hung about them, but this time, it was a normal mist that came with the sun. Where but hours before they were a vibrant troop of knights more than 70 strong, polished and ready, full of life and fight, now they were a troop of the dead. Nine weary men, bloodied, beaten, and bruised rode amongst scores of riderless horses that bore dozens of the dead.

On the way, Par Tanch approached Claradon. He spoke in a stronger, deeper, and steadier voice than was his custom. "Claradon," he said, taking care that no one else overheard. "Though I know this timing is poor, I must advise you that the Order of the Arcane, the High Council, and likely the Crown, for reasons of their own, will never allow the events of last night to be commonly known. They will cover them up. Some story will be fabricated to account for the battle, the howling in the woods, the fog. They will force you and your officers to swear to never reveal the truth."

Claradon's eyes narrowed as he was taken aback by Tanch's words. "And what if I don't go along with such lies? What if I insist that everyone know the truth of how father and Sir Gabriel died?"

"Then, they will deny the truth and call you a liar in public and even in private. When they're done, they will destroy you. You will lose the Dor and your good name, perhaps even your very life."

Claradon's eyes were wide with shock or disbelief. "Would they really go so far? Could they?"

"They would, they could, and they have done such things before. I have seen it."

"King Tenzivel has always been a friend to us. He would never allow this."

"The king is old, Claradon. Dark voices whisper in his ear these days. Things are changing in Lomion, my friend, and not for the better—we can't count on the king's support, though even if we had it, it may do us little good. The real power these days lies with the High Council, and in particular, with the Chancellor."

"Barusa of Alder?" said Claradon.

"Aye. As you well know, he's no friend to the Eotrus and never has been. Let us be the ones to create the tale that the Council hears. That way, we can be assured that Lord Eotrus, Sir Gabriel, and the others are honored as the heroes that they are."

"I don't like the sound of what you suggest,

but I'll hear you out."

"I don't like it any more than you do, but it must be done. We can say that a pack of trolls came down from the mountains and caused all the trouble. There was a time when trolls rampaged through these lands, and caused much havoc and death. Though rarely seen these days, they are still widely feared and considered extremely deadly. Any knight that fell in battle to a pack of such beasts whilst protecting his lands would be rightly named a hero."

"And how would we explain the wailing in the night?"

"We will say it was the trolls. Few alive in these parts have ever heard the call of a troll. If we say that that is what they heard, most would believe us."

"And the fog, and the explosions the night father was lost?"

"A freakish storm, nothing more. Claradon, I know this is difficult, but we must do this. We must protect the Eotrus name or your enemies will use this opportunity to destroy your House."

"I didn't know we had those kinds of enemies. The Alders never liked us—that feud goes back so long I don't think anyone even remembers how it started. And we've never got on well with the Dantrels or the Tarns, but I never thought of any of them as enemies—not the kind that would want us dead. I just thought of them as rivals, nothing more."

"I don't want to sound harsh, especially considering what has just happened, but you have been naive. The Eotrus have true enemies—every noble House does. The vultures will begin to circle all too soon and we have to be ready for them. Our wisest course of action is to not show weakness and to give our enemies no excuse to speak out or move against us."

"So we must speak of trolls."

"Aye, my friend. We have little choice in this. Besides, we will always know the truth. The people will know that our comrades died as heroes defending Eotrus lands. What does it matter that people think they fell to trolls rather than demons of Nifleheim? A hero is a hero."

Claradon paused for some moments gathering his thoughts. "For the sake of my brothers, I will go along with this. But know well, if it were only my position and my life at stake, I would tell the Order and the Council to go to hell, and the Crown too, if need be."

"I don't doubt it, Master Claradon."

"What of Paldor? He is likely telling the tale even now. The whole Dor will hear of it by the time we get back."

"His head was hard hit in the battle. He became delusional and wandered off. He didn't know what he was saying."

"You think of everything, don't you?"

"It's a wizard's job, sir. I try to make myself useful. We will not be able to keep the truth from the senior knights at the Dor. You will have to swear them to secrecy and all of us here as well, of course."

"It will be done. As for useful—you're a lot more than just useful. I saw what you did in there. I saw the hammer you conjured and used against that thing when we needed you. You came through—and with powers that I never dreamed you had. Thank you. I mean that."

Tanch's eyes grew watery. He nodded, though no words escaped his mouth. He had finally made himself useful.

Claradon awoke in his bed to Ob shaking him. "Get off your duff you lazy bugger. The men are gathering in the Odinhome already. We need to get you down there right quick. Mister Know-it-All, fancy pants, is giving a speech. The boys need to know you're the boss now, not that foreigner, nor anybody else."

Claradon's head still spun from an almost unbelievable tale Ob told him the previous night while he stood by the wounded Gnome's bedside. He had to push that story aside in his head, however hard that might be. The last days seemed a maddened dream. Claradon pulled himself together as best he could. He splashed water on his face, combed his hair, strapped on his sword belt.

"How is your arm?" said Claradon, though he only glanced at Ob as he spoke—his attention focused on waking up and getting ready. "After how you looked last night, I thought you would be bedridden for days, but you seem as spry as ever this morning."

"Mister Fancy Pants's witches' brew did the trick," said Ob. "It's not natural, that stuff. Must be some sorcery; some stinking potion made of who knows what foul gunk. Probably black sorcery whipped it up—with my luck, the kind what sucks a man's soul out. I would rather have a bad arm, or no arm, than risk that."

"It was just a healing draught," said Claradon. "Herbs and such, I'm certain."

"You think so?" said Ob. He pulled up his sleeve, exposing his forearm. "Take a look." There was no wound; no scar, not a trace. "It feels a bit stiff is all."

Claradon's eyebrows rose. "Well, if it is sorcery, you should be grateful. It was an ugly wound. If it had gotten infected, it could have been the end of you."

"Take more than an infection to put me down," said Ob. "All the same, I should be grateful, but I'm not. Such things always come with a price, but it's usually a price that you wouldn't want to pay."

"Maybe it was just a powerful healing draught," said Claradon.

Ob's eyes narrowed. "Maybe."

In the interests of secrecy, knights guarded the Odinhome's doors and only admitted ranking knights who knew the truth of what happened in the wood. When Ob and Claradon arrived, Theta stood on the central dais addressing the men who were seated about the hall. The knights rallied around him, bristling for a fight, enraged as they were over the loss of their lord and their comrades. Each time Theta spoke the knights quieted down to listen.

"We must destroy his body," Theta boomed in his strong, steady voice. "When we do, we will be killing Korrgonn, not Gabriel, for Gabriel is already lost to this world; his body now nothing but a stolen shell, occupied by a monster—a true monster out of Nifleheim. Destroying it won't be easy. Korrgonn not only has all of his own knowledge and skills, but he may also have Gabriel's. That would make him far more dangerous than ever before. No one will be safe until we put him down. And do not forget the skull-faced demon—that creature was Mortach of Nifleheim. He must be put down as well."

"Two Lords of Nifleheim running about," said Tanch. "It is the end of the world for certain. We're all doomed."

Artol stood up. "We must find them and kill them for what they've done, however difficult the task."

"We will track our enemies to the ends of Midgaard, and beyond if need be," boomed Theta. "We will cleanse the world of their plague."

A cheer erupted in the hall; the knights rose to their feet and shook their fists.

"There can be no other course of action," boomed Theta.

After the noise died down, Tanch spoke. "It sounds as if we are about to embark on a major undertaking. Though it pains me to say it, my delicate back isn't up to the challenge, for old battle wounds plague me. No doubt, I can do far more good remaining here at Dor Eotrus, supporting young Sir Ector, than I could in the field."

"Are you the stinking House Wizard or not?" shouted Ob as he and Claradon made their way down the steps.

"I suppose," said Tanch. "Though no formal appointment has yet been made."

"Par Tanch," said Claradon when he reached the dais, "I will need you in this. You will come with us. We will go back to the Vermion, to the circle, and pick up the trail of the Nifleheim lords. We will make them pay dearly for what they did. We'll not return until we rid this world of them."

"All right, Mister Fancy Pants, move aside," shouted Ob as he and Claradon approached the lectern. Theta glared at the Gnome, stood his ground, but said nothing.

"Claradon is here now and will be taking over." Ob faced the gathered knights, his arms upraised. He motioned for quiet. "Brother Claradon, as first son of House Eotrus, and upon Lord Aradon's passing, is now Lord of the Dor, and Patriarch of House Eotrus. You will serve him with the same respect and honor with which you served Aradon afore him. And if you don't, I'll rip your stinking heads off and feed your dead corpses to the dogs."

"Long live Lord Claradon," boomed Artol from amidst the knights.

"Long live Lord Claradon," shouted all the knights in response.

"And death to the Lords of Nifleheim," boomed Artol, raising his fist to the air.

"Death to the Lords of Nifleheim," boomed the whole company in retort.

"I guess we won't be going home anytime soon, Lord Angle," whispered Dolan.

"Not for some time, I think."

"When do you think them evildoers will leave

us be so we can live like regular folks?"

"When I have killed them all; not before."

END OF VOLUME 1

THE FALLEN ANGLE
Volume 2 of the Harbinger of Doom Saga

"How do you know these things? Who are you, Theta?
Who are you really?"
— Ob to the Lord Angle Theta

PROLOGUE

I've got it," said Theta as he recovered Sir Gabriel's dagger, Dargus Dal, from an opening that he had made in the vast heap of stone rubble—the collapsed remains of the ancient Temple of Guymaog in the Vermion Forest. Only one night previous, that place had been a scene of otherworldly horror, wherein somehow opened a gateway to the nether realm of Nifleheim, the very hell of myth and legend. A great battle ensued between the knights of Dor Eotrus and the Nifleheim lords and their minions before the open gateway was sundered and forever held fast. The dead of both sides lay broken and strewn about the ruins, putrefying in the chill morning air.

With the gateway closed, the monstrous armies of Nifleheim were barred from entering the world of man and laying it to waste, but two of their dread lords had made it through to Midgaard and were on the loose—one, a skull-faced monster called Mortach, the other, Gallis Korrgonn, son of Azathoth. Through foul magic, Korrgonn possessed the body of Sir Gabriel Garn, greatest hero of the Kingdom of Lomion and weapons master of House Eotrus.

"Is it damaged?" said Dolan as he scooped black ichor (the remains of some creature of Nifleheim) from another hole into a wide-mouthed flask while holding his nose.

Theta held up the long dagger and closely examined it. "It is intact," he said smiling. "Its edge, still keen; 'tis truly a wonder. It's good to hold an Asgardian dagger in my hand again; it has been long years."

"I can't believe you found both it and the shards of that orb thingy," said Dolan. "That necklace sure comes in handy, it does," he said, referring to the curiously bent and twisted ankh that hung from a chain about Theta's neck. "How did it find them through all this stone? What is its magic?"

Theta shrugged.

"Are you ever going to tell me how it works?" said Dolan.

"No."

"Didn't think so. What are we going to do about the wizard? He's still spying on us from behind that rubble off to our left; must think we're deaf and blind."

"As noisy as he is, I smelled him first," said Theta.

"As did I," said Dolan. "He has got a weird stink about him."

"It's some kind of oil he smears in his hair," said Theta. "That and his thumping about make him less stealthy than a thunderstorm."

"Why do you figure he puts that stuff in his hair, anyways? Does he think women like it?"

"Wizards are a strange lot," said Theta. "I don't waste much thought on them. I grow tired of his lurking, so you had best invite him over."

In a flash, Dolan's bow was in his hand, an arrow knocked and set to flight. The arrow buzzed through the air and struck the remnants of a stone column inches from Tanch's head, which set him reeling backward on his rump, screeching in alarm.

"Show yourself," called out Theta.

"Don't shoot; it's me," yelled Tanch. "It's just me, Par Tanch Trinagal," he said as he stood up and stumbled forward.

They waved him over.

"Out for a stroll, wizard?" said Theta.

"I was just—I was—I wasn't—I mean—I didn't—"

"If he keeps babbling," said Theta, "Shoot him between the eyes."

"Aye, boss," said Dolan as he raised his bow again, this time at point blank range. Tanch's eyes went wide and then promptly glazed over and he fell backward in a feint.

Theta and Dolan both chuckled.

"Make sure the fool is alright," said Theta, "and then let's finish up here."

Dolan moved to Tanch's side and knelt, then froze, cocking his head to the side as if listening for something.

"Thetan," said a strange, womanly voice on the wind. The sound was drawn out and otherworldly, but what it said was distinct enough.

Dolan's bow was back in his hand and he pivoted all around, searching for the speaker.

"Thetan," said the woman on the wind again.

Theta was on his feet, his falchion in his left hand, his shield in his right. He crouched and turned this way and that, but could not find the source of the voice. As his eyes passed over Dolan, he noticed that his manservant looked odd, as if paralyzed or frozen in place. "Dolan," he said sharply, but Dolan did not reply, nor did he move. Tanch too was stone still. "Dolan," he shouted again, but to no avail.

Theta caught a glimpse of movement from the corner of his eye, and turned toward it. A blur of cloth, perhaps a woman's shawl, passed behind a pile of rubble, though the pile was too narrow to conceal a person, and yet, whatever it was, was gone. The scent of flowers and springtime appeared in the air, though winter was fast approaching.

"Show yourself," said Theta, menace in his voice.

"What have you done, Thetan?" said the wind. "What mischief have you wrought this time?"

Each time the voice spoke, it came from behind Theta, and when he spun toward it, he saw only the merest glimpse of a translucent gray fabric that trailed behind someone or some thing that moved too fast for his eyes to follow.

But Theta knew nothing moved too fast for him to see or for him to stop. His mouth dropped open; his brow furrowed in surprise. He pulled his sword and shield close, and crouched, all his energies poised to spring into action, to crush whatever threat that thing represented.

"Did you open the portal, Thetan? Did you open the gateway?" said the woman on the wind, her voice bittersweet. "Tell me; speak the truth; speak the truth."

Theta stopped turning toward the voice, for there was no hope to catch it. Its speed was beyond him. He stood ready; all his senses heightened to their limits. He pulled his shield closer against his chest, close enough that his thumb grasped his ankh. When he touched it, it pulsed with eerie light. He called on that relic, as he had so many times afore, mouthing the secret words that empowered it. He commanded it to reveal whatever it was that taunted him.

"Your tokens hold no power over me," said the wind.

And it spoke the truth, for the ankh failed Theta, though it had rarely failed him before. It was as if the speaker was invisible to the ankh, just as it was nigh invisible to Theta. Or was it even there at all? Was this all just some figment in Theta's mind; madness come over him at last?

"Did you open the ever-barred door?" it said, its tone demanding an answer.

"No," said Theta. "I closed the gateway to Nifleheim."

Silence ruled the scene for several moments.

"Do you speak the truth, Thetan—you who they call the Prince of Lies?"

"I closed it."

"So you say, but your heart and your mind are closed to me. I cannot see within them, just as I could not see within that temple the other night, though my eyes pierce all darkness throughout the world, and into the hearts and minds of all the world's children."

"Who are you?" said Theta.

"You have seen me before. Am I so easily forgotten?"

Theta's eyes narrowed. "You were at R'lyeh."

"There and elsewhere. I have watched you since the dawn of time," said the voice, now from close behind Theta.

He spun, and there before him, mere inches away, was a tall woman, or some thing that took a woman's shape. She was strangely insubstantial, for he saw clear through her, but then, as the moments passed, she became as solid, as real, as any woman he had ever known. Her skin was gray but smooth, without lines or blemishes; her hair, green as springtime's grass; her eyes, piercing blue like a mountain stream; her dress, gray and flowing and lithe; her features, young and beautiful beyond compare with curves to make any woman brim with envy; her voice, soft and melodic, but haunting.

"What do you want?" said Theta, holding back the swing of his falchion, perhaps for curiosity's sake, or perhaps for something more, though she was now well within his range.

"I want you to keep safe the world," said the woman. "As only you can."

"That is all I have done for years beyond count."

She put a gentle hand to Theta's face and caressed his cheek. "I wish that to be true more than I can say. I need that to be true, for I foresee great calamities ahead. Midgaard will need your sword and your strength to weather what is coming or all may be lost. She needs you now, more than ever."

The woman leaned forward and brushed her lips against his, gently at first, then stronger.

"Do not betray me, Thetan," she said when she pulled away, though he could not be certain whether that was a plea or a threat. And then she was gone. She faded away to nothingness right before his eyes.

"What was that?" said Dolan. "That voice on the wind?"

"What?" said Tanch as he pulled himself to a sitting position. "What voice?"

Then from the east came the sounds of many horses and men.

"The Eotrus," said Dolan. "They come to collect their dead."

I
RIKER'S CROSSROADS

The old stone inn at Riker's Crossroads was in a shambles: tables overturned, chairs and windows broken, the front doors torn off their hinges, blood spatter on walls and floor. Four armed men—three tall, the third shy of four feet—entered the place guided by the village elder. A few dejected villagers respectfully bowed their heads and offered solemn greetings to the new arrivals as they carted out smashed furniture and piled it out front for repair or disposal. A modest contingent of rugged soldiers equipped with gleaming armor, sword, and shield, stood watch outside, and surveyed the damage to the village.

The stooped and gray elder paused a few feet beyond the threshold and turned toward the youngest of the four visitors.

"Master Claradon," he said in a soft but raspy voice, "it is very kind of you to look into our troubles so soon after your own grievous loss." The two shook hands; the old man softly gripped the young knight's hand between his as tears welled in his eyes.

"We were so sorry and so shocked to hear of your father's passing. The people all dearly loved him, you know. Our deepest sympathies to you and your good brothers."

Claradon nodded. "Thank you," he said as he gently pulled his hand free.

"At least he died as he lived, a hero, protecting

us all," said the elder.

"You heard then that it was mountain trolls?" said Par Tanch, a middle-aged blond man with a curious silver circlet over his brow and a long wooden walking staff banded in silver in his right hand.

"That we did, your wizardship, sir. And we were shocked by that too. Not since I was on my grandfather's knee have I heard tell of trolls hereabouts. These days, the young folks don't even believe in them. Children's tales they call them; bogeymen and figments they mark them. But we know different, don't we, your lordships?"

Tanch spoke up before Claradon could respond. "That we do," he said. "The trolls have been lurking in the deep mountains for untold years, breeding like rabbits in their filthy warrens. They are patient creatures. As we have been going about our business, they've gathered their strength and bided their time, waiting to strike at us unawares and lay waste to our lands as they did in olden days."

The old man's mouth was open, fear and shock filled his face.

"But the Eotrus were ready for them," said Tanch. "They did not catch us by surprise; our scouts marked their movements well. We knew when and where they would strike, and it was we that took them unawares. Lord Eotrus took to the field in force and led the assault himself. We crushed them before they threatened our towns and villages, and even before a single farm was overrun—though the price was terribly steep. Not only did we lose our liege, but many of his best

271

and bravest fell at his side."

"A terrible price, indeed," said the elder. "Lomion won't see the like of Aradon Eotrus or Gabriel Garn again; not for long years, I expect. Talbon of Montrose, Brother Donnelin, Stern of Doriath—the best men of the North, the best men of our age, all fallen in a single day. I still can't believe it. Heroes they were, and all their men with them; true heroes, like them from the sagas and legends of ages past. And just like them olden heroes, their deeds will be remembered in song and story long after all alive today are gone to dust."

"Hear hear," said Tanch.

The old man stepped close to Claradon and looked about to make certain the villagers weren't watching before he spoke into his ear. "The old folk whisper about dark things stirring in Midgaard again, and not just in the mountains, your lordship. Things not seen in an age. Things far worse even than trolls, if you'll forgive me."

"Why do they think that?" said Claradon.

"We've heard things of late—frightful things from rangers, mountain men, and the merchants what pass through here on to Lomion City, Kern, and parts foreign. Until the other day, I thought it all humbug and babble, but then that rabble came and sacked our inn. They killed old Riker, your lordship. Right over there, behind the bar—the bastards."

"We have always been and felt safe here, sir, what with you fine noblemen of House Eotrus protecting our village and watching over our folk. That day was none different. It was your men what stood up to them killers, though it did no good, since they was so outnumbered, and if you'll forgive me, outskilled."

"Who were they, and how many?" said Claradon.

"It was brigands what done this thing, your lordship," he said as he guided the group toward the bar. "They came in on horseback. Had a big carriage with them. Probably twenty of them."

"A carriage!" said Ob, the tiny man.

"Was it a covered carriage or an open wagon?" said Theta, the tallest and broadest of the four visitors, as he stepped toward the bar. Theta moved smoothly and quietly as if born to the thick plate armor that he wore beneath a long, midnight blue cloak that hung open at the front. His steel armor was enameled deep blue and featured a grand coat-of-arms intricately inlaid with gold. He spoke with a slight accent that was hard to place, save to say that it was foreign.

"A covered carriage, sir, it was. Fancy-like with doors and curtained windows as you would see in Lomion City amongst the nobles."

"How many of your folk were hurt?" said Claradon as he found a sound chair and sat down, his heavy plate and chain armor clanking against the wood.

"Besides Riker, they killed dead all five of your soldiers that were stationed here, your lordship. Good lads every one, always respectful to us elders and the womenfolk, they were. Young Sergeant Jerem was set to marry my grandniece

273

next month, and now he's dead, the poor boy, and she is brokenhearted. And they gutted old Thom Butcher because he stood with them. He passed this morning, old Thom did. We put him and the soldiers in the icehouse for keeping until you folks investigate things all proper-like. Besides them, Riker's two serving girls were bruised and battered, but they will live. And of course your soldiers what rode in on patrol fell too."

"What?" said Ob.

"What soldiers?" said Claradon.

The elder looked surprised and taken aback. "I thought you knew, your lordships. Didn't the baker's boy tell you?"

"He said our soldiers were killed," said Ob, "but nothing about a patrol. We thought he meant only the men stationed here."

"Then I'm sorry to bring you more ill news, my lords. It was young Sir Bareddal of Hanok Keep and his men. They rode in just as things went bad. We thought we were saved—that they would show them brigands a thing or two. And they did. Bareddal fought like a demon, but they bested him, the scum, with swords and magic, and all his men with him: all five of them dead. They used magic on him—real magic—if you can believe it. I never seen nothing like it."

"Blasted scum!" said Ob. He slammed his pointed boot into the bar with such force that it crashed through and lodged in the thick oak panel. "Bareddal too, blast it all."

"We put them in the icehouse, along with the others," said the elder, his voice unsteady, clearly unsettled by the Gnome's rage. "Wrapped them

274

up as respectful as we could, but I'm afraid we had to pile them atop one another, for lack of room."

Theta pulled the Gnome free of the bar with one hand, then leaned over the counter and looked about.

Ob glared at the big knight, not caring to be manhandled.

"The cash box is still here," said Theta.

"They left in a great hurry, sir," said the elder. "I expect that's why they left it; the silver had spilled out and it would've taken a spell to purse it. We collected it all up right and proper. Drogan Blacksmith is holding it for safekeeping until it can be dispensed all legal and such to Riker's heirs."

"You going after them, your lordship?" said the elder as he turned back toward Claradon.

Claradon didn't answer. He stared glassy-eyed about the wrecked inn.

"I'm just asking because if you are and you don't mind my saying—you will need more men. A whole company of your finest, I would expect. Even besides that they got wizards amongst them, these weren't no ordinary highwaymen."

"Describe them," said Theta as he scanned the room, his hand resting on the strangely misshapen wooden ankh that hung from a chain about his neck.

"Some weren't Volsungs, sir, if you can believe it. Lugron, or part Lugron, I would call them. And some looked fouler still, like no one I've seen afore. And even them what were Volsungs were the lowest types, except for their leader that is."

"It was the strangest thing—he looked much

like Sir Gabe." At that, Claradon perked up in his seat and hung on the old man's words.

"Enough to be his twin, I would say, except for his eyes and that voice. His eyes were odd— golden in color and they glowed. Whoever seen anyone with gold eyes afore? And glowing? I sure have not; it's not natural at all, at least not for Lomerians—I can't speak for stinking foreigners. Carried a big black sword he did, and his voice was deep and raspy. I will never forget his name— Korrgonn, they called him. What kind of a name is that anyways? Something foreign, I expect. Lomion is getting overrun with them types of late, if you ask me."

"Had you seen any of those men before?" asked Theta.

"Not a one."

"Did they have a captive?" said Claradon. "A prisoner?"

"No, my lord, not that we saw, but I suppose they could have held somebody in the carriage. It was more than large enough; the biggest I've ever seen."

"Did you catch any other names?" said Theta.

"I don't recall them; though I'm sure I heard some. One I think they called "Ginalli" or "Ginelli" or some such. Don't know what kind of name that is, neither. Stinking foreigners—no good bandits, every one. Let one in, and pretty soon, you are infested with them—pockets picked, and cupboards bare."

"When did they leave and which way did they go?" said Ob. "Speak quick man."

"They flew out of here near dusk, day before

yesterday, headed toward Lomion City."

"Let's go," said Ob.

The four made haste for the door.

Theta turned. "You said they left in a rush?"

"That they did. They were chasing somebody, your lordship. Some fellow what wore a black cloak and hood. We've seen him in the inn now and again, but he keeps to himself. Don't even know his name."

"Were they looking for that man?" said Theta from the doorway. "Was that why they were here?"

"I don't think so. The cloaked fellow tried to help old Riker and your soldiers, but when they fell, he ran for it, and they were at him. Brave fellow, braver than me anyways. Hope he got clear."

As Claradon exited the inn, he stepped amidst a bustle of activity: a crew of villagers were making repairs to the inn's door and wooden balustrade; others pored through the broken furniture piled in the street; a squadron of Eotrus soldiers sat astride their horses, waiting; a stream of citizens were going about their daily toils, sullen expressions on their faces; other folks stood about, watching the soldiers, seeing whatever there was to see. Suddenly, a striking, middle-aged woman stood before him, her face stern but bursting with grief. Just as Claradon recognized her, she slapped him hard in the face, harder than he would have thought her capable. The street went quiet almost immediately, and all eyes and ears turned toward them.

"Why?" she said, her eyes pleading. It was

Lady Alana of Forndin Manor. "Why?"

Her blow shocked Claradon; his mouth dropped open; he couldn't think; he didn't know what this was about.

"My husband collapsed when he heard the news—his heart. He's on his deathbed even now. I've lost them all—all of them. You've taken them all from me. Why? Why? We've always been loyal. We've done our duty and more. Couldn't you have taken just one of them into that battle? Why all three? Tell me, why?"

Tanch and Ob stood by, both at loss for words, not knowing what to say or do.

"I—they—I didn't know—I didn't think—" stammered Claradon.

"You didn't think?" she shouted. "You didn't think that there was anything wrong-headed about taking three sons of one of your vassals into a fight with trolls? Because you didn't think, my boys are dead. Because you didn't think, House Forndin has no heirs. This is the end of us—after this generation, House Forndin is no more—dead—and all you can say is, 'you didn't think?'"

"We took only the best knights with us, my Lady," said Ob. "Handpicked for their skills and bravery. Erendin, Miden, and young Talbot each gave a good account of themselves. Took down no fewer than a half dozen trolls between them. Your husband would be proud of how they fought—how they defended their liege, just as he did in years past. They brought honor to Forndin Manor and to the Eotrus."

Lady Alana's eyes brightened and pride appeared on her face at the Gnome's words.

"They were my friends," said Claradon. "Their loss pains me too. I'm very sorry."

"They were my sons," said Lady Alana sharply. "My only sons." She turned and walked away, tears streaming down her face, her nervous servants following on her heels.

"**R**iker was one of the good ones," said Ob as they rode down the wooded lane. "An old war dog he was; tough as nails. Fought in the campaigns with Aradon, me, and Gabe back in the day; was with us at Karthune Gorge and the Nikeatan Gap. A loyal and true friend; a good Eotrus man; a man of honor. Never once had to pay for an ale or a bottle all the times I've been through here. At least he went down fighting. That's fitting for men like us. That's how I want to go, anyways, when it comes time."

"We've lost too many dear to us in recent days," said Claradon. "Let's hope Riker was the last."

"At least we know which way Korrgonn went. A blind Dwarf could follow these wagon tracks; they're the deepest I've ever seen. Twenty or more of them, he said, but there are tracks of only eight horses besides those that pull the carriage."

"The rest of the men must be riding in the carriage," said Claradon.

"Ten men piled inside wouldn't be enough to make tracks as deep as we've been following," said Ob. "What do you make of it, Theta?"

"Fear often makes a man see more enemies than there are," said Theta. "And the carriage may be heavily loaded with stone or metal."

"That's as good a guess as any," said Ob. "We'll not know the truth until we find them, I expect."

"If they're headed to Lomion City, will we catch them before they get there?" asked Theta.

"By the tracks, I would say they're moving fast, very fast, considering the load they're pulling. Keeping that pace, with the start they have on us, they will beat us to the city by some hours. That's assuming no stopping for the night. If they set a camp, we will catch them."

"The men with Korrgonn," said Tanch, "must be the very same cultists that buried those coins and placed the magical orb in the old temple ruins in the Vermion."

"Still a genius, I see," said Ob.

Tanch ignored Ob and turned toward Theta. "Did you recover any fragments of the orb?" said Tanch—a question he had waited to ask until Claradon and Ob were there to hear both it and Theta's answer.

"I did," said Theta.

"What will you do with them, Lord Theta?" asked Claradon. "Do they still pose any threat?"

"They do, but only in the wrong hands. I will see to it that that doesn't occur."

"I would like to study the shards," said Par Tanch. "They may hold valuable secrets. Secrets that could aid us in dealing with those that opened the gateway."

"Secrets they hold. Also temptation, madness, and death. It's better that they be left alone."

"If I could just study a few fragments—"

"No," said Theta, louder. "If you experimented

with them, you might fall under the thrall of the dark powers. I can't allow that. No one touches the shards, and there will be no more discussion about it. Understood?"

"There he goes again, giving orders," said Ob. "Proclaiming edicts, issuing commands. You're good at that, aren't you, Mr. Fancy Pants? I say those shards belong to the Eotrus and it's us that should be doing the deciding about them. I say you and the hedge wizard are both idiots. Do you want those orb chunks getting in the hands of some other nutcases? You want some more magical doors to Nifleheim opening up in our backyard? Darned fools, one and all. Destroy them I say. Ground them to dust and fling them to the winds."

"There are kernels of wisdom in your babbling, Gnome," said Theta. "But such things as these shards cannot easily be undone. There are those who would seek even their dust to use in vile rituals. Better that I keep them close at hand until I can dispose of them properly."

"Riders approach," said Dolan, a pale wiry man riding ahead of the others. "Looks like part of somebody's army."

A group of about a dozen heavily armed horsemen approached from the south dressed in the livery of the Guard of Lomion, capital city of the realm. One wore the armor of a royal knight of the Myrdonian order. The two groups stopped as they neared each other.

"Make way for emissaries of the Crown," said the Myrdonian.

"You're riding through Eotrus lands, laddie,"

said Ob, "and being as I am the Castellan of Dor Eotrus, I will ask you your business."

"My business is with your master, Gnome," he said with disgust, "so make way."

Beside Ob, Sergeant Artol signaled to the other Eotrus men and they surrounded the Myrdonian's soldiers, weapons drawn and leveled.

"You had best be a sight more polite, boy," said Artol, "or we might get a wee bit cross with you."

The Myrdonian looked around with uncertainty. His men were but fresh-faced boys decked out in shiny new armor, whereas the Eotrus men were plainly grim veterans.

"I'm his master," said Claradon. "What is your purpose here?"

"Are you Claradon Eotrus, son of Aradon?" he said, the confidence and bravado gone from his voice.

"I am Claradon."

"Claradon is the Lord of Dor Eotrus," said Ob. "And you will address him as such, Myrdonian."

"He's the lord of nothing," said the knight, somehow rediscovering his courage, "unless the Council says he is, which is why I'm here. I bear a writ from the High Council. You are commanded to travel posthaste to Lomion City to meet with the Council on the matter of the succession. I'm to escort you."

"Word travels fast hereabouts," said Dolan.

Ob took the writ from the Myrdonian's hand and read it. "Barusa's seal," said Ob, holding it up so that Claradon could see it. He turned back to the Myrdonian. "Lucky for you, we're heading just that way. Eat our dust." The group galloped past the emissaries and on toward Lomion City.

II
INQUISITION

"**M**y father is dead," said Claradon as he stood before the High Council in ancient Tammanian Hall. "More than eighty of House Eotrus's finest knights and soldiers are dead; all lost defending our lands. It was you, Chancellor Barusa, that penned the writ inviting me to these chambers to receive formal appointment as Lord of Dor Eotrus, and now, despite my written account and having heard the tale twice from my lips, you still question me. What are you about, Chancellor?"

"What am I about?" bellowed the Chancellor— a tall, fit man of gray hair, pasty face, and middling years—from his perch high above the audience hall on the councilors' mezzanine. "How dare you question me, you young pup. You are most certainly not here to be handed a Stewardship; you are here to answer this Council's questions, and answer them all you will."

An ornate wooden door on the mezzanine slowly opened with a loud creaking noise, though the sound came not from the door, but from the throat of he who opened it. Prince Cartegian, King Tenzivel's son and heir, entered the chamber, richly garbed but unkempt and wild-eyed. The Council's guards rolled their eyes and snickered at the prince's appearance, while the councilors attempted to ignore him. When the prince was certain that he had everyone's attention, he tiptoed across the mezzanine in melodramatic fashion and took the center seat, the place of the king.

To Cartegian's left sat the Vizier, a hawk-faced man of long white beard and evil visage—his face so thin that his pale, mottled skin covered little more than bone.

To his left sat Councilor Slyman, Master of Guilds and gluttony, his belly reaching for his knees. Past him was Lord Jhensezil, Preceptor of the Odion Knights and wealthy landowner. Farther on was Field Marshal Balfor, commander of the Lomerian army. An array of medals lined the prominent arc of the marshal's midsection, which was partly hidden behind a broad black beard streaked with gray. Beyond Balfor were empty seats—odd for a formal council meeting.

To Cartegian's right was Barusa of Alder, followed by Bishop Tobin of the Churchmen, long now stooped and in his dotage, and Lord Harringgold, Archduke of Lomion City—highest official in the kingdom save for the King and the Chancellor. Beyond Harringgold were the Lady Dahlia of Kern, renowned diplomat and scholar, and the Lady Aramere of Dyvers, her hair dyed blue and piled high, as was her city's fashion. Several personal attendants and armed bodyguards shadowed each councilor.

Myrdonian Knights guarded each entrance to the chamber and the two grand, sweeping marble staircases that connected the audience hall to the mezzanine. The hall's perimeter burst with all manner of perfumed courtiers, ladies in waiting, dandies, toadies, and lackeys, chattering softly but hanging on each word that the councilors spoke. At the center of the audience hall was the petitioner's dais: a movable round platform that was two steps up from the audience hall's floor. The petitioners were separated from the courtiers only by the circular railing that hugged the dais's perimeter, and by a cordon of Myrdonian Knights that surrounded it. Claradon stood tall at the dais's wooden lectern. Ob and Tanch flanked him.

Barusa made no pause at Cartegian's entry and continued his tirade, his voice booming and resonating off the majestic, domed ceiling, gilt in silver and bronze, and magnificently coffered with rare hardwoods. "You are the one that presented this esteemed Council with an implausible and incoherent account of the death of your father and liege. You stand here churning a fairy tale about mountain trolls. Preposterous!"

"Why are we surrounded by armed guards, Chancellor?" said Claradon. "Are we your prisoners, sir? Perhaps you will throw us in irons next?"

"Not yet, but we will see," said Barusa with a sneer. "I will have the truth from you, Eotrus, one way or another. Tell me what really happened out there? Come clean with the truth now, or I vow, you will regret it."

"I had a troll once," said Prince Cartegian as he perked up in his seat. "I scooped out his eyes with a soup spoon and swallowed them whole. I fed the rest of him to my cat—not all at once, of course. He bled green blood, you know, and squealed like a pig; most delightful—the troll, not the cat." The prince slumped back down in his seat, closed his eyes, and went quiet.

286

"I have told you all there is to tell," said Claradon as he gazed in disbelief at Cartegian. "And where is King Tenzivel? Does he no longer preside over this Council?"

"Alas, the king is ill," said Barusa. "Until he recovers, Prince Cartegian represents the Crown on this Council."

"The cat just died, but I didn't throttle him," said Cartegian, awakening. "He did it to himself; he had it coming, you know." The prince closed his eyes again as drool slid down his chin.

"And how can he do that when he's not of clear mind?" said Claradon. "And what of Baron Morfin, Lord Glenfinnen, and the other Council members? Tradition dictates that all councilors be present at a stewardship assembly. Are they ill as well? What goes on here? What has become of this Council?"

"Do not presume to lecture us, young Eotrus," said Councilor Slyman, dressed in festival finery stained with his last meal. "The workings of the High Council of Lomion are none of your affair and we will not debate them with you no matter—."

"If you must know," said the Vizier in a slow and droning voice that somehow commanded the room, "Morfin is dead by his own hand." He paused to study Claradon's reaction before he continued. "A troubled soul was he, Morfin. Unable to cope with the stresses of his duties and responsibilities. An unfortunate weakness of character. Yet we who knew him these many years honor his service and miss his council. But we must carry on with the affairs of the realm, you understand. The other Council members are merely away on state business or other pressing personal matters; nothing of any concern to you. I trust you find this explanation, satisfactory, young Eotrus?"

Claradon nodded for politeness's sake, if not in agreement.

"Good," said the Vizier. "Unfortunately, I do not find your explanation at all satisfactory. No trolls have been reported in Lomion for three generations—"

"More likely than not," said Slyman, "even back then, they were only figments to scare the misbehaving whelps."

"Indeed," said the Vizier. "And yet here you stand before us, spinning a tale of troll attacks; a veritable invasion that has scores of our citizens dead in open battle. Troubling, I find this story, young man, most troubling, and most unlikely."

"If I might interject a few thoughts," said Lord Harringgold, a tall man of regal bearing and piercing eyes. "Good Councilors, we know all too well that each of our duties and responsibilities have grown more burdensome since the onset of the king's illness, leaving us little time to matters outside the norm such as this. No doubt, most of us have had little opportunity to fully digest and reflect upon the written account provided by Brother Claradon. I, however, was fortunate to have a break in my schedule that permitted me to study the report in some detail, and I must say, that having done so, however surprising the news of trolls abroad in our lands, I find the account of Brother Claradon quite thorough and complete. I would add that his account has been duly corroborated by the men of good name that stand with him."

"Ha," belched Barusa, triumph in his eyes. "A Gnome, a befuddled hedge wizard, and a foreigner too barbaric and cowardly to even doff his weapons and enter these sacred chambers. Bah! Men of good name, indeed."

"I will put it straight to you, Eotrus," said the Chancellor. "I think you and your compatriots conspired to murder your father, either by your own hands or through some proxy—perhaps that foreign mercenary of yours—to take the Eotrus lands for your own, before your time. And unless you can prove otherwise, I intend to see that you—all of you—pay for these crimes."

"You are out of line, Barusa," said Ob, shaking his fist. "Way out."

"Your Excellency—Lord Eotrus's death—it happened just as Master Claradon described," said Tanch, panting. "Mountain trolls they were. Many, many trolls. The beasts set a coordinated attack on Eotrus lands. We fought them as best we could. Only the heroism of—"

"So where are the carcasses?" said Barusa. "Show us these dead trolls that we might know the truth of this tale."

"We burned them," said Ob sharply. "Only way to keep them things down for good. Nothing left but ash."

"Preposterous," said Barusa.

"And most convenient," said Slyman.

Lord Jhensezil, tall, broad, and muscular, but graying, leaned forward in his chair. "Hunters have reported troll spoor deep in the mountains, north of Eotrus lands, in recent years."

"Superstitious country folk," said Barusa. "Their accounts are not relied upon by this Council. Eotrus, can you at least tell us what happened to these mysterious brigands that you claim that you were tracking? The ones that attacked that little trading post—Riker's whatever it is called."

"As I said, we lost their trail at the city gates. We can't track horses on cobblestones, Chancellor."

"Well then why has no one else seen these brigands? The patrol that escorted you here saw nothing—no mysterious carriage, no strange riders. Did they just vanish or did you burn them to ash with the trolls?"

Claradon stared at him with clenched teeth, shaking his head.

"Admit it, wolf's-head, there were no brigands," said Barusa. "The soldiers stationed at Riker's found out about your conspiracy—your treason—and sought to expose you, so you and your fellows disguised yourselves and sacked the inn, killing those good men, not to mention several innocent Lomerian citizens. Admit to your crimes, Eotrus, and this council may find a measure of mercy for you."

"You sniveling turd," said Ob as he fingered the empty sheath where his sword hilt would be.

"This is madness," said Claradon. "You have no basis to level such charges against us. This is a total fabrication."

Lord Jhensezil rose to his feet. "I for one see no reason not to accept Brother Claradon's account of these events. No evidence has been presented that contradicts any portion of his story. Might I remind this Council that Brother Claradon is a respected member of the priestly knights of the Caradonian Order and a nobleman in good standing with the Crown."

"Reason and logic contradicts his story," said Guildmaster Slyman.

"Neither of which you are well acquainted with," said Jhensezil.

Slyman looked confused, trying to grasp Jhensezil's meaning.

Balfor slammed his fist the table as he eyed Jhensezil. "Always ready with your insults, aren't you? If only your judgement were as sharp as your tongue."

"I agree with Jhensezil," said Duke Harringgold. "We have seen no evidence to dispute Brother Claradon's account. I move that we formally accept the report he has submitted, and further, move at once to confirm his appointment as Lord of Dor Eotrus. I call for a vote."

"I second his call," said Lady Dahlia, flaxen-haired and statuesque, but fading.

"Hear hear," said Jhensezil.

"Now wait just a minute," said Slyman. "A moment ago we were about to slap the boy in irons for treason, and now you want to anoint him Lord of a Dor?"

"Perhaps matters are moving too quickly here," said the Chancellor. "What say you, Bishop Tobin?"

"Hmm, perhaps it would be prudent to proceed with caution and due diligence in this matter," said

Bishop Tobin, an ancient figure who seemed asleep except when he spoke in his deep, halting voice.

"At the very least an investigation is in order, don't you agree?" said Barusa.

"Oh, most certainly, an inquisition is warranted," said the Bishop. "We must be thorough; the guilty must be punished. Justice demands it."

"Indeed," said Barusa. "And in the meantime, we shall appoint a Regent to run the affairs of Dor Eotrus until this matter is resolved."

"There will be no stinking Regent," shouted Ob. "That Dor belongs to the Eotrus and there it will stay. You have no right—no right at all."

"You are the one with no rights, Gnome," said Barusa, raising his voice. "All too long we have suffered your degenerate people in our midst. What with your hoarding of ill-gotten wealth and your foul-mannered ways, not to mention your stench. You are throwbacks to times past and best forgotten. Your betters command these lands now, as is our sacred right. Your welcome here will soon be worn out."

Prince Cartegian bounced forward in his seat. His eyes grew wide and wild. "It's fun to hunt Gnomes," he said with an evil smile. "Your heads make such good trophies. I have a spot for you on my mantle. Gnomey, the troll killer, stuffed on my mantle; it will be wonderful."

"Why I ought to rip your stinking heads off, you slimy sons-of-Lugron."

"That remark will cost you a month in the deepest pit I can find for you, little man," said

Barusa. "Guards!"

"To the pit, to the pit with him," said Cartegian, capering about in front of his chair. "Throw the little bugger in the pit. Just give me his head; his head for the mantle."

"Stop," shouted Claradon, his tone and outstretched arm halted the guards in their tracks. "Chancellor Barusa, this madness will not stand." Claradon took a deep breath and cleared his throat before continuing. "By the rights granted me by the *Book of the Nobility*, I demand satisfaction."

Lord Harringgold started violently in his seat.

"What say you?" said Barusa as he rose to his feet with furrowed brow.

"Pipe down, boy," said Ob, "afore you get yourself killed dead."

"Chancellor Barusa, you have publicly accused me of murdering my father; you have called me a liar, a conspirator, and insulted and threatened the Castellan of my fortress. I cannot let this stand. I call upon the Fifth Article of the Rules of Nobility. That decree gives me the right to challenge you to single combat, fair and honorable. And this I do. I trust this Council is still bound by the traditional laws?"

Lords Harringgold and Jhensezil cringed and squirmed in their seats as Claradon spoke. Par Tanch covered his eyes and shook his head.

"Have you the courage to accept my challenge, or do you recant these offenses?" said Claradon.

"I recant nothing, you pathetic upstart. I will—"

"Upstart," squealed Cartegian. "My cat was an

upstart."

"Hold," shouted Lord Harringgold, nearly jumping from his seat. "Brother Claradon, think carefully before you invoke this right. Barusa is a renowned sword master, far beyond your ken. Surely, if you had known that, you wouldn't have put forth that challenge. Withdraw it now, before he accepts, and it will be forgotten."

Claradon stood straight and tall; his chin held high. "I know the Chancellor's reputation, both fair and foul. My challenge stands."

The Duke sank slowly back into his chair. "So be it then," he said, his eyes downcast.

"And when will this duel take place?" said Slyman eagerly.

"Now," shouted Cartegian as he pounded his fist to his chair's armrest. "What better time than now? Someone bring me my cat, and my slippers. I demand a turnip."

Ob grabbed Claradon by the arm and pulled him down to whisper in his ear. "You're a darned fool, boy, but if you must do this, call for it now. Otherwise, he will lay a trap and his henchmen will kill us all for sure."

"My thoughts exactly." Claradon straightened. "I demand that the duel be immediate. Here and now."

"I need not comply with this," said Barusa, waving Claradon's words away in disgust. "Tomorrow at noon will suffice." He turned as if to leave the hall.

"Run away, run away," cackled Cartegian as he squatted atop his chair. "Scaredy-cat, scaredy-cat. Barusa is a scaredy-cat, and I know what to do with cats."

Barusa halted and glared at the crazed prince.

"Actually," said Lord Jhensezil, holding up a copy of the referenced text, "the decree specifies that the duel be immediate, unless the challenger chooses to postpone it or unless his opponent is ill, injured, infirm, or otherwise incapacitated."

"Do you claim such illness or infirmity, Lord Chancellor?" said Jhensezil.

Barusa shot him an evil glare. "Very well. We will do this now," he said through gritted teeth. But then his tone changed. "We must of course always comply with the law, until at last the laws are changed," he said sardonically, an evil grin across his weathered face.

"Yes, change the laws," said Cartegian. "All the fun things are illegal. The laws are so tiresome, such bother—let's burn them all. Make them ash, just like Gnomey's trolls."

"For too long we've looked upon the law as written in stone, unchanging forevermore, but that is backward and unjust," said Barusa. "Our laws must be living, breathing documents that change with the times or else they make no sense. This challenge proves that. The days of duels are long past and best forgotten, but yet here we stand, with the old laws as they are, and so, a duel it must be. A duel to the death."

"The Sergeant of the Guard will recover Brother Claradon's sword from the antechamber," announced Lord Jhensezil. "Prepare yourselves, gentlemen, and may Odin's hand guide the righteous to victory."

Ob and Par Tanch gathered close about

Claradon and spoke in hushed tones, careful that no one could overhear.

"Now you've done it, boy," said Ob. "You've really made your bed this time."

"I'm afraid I won't be able to assist you, Master Claradon," said Par Tanch. "No sorcery can be used undetected in these chambers; you are on your own in this reckless endeavor."

"I had no choice. I can't let him put a Regent in; it's the same as handing over the Dor to the Alders. I would rather be dead."

"You soon will be, unless the luck of the Vanyar shines full on you," said Ob. "Just a minute," he said, his face brightening. "I bet them laws allow you to choose a champion to stand in for you. Name Theta—Mister Foreign Fancy Pants is darn good with a sword; he might be able to best Barusa."

"I've little doubt that he could, but I will not put this burden on him. This is my fight."

"Then name me. I'm your Castellan; let me stand in for you. I can thrash that pompous lout for sure," he said, puffing out his little chest.

"No, Ob. Like you told me after we lost father— I'm the lord of the land now. This fight is mine."

"You're a brave lad, Claradon," said Ob. "A credit to the Eotrus name. Aradon would be proud of you today, and so would Gabe. If you are set to this course, I will tell you what I know. I've seen the old man fight—strong as an ox he is, and quick like a Gnome despite his years. His skill with the blade is great, but he has his flaws. Lean down, boy, so I can tell you quiet-like."

The sergeant of the guard exited the

chambers, closing the massive oaken doors behind him. On a couch in the antechamber, Lord Angle Theta sat in full battle armor, his back to the wall. Across from him sat Dolan Silk, his manservant. A guard stood at each side of the Council Chamber's doors; two others, and a Myrdonian Knight stood near a huge, locked cabinet within which were housed the weapons of those visitors within the chambers.

"By order of the Council," said the sergeant, looking toward the Myrdonian, "I'm to bring the Eotrus his weapons."

"What say you?" said the Myrdonian.

"There's to be a duel—the young Eotrus against the Chancellor; the boy called him out. The Council calls for his sword."

At this, Dolan stood up, a look of surprise on his face. Theta raised an eyebrow.

"A duel?" said the Myrdonian. "You jest?"

"It's true. The Chancellor accused him of killing his father, so the boy challenged him."

"Will it be to the death?" said Theta, suddenly standing behind the sergeant.

"Almost certainly, yes," said the Myrdonian. "Unless the victor shows mercy. Since that will be the Chancellor, there will be no quarter given."

"Dolan," said Theta, "turn over your arms to these men, and go within to watch."

As Dolan doffed his weapons, Theta whispered in his ear. "If there's foul play, come out at once or give sign."

Theta leaned casually against the counter, carefully positioning himself within arm's length of the Myrdonian knight while gauging the precise distance from there to each of the other guards. His gauntleted hand at his hip, just inches from the hilt of the massive falchion that hung from a bejeweled leather belt at his waist.

The sergeant took up Claradon's sword and reentered the Council chambers, Dolan following.

Claradon and his comrades stepped down from the petitioners' dais. Attendants pushed it to the side of the hall, and ushered the various aides and courtiers well away from the action. Chancellor Barusa strode down the steps from the mezzanine and strapped on his shield.

"50 silver crowns on the troll," shouted Cartegian. "Even my cat could take the other one."

Barusa stepped to the center of the hall, as did Claradon. "I always expected to cross blades with your father," said Barusa quietly. "All the easier since it's you, boy. Now Dor Eotrus will go to the Alders and your family will fade to nothing."

Claradon's eyes were wide with fear, his face grew pale, and sweat beaded on his forehead as Barusa drew close.

"Realizing the stupidity of this challenge, whelp?" said Barusa. "Too late now to withdraw. Soon you will be as dead as your father, but not before I have sport with you."

"Perhaps you will kill me, but my brothers will stand against you," said Claradon, his voice wavering. "They will avenge me."

An evil grin formed on Barusa's face. "Your brothers are already dead; I have seen to it."

Horror and shock covered Claradon's face and his sword clattered to the floor.

Barusa rolled his eyes. "Dead gods, you

sniveling cur—pick up your sword."

Claradon did so, his eyes wide, pleading.

"Who ate my cat?" shouted Cartegian. "He's nothing but skin and bones."

"Are you ready?" called out Lord Jhensezil. Both men signaled that they were.

Barusa stepped in and slashed his blade back and forth, as much flourish as attack, all designed to test and probe his opponent, to gauge his skills and take his measure. Claradon put up the slow and clumsy defense of a frightened youth with no real combat experience. His sword visibly shook from his terror. All he could do was clumsily parry the Chancellor's punishing slashes, backpedal, and sidestep in awkward fashion. It was plain for all to see that he was far overmatched and wanted nothing but to run, to flee.

Barusa toyed with him for several minutes, beating down his defense with broad, powerful strokes, holding back his killing thrust. Claradon managed a few weak slashes, all ineffective. Winded from the strain, Claradon looked as if he were about to drop.

"Pathetic whelp," said Barusa. "You have even less skill than courage, and this grows tiresome. Give my regards to your father."

Barusa pulled his shield to the right, better covering his torso and swiftly raised his sword for an overhand strike designed to crush Claradon's skull and end the duel. Just as Ob has advised him, Claradon sprang to his left, all sign of fear and fatigue dropped from his face, and slashed his heavy blade with blazing speed and great power against Barusa's side, just below his armpit. The sound of cracking ribs erupted through the hall, though Barusa's heavy mail held, saving him from a mortal wound.

A roar of surprise went up among the attendants, courtiers, and guards alike. The councilors gasped and jumped to their feet; even Bishop Tobin came alive and bounced up.

The Chancellor groaned and staggered forward, then dropped to his knees, coughing blood. His sword clattered to the floor and his right arm hung limp.

"Off with his head," screeched Cartegian. "His head for my mantle."

Claradon moved smoothly to Barusa's side, kicked his sword away, and placed his blade against the back of the Chancellor's neck.

Several Myrdonian knights pulled their weapons and moved forward. Dolan dashed for the door to the antechamber.

"Hurry boy, finish him," yelled Ob as he drew a hidden dagger from beneath his vest and moved to engage the Myrdonians, Tanch beside him—his palms glowing with an eerie light stemming from his wizardry.

Ob kicked the closest Myrdonian in the groin and he went down in a heap.

Tanch and Ob now stood back to back with Claradon.

The Duke's men moved toward the Myrdonians, but they were far outnumbered. "Hold," shouted the Duke from his place in the gallery. "Let no one interfere."

Most of the Myrdonians surrounded Claradon and his comrades, though none dared attack with

Claradon's blade at their master's throat. The rest held back the Duke's men. There they stood in standoff for several moments, the leaders no doubt calculating the odds of victory for their own.

The Vizier, still beside his seat in the gallery, lifted his hands from within his sleeves, preparing no doubt to weave some sinister sorcery. Before he could execute it, the cold steel of wide blade pressed his nape.

The Vizier gasped in surprise, as he had heard no one approach. A thin line of blood trickled down his back, staining his collar.

"Recall your dogs, wizard," whispered a deep voice in his ear.

"Stand down," shouted the Vizier after but a moment's pause. He chanced to turn his head and gaze on his besieger. Lord Theta stared back at him.

The Myrdonians withdrew from Claradon, though slowly, begrudgingly, as if the Vizier's orders meant little to them.

"Do you recant your accusations against me and mine?" boomed the young patriarch of House Eotrus, loud enough for all in the hall to hear.

Barusa's eyes burned with hatred. He spit blood through clenched teeth.

"Speak now or your life is forfeit," said Claradon.

". . . I recant," said the Chancellor coughing up more blood.

"His blood is red just like my cat's," bellowed Cartegian as he capered about.

Claradon stepped back and put up his sword.

"You will regret this, Eotrus," said Cartegian.

"Just like my troll."

Harringgold stood motionless. "Let no more threats or accusations be heard against the heir to House Eotrus," said the Duke. "He has proven his quality before the gods and all those gathered here today. Henceforth, he will carry the mantle of his house and let no man challenge him for it."

Urged on by Ob, Claradon and the others quickly made their way out of the Council chambers, carefully stepped around the unconscious soldiers Theta had left in the antechamber, and fled Tammanian Hall.

III
THE SHADOW LEAGUE

Later that day, in the grand citadel of Dor Lomion, the highest point within the walls of ancient Lomion City, Duke Harringgold held secret council with Claradon Eotrus and his retinue. Gathered about a large oval table, Harringgold sat at one end, Claradon the other, their men in between. Harringgold's trusted guards stood as silent sentinels about the door and in this corner and that. At Harringgold's right hand sat Lord Samwise Sluug, the tall, lean, and dangerous Preceptor of the Rangers Guild and master of Doriath Hall. At his left was Sir Seran, the Duke's nephew: clean-cut, shiny armored, and young. With Claradon were Ob, Tanch, Theta, and Sir Glimador Malvegil.

"Lord Harringgold," said Tanch, "the Eotrus greatly appreciate your hospitality and generosity in boarding us during our stay in Lomion City. After our adventure this morning, safe harbor in the city may well have been hard to find."

"The Eotrus are welcome in my fortress," Dor Lomion, "as always and ever. I counted Aradon a trusted ally and friend of long years. I hope to say the same of his heir."

"As do I," said Claradon.

"Curious then," said Ob, "that your guards have shadowed our every move since we arrived, two to each of us, and all skittish-like."

"That watch was set at my urging, Castellan,"

303

said Sluug. "I meant no offense by it, but caution is prudent in the best of times, and these times are growing dark, as I'm sure you will agree."

Ob nodded begrudgingly and swallowed back whatever wisecrack sought to stumble out.

"Brother Claradon," said Harringgold. "Please share with us the tale of what truly happened to your father and his men."

"The whole truth this time," said Sluug. "Not the tale of fancy you told in Tammanian Hall."

Claradon didn't immediately respond.

"I want to help you," said Harringgold, "but I can't if you don't trust me, and my help I believe you require, despite your victory today."

"You have ever been a friend to the Eotrus, my lord. I have not forgotten that."

"And today was none different," said Ob. "You spoke up on Claradon's behalf when you could've kept silent and safe. We will not soon forget that. But your words served your own purposes as much as ours. Ain't that so?"

"We have common purpose," said Harringgold. "That's nothing new and no secret."

An uneasy silence ruled the room for several moments before the Duke spoke again. "All I can say is that within this hall, you are amongst friends and should speak freely."

Claradon nodded. "Very well, but the tale will take some time."

"The servants are bringing wine and hot tea and I have already cleared my schedule," said the Duke.

Claradon and Ob, supported now and again by Tanch, told all that there was to tell about the recent events in the Vermion Forest—the tragic deaths, the otherworldly monsters, the mystical gateway to Nifleheim, and the sinister Temple of Guymaog. They answered the many questions posed by the Duke and Sluug as best they could. Theta listened and watched, but said nothing. Eventually, the conversation turned back to the killers that attacked Riker's Crossroads.

"I have made it my mission to hunt down Korrgonn," said Claradon. "I will not rest until he and his evil band are dead."

"If I were you I would feel the same," said the Duke. "But there are other grave matters to consider before you venture on that course."

"Such as the madness that's overtaken the Council?" said Claradon.

"Indeed," said Harringgold. "Madness is as good a word as any to describe it. The High Council is one of Lomion's greatest achievements. It has allowed us to maintain the traditional monarchy while placing nearly all the decision making into the hands of the mercantile, military, administrative, and religious leaders of the land— all the while maintaining a balance of power amongst those divergent groups. But as you saw today, the Council is corrupted—a mockery of its former self. For all practical purposes, the High Council is no more, and may never be again."

"What of the Council of Lords?" said Claradon.

"It fares better, but not by much," said Harringgold. "Paranoia and fear rule there as much as anything, placing the Lords in impotent disarray."

"And sadly, young Eotrus, the mercy you

showed today may cost us dearly in the days to come. A new power is rising is Lomion. A dark power of which today you saw only the merest glimpse. The death of Barusa might have turned the tide in our favor, or at least slowed it, giving us more time to prepare."

"Or, it may have made things worse," said Sluug.

Harringgold shrugged. "Who can say?"

"What is this dark power?" said Claradon. "What madness assails Lomion? Tell me."

"The Shadow League, or the League of Shadows, as some call it," said the Duke as he carefully surveyed the faces of his guests. "Have any of you heard those names before?"

They indicated they had not.

"Others call it the League of Light," said Sluug. "Have you heard of that?"

Again, they had not.

"By whatever name they go," said the Duke, "they are an alliance among various corrupt churchmen, organized criminal groups, rogue wizards, and bizarre cults. I believe House Alder figures prominently in the League's hierarchy, and with the League's support, the Vizier recently gained control of the Tower of the Arcane."

Tanch started at this and his eyes grew wide.

"The members of The Shadow League are not of one mind, however. They fight for position, striving to gain power and control within their treasonous alliance. It's this struggle, I believe, that causes Barusa and the Vizier to vie with each other, and only due to that infighting does the High Council survive at all."

"The tale of how all this came about is long and complex. What I can say now is that Barusa effectively rules in the king's stead. His majesty, King Tenzivel, is rarely seen, and likely only still lives because his bodyguards never leave his side and haven't yet been corrupted. He is a prisoner in his own palace. Barusa controls the Myrdonians, and through proxies, he commands nearly the entire City Watch. Cartegian is his puppet, though a dangerous, unpredictable, and unreliable one. Slyman is Barusa's lackey. He controls the guilds, their wealth, and their soldiers. But the Vizier may be the worst of them all—manipulating events from behind the scenes. He is subtle, smart, and devious. 'Twas in a bloody coup several months ago that he wrested control of the Tower of the Arcane from the Grandmasters."

"Word on the streets is that Grandmaster Pipkorn was killed in the fighting," said Sluug, again studying the others' reactions.

"But we know better," said Harringgold. "When all was lost, Pipkorn fled the tower and went into hiding, though he has not been seen publicly since."

Tanch shook his head in disbelief. "How could that happen? No one could defeat Master Pipkorn. I can't believe this."

"Nevertheless, it is the truth," said Harringgold. "Marshal Balfor commands the city's standing army, but grovels at the Vizier's feet. What hold the wizard has over the old war dog, we know not. Bishop Tobin ostensibly represents the Churchmen, but his true loyalties are unclear—all that I can say for certain is that he is not nearly as addle-pated as he puts on. Lady Aramere's loyalties are also suspect."

"And Lord Jhensezil?" said Claradon.

"He stands firmly with us, as do most of the Noble Houses and the Church Knights. Lady Dahlia of Kern is with us, and Lord Glenfinnen, and a few others. I, of course, command Dor Lomion and its garrison—though even here skulk spies for the League. Lord Sluug commands Doriath Hall and all its rangers and agents—our eyes, ears, and good right arm, although even within Doriath's hallowed halls, we suspect lurk spies of the enemy. For too long we focused our gazes on enemies outside Lomion, while those within grew in strength, infiltrated our ranks, and poisoned us from the inside."

The chamber's door swung open and the conversation halted. Claradon turned to see a tall, swarthy man framed in the portal. Dressed in gray and black, head to boot, he surveyed the room for a moment, and then stepped in, the guards paying him no heed or homage.

"The name of this devil you will know," said the Duke, pointing toward the new arrival, "though not his face. Meet Dark Sendarth."

Tanch gasped.

"The Dark Sendarth?" said Ob, a look of amazement on his face. "The master assassin? Most deadly killer to ever walk Midgaard?"

"The one and only," said Sendarth with a smile on his lips but not his eyes.

"Somehow," said Ob, "I expected someone shorter."

"Ha," laughed Sendarth as he approached Theta. "It was your sword that shaved the back of the Vizier's neck today," said Sendarth. "Yet you didn't take his head."

"Nor did you," said Theta, "though you lurked behind a curtain not six paces away."

Sendarth smiled. "We were outnumbered five to one. Had I killed the old skunk, we might have lost the Duke in the ensuing battle. That I couldn't risk. I would like to know how you knew I was there, never having looked my way.

"I have my ways," said Theta.

"You always did," he said. "It has been a very long time."

"So it has," said Theta.

Sendarth extended his arm and they firmly clasped hands.

"Friend of old times," said Sendarth.

"Friend of old times," said Theta.

"It figures; birds of a feather," said Ob under his breath. "I think I'm gonna be sick."

"Claradon, my list of allies is all too thin," said the Duke as they retook their seats. "I need people I can trust in positions of power, and I need them to stay alive. After the enemies you made today, you will have a bounty on your head. It is not safe for you to remain in Lomion City. Outside this fortress I can't guarantee your safety. If you pursue your course and go after Korrgonn, the Chancellor's men will surely track you down. I cannot allow that. As you well know, Dor Eotrus has great strategic value, situated as it is between

Lomion City and the City of Kern. That trade route must stay open. Your lands must stay secure."

"My brothers—" said Claradon

"Are young and inexperienced," said the Duke. "I need you to hold the Dor. Your brothers will assist you. I've sent men to collect Jude and Malcolm and bring them here in the morning. I understand that they've been staying at the Chapterhouse of the Knights of Tyr. It seems young Malcolm has nearly completed his training and will soon be knighted."

"You're very well informed, my Lord," said Claradon.

Harringgold nodded but offered no more. "I know that abandoning your mission will be difficult, but for the greater good you must do this. You must go home."

Claradon looked dejected and stared down at the table.

"I will send a squadron of my men to escort you and your brothers back to Dor Eotrus, and they will remain there to bolster your garrison."

"And I will provide a squad of rangers as well," said Sluug.

"Listen here, Harringgold," said Ob. "If you think we're gonna let Korrgonn get away with what he did, you've another thing coming."

Theta pounded fist to table, startling all. "Korrgonn must die," he said in a slow commanding voice. "That is far more important than trade routes or your petty politics. Korrgonn will be the glue that will bind The Shadow League together. Do you understand that? Do you comprehend what he is, what he can do? He cannot be allowed to roam free."

"I understand that that is one possibility," said the Duke. "I also understand that Korrgonn may not be the threat that you think he is. But I agree he must be stopped. I'm just saying that Brother Claradon is needed elsewhere. He will not be the one to stop Korrgonn. That duty must fall to others."

"I will stop him," said Theta. "What aid can you offer me?"

The Duke seemed taken aback. He looked toward Sendarth.

"If there is one man alive that can stop any other," said Sendarth. "Theta is he."

"Rare praise that is, indeed. Rare praise. Then you have my support, Lord Theta," said the Duke. "And you, good Castellan? Will you pledge your axe to this quest?"

"You expect me to abandon Claradon and serve under Mr. Fancy Pants?"

Harringgold glanced at Theta's ornate armor. "Yes," said the Duke with a grin.

Ob looked the Duke up and down with narrowed eyes. "It's because I'm short, isn't it?" he said. "Never judge a Gnome by his size, Duke."

Claradon shifted his feet uneasily. "I—but—"

"Never fear, Claradon, Ob will only be taking a temporary leave from your service—hopefully, it will be a brief one. He can return to his post as Castellan of Dor Eotrus when his mission is complete."

Ob turned toward Claradon. "Laddie, can you manage without me for a time?"

"I will manage. You and Tanch should go."

311

"Me?" blurted Tanch. "Oh heavens, no, Master Claradon. My delicate back could never withstand such a mission. I must protest. My place is at your side. I—"

"You will go with Lord Theta," said the Duke. "Such is my command."

The Duke turned back toward Theta. "As for what aid I can offer, I will have my agents scour the city for any signs of Korrgonn, his men, and that strange carriage. Until they're found, there is little more to be done. In the meantime, I advise that you consult with Grandmaster Pipkorn. He is the most formidable wizard loyal to our cause, and a source of vast knowledge. Sometimes, even Sluug envies Pipkorn's network of spies. How he gathers the knowledge he does, we may never know, nor does it matter much, as long as shares with us what we need to know, when we need to know it. So speak with him."

"He guards his knowledge like a dragon guards its treasure," said Sluug. "He will not give it freely."

"Nevertheless," said the Duke, "if any can tell us more of Korrgonn or his followers, it is Pipkorn."

"Take this talisman," said the Duke as he produced a curious star-shaped jewel from his pocket and handed it to Par Tanch. "On the morrow, it will lead you to Pipkorn's retreat, though it will likely only work for a wizard. Show it to him, and he will know that I sent you. Until then, enjoy a hot repast and a good night's rest here in Dor Lomion."

IV
THE BLACK HAND

The last of them went down—cleaved in half by Theta's falchion. Geysers of blood gushed everywhere as the Duke's guards charged into what was once a cozy guest suite, beautifully adorned in the Old Lomerian style, but was now a butchery of flowing blood and spilled entrails, more slaughterhouse than home.

Several corpses soiled the exotic carpet, some still twitching as such are often wont to do. The dead wore the Duke's livery, confusing the guards. The Duke's guest, a hulking foreign knight, stood beside the bed, nightshirt drenched red; his face and pants splattered with blood; bloodied falchion in his left hand. His expression best described as annoyed; his aspect, calm. He stood unmoving, staring at the guards with his piercing blue eyes— and there they all still stood when the Duke and his personal bodyguards dashed down the hall to the apartment's entrance. The guards made way, relief on their faces at the Duke's arrival.

Harringgold's mouth dropped open as he entered and took in the sight and the stench of the dead.

"Are these yours?" said Theta, menace in his voice as he pointed to the dead with his right hand. Blood dripped from his sword and made a plopping sound when it struck the red puddle beside his feet.

"What happened?" said the Duke.

"They came to kill me," said Theta. "They failed."

"I assure you, sir, they acted on no orders of mine," said the Duke as he cautiously watched Theta's sword arm. Harringgold motioned to the guards and they adjusted the corpses so that their faces could be viewed.

Harringgold's jaw stiffened when he recognized the first of them. "This one has been in my employ some five years," said the Duke pointing to a decapitated head at the foot of the bed. "And this one has worked as a guard for a few months, I think, perhaps a year. The other four I don't recognize."

"Nor do I," said the guard captain from the Duke's side.

"Search the bodies," said Theta, still standing tensed.

The Duke nodded to the guards and they began to search.

"Looking for what?" said the Duke.

"A tattoo, a scar, a strange coin, or some other such sigil, sign, or token."

After some minutes, the guard captain reported their findings. "Two bear the mark of the Black Hand on their shoulders."

"That's it then," said the Duke. "They're paid assassins. Check on our other guests at once." The guards did so.

"These others each wore a gold coin hung from a chain about their necks," said the guard captain.

"Put the coins down on the bed," said Theta as he strapped on his sword belt. He wiped his falchion clean on the sheets before sheathing it.

"The Chancellor wasted no time," said Harringgold. "I didn't expect this, especially not here. Not in my own home."

Theta studied the coins for a time, wrapped them in cloth, being careful not to touch them with his hands, and pocketed them.

"It is still some hours until dawn," said Theta. "I will need another room."

"Of course," said the Duke, seemingly surprised at the request.

"One with a bath, and some bandages, and a few guards at the door that you can trust more than these."

"You will have it. I don't know what to say, this should never have happened in my fortress."

"You are right, it shouldn't have," said Theta, giving the Duke an ice-cold stare.

"I will stand the watch myself," said the guard captain, "with your permission, Duke."

Harringgold nodded.

Servants led Theta to another room, two floors up. Ob appeared along the way and walked beside Theta.

"You hurt?" said Ob.

"No."

"Good, but it's not over, laddie. The scum won't stop coming. Once The Hand has a contract, they never give up. Not ever. They took five years to track down old Par Tandar in Minoc—he was hiding out as a cobbler—but they got him—hung his head from a lamppost out in front of the Tower of the Arcane. Not one witness. Theta, your only chance is to head for the hills and not stop until you're back home—wherever it is you hail from."

"What makes you think they're only after me, Gnome?"

Ob paled. "I—just figured you had crossed the wrong sort somewheres about, that's all. You think the Alders set them on you? On us? This fast? Bloody hell; that's all we need. If you're right, we're really in the deep stuff."

"I will deal with the assassins as need be, but it won't be by running. Let's focus our attention on tracking down Korrgonn and Mortach—they are the real threats. Everything else is unimportant."

"Don't underestimate the Black Hand, Theta. If you do, you just might get dead."

"Don't underestimate me," said Theta.

V
TO PIPKORN WE WILL GO

The guards that escorted the Eotrus men were helpful guides and kept them from getting lost in Dor Lomion's halls, which were vast, even cavernous, and made Dor Eotrus—a large fortress by all accounts—feel small and provincial. In the morning, the Eotrus group gathered in one of Dor Lomion's well-appointed lounges to break their fast and have council. Each man in the group attended the breakfast in casual dress; no armor to be seen, though each girded a sword or axe at their hips.

The round room in which they gathered was at the very top of one of Dor Lomion's turrets and had a high peaked ceiling of exposed timbers and very tall glass windows that looked down upon the city far below—an incredible view matched by few windows in all the city. The room's walls were paneled in thick wood and gave it the feel of a rich manor house, not a musty and cold castle. Leather clad chairs, thick wooden tables, a large hearth with a crackling fire, and exotic carpets populated the room, which was accoutered with silver wall sconces and oil lamps, candelabras, bookshelves, maps, and a well-stocked bar, which Ob enjoyed sampling. Not a room offered to casual guests or commoners, was this. The Duke no doubt felt guilty over the previous night's events.

Meticulously dressed and well-mannered

317

servants laid out a buffet of pastries, fresh breads and butter, local fruit, and drinks, including mulled wine and hot cider, before exiting the room, leaving the group in private.

"Jude and Malcolm are expected to arrive later his morning," said Claradon. "The Duke has us scheduled to set out immediately thereafter for the Dor. I'm just not sure what to do. Do I follow Harringgold's orders, go back home and hide under the bed, or do I go after Korrgonn, with you?"

"I'm not much for following orders, as you well know, laddie," said Ob, "but this time, maybe it's for the best. Me and Lord Bigshot can take care of Korrgonn."

"Lord Theta," said Claradon. "I would ask your council as well."

A steaming mug of hot cider in his hand, Theta leveled his steely gaze on Claradon. "Your path does not lie on the homeward road."

"Are you saying that I should come with you? I would be going against the Duke's orders."

"Don't confuse the boy, Theta. He belongs at the reins of the Dor, in his father's stead, not fighting such as Korrgonn and his ilk."

"You seek to send him home to protect him, to keep him from harm's way," said Theta, "but he needs no protection, and he's no boy, in age or experience. He proved his quality in the Vermion and again against Barusa—of that there can be no doubt. His path lies with us."

The hairs on the back of Claradon's neck stood up and the blood drained from his face. "Once, not long ago, you told me that those who share your path are not long for Valhalla."

Theta smiled a thin smile. "Nevertheless, such is your path."

"Meaning no disrespect, Lord Theta, but I beg to disagree," said Tanch. "I think Master Claradon should head home; he mustn't go against the Duke's orders. Stopping Korrgonn is no longer Claradon's first priority. His other duties must take precedence."

"Wizard, you are as shallow and simple as a one-eyed drunken Dwarf," said Ob, a large goblet of mulled wine in hand.

"What say you?" said Tanch, outraged.

"Harringgold wants Korrgonn dead as surely as we do," said Ob, "even though he doesn't believe he's the threat that Theta says he is. But the Duke wants us to take Korrgonn's measure so that he doesn't have to. We are to take the risks, not him and his. That's why he pushed you and me both to head off with Theta."

"If we kill Korrgonn and come back heroes, we've served his purpose and we're all best pals—as he will have backed us. If we get dead, that will give the Duke a good measurement of Korrgonn's strength. He will use what he learns to put his own plan together, with his own men, to stop Korrgonn. We're the fodder, magic-boy—make no mistake of that. We're to be pushed out in front, to test and probe the enemy. Expendable assets we are—pawns, just like in Mages and Monsters."

"And if we do end up dead, Claradon will come to rely that much more on the Duke, bringing Dor Eotrus more under his influence—under his control. That is his plan; I have no doubt. You can never fully trust a politician, and that's what the Duke is, and that's the truth."

"You're mad to think that Lord Harringgold is so manipulative," said Tanch.

"And you're a fool not to see that he is," said Ob. "Harringgold is a crafty one. He didn't get to be Archduke of the greatest city of Midgaard by his good looks alone."

"He is the Duke," said Tanch. "Deserving of respect and—"

"The Chancellorship deserves respect too, but Barusa is still a snake," said Ob. "Open your eyes, Magic Boy, and see the world the way it is. You're walking around in a fog."

"I don't know if I'm cut out for this," said Claradon. "I'm not ready, not yet, anyway."

"That is much of what the Duke is after," said Theta. "To take your measure, not just to have us take Korrgonn's."

"My measure? What do you mean?"

"He means that at the duel yesterday, the Duke learned you're a warrior to be reckoned with, so he wanted to learn more," said Ob. "To size you up, to see if you're made of solid stuff or slippery slop. Any man can judge strength that's in his face. But you showed guile yesterday, pretending the fool and coward until your opening came. That takes smarts and discipline. The Duke didn't expect that from you. He wants to learn more. That's why he asked us here—it wasn't just to hear our tale of what happened in the Vermion."

"I don't know what more he could have learned about me from our discussion," said Claradon.

"He learned that you rely on your comrades," said Theta. "That the guile you displayed at that duel may not have been only of your own making."

Ob raised an eyebrow. "I hadn't thought of that," he said. "Another reason to split us up. Easier to read the boy and control him without us hanging about. Mayhaps Harringgold is up to even more than I thought. Could he want the Dor for himself?"

"I can't believe that," said Claradon. "He was a good friend to my father. He wouldn't betray us."

"There is no doubt that the Duke has an agenda," said Theta. "Most of which he's kept hidden."

"Hmm—dark times," said Ob, a pensive look on his face. "Dark times."

"I have much to consider and little time for consideration," said Claradon. "No matter my decision, I can't go with you now. I must await my brothers and have council with them."

"In the meantime," said Ob, "we'll go track down Old Pointy Hat Pipkorn in whatever hole he's hiding in and see if he can help."

"You have no respect at all for anyone, do you?" said Tanch. "Not even for the Grandmaster of the Tower of the Arcane."

"Nope," said Ob.

Somehow, while holding the ensorcelled talisman, Tanch knew which way to turn, though he knew not their destination, nor their full route. He led the group through the fair districts of Lomion City and then down into a seedier neighborhood called The Heights. There, the broad avenues gave way to alleyways, narrow and grim. The streets became a maze and all manner of ruffians, beggars, and vagabonds prowled the ways. A far cry from the beautiful, tree-lined lanes of the High Quarter or the Mercantile District, but no worse than the coarser sections of other cities of the realm.

Despite the nondescript cloaks worn by the group, the wary denizens of The Heights marked their passing. Some folk made way for the sturdy group, and others stood glaring from doorways, windows, and darkened alleys. Not a place for an outsider to pass safely alone this was.

"Just where are you taking us, Mister Tanch?" said Dolan.

"To Master Pipkorn, I hope," said the wizard. "Assuming that this thing actually works."

"Where is Old Pointy Hat hiding?" said Ob.

"I can't say, I'm afraid, though it seems we're heading for Southeast."

"Southeast! Oh, that just beats it," said Ob. "All we need."

"It can't be much worse than this place," said Dolan.

"The Heights are a palace compared to Southeast," said Ob. "Good thing I brought my axe."

"You bring your axe everywhere," said Tanch.

"Gnomes are always prepared. That's why we're so long lived."

"How much farther, Mister Tanch?" asked Dolan.

"We're there, laddie," said Ob gesturing ahead.

Before the group was a high stone wall, many feet thick, with a massive wood and steel gate and iron portcullis, both open. Several armed Lomion City guardsmen stood about and approached when the group made to pass through.

"Good afternoon, gentlemen," said one of the guards, apparently the officer in charge.

"Afternoon," said Ob loudly, standing on his toes to catch the officer's eye.

"This is Mideon Gate; beyond lies Southeast," said the guard. He addressed Theta and took no notice of Ob. He stared as if expecting to see surprise at his announcement and for the group to turn away.

"We know where we are, man," said Ob. "We're not daft you know. Now stand aside so we might pass."

The guards did not make way.

The officer narrowed his eyes and scanned the group with suspicion. "What is your business in Southeast?" he said, still addressing Theta.

"Our business is our own, laddie," said Ob. "If you move yourself aside, quick-like, I may not have to step on you."

"No one passes this gate," said the officer in a stern voice, only now taking notice of Ob, "unless they state their business and sign their names in the logbook, by order of the Crown."

"And then may we pass all friendly-like, laddie?" said Ob.

"Aye," said the officer.

"Then give me the logbook, bucko, and sign I will."

The officer motioned to one of his men, who

passed Ob the logbook and a quill.

"Here's the spot for our names, I see," said Ob as he studied the book. "Too Tall is what they call me, and my friends are Scaredy Cat, Pointy Ears, and Mr. Fancy Pants," he said, writing each name in turn. He passed the book back to the officer who stared at it dumbfounded.

"As for our business—my friends and I are headed to the Brown Boar Inn to get famously drunk and beat people up.

The officer's mouth was open, but no words found their way out.

"Let's go," said Ob as he pushed forward passed the guards. They stared after the group as they made their way.

"The gates close at dusk," called out the officer, "and don't open again until dawn. Believe me, you don't want to get stuck in there after dark."

VI
EDWIN OF ALDER

Populated with a mix of residential buildings of rotting wood, decaying brick, and crumbling mortar, houses of ill repute, riotous gambling dens, seedy taverns, flea infested boarding houses, and fetid beggars' hovels, Southeast was the foulest district in the otherwise fair city of Lomion, capital city of the Kingdom of Lomion.

A clinging mist continually hung over the district, sometimes even permeating indoors. The whole place radiated a sense of vast age and decay. An inexplicable malaise afflicted those goodly folk that braved its narrow streets and dismal alleyways. Those who lingered would oft grow morbid, grim, and even violent. Some said a strange vapor within the mist caused that madness; others attributed it to wizards' spells gone awry in ages past.

"Not a fit place for proper folk," said Ob as he eyed the ill-kept buildings that precariously leaned over both sides of the lane that they walked down, blocking out much of the day's light. "Dark, dismal, and dirty—always been that way, Southeast has. Mostly folks up to no good are seen hereabouts—cutthroats and scoundrels, the lot of them."

"And Gnomes," said Tanch, the Duke's talisman in his hand.

Ob narrowed his eyes and glared at the wizard. "It's true: a Gnome or two has lived around here over the years. Mind you, they are southern Gnomes, from Grommel or Portland Vale, not Northerners like myself. My kin have more sense."

"Things have gotten worse in Southeast in recent years," said Tanch. "I have heard that most common folk, including the beggars, have fled or gone missing. Even the thieves' guild moved out, as did most everyone else of sound mind. Only the crazies are left, and there are plenty of them, or so I hear."

Theta grabbed Tanch by the arm. "This is not a place to be cornered in. Why did you have us leave our horses?"

Tanch winced from the pressure on his arm. "Forgive me—Lord Theta—but there—is something about the place—makes animals wild." Theta released him and Tanch rubbed his shoulder. "It has always been that way, and grown worse of late, I'm told. If we had taken horses in here, they would've tried to throw us and run off."

"He's right," said Ob. "Animals not accustomed to this place lose their heads and panic. I've seen it happen. The place isn't quite natural; some wizards mucked it up ages back. Stinking wizards."

Par Tanch looked stricken but offered no retort.

"Them fellows following us have horses," said Dolan, "and they're getting on good enough."

"What?" said Ob. "Following us?" Ob cupped a hand behind his right ear. "Be silent," he said, pausing to listen. "Oh boy, you're right, I hear them coming. I thought I heard something a minute ago, but the darned wizard distracted me, as usual. Stinking wizards." Ob glared at Tanch and took a swig from his wineskin.

"Let's get out of this alley before they're on us," said Theta.

"Who are they?" said Ob. "That is what I want to know."

"Somebody's soldiers," said Dolan. "They've been following us since before we entered Southeast, hanging well back, trying to stay out of sight. I caught a glimpse of them a couple of times."

The group picked up their pace, but so did their shadows. The talisman led them from narrow alley to narrow alley, with no wide way to turn off in to. Shutters slammed closed on upper floors as they passed. Theta halted and turned about. "They're coming up."

"What do we do?" said Tanch. "Run? Hide? Perhaps we should surrender?"

"Keep quiet," said Theta.

Horses walked up the way behind the group, hooves echoing on the cobblestones, two by two, taking up nearly the full width of the narrow alley, their numbers unclear in the mist and gloom. The riders wore the chain mail vests and leather hauberks common to the soldiery of the wealthier classes, beneath dark-brown cloaks, save for their perfumed leader, swathed in a red silken cloak and pantaloons and black leathern armor.

"Look what we have here," said the leader, a handsome, dark-haired man in his thirties, as he struggled to keep his skittish mount under control. "Scared little rats scurrying down the alley. Stand aside rats and let your betters pass or we will run you down." He and some of his men had hands to sword hilts, blades sheathed; others held steel crossbows, primed to fire.

"Laddie, just who do you think you are to be speaking to honest folk like that?" said Ob.

"I am Edwin of Alder," said the rider. "You, on the other hand, are a half-grown mongrel rat by the look of it. Step aside, rat, so we may pass."

"Ob, we've no time for this," Tanch hissed from a shadowy alcove that he had stepped into. "Just let them pass."

"They're not just passing," said Dolan quietly. He edged into the shadows, unslung his bow from his shoulder, and reached for his arrows.

"He's Barusa's nephew," whispered Ob. "Seeking to settle the score with the Eotrus. He's here for blood."

"Perhaps you would care to step down, laddie, and see if you can push me aside?" said Ob.

Edwin smiled. "That I would, Dwarf."

"I ain't no stinking Dwarf, Alder."

Edwin stepped down from his horse, eyes fixed on Ob, but wary of Theta who stood close by. Four of his men dismounted beside him. "You think the Eotrus can disgrace my uncle and my House and get away with it? You can't. Where is your brave new lord? Did he run at first sight of us? Or is he hiding in the shadows, all atremble?"

"Lord Eotrus is not with us, laddie. If it's him you're after, you're out of luck. Best you get gone, afore there's any more unpleasantness."

"I'm afraid there will be a good deal of unpleasantness before I'm done with you, Dwarf," said Edwin as he drew his sword. His men did the same. "They say that despite his size and stench, the Castellan of Dor Eotrus is a sturdy warrior. Well, so am I, as you will soon see. Are you ready to die, Dwarf?"

"I'm ready to give you a lesson, pig, just as Claradon did to your stinking uncle."

Edwin sneered, stepped forward, and spun his blade in a whirling, looping pattern to this side and that, faster and faster, impressively so. Ob's axe was in his hand in an instant, his eyes darting back and forth following Edwin's blade.

Edwin sprang forward and his blade crashed down, aimed for Ob's head. But then Theta was there, and blocked the blow up high with his massive falchion, though in truth, Ob's axe was well positioned to parry the strike without aid from anyone.

Edwin grunted at the impact and recoiled as the big knight stepped around Ob and moved toward him. Edwin's upper arm felt afire; his sword dropped from his grasp; his fingers and forearm unresponsive, shaking, and numb.

"Did I ask for help, Mr. Show-off?" said Ob to Theta.

Edwin tripped as he backpedaled, landed on his rump, and rolled beneath the nearest horses, desperate to get clear of Theta. "Shoot him, you fools," Edwin shrieked.

Two crossbow bolts hurtled at Theta's chest from point blank range.

Theta's sword arced purposely to the left and then to the right, each bolt twanging off the flat of the blade.

The crossbowmen's eyes went wide with shock.

"That was a mistake," said Theta.

A moment later, an arrow protruded from the forehead of one crossbowman, and then the other, courtesy of Dolan's bow.

A rider bore down on Theta, yelling a battle cry. Theta blocked the rider's slash with his shield and lopped the man's arm off with an overhand strike of his war blade.

Dolan put an arrow through the throat of another of Edwin's men, while Ob and Tanch engaged two more.

In moments, Edwin found himself alone, a half dozen of his men down and dead, the rest fled with all their horses. Edwin spun around, disheveled, and in disbelief at what had so quickly happened. Abandoned and vulnerable, his sword on the cobblestones halfway between him and Theta.

A horse trotted up from behind and when Edwin turned in relief, expecting one of his men to his rescue, a blade sliced deep into his cheek, rending him to the bone from temple to chin.

Edwin screamed in agony, clutched at his face, and gazed in horror at his bloody hands.

Claradon had struck the blow.

"Aargh!" Edwin staggered against the alley wall and sought to stave the flow of blood from his ruined face. "You cowardly bastard," yelled Edwin as blood streamed from between his fingers. "I will see you all dead for this. Every one of you."

Claradon fronted Edwin again, his sword tip inches from Edwin's throat. "Trouble us no more,

Alder, or next time I will take your life, not just your looks."

"Let me cut the scum down, boy," said Ob marching forward.

"Dead gods," called out Tanch. "Stop this madness for Odin's sake. Let him go."

Claradon motioned Ob back. "Get you gone, Alder, and trouble the Eotrus no more. Twice this week we've shown your House mercy; we will not do so again."

Edwin turned and staggered down the alley, cursing Claradon all the while.

"We don't need an all-out war with the Alders," said Claradon, "which is what we would have if we had killed him."

Ob clearly didn't agree but held his tongue.

Dolan inspected each of Edwin's fallen—pockets, purse, and weapons.

Tanch faced his comrades, flushed and exasperated, arms out to his sides, palms upraised. "Is this what we have come to?" he said, his voice wavering. "Cutting down noblemen in the streets? Picking the pockets of the dead," he said pointing to Dolan. He stormed up to Theta. "These were men of Lomion, not monsters conjured from Nifleheim. They have families—parents, wives, children. Their lives have value." He turned back to the others. "This is a civilized land," he said, his voice growing ever shriller. "There are laws; there are laws. There will be consequences. You can't just kill retainers of a noble house and expect to get away with it. The repercussions will be grave and—"

"You've killed men before," said Theta.

Tanch was taken aback; he took a step back, unsteady; his mouth continued to move but nothing more came out.

"They started it," said Ob to Tanch. "Don't poke the dragon and expect not to get dead, I say." He looked toward Claradon. "What are you doing here, boy? You're supposed to be off home with your brothers."

"Jude and Malcolm arrived early; we talked and I sent them back to the Dor. I couldn't go with them; I need to see this through. It was all I could do to keep them from coming with me."

"You've made your choice then, laddie," said Ob. "Let's hope it was the right one."

"Eotrus." Theta wiped clean his blade and sheathed it. "Next time you have an enemy at your mercy, show him none—you will live longer."

"More Nifleheim trinkets," said Dolan as he rose from beside one of the corpses. He passed Theta several embossed gold coins, very similar to those they encountered in the Vermion Forest, and those recovered from the would-be assassins in Dor Lomion. "It seems these are quite popular around here."

"It's the callousness," said Tanch shaking his head. He looked toward Dolan who held yet another gold coin lifted from one of the dead. "The casualness of it all. You disgust me. Have you no decency at all? No regard for life?"

"Not sure," said Dolan. "Should I?"

"Did you notice, Mr. Genius, that the Alders started it?" said Ob. "They came to kill us, you fool, so close your trap, and fire that talisman thingy back up. We're not done for the day yet."

VII
GRAND MASTER PIPKORN

"Petitioners, Master Pipkorn," announced the aged retainer. "Five in all; not one have I seen before. They refuse to doff their weaponry, and, most surprisingly, they carry a locator talisman. They say that Archduke Harringgold sent them."

Pipkorn looked surprised. "Do you recognize it? The talisman."

"It does resemble the one that you gave the Duke, Master, but I cannot be certain."

"What is their business?" asked Pipkorn, a hint of tension in his voice."

"They won't state their purpose to any but you, Master. I have rarely seen a stranger lot. Their spokesman is a foul-mouthed Gnome called Too Tall. One of the others, an adept from the Tower—though I don't know his face. Another is a young knight, a nobleman by the look of him: sturdy and tall. The fourth is of part-elvish blood: ears pointed and pale skin of a sickly pallor— probably southern stock from the White Wood or perhaps farther afield."

"And the fifth?"

"A garish behemoth of polished steel and chiseled stone with a strange accent that I can't place. Carries two swords, as if one isn't enough— both of some curvy, foreign design. I would have marked him an old knight-errant, but his suit of plate is more intricate than a tourney marshal's. Probably his great grandpop's ceremonial armor.

As impressive as he looks, likely as not, neither the armor nor he has seen a real battle."

"And they won't yield their weapons?"

"Not a one."

"Show them to the rotunda. I will be there directly."

The thick stone slabs that comprised the rotunda's door were banded in burnished steel and set on ingenious pivots that swung them inward with nary a touch—almost of their own accord. Beyond lurked a circular chamber of thirty-foot diameter and murky depth. A vast and cryptic design of bizarre geometry was etched in faded pigments across the chamber's stony floor. Torches hung from cast iron sconces about the perimeter, but no doors or windows did they brighten; the room, a barren expanse of cold hard stone, save when one looked up.

A torch-illumed, domed ceiling capped the room. It bore designs geometric and pictorial—depicting scenes of fearful, non-Euclidean geometry, juxtaposed with fanciful renderings of mythological beasts battling heroes of yore. A masterwork in its day, now darkened and stained from untold years of smoke and decay. More than that, those who gazed at it too long grew faint or confused—a strange effect, not uncommon in Southeast, but stronger here than elsewhere in the district.

A mezzanine encircled the chamber on high—twenty feet above its lonely slab, though well below the great dome. Adorned with a balustrade of grey stonework, the mezzanine empty, save for a stony throne of black upon which sat a cloaked figure.

After the group stepped into the rotunda, the great doors swung closed behind them with a finality that declared that they would not open again that day or any other. Theta and Dolan stepped into the shadows, one to each side of the entry.

Within that odd chamber, the group felt small, insignificant, intimidated. An unnatural atmosphere akin to the hellish temple of the Vermion chilled them to the bone.

"Who seeks Grandmaster Pipkorn?" said the foreboding figure upon the throne, his voice resonating with the domed ceiling, his face concealed by his cloak and the chamber's shadows. "Speak you your names and your business."

Claradon looked to Ob—a worried expression covered his face.

Ob stepped forward. "I am Ob A. Faz III, Castellan and Master Scout of Dor Eotrus," he said, steamy breath rising from his mouth as he spoke, though it should not have been so cold inside. "With me is Brother Claradon Eotrus, Lord of Dor Eotrus. We seek your council in these dark times, if Pipkorn you be."

"You have a sorcerer amongst you," said Pipkorn. "Let him step forward."

Ob looked annoyed, and turned toward Tanch who stared at his feet. The wizard shivered in the cold that dominated the room, but dared not advance. Claradon motioned for him to step forward and he did, albeit slowly and tentatively. "It is I, Master Pipkorn, Par Tanch Trinagal of the

Gray Tower, House Wizard for the Eotrus."

"Talbon of Montrose is House Wizard for the Eotrus."

"I beg your pardon, Master Pipkorn, as it is not my place to contradict you, but I regret to inform you that Par Talbon fell, along with his liege, Lord Aradon, two weeks ago, deep within the Vermion Forest."

Silence ruled the chamber for some moments.

"These are losses of consequence," said Pipkorn. "The Eotrus have my sympathy."

"We thank you for that," said Claradon, stepping forward, his voice as shaky as Tanch's. "We need to speak plain and true with you about dark tidings."

Silence.

"Perhaps, your wizardship," said Ob, "we could retire to a tabled room and sit a spell as we talk?"

Silence.

"I would surely like not to shout and rather look," said Ob. "Not to mention, my neck is getting rather stiff looking up."

"We can hear and see each other well enough," said Pipkorn.

Ob sighed. "We have come to speak of The Shadow League, or The League of Light, as some call it."

Silence.

"We're trying to find a man called Korrgonn— a Leaguer by all accounts but new to Lomion," said Ob. "Has a group of nasties with him. They travel with a strange carriage."

"Why come to me with such questions?"

"Harringgold pointed us your way. The Duke

says that the League is no friend to you, nor you to them. We expect that you keep track of them as best you can."

"Why do you seek Korrgonn?"

"He and his killed several of our folk some days back."

"In the Vermion?"

"At Riker's Crossroads."

"Did Korrgonn have a hand in Aradon Eotrus' death?"

"That was trolls, down from the mountains north of us. They come with the mist, in the cold years, every now and again; always with the mist."

"I have heard such stories before, many times, but not in long years," said Pipkorn.

"Do you know anything about Korrgonn, or not?" said Ob.

"Perhaps I do. If I do, I might tell you, but not unless you tell me what really went on in the Vermion. How did Aradon Eotrus meet his end, and how did Talbon of Montrose fall?"

Silence.

"Then of Korrgonn, you will learn nothing from me."

Ob's cheeks grew red and his jaw stiffened as he clenched his teeth.

"Now look here, Mister Wizard, this Korrgonn fellow is as bad as they come and we're to stop him. If you are on our side, you should help us. But perhaps you're not. Maybe you've gone over to the League or maybe you're not Pipkorn at all, but some cloaked imposter whose mother was a Lugron," said Ob, his voice growing steadily louder. "Take that stinking hood off, come down here, and talk to us like men, or so help me, I will get up there somehow and tear you limb from limb."

Theta chuckled quietly from the shadows.

There was a pause, and then Pipkorn let out a long, slow laugh. "Well spoken." Pipkorn arose, turned, and exited through a door that appeared at his back, though it wasn't there before or at least went unnoticed.

After some moments, the great door to the rotunda opened behind them and there stood Pipkorn: a stout man of average height and of late middling years, with a bushy blond and gray mustache. Mostly bald, he had a large boil at the top center of his forehead.

"I am Pipkorn," he said in a confident, booming voice, though much diminished from its sound on high. His black robe and cowl gone, he wore a strange knit shirt that extended up to his chin, gray breeches, and soft leather boots.

Claradon, Tanch, and even Ob, stood agape, intimidated in the presence of the world's most renowned wizard.

Theta stepped from the shadows and Pipkorn met his piercing gaze. Pipkorn's eyes grew wide, his hands fidgeted against his sides, and he took a half step back. The glow vanished from his face and he seemed to physically diminish; he looked as if he was about to turn and run.

The slightest grin formed on Theta's face. "Greetings, wizard," said Theta.

Pipkorn let out a sigh. "Greetings—I had no idea that you were one of my guests. If I had, I would have made more suitable arrangements. My apologies."

"You're slipping in your old age, Pipkorn," said Theta. "Lord Angle Theta is not easy to miss, the shadows of your chamber notwithstanding."

"Indeed," said Pipkorn with a knowing nod. "Let us retire to the drawing room. There we can converse more comfortably."

"Are you kidding me?" muttered Ob. "He knows Old Pointy Hat too?"

Pipkorn turned and extended his arm toward the hallway on the right. The men filed past.

"After you, Lord Theta," said Pipkorn when only Theta and he remained.

Theta shook his head and pointed at Pipkorn and then down the hall. He would not allow Pipkorn to walk behind him. The wizard turned and headed stiff-legged down the hall, wiping his brow as he went. Theta followed, his hand never leaving the hilt of his falchion.

Unlike the menacing audience chamber, Pipkorn's drawing room was warm, with dark paneled wood, a large fireplace, and plush carpets of exotic origin. The rosewood table at its center, inlaid with a thick marble slab, hosted the group. The aged servant laid out platters of food and filled goblets with red wine.

Pipkorn spoke from the high-backed chair at the table's head while munching on cheese and crackers, crumbs collecting on his shirt. "Men and a carriage that match the description of your brigands entered Southeast yesterday morning. Several of them were on horse, more than a dozen others rode in the carriage; one of those matches the description of your Korrgonn. His companions include several captains of The Shadow League—most of them wizards: necromancers, chaos sorcerers, and the like. Some of them are not Volsungs, or at least, are Volsungs no longer; perhaps demon spawn or something else, I know not. Several Lugron also travel with them. A most unsavory lot they are. The carriage itself is magical. Rarely have I seen such as it. Its dweomer is powerful and harkens back to olden days. Above it and that entire unholy group is a sorcerous mantle nigh impenetrable."

"So you can't track them," said Theta.

"Not by magery, but my spies track them afoot. These Leaguers, however, are alert and on their guard; my agents can't get close."

"So you lost them."

"No, we just haven't got close enough to overhear their plans or to cull their numbers."

Theta looked surprised. "Then you know where they are?"

"I do. But you must understand, these men are formidable and well protected. They have many supporters. You can't just storm the place—it would mean open warfare in the streets."

"We cannot delay; Korrgonn's power will only grow. Speak quick, wizard, where are they?"

"At the Temple of Hecate, here in Southeast."

Pipkorn looked about to gauge the men's reactions.

"All we need," said Ob as he shook his head. "More damn chaos worshippers—stinking anarchists and Nifleheim lovers, one and all."

"We're doomed," said Tanch.

"The Hecate compound appears to be an abandoned warehouse, but that's a front. The Hecates control the place and run it like a fortress."

"Why doesn't the watch go in and clean them out?" said Claradon.

"The watch has been corrupted," said Pipkorn. "Just as have many parts of our government, including the High Council—as, no doubt, you noticed yesterday."

"What is their strength?" said Theta. "Their numbers?"

"That is not clear," said Pipkorn, "but enough food goes into that compound to feed two hundred folk. I would think near half of them could bear arms if pressed."

"Two hundred?" spat Ob, shaking his head. "Our own private little war."

"This is getting out of hand," said Tanch. "We can't take on two hundred fanatics."

Theta turned to Tanch and stared, eyes narrowed, until Tanch flinched and looked away.

"Master Pipkorn," said Claradon. "Korrgonn and his men must be brought to justice. Will you aid us in this?"

Pipkorn paused for some moments before answering. "I will give you what support I can, but I must work from behind the scenes for reasons both complex and private."

"A moment ago, you complained that your agents couldn't get close enough to cull their numbers," said Theta. "Have you a force that can aid us or not?"

"No," said Pipkorn. He flushed red and looked

down at the table for some moments before continuing in halting fashion. "A man—fallen from power—sometimes pretends to hold on—to more than is truly left. I trust, my lord, that you will forgive an old man for that. I will redouble my surveillance of the Hecates and send word to you of anything I learn. I regret that is all the aid that I can offer you."

"Any other questions for the good wizard?" said Theta. There were none. "Then I would speak with him in private."

"But of course," said Ob sardonically, rising, but taking his wine goblet with him.

Theta spoke not again until the others left the room, closing the door behind them. Claradon and Tanch headed to the main entry hall. Claradon couldn't help but smile when he looked back and saw Dolan's ear and Ob's too plastered to the drawing room's door.

"You no longer trust me, my lord?" said Pipkorn.

"What makes you think I ever trusted you?"

"You're tensed—ready to spring and cleave me in two should I make a false move."

"If you think of making a false move."

Pipkorn smiled.

"I have seen too many men that I knew of old, turn down the dark road," said Theta. "Even some who were known for ages to be noble and true."

"Another effect of the damnable plague," said Pipkorn. "For all my power, even I am not immune to its degenerating effects. It gnaws on the mind, saps the will, and scrambles the conscience. No evil in all creation has ever been so insidious and so persistent. And yet here we are, long years after the coming of the plague, and little the worse for it."

"We bear the scars," said Theta solemnly. "You had more hair back in the day and it wasn't so gray. And you didn't limp."

"Your memory is impressive, Lord Theta, but it's my art, not my age that has bleached my hair. The sorcery has its own draining effects, I'm afraid. As for the limp, that's new, and was courtesy of the Vizier. The bastard flung a chair into my kneecap—broke it rather badly; haven't found the correct spell to mend it, so it's healing the old-fashioned way."

"They say you fled and that you're in hiding."

"True on both counts. I do hope you weren't followed here; I wouldn't want to give up this place—so few decent spots left in Southeast."

Theta looked at him quizzically.

"The Vizier has many supporters in the Arcane Order—others like him who lust for power for power's sake. I no longer know whom I can trust. Let him have the darned Tower—just a building after all. What matters are the wizards of the order. Those of good conscience have fled to parts more secure; they bide their time, as do I. Would it be too much to ask, that you lend us your support?"

"I have no interest in the squabbles of wizards."

"You know that there's much more to this than that; all of Lomion is at stake. We're one sword thrust or one poisoned apple away from Cartegian ascending the throne—and the Chancellor will soon follow him."

"I'm only involved here to vanquish Korrgonn. I have no interest beyond that and little stomach for politics."

"But you should, my lord. Lomion is beacon of hope for this forsaken world. It's the center of trade, knowledge, and art. One million souls ply its streets at last count. Not since the days of Asgard has there been such a city. It must not fall to darkness."

"That it is large, there's no doubt, but what I have seen is already dark and squalid. A city long in its decline; a beacon no longer, if ever it was."

"Then you have seen too little or have gone blind with age. Have you walked the gardens of Rasool or gazed on the Fountains of Findin at midnight? Have you browsed the Museum of the Ancients or strolled the marbled halls of Odin's House on Hightop Hill? Have you quaffed a flagon of Elven Enerquest at the Pfister or dined in Pequod's Rest? No, my lord, too little of Lomion fair have you seen; far too little to judge."

"Perhaps this be true. I did only arrive in this city yesterday, wizard, and I have been a bit busy with Chancellors, Dukes, secret plans, and crotchety wizards—leaving little time for the culture and tourism. In any case, I have little doubt that I will see more of the dark before any of the light. I wouldst find Korrgonn before his powers grow. He must be put down before he can call up others of his ilk."

"I find it hard to believe he is as you say. Only at the beginning of the plague did such creatures enter Midgaard. Who could open such a gateway today? Who is so mad and foolish and so filled with power?"

"Name him I cannot, but the gateway was opened and through came Korrgonn. Is there anything more you can tell me of his movements or of those with him?"

"I can tell you that if you storm the Temple of Hecate with five men, you will not succeed. They are too many, even if you get the best of them somehow, the others will melt, and the whole endeavor will profit you nothing."

"Don't presume to lecture me on tactics, wizard, and I will not tell you how to make foul stew in your cauldron or instruct you on the proper techniques of turd readings."

Pipkorn paled. "I meant no offense, Lord Theta," he said as a bead of sweat rolled down his temple.

"If he was offended, old boy," whispered Ob from beyond the door, quiet-like, so that only Dolan heard, "I expect you would be dead."

The meeting over, Theta made for the door. "Rascatlan," he said over his shoulder, "If Korrgonn is expecting me, I will visit you one last time." He stood motionless for a few seconds before striding down the hall. Pipkorn closed the door, turned his back to it, slumped against it, and let out a sigh as beads of sweat trickled down his forehead.

VIII
THE TEMPLE OF HECATE

From darkened alley, Claradon watched a near continuous stream of cloaked figures approach the entrance to the decrepit warehouse that housed the Temple of Hecate. Four guards stood at the doors and inspected tokens that the figures displayed when they approached.

"Hecate's temple is well guarded," said Tanch. "Unlikely that we could sneak in. Perhaps we should turn back before we're seen."

"I'm not inclined to," said Theta.

"What do you propose?" said Ob. "Just a knockety knock and a 'by your leave' at the front door? Perhaps if we ask nicely, they will bring old Korrgonn out all trussed up like a holiday pig for our pleasure."

Theta ignored him.

"We will need more men for certain, if we hope to accomplish anything here," said Tanch. "Don't you agree?"

"Would the Duke give us soldiers?" said Theta.

"Maybe he would send some of Sluug's rangers," said Ob, "but not his guardsmen. With the rangers, the Duke and Sluug have deniability—the rangers guild being all secretive and such. Few know their members' faces or names. If they're captured, Sluug could disown them, and the Duke might come out clean. Guardsmen are a different thing. Putting them into action would bring open warfare between the

346

Harringgolds and the League. From what we've seen, the Duke is not ready for that. Even if he gives us a squad or two of rangers, them plus our men, won't be enough. The place is too big; there are too many in there."

"Where does that leave us?" said Tanch.

"Perhaps a bluff," said Claradon. "The tokens they're showing the guards look like the coins that we found on Alder's men; maybe they were headed here all along, and we were just targets of opportunity."

"Show the guards the coins, and we're in," said Ob, his face lighting up. "That would be a bold move, for certain. Reckless even."

"Do we have enough coins?" said Claradon.

Theta held out his palm, displaying several coins. "We do."

"Excuse me, dear friends," said Tanch, "but we agreed this would be a reconnaissance mission, not an assault—that's why we didn't take the rest of our men. We should go back and get them and whatever other help we can muster if we're to even attempt to storm this place. Artol, Glimador, and the others are waiting for us in Dor Lomion— there is no reason for us to do this alone."

"A soldier must take the opportunities that present themselves," said Theta. "If we leave and come back with more men, the enemy may have dispersed; we may lose Korrgonn's trail. I can't allow that. We're going in."

"This is madness," said Tanch. "What—how?—"

Ob chuckled. "It is madness, alright, but I like the sound of it. Walk in all la-de-da with a small group, take out Korrgonn before they know what's happening, and run it. Bold and reckless, but it just might work."

"I can't go along with this," said Tanch. "You will be the death of us all. What can we five do against an army of madmen?"

"Look, listen, and learn," said Theta, "while keeping silent."

"You think your delicate back can handle that, Magic Boy?" said Ob.

Tanch gave up and said nothing else.

Soon the stream of cloaked figures that approached the temple subsided, but they waited some minutes more.

"Enough lurking," said Theta. He strode from the alley, cloak pulled close about him, hood up. The others scrambled after him. Theta displayed the coin as he approached the guardsmen, but did not pause or slow his stride as he went past. The guards looked at the coin, but made no move to stop or question him. Beyond the door was a small antechamber. Decrepit hallways of rotted wood, musty air, and peeling paint led in three directions, and a stair led down. The stair was new and wide, of thick, rough-hewn, unfinished timbers. Theta peered about for a moment, and then proceeded down, the others following.

The stair emptied into a large room with marble tiled floors and paneled mahogany walls inset with hundreds of wooden pegs upon which hung cloaks and outerwear of all descriptions. The room's perimeter was lined with many large trunks and wooden crates, most empty, but a few contained blood-red, hooded robes.

At the far end of the room stood two ornately carved wooden doors banded in copper. From beyond those, many voices could be heard.

Ob and Dolan rummaged through the crates, examining the robes. They tossed one that looked like it might fit to each of the others, and they all put them on.

A tall, lanky man garbed in leather and girded with steel dashed down the stairs with such speed that he slid several feet across the marble floor. His suit and sword were of a style common to sea captains and naval officers.

"Did the service start yet? Did I miss anything good?" he said as he grabbed a robe from the nearest crate. He pulled it over his head and put up the hood though it was a size or two too small. "I hate to be late. I'm not the last, am I?" he asked Theta.

Theta didn't respond.

"Name's Fizdar; Fizdar Firstbar the Corsair, first mate of *The Black Falcon*," he said standing tall and sticking out his chest.

Theta stared at him, expressionless.

"Surely you have heard of *The Black Falcon*? Dylan Slaayde's ship? Scourge of the seas? The ship that did Minoc run in four days flat?"

Theta, still expressionless.

Fizdar shrugged. "What's your name?" he said.

With no expression on his face, Theta spoke in a slow, measured, and cold voice. "Mister Fancy Pants."

Fizdar looked down at Theta's legs, but his long red robe covered whatever pants he might be wearing. "I'll take your word for it. And what do you do?"

"He kills people what ask too many questions," said Ob.

Theta smiled.

"Smashing," said Fizdar smiling back. "I always wanted to be an assassin. You probably work for The Hand, right? Darned tough bastards you men are, or so I hear." Fizdar looked Theta up and down and seemed properly convinced of Theta's toughness. "Glad to meet you," he said extending a hand that Theta ignored.

"Maybe we should get inside before the whole thing is over with," said Ob as he pushed Fizdar along toward the doors.

The moment Fizdar pulled one door ajar, the jabber of hundreds of talkers filled their ears. The open door revealed a cavernous chamber, far larger than they ever would have imagined, crammed with wooden pews and red robed cultists. Some few thousands filled the chamber's seats over which hung a heady cloud of pipe smoke and incense. Scores more cultists stood or milled about along the sides of the auditorium, having found no suitable seats up close. A throng it was—a gathering of all the cultists of Lomion City, it must have been.

The ceiling was almost lost in smoke and darkness some thirty feet above. The walls were paneled in rich woods and the floors tiled in polished marble. At the far end of the place was a raised stage upon which sat a dozen or so richly clad figures. Their robes were of intricate design, each different and ornate as a noble's coat-of-arms. At the stage's center, a basalt altar, plain in features but imposing in stature. Guards with red tabards stood in groups about the chamber's perimeter.

"Dead gods, so many," said Tanch quietly, though Fizdar heard him.

"Our numbers grow every day," said Fizdar. "The good news spreads and attracts the masses. We've merchants and judges, wizards and knights, lords and ladies, and even Councilmen swelling our ranks now. Now we will see real change in Lomion. We will take our country back."

The group made their way to a pew near the back, not far from the door.

IX
THE OTHER PATH

A stately man in ornate red and black priestly robes gripped a golden staff topped with a polished gemstone as he walked across the stage to a lectern beside the altar. At the sight of him, a hush came over the crowd. This man wore no hood or cowl. He was middle-aged, handsome, with receding gray and black close-cropped hair, deep booming voice, and the wild, shifty eyes of the fanatic.

"Silence," he boomed, though the place had already gone quiet. When he spoke, the large red stone atop his staff pulsed and glowed with a dim, eerie light.

His voice was robust and distinct and held a strange melodic tenor that was captivating and hypnotic. "As with each gathering, today we welcome many new friends to our family," he said. "The duty falls to each of us to make them feel at home and at ease amongst us, so that they may experience the love and joy that is our family and our faith. To be one with us and one with the Lord our god."

"I greet you tonight, my brothers and sisters, one and all. For the newcomers—know that I am Ginalli, High Priest of Azathoth, the one true god. I have the honor of shepherding this growing flock."

"You all know that we are in challenging times. Many forces align against us. Darkness and evil

352

seeks to undo us from all sides. Of late, troubling rumors have spread through our family. Rumors of gods walking Midgaard. Rumors of impending doom. Rumors of an ancient evil risen from the ashes of time to threaten us and all we hold dear. I have called this special gathering of all our flock to put an end to these rumors and to your fears, and to fill you with the everlasting and pure truth of the one true god. For through truth, faith, and unswerving adherence to duty do we become closer to the Lord."

"Let us begin our holy service with the prayer of the faithful." Ginalli lifted his staff and soundly thumped its end on the stage, the booming echo of the impact reflecting off the chamber's ceiling and walls. At the same time, the unnatural, crimson glow that emanated from the stone at the staff's apex brightened.

"First and always, know that Azathoth, and we that follow him are family, your family—the only family you will ever truly need."

"The faithful are our family," chanted the cultists in practiced fashion—more than a few reading from booklets that they held in their hands. "And Azathoth is our father."

"Blessed be the Lord," chanted the cultists.

"Cast off your earthly ties and be beholden to none, save Azathoth your lord, and his family, his faithful."

"It is right to cast off our earthly ties," they chanted.

"Azathoth, father to us all, teaches us that each man is of equal value to all others and entitled to the same benefits, and happiness, and respect."

"We are all equal and deserving," chanted the multitude in near unison.

"But equality eludes us, not through our faults, but through the faults of others—those of the disbelievers, the sinners, the hypocrites, and the hoarders of wealth. I say to you, why should some loathsome nobleman or disbelieving, fatted merchant be permitted to lounge in a grand manor house while you starve in a hovel or sleep in a ruin on the cold hard ground? Should he not share his home and table with you and yours, as would your brother or your father?"

"His home and table are rightly ours," chanted the faithful, many beginning to sway from side to side as they spoke, listened, and stared.

"What of his horses, his land, his fine clothes? Are you any less worthy than him to partake in these pleasures?"

"We are worthy and deserving of all," they chanted, now in almost monotone fashion.

"Is he better than you? More deserving than you? Azathoth teaches us, he is no better."

"No one is better than I," they chanted, Dolan now joining in, just a bit out of sync with the others, as he knew not the refrain.

"Why should your neighbor have a beautiful, buxom wife kept only to himself while you are alone and miserable? Why should you not be free to enjoy her favors as well?"

"Let her favors be freely given to us," chanted the faithful.

"He must share what he has with us, and if he does not—if he dares refuse to obey the divine laws, the very will of the one true god, then he is no believer."

"A heretic we will mark him," they chanted. "A traitor we will name him."

"From him, we must take all," said Ginalli. "Such is Azathoth's will."

"Such is Azathoth's command," spoke the enthralled. Ob now mumbled along, glassy eyed and expressionless.

Theta shook his head and clenched his jaw.

"In this way, the greedy, the hoarders of wealth and ill-gotten gain will come to know poverty and loss and loneliness and despair."

"Let them know despair," they chanted.

Tanch's eyelids became droopy, his expression dazed. His chin rested on his chest.

"Those who repent among them will come to see the wisdom of the one god's ways—the wisdom of his justice and equality and shared prosperity for all."

"The repentant will come to know the Lord."

"And if the disbeliever resists, we must take all that he has and all that he ever will have, for the good of all."

"Even unto his life," they chanted, shaking their fists in the air—Dolan, Ob, and Tanch among them. Claradon felt sleepy; he fought to keep his eyes open.

"Even unto his very soul," said Ginalli. "Deliver his black, wicked soul to Azathoth who will cleanse and purify it, mercifully gifting the disbeliever with another chance to find a place among the faithful when he is reborn anew on Midgaard, his sins washed away. Such is Azathoth's boundless goodness and mercy.

"Some things never change," said Theta under his breath as he recalled a far-off day when he stood beside Azathoth, and when he was known not as the Lord Angle Theta, but as The Lord's Arkon, Thetan.

"How long will it take them to reach Pergillum?" said Gabriel, alight in polished, silvered armor.

"Three days," said Azathoth, a glowing figure in white—at once beautiful, but indistinct.

"A hard journey on foot carrying such a burden," said Thetan as he sat atop a boulder to Azathoth's right, clad in armor similar to Gabriel's, though golden in hue.

"The stones of my law are heavy, 'tis true, and its vessel is the heavier, but my faithful must bear it, though they will strain and stumble."

A long line of pilgrims and soldiers stretched out in the valley far below and before them. At the vanguard of the host was a large, rectangular chest of golden hue, supported by poles needled through golden rungs bolted to the chest's sides. Atop the chest, a golden tapestry and two golden statues honoring the Lord's greatest servants, his Arkons. Twelve large men bore the poles on their shoulders, six to a side. Ornate tapestries hung between the men's shoulders and the chest, preventing direct contact between the men and holy vessel. As they passed over the rocky ground, a man on the right stumbled and went down; the bearer behind tripped over him and fell headlong to the rocky soil.

The chest overbalanced and pitched forward.

All the bearers on the right side fell, their pole spearing into the ground. As the chest tipped, threatening to crash to the rocky ground, a large soldier lunged in and steadied it. When his bare hands touched the side of the chest, Azathoth stood, anger flashed on his face, his glow turned from white to blood red. With the soldier's momentary aid, the bearers regained control of the chest and brought it gently and safely down. The soldier dropped to his knees and broke into a prayer imploring Azathoth's forgiveness for daring to touch the holy vessel. He knew well the terrible penalty for such irreverence.

Azathoth raised his hand to the heavens—

"Please, my lord," said Gabriel. "The man sought only to safeguard your holy word."

Azathoth pointed the index finger of his right hand, first at the heavens, and then at the soldier. A bolt of lightning fired down from on high and pierced the soldier's chest, leaving a massive, blackened wound behind. His corpse collapsed to the ground. Those around him wailed in horror, cringed in terror, and beseeched the Lord's forgiveness and mercy.

"He broke the holy law," boomed Azathoth. He turned toward Gabriel with wild eyes that still glowed red, "and for that he had to die."

Gabriel's eyes grew wide at Azathoth's reaction, and his face went white; the hairs stood up on his neck.

"A harsh penalty," said Thetan, concern and confusion filling his face, "for one who sought only to do good."

Azathoth turned toward Thetan. "Harsh,

indeed," he said, his aspect now returned to normal. "But necessary, and all part of my grand design for the world of man. Had that man lived, the tapestry of mankind would have taken turns toward darkness, turns toward chaos that I cannot allow. Never fear, all you need know of this and more will be revealed to you, my henchmen, in due time. Such is my will."

"Yes, my lord," said Gabriel.

"As you say, my lord," said Thetan as he stared at the ground.

"**G**lory to the merciful lord," chanted the cultists.

"This, the one true god teaches us. This is the way; this is his command and by following it, we will help to bring about an age of peace, an age of shared prosperity, of equal outcome, and happiness for all. A world where there is no poverty, no homelessness, no hunger, and no war. The world owes us no less."

Claradon's vision narrowed until all he could see was the red glowing stone of Ginalli's staff; all he could hear was the sound of Ginalli's voice.

"The world owes us no less," they chanted. Claradon mumbled along, his will no longer his own, as if in a trance.

"The kingdom owes us this—and it must provide or we will bring it down in Azathoth's holy name."

"In Azathoth's holy name," shouted the faithful.

"Down with Tenzivel," said Ginalli. "Death to Lomion."

358

"Death to Lomion!" chanted the enthralled, fists pumping in the air.

"This is the path to Azathoth. This is our path—the path that we have no choice but to follow. The one truth path."

"We will follow Azathoth's holy path," chanted the gathered faithful. "This we vow. This we vow."

Claradon snapped from his trance when Theta cuffed the back of his neck and stamped on his foot. They gave Ob, Dolan, and Tanch the same treatment to free them from their daze.

Ginalli grinned from ear to ear as he scanned the mesmerized audience, his staff now quieted.

"I am proud to stand before you tonight my brothers and sisters. But despite the solemn vows that we have spoken tonight and many times afore, we, Azathoth's faithful, have oft strayed from the holy path. We have strayed from the will of our lord and master. Too long have we tolerated the evil rich, the hoarders of wealth; too long have we tolerated a corrupt government whose secular laws inhibit our freedoms. Too long have we tolerated the hypocritical Churchmen who call themselves good but do only evil. Too long have we tolerated the wicked among us. But Azathoth has not forgotten us, he sees our plight, he knows our hearts and our minds. To us, his faithful, his earthly family, Azathoth has sent two of his greatest servants, his most loyal followers and lieutenants to show us the way to salvation, to put us back on the path to righteousness and to lead us into battle against the unbelievers. To us, the Lord has sent Lord Mortach the Merciful and Lord Gallis Korrgonn the Just—the glorious son of our lord, Azathoth, himself."

From beyond the doors at the rear of the stage emerged a giant, skull-faced monstrosity of articulated black armor and massive white sword alight with otherworldly fire. Beside him, a striking-looking tall man of golden eyes. The Nifleheim Lords strode to the black thrones behind the altar and sat.

Gasps and murmurs raced through the crowd.

"It's true," shouted one of the faithful. "The Arkons of the Lord are here."

"They walk amongst us," called out another.

Several people fainted. Many others fell to their knees and covered their heads. Some began to pray.

"It's judgment day," yelled one cultist.

"Judgment day," screamed another. That man pulled out a long dagger, and held it before his chest in both hands. "Dear lord, take my soul," he yelled, and plunged the dagger deep into his own breast. He collapsed in a wellspring of blood. Those around him gasped in shock and backed away.

Ginalli's eyes went wide and his mouth dropped open at the sight of this.

"Judgment day," yelled the enthralled.

Several others in the crowd pulled out daggers and stabbed themselves, or those standing next to them. Screams erupted throughout the crowd. People backed away in fear from the dagger-wielders. The crowd began to panic.

Ginalli waved his hands, slammed the butt of his staff on the stage, and raised his voice to catch the crowd. The staff's head glowed much brighter than before and pulsed, seeming to cry out.

"Hear me my brothers and sisters," shouted Ginalli. "Hear me!" The crowd quieted down— Ginalli's intervention staying the hands of several other would-be martyrs and murderers. "The sacrifices of our brethren," pointing to those expiring on the now crimson floor, "will bring great favor on us by the lord, but he has other tasks for the rest of us. He wants us to live and spread his word to the unbelievers, so stay your daggers and put them away."

"These holy messengers," pointing now to Mortach and Korrgonn, "these Arkons from the lord are here to aid us in the coming struggles, to help us to bring about Azathoth's will. We will serve them and obey them as we would our lord himself."

"So shall it be," said Ginalli, upraising his hands.

"So shall it be," chanted the faithful.

"It is not our blood, it is the blood of the unrepentant infidels that Azathoth commands be spilled."

From offstage, six of the faithful carried a large, richly dressed man who was bound and gagged.

"This man is a hoarder of wealth," said Ginalli. "He would not give the scraps from his table to a starving beggar child. He forbade one of our finest brethren to marry his fair daughter. He refused to pay the faithful's collectors the just tithe asked of him so that his ill-gotten wealth could be equitably divided amongst the worthy. Worst of all, he struck one of our brothers when he called on him to collect what is rightfully ours by Azathoth's laws. In this life, his soul is beyond saving; his evil runs deep. We must send him to the Lord for cleansing. It is the merciful thing to do."

"Send him to Azathoth," yelled several in the crowd.

Others took up the cheer. "Send him to Azathoth! Send him to the Lord!"

"The Lord will cleanse him and his black soul," said Ginalli. "Azathoth will wash the evil from his stony heart and scour the blight from his black soul. And through Azathoth's grace, he will be reborn anew, pure, and unblemished. The Lord's infinite mercy will provide him another opportunity for a pious and faithful life."

The guards tore the merchant's clothes, exposing his bare flesh.

Mortach rose and strode up to the altar, the merchant tied down and helpless before it. The Nifleheim Lord's massive form, its head naught but whited bones and glowing golden eyes, loomed over the merchant. Mortach pulled a long curved dagger from its belt.

"The dagger of salvation," called out Ginalli.

"The dagger of salvation," boomed the cultists in retort.

Mortach held the dagger high in both hands, and moved it slowly from side to side, displaying it to the faithful. Mortach mouthed words that none could hear save perhaps the doomed merchant, though few failed to see the long forked tongue alight with hellfire that wagged in its mouth as it spoke. A drop of spittle fell from Mortach's maw and landed on the merchant's shoulder, sending him into convulsions when it seared his mortal flesh.

Mortach grasped the blade in his right hand and placed the tip against the merchant's throat. The merchant squirmed, desperately trying to free himself, but his bonds held fast, his face a mask of fear and horror. Through his gag issued the stifled moans and gasps of a man begging for mercy, pleading for his life; his entreats, unheard and unacknowledged.

Mortach plunged the blade into the base of the merchant's throat and drew it, slowly and deliberately, from neck to groin; a vicious wound more than an inch deep. The man struggled and tried to scream, but his gag stifled his cries.

"See how he suffers," shouted Ginalli. "Even now he fights the will of our lord and master. Even now he rejects god."

Blood streamed over the altar and drained into the gutter system along its edges, funneling down into a large goblet. Mortach sliced the man's wrists, increasing the flow of his lifeblood.

Ginalli spoke again when the goblet was full. "Is there any forgiveness, any mercy, for so vile a creature as this who does not repent even at the end?" said Ginalli.

"Mercy," shouted much of the crowd.

"Yes, my brothers and sisters," said Ginalli. "Mercy we shall show him, despite his despicable ways."

Mortach plunged its knife into the center of the merchant's chest, piercing his heart and ending his misery.

"Mortach the Merciful," shouted Ginalli.

"Mortach the Merciful," shouted the cultists.

Three guards cut the merchant's bonds and carried his corpse away while others dragged a second man to the altar and bound him upon it. Several other citizens stood bound and well guarded in the wings, awaiting their turn upon the altar.

"We can't just sit here and watch this," whispered Claradon, squatting so he could speak in Ob's ear.

"Quiet, lad," said Ob. "There is nothing we can do but watch, or else die with them. Far too many of these lunatics."

"We should try. If we work our way to the front, we may be able to save one or two of them."

"Don't be an idiot, boy. Even Mr. Fancy Pants couldn't fight his way clear of this place. There are thousands of them, for Odin's sake—we've no chance, no chance at all. Just put your teeth together and watch."

"I can't look," said Claradon from beneath his cowl.

Ob grabbed Claradon's forearm and squeezed it so tightly that Claradon thought his arm would break. "Keep your eyes open, boy," growled Ob. "Never forget one moment of this, and bring it to mind any time you think to give up this fight or come to peace with these scum."

Claradon heeded Ob's direction. He watched it all. The spectacles at the altar went on for some time. Bound and gagged citizens were dragged out and tied to the altar, one after another. Various and sundry charges were leveled against them, though no evidence or defenses were ever presented. The results were always the same; each of the accused was cut, bled, and ultimately murdered by Mortach. Their spilled blood filled goblet after goblet.

Mortach took a sip of the blood that filled each goblet, and then passed them in turn to Korrgonn who similarly imbibed. The sacrifices completed, one final goblet was brought forth and placed on the altar.

Korrgonn stepped up to the altar holding a blade in his right hand. He held up his left hand, fingers spread for all to see, and placed the dagger against one of them. And then he cut it, and the cultists gasped in horror, their reactions, far more profound and emotional than any they offered the sacrificed citizens. Three strokes and the finger was severed. Korrgonn dumped it into the goblet. He let the blood drain freely from the stump, filling the goblet to the brim.

"Through Lord Korrgonn's divine body and holy blood, the very life essence provided him by his father, Lord Azathoth, shall we be blessed," said Ginalli.

The cup of Korrgonn's flesh and blood was passed to Ginalli and to each of the menacing figures seated on the stage, the Arkons of The Shadow League, their faces hidden behind dark red cowls. Those who were partly visible wore features frightening to behold: Lugron and demon blood surely polluted their veins.

A drop of Korrgonn's blood was poured into each sacrificial goblet, which was then topped off with water. The unholy brew was stirred with snake-headed daggers and then passed out to the faithful—each cultist obliged to drink. Some in the crowd fought for the goblets, and gulped down their gory contents, greedy and frenzied. Others seemed reluctant, but drank nonetheless. A chalice reached Ob, who raised it to his lips and pretended to drink, and then passed it to Theta. Theta grasped the goblet strangely betwixt both gloved palms, and then passed it to Claradon, making no pretense at drinking it.

"Your gloves," whispered Theta. Claradon saw that Theta touched the cup only with his fencing gloves, which covered his palms and the backs of his hands, the same as Claradon's. Claradon did the same, keeping the exposed flesh of his fingers clear. He pretended to drink, but he did not let the liquid or the cup touch his lips, and then passed it to Fizdar. As the cup changed hands, the tip of Claradon's pinky touched the befouled metal. A wave of searing pain crashed through Claradon, threatening to send him to his knees. Theta grabbed him under the arm and steadied him. Those around paid little heed, as many swooned and more than a few vomited after imbibing the foul draught. No one save Claradon was burned. He bore a blackened fingertip for the rest of his days.

X
HE WHO CANNOT BE NAMED

Ginalli resumed his place at the lectern. "With the aid of the heavenly servants of our divine lord, nothing can stop us. Nothing can prevent us from cleansing Midgaard of its evil."

"There is one who is a threat," said Korrgonn in his booming, raspy voice. "Tell them priest; speak the story of the traitor."

Ginalli looked startled, but quickly regained his bearing. "Yes, my lord," he said. "In the before time, when the world was young, the Arkons served Azathoth in the blessed land of Vaeden. The holy Arkons served the Lord in all his good and just works and shepherded the race of man from primitive barbarism toward civilization. You all know the story of he who was the most beloved of all Azathoth's servants—he whose name has been struck from our memories and our sacred scrolls. That one betrayed our lord and master. Azathoth merely commanded him to punish some vile evildoers—to hold them justly accountable for their wickedness, for their crimes; but he refused—he refused to obey the lord. Instead, he sided with the dark powers, with all that is vile and evil, and soon became the antithesis of all that is good. And his corruption spread."

"He gathered unto him all the depraved, the shunned, the pariahs, and launched an unholy rebellion against our dear lord. For this, he and his minions were cast out of Vaeden and thrown down to Midgaard in disgrace. His rebellion was crushed, but his exile brought him not to repentance and only served to expand the depths of his evil.

"He sought out the gates of Abaddon, and using unholy, forbidden magics opened them, setting loose demon spawn and all manner of vile creatures on our dear Midgaard. Untold thousands died at the hands of those wretched monsters, and at those of the traitor and his dark minions. Our lord wept for a hundred years over the evil done to his children. So hurt was he by these happenings, he withdrew from our sphere, withdrew from our lives.

"It is said that the Lord resides now at the very core of the universe; waiting for the glories of his creation to be restored and for all life to worship him again with all their very being. Before he left us, he rewarded his faithful Arkons, those beloved of him that fought against the traitor. They ascended to the paradise of Nifleheim where their powers were enhanced in wondrous ways beyond measure—the better to serve our lord. And through their power and our faith, these Arkons can on occasion travel back to our world to aid us in the struggle against evil.

"This story has been told in various forms for ages beyond record. Legend holds that the traitor walks Midgaard still. We call him the Bogeyman, the Prince of Lies, the Traitor, the Harbinger of Doom, and myriad other blasphemous names. What you didn't know, my dear brothers and sisters, is that the Harbinger of Doom is no mere fable, no will-o'-the-wisp. He is a real being—the embodiment, the very personification of evil. And he is near. He is amongst us. He is in Lomion."

A gasp and shudder permeated the audience.

As Ginalli scanned the crowd, Claradon looked over at Theta who stood tensed; he adjusted his hood, his left hand on his sword hilt.

"Who is he?" shouted one cultist. "Where is he?"

"What name does he go by?" yelled another.

"He must be destroyed," shouted another.

"Where is he?" shouted the audience. "Where is the traitor? We must bring him down. He must pay!"

Korrgonn stepped to the front of the stage, raised his arm, and pointed directly at Theta.

"He is there," boomed Korrgonn.

"Oh, shit!" said Ob.

"Oh, shit!" said Tanch.

"Oh, shit!" said Claradon.

"Who's he pointing at?" said Dolan.

The crowd gasped, and yelled, and parted about Theta.

"Run," said Theta as he grabbed Fizdar about the shoulder; a confused look filled the seaman's face. "Kill the traitor," boomed Theta. Then he flung Fizdar toward the crowd—Fizdar's face in a panic.

"Not me," yelled Fizdar. "It's not me!" he said, but few could hear him and no one cared.

Dozens dived in, fighting to tear Fizdar to pieces.

Korrgonn turned toward Mortach. "Go after him. Kill him."

Mortach leaped from the stage and thundered

after Theta, tossing aside any that blocked its path.

The crowd panicked, screaming and shouting; people fled in all directions, running for the exits. The guards blocked the doors, but the crowd barreled through them. Theta and Ob rushed from the auditorium and through the cloakroom; around them, the crowd spilled over the trunks, crates, and coats. More than several cultists went down and were trampled. Theta barreled through anyone in his way and bounded up the stair to the entry hall above, Ob close on his heels.

Mortach tore through the crowd, knocking his own followers aside like chaff. "I see you traitor," he bellowed.

As Theta and Ob reached the foyer, a shriek of cracking wood sang out. The panicked cultists ahead screamed when the rotted floor beneath their pounding feet dropped away and sent them toppling into darkness. With too much momentum and untold cultists on his heels, Theta couldn't stop, but managed to veer to the side, and skirted the edge of the jagged opening, Ob following. Like lemmings, the cultists behind poured over the edge, and screamed and flailed away as they fell. Those who tried desperately to halt were shoved over the edge by the panicked crowd behind.

Theta and Ob dashed down a side corridor, which promptly collapsed behind them, swallowing those few cultists who had been able to follow in their path. Groaning beams ever threatening to give way beneath their feet, Theta and Ob made their way quickly but warily through a maze of darkened, cobwebbed corridors filled of rodents, refuse, and rotted wood. After a time they came upon a dead end, blocked by a thick steel door.

"A draft," said Ob as he neared the door.

"It's an outside door," said Theta as he tried to open it. "Held fast."

Ob studied the door. "It is melted against the frame. Wizard's work. Should we go back? Try another way?"

"They've probably blocked all the exits, save the one at the front," said Theta. "We must force our way through the door." Theta pulled off his robe, produced a war hammer from his belt, and jammed its pointed end between door and frame, attempting to pry the door open.

"Hurry, Theta," said Ob, looking over his shoulder back down the darkened hallway. "Hurry."

Sounds of heavy boots on rotted wood filled the air.

"**S**omeone approaches," said Ob.

"It is Mortach," said Theta, as he strained against the door. Moments later, he had wrenched a section of the half-inch thick steel plate at the bottom of the door away from the frame. Too small a breach for Theta, but wide enough for Ob to squeeze through.

"Go through," said Theta, holding the bent plate in place, his muscles straining.

"I can help," said Ob.

"Not this time. Get clear. Go!"

Ob slipped through. Theta released the plate and it sprang partially back into place. He stood and drew his falchion. Mortach of Nifleheim emerged from the darkened hall.

"Greetings, Mikel," said Theta.

"I be Mortach," it said. Steaming saliva dripped from its skeletal maw.

"Not always. Once you were a man. Once you were my friend."

"No longer," said Mortach. "Not since you betrayed our lord."

Theta shook his head. "'Twas he that betrayed us; after all this time, can you not see that? Can you not see the path of ruin on which you dwell?"

"You are mad, traitor. I have ever followed the way of the lord; I have ever been faithful. 'Tis you who have strayed. 'Tis you who are evil."

"I am evil? You are the ones that murder; you

are the ones that drink the blood of innocents. How many died beneath your knife today? And you call me evil?" Theta's voice grew loud and bitter. "You broke down those doors all those years ago, and murdered those children before their parents' eyes. If that is not evil, what is? I have not forgotten that black deed. It endures as a stain upon the world, and upon your very soul; if a soul you still do have. Being good is doing good and being evil is doing evil—a simple axiom. Is it truly beyond you?"

"We tread old ground, Thetan, ground long since trampled and best forgotten. I will say once more as I have said afore: just because your puny mind cannot grasp the greater good of Azathoth's holy plan doesn't make that plan evil, but it does make you a blind fool unworthy of the honors once afforded you. If only you could see clearly you would know that Azathoth is love and goodness and justice and that following his commands, his laws, is doing good—it cannot be anything but."

"Why did you lose your faith, Thetan—you who were most beloved and greatest of us all? Why did you betray us?"

Mortach's question brought Theta back, for the merest of moments, to a time ages past.

"There is good in nearly all these people," said Thetan as thunderous rains pounded down about him, Azathoth to his left. Below, a roaring torrent of water flooded through the streets of a large town, sweeping people, livestock, and less sturdy structures away. Only the tops of the tallest spires could be seen in the nearby valley, already fully engulfed.

"They have turned their backs on me," said Azathoth. "They worship false idols, fake gods, and their own riches. Their black deeds make me regret creating them. Even now, few repent for their sins. They have brought this fate upon themselves. Only the one family deserves saving."

"You have shown them your terrible power these last days, my lord; surely you are moved by their entreats for forgiveness, for mercy. Let them live, Lord, I beg you."

"Thetan, most loyal and greatest of all my Arkons, you have ever been a voice of restraint and compassion. This I value and love, but know this: my plan, my vision, is long and bold and deep and know that though you cannot see the good of it, I can. Know that in the end, this path is the righteous one. You must have faith."

"Why not then at least take them into Vaeden; why make them suffer in the depths?"

"One will come whose sacrifice will free them. It is all part of my plan, so fear not. One boon I will grant them. No matter their future transgressions, never again will I destroy the whole of Midgaard by flood."

The floodwaters rose farther and the buildings washed away, great and small. Screams of the drowning carried on the winds. Tears welled in Thetan's eyes, and trickled down his cheeks, mixing with the pounding rain.

"**M**ikel, after all these ages," said Theta. "After all you have seen, all the pain and suffering you have caused, do you still truly think you are on the side

374

of right and truth and justice?"

"I am on the side of Azathoth—as I always have been and ever will be," said Mortach. "I ask you one last time before I send you to your fate: why did you betray us?"

"Because Azathoth went mad. Because Azathoth became twisted and corrupt." Theta's voice rose and nearly shook the building. "Because he commanded me to do things for which I will ever be ashamed. Because his wickedness corrupted the Arkons and blinded us all. Even now you walk in a fog. By all that is holy, have you looked at yourself? Have you looked at what you have become? You are a monster—a thing."

"Tis you who walk in a fog, Thetan. I hoped that there was still some remnant of goodness in you, however small. I hoped that I could reason with you and bring you back to the Lord, but you are lost, Thetan. There is no saving you; I see that now." There was no flesh upon Mortach's face to read, but his voice harbored hesitation, and even fear. "I regret this reunion can only end one way," he said, raising his blade in salute, "by the old way of the sword."

"So be it," said Theta.

"My powers have grown," said Mortach, "far beyond your ken. And for all your long years, you are still but a man, nothing more. You are no match for me."

Theta grinned. "Then come forward, Mikel, and show me your quality."

Mortach made no move forward. "Even if you slay me, Thetan, this will not be over. You will not be free. You will never be safe; never be at peace. The Arkons will come for you and there will be nowhere to hide. You will pay for driving the Lord from us. You will be haunted and hunted down through all the years. And you will be alone."

"With Gabriel's passing, you are the last of the fallen. You stand alone. You will die, Thetan—and the Arkons will lay your corpse upon the holy altar of Haerg, and we will devour your soul."

"No, brother. Your brethren will not come for me. I will come for them. I will kill them all. Every one. Know too that Azathoth did not abandon you, brother. He is gone from the world for one reason and one reason only: because I killed him and cut out his black heart."

Mortach's eyes grew wide and he momentarily froze. Theta leaped toward him, blade burning bright.

Ob pressed against the far side of the steel portal, seeing nothing of the scene beyond, but hearing every word, every movement, every breath. A quick advance; a loud howl followed by maneuvering booted feet, and a clash of steel louder than Ob had ever heard. Blows of incalculable, titanic force followed one upon another at speeds incredible for rapiers or foils, but these were heavy battle blades. How the blades themselves survived the clash, unknown. On and on it went; a duel for the ages. Finally, a series of blows struck flesh and severed bone; fountains of blood erupted from some mortal wound (all sounds that Ob knew all too well and could never mistake). A crash. One was down. One was dead.

Ob backpedaled from the building, too afraid to remain at the door, too stunned to run. He squatted some feet from the door, straining to hear any sound from within, poised to flee, but he couldn't flee—he had to know which one yet lived.

Some moments passed, and then Ob's courage returned and his curiosity moved his ear again to the door. Sweat dripped down his brow just as a mighty blow from within struck the door and sent him reeling. Ob crashed to the ground, rolled, and was on his feet in an instant. A second blow battered the door, bending and bulging the heavy plate in its frame. Ob had seen enough. He could not take the chance that it was Mortach that lived. He had to get clear. He turned and fled to a darkened alley across the way and dove behind some crates.

A series of titanic blows struck the door and crushed it ever outward. Finally, it burst free and crashed down, blasted from its hinges. A figure stood shadowed in the doorway for some seconds, then stepped outside.

Theta. It was Theta. He stood straight and tall, chin high, and looked up and down the way, holding his massive battle hammer in his left hand. No one was about. A large sack dangled from his right hand, filled of something rather large, rather round. Theta walked to the alley in which Ob hid, looking this way and that as he went. Ob remained hidden—having heard what he heard, he was too frightened to move. When Theta reached the alley, he staggered against the wall, then turned and slumped down—his back against the hard stone. He groaned with pain and slumped over unmoving for some time.

Ob was rooted, frozen. He could not believe what he had heard. Theta is he who cannot be named; Theta is the Slayer, the Bogeyman, the Widowmaker, the Harbinger of Doom, the Prince of Lies, The Great Dragon, the Traitor. How could that be? Is he truly evil? Can the legends be wrong? Would Theta let him live? Ob dared make no sound. He could barely breathe.

Dear gods, thought Ob. Theta said that he killed Azathoth. It had to be a boast—a distraction—a subterfuge—to unbalance Mortach and give Theta the edge he needed against that monstrosity. But could it be true? It would explain Azathoth's disappearance from the world. That would mean that Theta had killed a god. I'm doomed and so are we all.

Theta stirred and pulled a flask from his belt— the one that contained that witch's brew that he had used to heal Ob's injured arm after the gateway to Nifleheim closed. He sipped from it, and then replaced it ever so slowly and carefully on his belt. He pulled himself to his feet.

Despite himself, Ob shifted ever so slightly, though no more noise did he make than a rodent's rustle.

Theta looked directly at him through the dark and advanced on him; Ob, frozen with fear. Theta reached down, grabbed the Gnome by the throat, and lifted him into the air. Ob's mouth opened as if to speak, but no words came out. His eyes bulged, pleading for mercy as his arms dangled limp.

"Speak not of what you heard between Mikel—Mortach—and I," said Theta in a cold hard voice. "Not one word. Not to anyone or you will join him in the void. Do you understand?"

Tears streamed down Ob's face and he gasped for air. At the sight of Ob's anguish, Theta drifted back again to the days of yore.

He stood upon a hill next to his lord, looking down upon a great city.

"Have the relics been placed as I instructed?" said Azathoth.

"Mikel and Gabriel have set them exactly as you commanded, my Lord," said Thetan.

"Good. Those below and in Gemorrda are amongst the vilest, wickedest creatures in all Midgaard. They must pay for their sins; their crimes are incalculable."

"My Lord, Mikel and Gabriel were attacked by a mob; they sought refuge in a home and were given safe haven."

"And that family will be spared," said Azathoth. "The rest, for the void."

"Surely there are others as good as that family. Had they sought refuge at another home, it may have been given just as freely. Would it not be better to kill only those known for certain to be wicked?"

"I have looked into their hearts and see nothing but cold evil, and in their black thoughts, carnal pleasures and murder. Their pollution must be wiped from the land before it corrupts others."

"What of the children?"

"Even they have been corrupted. It saddens me more than I can say, but their souls must be cleansed before they may again return to Midgaard."

"My lord, is there no other way?"

Azathoth paused before replying. "This is all part of my grand design, as you will see in due time. Keep faith, my beloved Arkon."

"As you say, my Lord."

After a time, as they stood there watching, the city exploded in flames. Thetan turned away, the screams of tens of thousands of souls pressing him back and tearing apart his heart.

Theta's eyes softened. He lowered Ob to the ground and released his grip. "I am not your enemy. Do you understand?"

Ob nodded, still gasping. "I—will—keep silent, I swear it."

"Let's make our way back to Mideon Gate before we're discovered," said Theta. "The gate will be closed soon, if not already. We must move with speed."

XII
MIDEON GATE

"**I**t's not even bloody dark yet, you stinking cowardly scum," shouted Ob, Theta at his side. "Open the gate. Open up!"

"The gate is shut for the night," called down a guardsman. "It will not open until dawn."

Claradon, Tanch, and Dolan charged from one street, weapons in hand, and joined Theta and Ob in front of the gate. "They're behind us," yelled Claradon. "A mob of them."

No sooner had he said that, than a horde of black-clad figures raced down the street and pulled up as they approached the sturdy group. From an alley crept other black figures, each held a drawn blade, club, or ax. Perhaps fifty, sixty, even eighty all told, though it was hard to tell in the deepening shadows of dusk. These assailants bore little resemblance to the cultists; these were rougher, dirtier, street thugs, dock scum, and the like. Paid killers, or so they appeared.

"Open the stinking gate," yelled Ob once more as he pounded his fist upon it. Dolan readied his bow.

Theta stepped forward until he stood closest to the gang of assailants. There he stood transfixed, expressionless, his falchion blade pointed up and resting against his left shoulder; his shield held in his right hand, close to his chest.

"Open these stinking gates you snooters or I will skin you alive," yelled Ob.

"It's you who will be skinned tonight, Gnome," hissed one of the figures at the forefront of the gang.

"What do you want with us?" called out Claradon. "Who sent you?"

"We're to kill you says the League," said the figure.

"So kill you we will," said another.

"Do you know who we are?" said Par Tanch.

"Five dead men—if we bother counting the Gnome," said the first figure. "We need know nothing else," he said, stepping slowly forward.

"Then you don't know that I am an archmage of the Tower and that this knight is Claradon—the Lord of Dor Eotrus—who only yesterday bested the Chancellor himself in single combat. Attack us, and you will die; that will profit you nothing."

The figure stopped his approach and looked to his comrades, uncertainty on his face. There were grumblings and murmurings amongst their ranks.

"We are many," said a gravelly voiced figure near the first.

"True enough," said Par Tanch. "We may not best you all, but the first five or ten or more that come at us will soak this ground with their blood."

"Step up now," said Par Tanch. "The ground is thirsty. Who will quench it first?"

Those men in front did not move, but looked at each other uncertainly. Those behind started to shift backward, slowly. Meanwhile, several figures moved up from the shadows in the rear. As they drew closer, it was clear these were not Volsungs at all, but Lugron, the dreaded enemy of humankind. They were here before us, an ancient, primitive, bestial people of the cold northlands.

"Kill them, you scum," bellowed a huge whip-wielding Lugron, "or the League will carve out your hearts." He flicked the whip, which snapped a few feet in front of Theta. As the Lugron made to step forward, Theta called out, "Dolan—the Lugron!"

No sooner had he said those words than an arrow struck the Lugron in his left eye and partially blasted out the back of his head. He fell backward as a chopped tree and crashed to the cobblestones. The other Lugron roared and charged forward, their Volsung comrades following.

Theta's sword sang, moving too quickly to see, and Lugron and Volsung alike died at his feet, showering the cobbles in blood and gore, just as Tanch had forewarned. Simultaneously, a rain of arrows hailed down from atop Mideon Gate, plowing through the ranks of the murderous mob. This crushed their charge and sent most of them scurrying for cover. A second volley dropped a half dozen more and scattered the rest. The gang ran from the scene, fleeing for their lives. The entirety of the battle consumed but a handful of heartbeats.

"Grim Fischer at your service," called out a Gnome from atop the rampart above Mideon Gate. A dozen of Sluug's rangers flanked him, bows in hand.

Mideon Gate opened.

"If you please, gentlemen, step lively now," whispered Fischer, "best we be gone from these parts afore more trouble finds us this night. Let's get us somewhere where we can sit a spell in safety and drink a tankard or two."

XIII
TRAVELERS' REST

"**B**eyond the farthest hill," continued Claradon as the group sat about him at a round table in the inn called Travelers Rest.

"Across the widest sea,
Atop the highest mount
Beneath the deepest ocean
Lies Asgard—shining, eternal, beckoning us home."

"That's a goodly one, but I'm not much for poetry," said Ob, "especially what type as don't rhyme. But I like that one, I do."

"I've got one," said Grim, looking about at each man at the table, and then fixing his gaze on Theta.

"Once was a time of peace and joy, the world was young, the days were long. Odin the All-Father ruled from a marble throne in shining Asgard in the Land of Vaeden. Beside him were the gods of old: Frey and Freya, Thor and Balder, Tyr and Heimdall, and on and on. Amongst their number was the evil one who shall never be named."

I know his name, thought Ob with a shudder.

"We call him the harbinger of doom," said Grim. "The evil one conspired with darkness and demon spawn; he sold his soul and his heart grew cold. He corrupted others with promises of power, wealth, and more base desires. Perhaps he wanted Lord Odin's throne, or perhaps his evil was for naught but evil's sake. Though he walked with the gods in Odin's halls, he was misshapen and foul of face and manner."

Theta rolled his eyes.

"Even before he betrayed us, none called him friend, for he had a kindly word for no one. In his madness, he set out to open the ever-barred door—betwixt Midgaard and the pits of chaos, the realm of death and horror. He prayed alone to demon lords and devils of the outer spheres, atop Mount Cantorwrought, in an ancient tomb. There he practiced the blackest unspeakable rites of wickedness, preserved on leathern skins and stone menhirs from the time before man—from the time when the demons ruled Midgaard. His rites completed, the cursed portal opened and out spewed the very hordes of hell, the spawn of Nifleheim. Dragon and wight, goblin and troll, ghoul and devil, all these and countless others flew through to Midgaard. This was the plague that beset mankind. These creatures did wreak havoc and horror to all corners of the world."

"What reward the dark powers paid the traitor is recorded nowhere, though it's said that he suffered the most vile and painful end imaginable, all at the hands of the monsters he aided. Some say that he escaped that fate and is here on Midgaard still—cursed to haunt the world forever, finding no comfort, no rest, no peace, forevermore."

"A grim tale, Mr. Grim," said Dolan.

"That it is. Very similar to the tale of the pagan god Azathoth and his Arkons, though, is it not?" said Grim, still staring at Theta.

"The stories of many religions oft have a common basis," said Theta.

"But how can they both be true?" said Dolan.

"They cannot," said Theta. "Not literally. But there is some kernel of truth contained in both, I expect, though the truth may be twisted by the tellers."

"Indeed," said Grim. "I think it curious nonetheless."

"I think it curious that you stood within Hecate Hall tonight and heard the Azathoth version of the tale just as we did," said Theta.

Grim's face grew beet red, and his eyes darted to Theta's hand, as if expecting him to go for his sword.

Theta's voice grew louder and quicker. "Where is your red robe, Gnome?"

All eyes looked to Grim.

Grim smiled a thin smile, and he took a deep breath before responding. "My robe was borrowed as I entered that foul place, just as were yours, and discarded as I left. I was the eyes and ears of Doriath Hall this night, as is my duty. Such things can be confirmed if you doubt me."

"Sonny," said Ob, "if he doubted you, I expect you'd already be dead."

Grim shrank in his seat; his face now white.

Theta smiled. He took a sip of sweet white wine and stared at the far wall of the inn, his back exposed only to the inn's brick wall, his thoughts drifting.

XIV
HARBINGER OF OUR DOOM

"**I** will bear the treachery and evil of this petty kingdom no longer," said Azathoth. "They defy me and deny me at every turn. They oppress and persecute my faithful."

"Their king and his subjects shall all suffer my wraith. My beloved, most loyal and greatest of my children—you shall have the honor of carrying out my just sentence."

"What would you have us do?" said Mikel as he stood beside Thetan, Gabriel, Bhaal, Mithron, and Arioch, Arkons all.

"You shall go into the city this very eve and visit every home. All the doors not marked by the signs and symbols of my faithful shall be sundered. You shall enter into them, pluck the firstborn from their beds or their mothers' bosoms, and slay them as their parents watch. Every home, every child firstborn of the unbelievers shall suffer this penance. Such is my will. Such is my command."

"Yes, my Lord," said Mikel and Bhaal. The others nodded.

Azathoth turned and walked from the chamber, followed by Mikel and Bhaal who were off to prepare themselves. Gabriel, Thetan, Mithron, and Arioch stood transfixed and looked to each other.

"We cannot do this," said Gabriel.

"And we cannot disobey," said Arioch. "He is

the Lord: all good, all holy—omniscient, omnipotent, and eternal. We are but men."

"He is mad," said Thetan.

They were silent for some moments before Gabriel spoke. "I agree," he said. "The Lord has gone mad. He does evil and calls it good."

"But his plan—" said Arioch.

"Is the road to ruin," said Thetan. "I will not murder innocent babes; not for him; not for anyone. To hell with his plan."

"To hell with us, if we stand against him," said Mithron.

"So be it," said Thetan. "We've stood by and allowed this madness to continue for far too long already. Each time we carried out his punishments, we thought we were doing the right thing, but we were not. In my heart, I knew that. There is blood on my hands that will never wash clean. It ends here, tonight. Never again will I do his bidding. Though it will surely mean my death, I will move against him on the morrow. Are you with me?"

"I am," said Gabriel. "I can't believe that it has come to this. But yes, I will stand with you, brother."

"As will I," said Mithron.

"Arioch?" said Thetan.

"I'm with you," said Arioch. "Though I fear that you are the harbinger of our doom."

END OF VOLUME 2

KNIGHT ETERNAL

By
GLENN G. THATER
Volume 3 of the Harbinger of Doom Saga

"Mine is a perilous road; those that walk
it with me are seldom long for Valhalla"
—Lord Angle Theta

PREFACE

The last few years were big for Thetian scholars. In 2006, Dr. Frank Smithwick of Brown University completed his long-awaited translation of the Fifth Scroll of Cumbria, long thought lost until donated to the Smithsonian in 2001 by a private collector. Professor Smithwick's painstaking translation of the twelve hundred year old documents revealed for the first time the lost tale of Angle Theta's relentless pursuit of Korrgonn following the Gateway incident. A portion of that translation, which I've updated into modern prose for readers of fantasy literature, forms the core of this book.

In 2007, archeologists from the University of Chicago discovered a cache of inscribed stone tablets in a cave excavation in the mountains near Grenoble, France. Carbon dating of pigments used in the inscriptions indicates that the tablets were created sometime between 2,400 B.C. and 2,600 B.C., making them some of the oldest written records of Thetian lore thus far found in western Europe. A crackerjack team of researchers from the University of Maryland at College Park, the University of Chicago, and Brown University, collaborated to translate the Grenoble Tablets in record time, their work revealing many previously unknown stories centered on members of The Shadow League. Two of these brief tales form the basis of the chapters herein entitled, "*Born Killers*" and "*The Orb of Wisdom*".

These latest discoveries, coupled with other

sources such as the Ningshao Jade Collection, the Olmec and Kish Tablets, the Derveni Papyri, the Scrolls of Corsi and Burdur, and others, conclusively demonstrate that despite these stories being relatively unknown today, the Thetian tales were widely read and reproduced for thousands of years throughout the ancient world. Thus, the influence of Thetian literature on mythology, folklore, and cultural traditions across the globe should not be underestimated and warrants significantly more scholarship.

2008 saw the publication of my novelizations of *The Gateway* and *The Fallen Angle*, two tales that have long lived in the core of Thetian canon, but which had never before been adapted into modern prose for the general public.

The hundreds of emails and messages I have received from readers of these tales have inspired me to continue to bring these fantastical stories to print. Some categorize these tales as mythology, others call them sword and sorcery or heroic fantasy, still others name them weird tales, but to me they are historical fiction, part of the rich but sadly little known literary legacy of the ancient world.

I hope that you enjoy this next installment of the Harbinger of Doom saga, entitled, *Knight Eternal*. Happy reading.

Glenn G. Thater
New York, USA

PROLOGUE

Ob flung the door open. "You can never tell anyone what I'm about to tell you, boy, or you and me both will get killed dead."

Claradon, pale and drained, and generally unkempt, rolled his eyes and stepped into Ob's chambers. The old Gnome looked even worse than Claradon did, his arm heavily bandaged, his face battered and bruised.

"What now, Ob?" said Claradon. "I can't take any more."

"There is much I've a mind to tell you, but I've got to lie down, my back is killing me." Ob closed the door and made his way through the large, cluttered sitting room toward his bedchamber. Claradon followed, though his thoughts drifted to the events that had just ravaged his life.

A few days prior, fanatical cultists gathered in secret in the Vermion Forest near the fortress of Dor Eotrus in the Kingdom of Lomion. Wielding ancient, forbidden magics, they opened a dark portal to the outré realm of Nifleheim, the very hell of myth and legend, allowing demons and their masters, the Lords of Nifleheim, to enter Midgaard, the world of man.

Ignorant of the cultists' activities, Aradon Eotrus, Lord of the surrounding lands and vassal to King Selrach Tenzivel, led an elite force of knights, wizards, and woodsmen into the Vermion to investigate reports of strange goings on. Amongst Aradon's veterans were the renowned Archwizard, Par Talbon of Montrose; the Master Ranger, Stern of Doriath; and Dor Eotrus's High Cleric, Brother Donnelin. For all their skills and courage, not a one returned.

In response, Brother Claradon Eotrus, eldest son of Aradon, gathered a troop of knights led by his mentor, Sir Gabriel Garn, and his friend Ob the Gnome. They were joined by an enigmatic foreign soldier called Lord Angle Theta. Together, they set out to learn Aradon's fate.

Hidden within a magical fog, deep within the Vermion, the group discovered the gruesome, mutilated, nigh unrecognizable remains of Aradon Eotrus's party outside an ancient, otherworldly temple. Plagued by a frigid, choking mist and mind-rending din, Claradon and his comrades assaulted the Temple of Guymaog, but arrived too late to secure the portal between the worlds.

With the gateway opened, three Lords of Nifleheim and a horde of lesser fiends trespassed upon the world of man for the first time since the very dawn of history. These monsters of Nifleheim had long filled man's tales of terror and plagued his nightmares, but had been only myth and legend. Now all that had changed. Monsters were real. Men's minds broke.

Bhaal of Nifleheim slew many brave knights before Angle Theta drove him back through the gateway with a magical lance—a relic of times long past. Mortach of Nifleheim bounded through the temple and escaped, later to join with the cultists that had opened the gateway. Sir Gabriel, greatest hero of the realm, died by the hand of the Nifleheim Lord, Gallis Korrgonn, while saving Claradon's life. Worse still, Korrgonn's life force passed into and took control of Gabriel's body, and enabled his escape into the night.

To close the doorway to hell, Claradon located and destroyed the shard of darkness that held open the gateway, sealing it forever.

After the brutal battle, the few survivors returned to Dor Eotrus, and at the wizard Par Tanch's urging, concocted a tale of rampaging mountain trolls to explain the night's tragic losses. Tanch warned that no mention be made of magic or sorcery and the like, as the government harshly suppresses the truth of such things, while the common folk believe them little more than children's tales and ancient legends.

That very evening, while the knights of House Eotrus began preparations to return to the Vermion to take up the trail of the remaining two Nifleheim Lords, Ob called Claradon to his chambers where he was recuperating from his injuries.

Ob's chambers boasted a hardwood floor, stained to a rich, walnut hue, though much of it was covered by teetering piles of books of every size and description–the overflow from the brimming shelves that lined the walls.

Well-tended fireplaces in both sitting room and bedchamber heated the apartment. Warm and cozy, the rooms, as always, smelled vaguely of pipe smoke. Empty wine bottles of exotic vintage were proudly displayed atop the mantles and the wardrobe. The more recent bottles overflowed the trash bucket, awaiting their ultimate fate.

All the furniture in Ob's bedchamber was sized appropriately for one of his stature, save for the bed, which was massive and high off the floor.

Ob stepped stiffly up a little four-step ladder and hopped onto the bed with a groan. He settled down on the thick mattress, wincing with every movement.

He reached out for his ale mug, but his hand met only empty air. "Darn."

The finely crafted night table beside the bed was Gnome-sized and far below Ob's reach high atop the bed. "Would you mind, boy? Give the crank beside the table a few turns?"

"What?"

"The crank, down there," said Ob, pointing down to a handle sticking out below the night table.

Claradon squatted down. Beneath the night table was a curious wood and metal contraption. Claradon turned the handle and the table rose smoothly up. Several more turns and the tabletop rose up to within Ob's easy reach.

"I had Donnelin make it for me. Cost me a bottle of '64. Worth it though, or else I'd break my neck leaning down for the mug. That fellow was always handy."

Ob paused, thinking.

"I will miss him. I will miss them all, dearly." Ob looked over to the large color portrait that hung on one wall. Aradon Eotrus stood in the center in full battle regalia; Gabriel, at his right hand, similarly clad; Ob at his left; then Brother Donnelin, Par Talbon, and Stern to either side, all wearing their finest, their features captured almost perfectly.

"The gaming table is still set," said Ob. "Just the way we left it. Me and Gabe were winning, but the others were giving us shot for shot. Now we'll never finish it. Not ever."

Ob grabbed a handkerchief from the night table and loudly blew his nose. Tears filled the old Gnome's eyes.

"We were together a long time, that group. Every one of them was like a brother to me. Now I'm the only one left." Tears streamed down Ob's face. "They're all dead, all of them."

Claradon tried not to look at the portrait, tried to keep his composure.

"I should've been with them. Who knows, maybe I could've made some difference—or at least, I could've died with them. I should have."

"We were with Sir Gabriel, at least," said Claradon.

Ob nodded. "It's good that you were beside him at the end; not good for a man to die alone."

They sat in silence for a time, grieving in their own way, until Claradon spoke again.

"We both need to get some rest. Your arm is badly hurt and my head still throbs; one ear hears almost nothing, the other rings without end."

"Aye, mine ring as well. A day or two will heal them, if Thor's luck is with us. As for my arm, thanks to whatever witch's brew Mr. Fancy Pants slipped me, it seems I will heal unnatural quick-like. No doubt that tin can will be claiming he

397

saved my life to all and everyone."

Ob lifted his ale mug and took several swallows. "There are some important things that you've a need to know. Things that maybe Aradon and Gabe should've told you long ago, but they did not, for reasons of their own. So now the telling falls to me."

Claradon grew paler, nodded, and leaned back into the cushioned armchair, jaw set, eyes staring straight ahead.

"When I first came to the Dor, long before I became Castellan, I worked as a scout for your father's grandfather who was the young lord of the House at that time. In those days there was a knight who was a good friend to your great grandfather. He would come to visit and go hunting with him in the mountains and such. This knight was a great weapons master, and during his visits he would often train the knights of the House in the ways of battle. His name was Gabriel."

"Quite a coincidence, but what importance does it have?"

"It's not a coincidence at all, boy, and that's the point of it. That Gabriel and our Gabriel were the same fellow. Gabe wasn't no normal man. He was old. I'm over three hundred, but to him, I was a child."

"That doesn't make any sense. Men don't live that long."

"Some men do, it seems; if men they truly be."

Claradon got up and paced. "I've heard stories of certain wizards, with their potions and such, that can extend life and maintain youth, but

Gabriel was no wizard. He was a soldier—a knight, a hero."

"I can't explain it, boy. I just know it to be the truth. Back in the day, after some years went by, Gabe stopped coming around. He had gone traveling about the world, doing hero stuff and such, I expect. I didn't see him again until one day, many a year later, when he showed up at the Dor.

"I was shocked when I laid eyes upon him. It had been decades but he looked as young as he did when I first came to the Dor.

"I was the only one that knew; the only one around long enough to remember.

"Gabe took me aside and told me that I had to swear never to tell nobody about his secret. So I swore. You're the first and only person I've done talked to about this, save for your father, and he already knew. I'm only telling you now cause they're both gone and you've a right to know."

"Father knew all this?"

"Your grandfather told him. Seems all the lords of the House knew, far back into olden times. Family legend says Gabe was a good friend to the Eotrus for many generations, long afore I came here."

"Did you ask him how he lived so long? Could he have had Elven blood?"

"I asked him, but he wouldn't speak of it, save to say he was no Elf. He said that there were others like him and that they would kill me dead if they found out that I knew about them. Gabe was never one to make idle threats or warnings, so I done believed him. You mustn't tell no one what I told you today, or they'll kill you and me both. You must keep especial quiet around Mr. Fancy Pants. I would bet my life that old Lord Angle Theta is one of them."

"Ob, from anyone other than you, I don't think I would believe a word of this, but after what we went through last night—"

"I've never lied to you, Claradon—."

"I know that."

"I've never lied, but there have been some truths like what I just told you that I've had to hold back. There's more to it, boy. It'll be difficult for you to hear."

"More? Tell me. Tell me and let's be done with this."

Ob took a swig from his mug and then placed it on the night table. Claradon sat down on the edge of the armchair.

"One time, when Gabe returned to the Dor after a mission doing hero stuff, he brought with him a small child—a mere babe."

"A baby?"

"A cute little bugger, as far as you Volsungs go anyways. He entrusted it to the care of your father. Then Gabe picked up and left again for a time. Aradon kept the child, and he and his Lady, who had no children yet of their own, raised him as their very own son, but for some darned reason, he never told the boy that he wasn't his natural father."

Claradon's face went white, his hands icy cold.

"How many years ago?"

"Twenty five."

Claradon's eyes slowly closed. Ob tried to pass

him the mug but Claradon brushed it away. They sat in silence for some minutes.

"So I'm not a true Eotrus."

"Don't ever be saying that, boy. You are as much an Eotrus as Aradon, Jude, or any of them. You are Aradon's son in every way that is important. Nobody would dispute that, not even Gabe."

"In the Vermion you said that I'm the lord of the land now. But am I? Or is Jude?"

"You are, Claradon. You are the Lord of the House now, answerable only to the King and the High Council, and don't ever forget it. And if you're smart, you will not tell Jude or anyone about this, ever. It can only bring trouble."

A vacant stare dominated Claradon's face.

"Was Gabriel my real father?"

"No, boy, he wasn't. All I can say about it is that your natural parents died when you was a babe."

Claradon reached for the mug.

***

While in pursuit of Korrgonn and Mortach, Claradon received a summons from the High Council of Lomion, ordering him to travel to Lomion City to receive official appointment as the new Lord of Dor Eotrus. Claradon found the High Council fractured into rival groups, some members supporting the traditional government while others were loyal to The Shadow League, a mysterious group allied with the dark powers of Nifleheim.

Chancellor Barusa of House Alder accused Claradon of conspiring to murder Aradon and claim Dor Eotrus for his own, before his time. To avoid losing the Dor to the Alders, Claradon challenged, and bested Barusa in single combat, thereby solidifying his claim to the Dor.

Aided by Harringgold, Archduke of Lomion, Claradon and his comrades tracked the Nifleheim lords to an old warehouse in the dread Southeast section of Lomion City. Disguised as cultists, they stumbled into a black mass attended by thousands and presided over by Ginalli, an Arkon and High Priest of The Shadow League.

Ginalli's sermon told the tale of the Harbinger of Doom, the ancient fiend of myth and legend that had long ago led a rebellion against the cultists' "one true god," Azathoth. Thrown out of the heavens for his treachery, this monster was cursed for all time and reviled by all mankind no matter what name or guise he took. Korrgonn stepped from the shadows and boomed that this harbinger of doom walked Midgaard still, though untold centuries had passed, and that he was here, in Lomion.

"Where?" shouted the cultists.

Directly at Theta, Korrgonn pointed.

Panic ensued and Claradon and his group fled. Mortach of Nifleheim pursued them and cornered Theta and Ob. Ob escaped through a hole while Theta confronted Mortach. The Gnome overheard all that passed between them. Theta admitted that in ancient days he had turned against

402

Azathoth, but claimed that it was Azathoth and his followers that were evil, not he. Mortach claimed that Azathoth is good, and that the Nifleheim lords merely carry out his bidding as part of a larger, holy plan beyond Theta's grasp. The two agreed, their argument could end only one way: the old way of the sword. And so, in a duel witnessed by none, and overheard only by Ob the Gnome, Lord Angle Theta slew Mortach, Lord of Nifleheim.

This meant that Theta was the Bogeyman, The Prince of Lies, the veritable Harbinger of Doom of myth and legend. Since the betrayal of Azathoth took place ages ago, this also meant that Theta was old beyond comprehension. Ob's mind nearly fractured as the truth of this settled in. Theta swore Ob to secrecy.

The group regrouped and vowed to continue their quest to destroy Korrgonn and the mad cultists that worshipped him.

Some weeks later...

I
THE MESSENGER

"To sate my thirst, I will drink thy blood—the blood of kings."

A cloaked figure shambled through the Outer Dor, a vibrant town of some few thousands that encircled the stone fortress called Dor Eotrus. The people gave the shambler wide berth, suspicious of strangers in those dark times. Hunched beneath a black cloak that concealed its face, the wearer's aspect remained unknown as he approached the entry to the Dor proper.

Several soldiers manned the guard post outside the entryway, passing the time with a game of dice. The tallest of the group, a gaunt veteran with a scar across his right cheek, stepped forward. He shivered from a sudden chill in the air.

"Halt, and state your business," said Sir Marzdan, watch captain of the gate. With each breath, steam rose from Marzdan's mouth, where there was none moments before. The shambler stopped before the captain, though he said nothing.

"Who are you?" said Marzdan after some moments. "Speak." Marzdan's fingers tapped his sword hilt.

"Messenger," moaned the cloak, though no steam followed from beneath its hood.

Marzdan eyed him with suspicion and wrinkled

404

his nose when he caught the fetid stench that emanated from the messenger. It wasn't the stink of a beggar, but something fouler, darker. The other guards took notice, put aside their game, and took up positions some feet behind their captain.

"What is your message?"

"Only for the Eotrus," he said in a slow, eerie voice that made Marzdan's neck hairs stand up.

"That will not get you in." Marzdan looked him up and down. "Who sent you here? Have you some token?"

"A token?" said the messenger. "Yes, a token I do have." The messenger slowly reached out his arm toward the watchman. The hand that emerged from beneath that threadbare cloak wore no human flesh. No skin, no muscle, no sinew concealed its naked gray bones. This was no mere messenger, but some creature out of nightmare.

Marzdan's eyes widened; his fingers locked around his sword hilt, though he didn't pull the blade free. "What—what are you?"

"Messenger," moaned the cloak once again.

Marzdan's face blanched, but he stood his ground and stared at the skeletal hand and the gleaming contents it held. A ring–a golden ring that bore the symbol of House Eotrus, the noble family that ruled the fortress and the surrounding lands.

"Make no move, creature."

Marzdan moved closer and plucked the ring from the boney hand, taking great care to touch only the ring.

"Wait here," said the knight. "I'll get word to the citadel."

The messenger stood still as a statue, silent as the grave. Marzdan cautiously backed away, his hand never leaving his sword hilt.

"I'm going to get Jude," Marzdan said quietly to his guardsmen. "You men stand fast. If that thing holds his ground, leave him be. Not a word to him, understand?"

"Not a word," said Harsnip, a skinny blond soldier not yet eighteen—his eyes wide, voice crackling with fear.

"If he tries to pass the gate, you're to cut him down. Whatever it takes, you don't let him pass. You're to protect the Dor. Understood?"

"Aye," said Baret, an older soldier with white hair. "We know our job, Captain. That bugger will not get by us, to be sure, but you be quick. Right quick."

"Right quick," said Harsnip.

"Aye, I will," said Marzdan, a wary eye still on the messenger.

"That arm—it's nothing but bones," whispered Graham, a stout soldier with big ears.

"Nothing but bones," said Harsnip.

"This is some sorcery, some foul magic," said Graham.

"It's foul magic, it is," said Harsnip.

"There's no such thing as magic, you fools," said Baret. "A damn trick is all, to fool us."

"A trick?" said Harsnip, a glimmer of a smile coming to his face. "Yeah, that's all it is. Just a trick. Not magic."

"To what end?" said Graham.

Baret scrunched up his face. "How would I know what's his mind, the stinking bag of bones? That's for bigger men than the likes of us."

"Bigger men," said Harsnip, staring over his shoulder at the messenger. "Foul magic, I think. Not a trick at all."

"What's that, boy?" said Baret.

"Me grand-mum told me to steer clear of magic, she did. She told me the old stories were more truth than fancy. Steer right clear of anything magic, or it'll be the death of you, Harsnip, she said. And she done told me not to join up with the guard too. Any magic already hereabouts will be at the Dor, she said, and any magic what comes around will head straight there, like a moth to a flame. She was right about that, it seems. She said the Dor would be the death of me, old grand-mum said. Said it just last week, right over Thorsday's dinner, she did."

"Steady, lad," said Baret, placing a firm hand on the young man's shoulder. "Just a messenger it is, bones or not. Nothing much to fear, not yet, anyways."

"What if—"

"I'll look out for you lad, if it comes to it.

"Thanks. I'm counting on that."

"Just remember your training."

"Aye," said Harsnip. "I will."

A group of men exited the keep's central tower and walked toward the gate. Jude Eotrus, a dark-maned hulk of crooked nose and squared jaw led the way. With him, his youngest brother, Malcolm, long and lean; Sir Marzdan; and several other knights and soldiers.

The messenger still stood by the gate, unmoved.

Jude held the ring before the messenger, then stepped back, wrinkling his nose and coughing from the messenger's stench. Marzdan stood protectively beside Jude, hand on sword hilt. The messenger, taller than most men, and as broad, more or less, came up only to Jude's jaw, and was barely half his breadth.

"What do you know about this ring?" said Jude from a safer distance, his breath steaming.

"It be the signet ring of House Eotrus, taken from thy father's hand the night he fell in the Vermion Forest, not one month ago."

"Who are you and how came you by it?"

"I be little more than dust. The ring was entrusted to me so that you would know that the message I bear be true." The creature pulled a piece of dusty parchment from beneath its robes and handed it to Jude.

Jude unfolded the parchment. It read:

Aradon Eotrus lives and will remain so if and only if you deliver twenty thousand silver stars unto our messenger tomorrow evening at Riker's Crossroads. Thence we will exchange the silver for the old Lord. No tricks or dead he'll truly be.

Jude's eyes grew wide. "It says that father is alive and this creature's master has him."

"What?" Malcolm's face flashed brick red and drew into a snarl; his fists opening and closing at his sides.

"Are you the messenger that will make this exchange?" asked Jude.

"Perhaps, perhaps not; who can say?"

"How dare you hold my father for ransom, you stinking dog." Malcolm pulled his sword, and before Jude could grab his arm, thrust the blade through the messenger's chest.

The messenger stumbled back and clutched at the sword with both skeletal hands.

Malcolm yanked the blade free.

No blood sprang from the creature's wound. No cry erupted from its throat; its torn cloak the only evidence that the blow had been struck.

Only gray dust marred the sheen of Malcolm's sword, but in no more than a moment, the fine steel blade turned to ash from tip to guard. Malcolm threw the hilt down as it too burned to ash before his eyes.

The messenger threw back its head, its cowl still cloaking its face, and laughed. Louder and louder it laughed—so loud that the men cringed and crushed their hands against their ears. It was a horrid, cackling sound of such unnatural tenor and fearful intonation as could not be voiced by the throat of man, though, mercifully, it lasted but a few moments.

"Well struck. Well struck," said the messenger. It shrugged off its cloak, revealing glowing, silver chains that criss-crossed about its body. From skull to foot it was little more than bleached bones affixed together by some strange gray tissue. It had two large eyes of blood-red pupil and sickly yellow sclera, and hands that ended in boney claws.

The messenger flexed its arms and legs, and strained against the chains. "Thy blow has freed me from my binding." Another flex and several links shattered. The chain fell to the ground in a heap. "I can now pursue my own course."

The creature vaulted at Jude, claws flailing.

Lightning quick, Marzdan grabbed Jude and pulled him clear—no small feat considering Jude's bulk.

The messenger veered and raked its claws across young Harsnip's chest; the boy's face froze in shock and horror. The blow met no resistance, as if the claws were insubstantial like those of some ghost out of a fireside tale.

Harsnip loosed a bloodcurdling scream. His face grew ashen; his skin wrinkled and shriveled. His hair grew instantly white and fell about his shoulders. For a moment, before he fell, his eyes locked accusingly on Baret's. Then Harsnip collapsed into a heap of dust, rotted clothes, and rusted armor.

The soldiers yelled, and hacked at the messenger, but their blades passed through it, doing it no harm. Each blade that touched the thing burned to ash, and those men too slow to throw down the hilts burned to ashes with them. The creature struck again and again and more men went down and shriveled to ash. Its touch was death, no matter the victim's courage, strength, or skill.

Whistles blew and calls of alarm sounded

about the keep. Jude led the men in a fast retreat to the central tower; the creature pursued at its own shambling pace. Soon, the booming claxon of the bell tower warned all the Dor of danger and roused the garrison to arms.

"Bar the door, and stand well back," shouted Jude after the last of the soldiers dashed through the portal.

The men crowded about the tower's entry hall and on the winding stair to the upper chambers. They heard screams and war cries from without as guards from other parts of the keep descended upon the messenger and died for it.

"What is that thing?" said Malcolm. "How do we fight it?"

"We wouldn't have to fight it if you weren't an idiot," said Jude. "Some monster out of Nifleheim. It's beyond our ken. I know not how to bring it down."

The messenger stepped through the door, though the door did not open. It passed through the solid oak, banded and reinforced in honest steel and iron, as if it were but empty air. Startled, the men jumped back. Many went down in a heap as they stumbled over those behind. Several crossbow bolts flew, passed through the creature, and embedded themselves in the door before they too burned to ash.

"To the chapel," shouted Jude, "Run."

Those on the stair turned heel and raced up the winding steps shouting the alarm as they went. Up and up they raced to the third floor, which housed the keep's place of worship. What men were still with Jude dashed in, closed, and barred the big double doors.

"What do we do?" yelled Malcolm.

"Holy water," said Marzdan.

The soldiers stood in a semi-circular line some ten feet from the barred door. Each held a basin of holy water, or one of the chapel's holy symbols or relics.

"We've no priests to bless the weapons," said Malcolm.

"Don't worry, young master," said Captain Marzdan. "They'll work. They have to."

Long seconds passed. A scream or two from without and below heralded the messenger's approach. Then it passed through the barred door, again as if it wasn't there. The room instantly grew frigid, the light from the sconces wavered and dimmed, and the air filled with the creature's fetid stench.

"Begone, creature," shouted Jude. "You can't enter this holy place. Begone."

"You be no priest," said the messenger. "You hath no power over me."

The men flung their holy water, dousing the spot where the messenger stood, though the water passed through it and the messenger paid it no heed. It moved forward, toward Jude.

Malcolm held a staff upon which was mounted an ancient, holy relic of Odin, father of the gods. He thrust it forward and pressed the end to the creature's forehead. This time, the weapon met resistance; the relic seared the messenger's skull and held fast.

The creature snarled and spasmed. It lashed out and grabbed the staff, howling in rage. Where its claws grasped the oak, the staff smoked and blackened and turned to ash. As a lit fuse, the destruction of the staff continued down its shaft. Eyes wide, Malcolm froze.

"Drop the staff," yelled Jude, his breath steaming.

Captain Marzdan dived into Malcolm and pushed him aside. Malcolm fell clear but Marzdan landed atop the decaying staff.

The captain's face froze in terror and he screamed—a lingering wail of agony and anger that no man there could forget for the rest of his days. Marzdan's hair went white, his skin paled and shriveled. In moments, the brave soldier was no more than an ashen heap with the shape of a man.

Malcolm writhed in agony and clutched at his left wrist; his left hand smoldered, flesh hung loose, white bone tasted the air.

"Yes," hissed the messenger. It thrust back its arms and its head as if in ecstasy, and then by some power born of hell, the creature grew—taller, thicker, darker. "Ah, the sweet blood of kings. I must have more." Its eyes locked on Jude, boring into his very soul. It shambled forward, toward Jude, ignoring all else.

Jude backpedaled through the room, sword held at the defensive. The knights and guardsmen fired crossbow bolts at the thing and threw weapons at it from all sides, all to no avail.

"What do we do?" yelled one man.

"How do we bring it down?" called out Baret.

As he neared the very back of the chapel, with little space left to run, Jude stopped and held his ground.

"What do you want?" he shouted. "Why do you plague us?" Jude's eyes darted from the beast to his wounded brother. Baret and Graham pulled Malcolm up and dragged him from the room.

"To sate my thirst, I will drink thy blood—the blood of kings," said the fiend, its eyes wild; foam dripped from its bony maw.

"To sate my hunger, I will burn thy body and devour thy soul."

"Can't we give you some mead and a chicken or two, perhaps a goat, and call our business done?"

"No," said the messenger.

"Some fresh venison then? Good Gnomish ale to wash it down? We've a keg from '58, brewed in Portland Vale."

The messenger lunged forward.

Jude stepped back and tripped over a chest that sat beside the chapel's lectern. The messenger's claws raked through the empty air where Jude had just stood. Jude landed on his rump, the stout, ironbound oaken chest before him, and knew at once what to do. He flung the lid open and sure and swift from within pulled a strange glowing dagger of silver hue.

The messenger recoiled and sniffed the air. It locked its eyes on the glowing dagger and growled. It flexed its claws and they began to change, to grow. In moments, they passed six inches in length; darkened, black as pitch; and sharpened to a razor's edge.

In one motion, Jude leaped to his feet and flung the ensorcelled dagger with all his power. It struck the messenger mid-chest, exploded through its sternum, and lodged there. The creature emitted a devilish wail to whither the soul and slay the spirit: a howl of such volume and pitch that near every man in the room dropped to his knees. It clutched at the dagger with both its taloned, skeletal hands, stumbled back a few steps, and collapsed to one knee.

"Curse you, Eotrus," spat the beast. "And all thy line forevermore."

Its eyes rolled back in its head. It fell backward, struck the marble floor, and exploded in a cloud of dust. The glowing dagger remained, embedded in a heap of foul black ash.

II
MAGES AND MONSTERS

"Don't play by any rules, just survive,
That is all that matters."
—Lord Angle Theta

Ornate figurines overran the tabletop. They were cast in the likenesses of soldiers, knights, elves, Dwarves, wizards, Lugron, and all manner of monsters, various and sundry—all beautifully painted and mounted on moveable hardwood bases inscribed with arcane symbols and numbers that represented their attributes. Two compact carrying cases of leather and hardwood, homes for the game tokens, sat open at the end of the table. Their outsides scarred and battered from long travels, the cases were heavily padded within to protect their precious cargo.

Two armed men sat on each side of the table, while a fifth—a shiny mountain of steel and grit called Angle Theta—observed from off to the side. Theta kept an eye on the game's progress while he skimmed through a dog-eared leather rulesbook and studied several unused pieces.

A tiny old man not much more than three-feet tall, of bulbous nose and big ears, shook his head and grinned. "A bad move, Magic Boy," he said to the fair-haired man that sat on the other side of the oaken table. "You should've moved your stinking Knight Champion while you had the chance. He's in range of my Mage and his back is

416

unprotected. He's worm food."

"Excuse me, Ob," said Par Tanch, "but I saw your Mage and I have intentionally ignored him. If you had been paying as much attention to the game as to your ale you would know that your Mage is too wounded to throw a spell, so he's no threat. I'm afraid you'll have to find another move."

Ob narrowed his eyes; an evil grin formed on his face. "You've forgotten, Magic Boy, my Mage has the Dagger of Shantii."

Tanch studied the table and his face paled.

Ob measured off the distance and moved the Mage directly behind the Knight Champion—a smug look on his face.

"That's a reckless move," said Tanch's teammate, Claradon, a large man, clad in a sharp gray shirt emblazoned with the crest of House Eotrus. "Magic dagger or not, the Mage doesn't have much chance of hitting the Knight, and less of finishing him off, even from behind."

"And next turn, I'll turn the Knight around and hack the Mage to pieces," said Tanch.

"If I kill your stinking knight, your game is over, as quick as that. You won't have enough points left to be a threat." Ob took a deep drink of ale from his mug "Start sweating." He picked up a pair of dice from the table—one of bone, one of metal. He placed them in an ornately carved wooden cup, shook it, and tossed the dice on the tabletop.

A six came up on each die.

Ob smashed his hands together. "Yes."

"Arrgh!" went Tanch and Claradon as they

jumped to their feet.

"What happened?" said Ob's teammate, Dolan, a pale, gaunt man of pointy ears.

"Double Doom," said Claradon. "An automatic hit and double damage."

Ob jotted some numbers on a piece of parchment with a feather quill. "By my count, your Champion is down, out, and dead as dead can be." He handed the calculation over to Claradon. "Game over."

Claradon looked over the numbers and shook his head in disgust.

Tanch leaned heavily on his wooden staff. "My back has been troubling me today; I'm just not at my best. Even so, it was a lucky shot."

"Not luck, Magic Boy. It was guts. In Mages and Monsters, just as in real battle, them with guts win the day more often than not. If you want to play it safe, you're hanging with the wrong bunch." Ob looked over at Theta. "Ain't that right, Mr. Fancy Pants?"

Theta continued to peruse the rulesbook and didn't bother to look over. "Is your confidence in your courage, Gnome, or in your dice?"

"Bah." Ob stood atop his chair and stretched as best he could to reach the Knight Champion figurine near the table's center. His fingers fell just short. Dolan jumped up and reeled the Knight in.

Claradon's eyes narrowed and he looked from Theta to Ob to the Double Doom dice that still sat on the table.

"I thought it was a good move, Mr. Ob," said Dolan.

"Thanks, boy."

Claradon reached to pick up Ob's dice, but the Gnome's hand darted out and snatched them away. "Those are my lucky dice, boy, get your own."

Claradon narrowed his eyes. "Let me see those dice."

"What? Why?"

"The dice, Ob. Now."

Ob put them in his pant pocket, a defiant look plastered to his face.

Tanch studied the exchange between his friends. "You cheated," said the wizard. "Those dice were loaded, weren't they?"

Ob looked taken aback.

"I thought it was just dumb luck, but you actually cheated."

"A wise man makes his own luck," said Theta. He closed the rulesbook and turned toward the others. "You didn't lose to Ob's luck; you lost to his skill, and to your own foolishness. You lost because you counted on him playing by the rules, and didn't check that he wasn't. That kind of mistake will get you killed out there. Don't make it again."

"But he cheated," said Claradon.

"His mage lives and your knight is dead with a knife in his back. How it happened really doesn't matter."

"You condone this treachery?" said Tanch.

Theta laughed. "Not so much in a game, but for real, when it counts, out there on some battlefield, yes. In battle, you must do whatever it takes to survive. You must use whatever edge you have. Don't play fair, don't give your opponent a chance, don't play by any rules, just win, just survive, that's all that matters." Theta tossed the rulesbook to Claradon. "That's your lesson for the day. Don't forget it."

"How did you know?" said Claradon. "How did you know Ob cheated?"

Theta smiled but didn't respond.

"He knew because I'm an old warrior and old warriors play the odds or they don't live to get old. I played way against the odds with that move, so he knew I must've had an edge: a big one."

"This game is too complicated for me," said Dolan. "I prefer Spottle."

A soldier clad in the livery of House Harringgold marched stiffly into the room. "Excuse me, Lord Eotrus; gentlemen. Duke Harringgold requests your presence forthwith in his drawing room."

"Is there some trouble?" asked Claradon.

"I fear so, sir. Your brother, Sir Ector, is in with the Duke."

Claradon stood. His face paled. "He's supposed to be at home."

III
AMBUSH

*"You want to be a hero, boy?
Live to write the history books."*
—Ob

Sir Jude Eotrus's massive destrier thundered forward at full gallop, adorned in steel barding and colorful caparison. Jude wore the traditional armor of the Knights of Tyr—a suit of steel plates tied to an undercoat and leggings of chain links. Armored gauntlets, greaves, and boots completed his protection. His steel helm hung from a saddle loop, his black cape fluttered in the wind. To his left arm was affixed a heater shield emblazoned with the Eotrus coat-of-arms.

Fixated on exacting righteous vengeance on those that sent the messenger against his home and claimed to hold his father captive, Jude stared forward, jaw clenched, only mildly aware that Sergeant Balfin rode beside him. Four more armored knights and seven sturdy men-at-arms rode behind them, dirt and gravel flying from their horses' hooves.

From the corner of his eye, Jude saw something large fall from a tree on the right side of the road.

"Pull up," yelled Balfin.

What?

A heavy rope sprang up across their path.

Zounds!

No time to stop. No time to turn or jump. The rope caught Jude's steed high on its legs, shattering them, just as he wrenched his boots free of the stirrups. The horse crashed to a halt, flipped head over hooves, and slammed to the earth. Jude rocketed forward, spun over once in the air, and sailed some dozen feet before landing on his back. He slid several yards along the dusty road, and aided by his momentum, gained his feet in an instant; the crash and howls of men and horses filled the air behind him.

Ambush!

Battered and disoriented, Jude drew his sword and assumed a defensive stance.

Is this really happening? I should've been paying attention. Sir Gabriel would have my hide.

Foreboding, armored figures emerged from the woods. Two men clad in blood-red armor with helms that covered their faces strode toward Jude with swords drawn. Behind them stalked a very tall, broad man in black-enameled armor, a dragon crest of red adorned his breastplate. Grizzled and scarred, armor gouged and dented: a veteran killer. Jude heard the rattle of steel and war cries of battle behind him.

No time to look. Is this real? My head spins; get ready. Cut them down. Quick. Jude backpedaled several steps to buy time to clear his head. *Behind me—something.*

Jude half turned and beheld a huge figure shaped like a man, but of brick-red skin, long fangs, pointed ears, and bald pate. An unspeakable union of man and demon, its very life a blasphemy and an affront to all that's holy. Far taller and broader than Jude, the creature stalked toward Jude, brandishing a massive, two-handed sword, chipped and stained with the dried blood of its last victims.

Dead gods, what's that? Can't fight that. Need help.

The red creature laughed at Jude's look of alarm, and then spoke in a rich baritone voice. "You look surprised to see us, boy. Did you think to find us asleep beside the road, waiting for you to swoop in and kill us like you did our messenger?"

It speaks? What is it? "Messenger? That thing was a monster, a demon."

"It was only sent to deliver our ransom note, nothing more," said Mort Zag, the red creature. "If it came to blows, the first was yours. You started this."

"You took my father!"

"We offered you a deal," said Ezerhauten, the dragon knight, in a deep gravelly voice.

"A fair deal," said Mort Zag. "Square and honest."

"But you came with your troops to cut us down," said Ezerhauten. "You have no honor, boy, none at all. Lord Korrgonn foresaw it; he foresaw your treachery."

"And now you'll pay dearly," said Mort Zag.

"Wait," said Jude. "We can—"

"No," said Ezerhauten. "The time for negotiation is past. We didn't want it this way, but you've given us no choice. Take him."

The two red-armored knights moved in.

"To victory and tomorrow," said Jude through

clenched teeth. He launched himself at the nearest of the two, barreled into him shoulder first before the man could bring up his sword, and sent him flying.

The other.

Jude spun in time to parry an overhand strike from the second knight, and launch a brutal kick to his groin. The man stumbled back a step and doubled over, stunned.

For father.

Jude spun his sword in a tight arc, a move taught him by Sir Gabriel, and separated the red knight's head from his shoulders.

Killed him. Can this be real? Behind me.

Jude turned and parried a blow from the first knight, now back on his feet. They exchanged several more cuts and thrusts while screams and shouts of the nearby melee echoed in the background.

He's good. Muscle him. Crush him down. Where's the dragon knight, and the red monster?

Jude pummeled the knight, smashing down with his sword over and over, beating the man back, before executing a Dwarven overhand strike. The red knight blocked the titanic blow, but the impact shattered his sword, leaving him nothing but the hilt.

Got him.

"For my father," Jude spat. He spun around, chopped down with all his might, and cleaved the man from shoulder to waist.

Dead gods, I killed him. Two down. Where are my men? Jude wrenched his sword free.

"The pup has sharp teeth," said Mort Zag.

"Your Sithians can't match him."

Must be quick, can't fight them both.

Jude feigned a move toward Ezerhauten, then spun toward Mort Zag, pulling a dagger from his belt. He launched it underhand, just as he had practiced with Ob a thousand times. The dagger caught Mort Zag in the throat, the monster's eyes wild with shock. He staggered back and clutched his neck as the wound spouted green ichor.

In a flash, a second dagger spun toward Ezerhauten. The knight brought up his sword and effortlessly knocked the blade aside.

Zounds.

"Time for a lesson, whelp," said Ezerhauten.

I can take him, I can beat them all.

The berserker's fury consumed Jude, body and soul; every ounce of his strength poured into each blow. He would crush his enemy. He would utterly annihilate him. He would have his revenge.

Two great swords flashed and sparked. Jude's sword thundered against Ezerhauten's, but for each powerful blow he struck, Ezerhauten struck twice, slashing and slicing into Jude's armor.

Jude roared in anger. *I'm hurt. He's too fast, too good. Gods, help me.*

Ezerhauten moved with blazing speed, parrying or dodging blow after blow after blow.

Toying with me. No chance. Hold out until Balfin can help.

"To the north is Asgard," shouted Jude. Blood dripped from his mouth.

"Asgard cannot save you, boy," said Ezerhauten. "Nor can Thetan."

As Jude raised his sword for another slash,

Mort Zag struck him across the shoulders from behind. Jude dropped to his knees, his strength gone. He was stunned, numb. His sword fell from his hands.

Mort Zag grabbed Jude, lifted him above his head, and threw him as if he were but an apple and not an armored man of well over three hundred pounds. Jude smashed into a thick oak some twenty feet away. He dropped down unmoving at its base.

Jude opened his eyes. Everything hurt. He felt cold, so cold. Blood streamed down his cheek. He coughed and spat up blood, and coughed again. Then everything hurt more. His vision was blurred, his mind clouded; it was difficult to breathe. He felt as if he floated in a fog. Then he saw Sir Gabriel walking toward him—strangely, Ezerhauten and Mort Zag walked on either side.

"Help me," Jude said. *I'm saved; it's Sir Gabriel.*

Sir Gabriel squatted down before him. His eyes glowed a brilliant gold, an eerie grin on his face.

Jude's eyes widened in alarm as he realized who fronted him now; his body shuddered in fear, though he had no strength to move, no command of his muscles. "Korrgonn," he said. "Please— don't kill me." *Can't abandon my brothers.*

Jude's vision grew dark and he saw no more.

***

"I told him not go," said Ector. Claradon, Duke Harringgold, Angle Theta, Ob, and several others gathered around the young knight in Harringgold's study.

"I told him it was a trap. We argued and finally he gave in and said he wouldn't go himself. He said he would send a squadron of knights and men-at-arms under Balfin. Next thing I knew, Indigo burst into my chambers saying that Jude just rode off leading a dozen men. One dozen. Not even a half squadron. The idiot."

"More muscle than brains is Jude," said Ob, nodding.

"Indigo and I rode after them with what men we could assemble in a few minutes.

We found them a couple miles north of Riker's Crossroads. They were ambushed. Twelve men dead, including Balfin, Mordekain, Mithras, and Desmond."

Claradon and Ob shuddered and winced as he spoke each name. Each one a friend and comrade of long years.

Ector took a deep breath before continuing. "Not just dead. They were mutilated. Unspeakable things were done to them. Some even looked—gnawed upon."

"Dead gods," said Tanch. "Madness, sheer madness. What did we do to bring this on?"

"What of Jude?" said Ob quietly.

"He wasn't there. They must've taken him."

"Did you search the wood?" said Ob perking up. "Could he have run for it?"

"His horse was down, dead in the road. They'd

pulled a rope up from the brush and tripped the lead horses. It looked like they fell at a gallop."

"He would've been thrown," said Ob.

"We found no trail leading into the woods. They took him."

"How many of them did you find?" asked the Duke.

"Not a one. They either took their dead with them, or none were killed."

"None killed?" spouted Ob. "Not likely. Twelve men of House Eotrus didn't go lightly, I'll tell you. Balfin is—was—an expert; Mordekain, a bruiser as strong as Jude, and Desmond was as tough as nails. Dropped twice their number at least, ambushed or not. They went down as heroes, and I will hear nothing different from nobody, understand?" Ob smacked his fist into his other hand and cursed under his breath.

Ector stared down at his feet for a respectful moment before continuing. "We came on to Lomion as fast as we could, chasing at their heels all the way. We got close enough to see them, but no closer."

"Who were they, and how many?" said Ob, still red-faced and bristling.

"Fifteen to twenty riders, plus a large coach that moves like the wind."

Claradon, Ob, and Theta exchanged glances.

"We followed them to the city, but lost them at the north gate. The guards let the brigands pass swiftly through, but held us there for many minutes. We were so close. It was all I could do to not cut the gatemen down."

"Did it seem as if the guards delayed you on

purpose?" said Harringgold. "To let the brigands get clear?"

"Maybe, but it's hard to say. A Myrdonian Captain gave us a difficult time, asking why we were riding so hard and what we were about. He just wouldn't listen to me or didn't care, and made no move to stop the coach despite my pleading."

"Did you get the Captain's name?" said the Duke.

Ector paused, thinking. "They called him Bartol."

Harringgold nodded. "I thought as much. Captain Bartol is the third son of House Alder, younger brother to Chancellor Barusa."

"Those stinking Alders are everywhere," said Ob. "Everywhere there's dirty dealings and backstabbings, that is. They've never been any good, not one of them."

The Duke stood up. "My men will find this coach." He strode off to dispatch his agents, leaving Claradon and his comrades alone in the study.

"That stinking carriage again," said Ob.

"It's The Shadow League for certain," said Claradon. "Why couldn't it just be brigands—pay some ransom and get Jude back? Instead, we've got the same crazies that killed father, Sir Gabriel, and the others. And now they have Jude too."

"We should've rooted them stinking cultists out years ago and been done with them," said Ob.

"Why do they want Jude?" said Claradon. "To what end? Haven't they done enough to our House?"

"We won't know why until we catch them,

boy," said Ob. "And catch them we will."

***

"The carriage went through Southeast," said Grim Fischer—a Gnome, and one of the Duke's agents. "Straight to the docks. They rolled it right up a gangway and onto a ship. Their outriders boarded too, along with their horses. They set sail as soon as they secured the carriage and horses below deck."

"Which ship was it?" asked Harringgold.

"*The White Rose*," said Grim. "It's the fastest ship in Lomion."

"Of course it is," said Claradon sardonically.

"A smuggler, reaver, and all-around ship of ill repute," said Ob.

"True enough," said Grim, "and captained by one Rastinfan Rascelon."

"A no-good raper and murderer, I hear tell," said Ob.

"That and more, but no one's given evidence against him," said Grim.

"And apparently in the employ of The Shadow League," said Claradon.

"More than that," said Harringgold. "We've suspected for some time that Rascelon is one of the League's Arkons—that's what they call their highest leaders."

"Did your men see Korrgonn?" asked Theta.

"He was there," said Grim. "He got out of the carriage just after they drove it onto *The White*

Rose. He sailed with the ship."

"Are you certain?"

"Saw him myself."

Theta turned toward the Duke. "I need a ship."

Harringgold didn't immediately answer.

"Will you give us a ship? We must track down Korrgonn. He must be stopped."

"I know your feelings on this, Lord Theta. Arranging for a ship that has any hope of catching *The White Rose* may not be an easy task."

"My Lords," said Tanch. "Let's not be hasty here. We've agreed that Korrgonn is a threat—we all want him gone. Well—now he's gone, of his own volition. Let him go, I say. Master Fischer has said *The White Rose* was heavily provisioned. That means a long journey, perhaps months or more, to who knows where. Just let him go, and keep watch for *The White Rose's* return. When it arrives—if it arrives—we can marshal our forces and be waiting for it with strength, on solid ground of our choosing. We will have the advantage. But on the river or at sea, any ship that we could send is vulnerable."

"They have Jude, you idiot," said Ob. "We're not to abandon him."

Tanch looked confused. "No—no—of course not," said Tanch, wiping his brow with his sleeve and looking for a chair. "I'm sorry. The stress of recent days has gotten to me. I didn't think—didn't know what I was saying. Of course, we must rescue Jude, of course, we must."

"Even if Jude wasn't with him," said Ob, "who's to say what evils Korrgonn will do downriver."

"Or what forces of his own he'll marshal,"

added Claradon.

"Remember, Lomion isn't just this city and our lands to the north," said Ob. "There are plenty of lands to the south too: Dor Malvegil, Roosa, Beringford, Dravilt, Dor Linden, Dover, and more. Stinking Korrgonn could do no end of mischief at any of those places. We can't sit back and let that happen."

"We will send ravens to the Lords Malvegil and Mirtise warning them of the threat," said the Duke.

"*The Rose* was provisioned for a long journey," said Grim. "Three days ago it appeared in the harbor, though no one saw it approach. Rascelon loaded it with all manner of provisions until the moment it sailed. They hauled aboard enough water and foodstuffs to sail all the way to Tragoss Mor, probably farther, without resupplying.

"So where could they be headed?" asked Claradon.

"Maybe they're going to Theta's lands, way out wherever it is," said Ob. "Perhaps old Korrgonn heard about your fancy wine cellar and wants to sample a vintage or two."

"Enough," said Theta. "I intend to follow that ship until I catch it, whether that be in ten leagues or at the very ends of the world. There will be no turning around, no letting him go. I will catch Korrgonn and kill him, and if it's possible, rescue Claradon's brother. Anyone that objects can stay here and hide under their beds. The rest of us will see this done." He turned toward the Duke. "You say that *The White Rose* is the fastest ship in Lomion; which one is the next fastest?"

432

Harringgold considered for a moment. "Any one of several Lomerian Cruisers—military ships. But I can't get you one of those—each is commanded by a Myrdonian Knight Captain and they all report to Marshal Balfor and through him to the Chancellor. The next best choice would be *The Black Dragon*. She's a smaller ship but she might be *The Rose*'s match in speed."

"My Lord, *The Black Dragon* is no more, at least in name," said Grim. "Slaayde renamed her *The Black Falcon* not long ago. Third or fourth time he has changed the ship's name and standard in the last few years, if I remember straight."

"Ah, yes, he is known for that." Harringgold turned back toward Theta. "*The Black Falcon* is a merchant ship captained by one Dylan Slaayde."

"The problem is, Slaayde is set to sail to Minoc with a load of marble, or so I hear," said Grim. "To make any good speed you would have to unload it before you set sail. That will take a day, maybe two, and we would probably have to buy the cargo off him to boot."

"Are there other options?" asked Theta.

"None that I know of that's near as fast and what could be ready much sooner," said Grim.

"Then *The Black Falcon* it is," said Theta, staring down the Duke.

The Duke stared back for a goodly time before responding. "Very well, I will arrange this with Captain Slaayde. I'll also assign some of my guardsmen to your command—as I fear you will need them before your journey is done."

"Can Slaayde be trusted, my lord?" said Claradon.

433

"To a point," said Harringgold. "He's a scoundrel and a menace to free trade; but he's no friend to the League."

***

"**W**hat am I supposed to do?" said Ector. He, Claradon, and Ob huddled together in the corner of Harringgold's den. "Father is gone. Sir Gabriel is dead. Brother Donnelin, Par Talbon, Stern, Marzdan, Balfin, Mithras, all dead, every one. Malcolm is badly hurt, now Jude is taken, and you, Artol, and Tanch are all going who knows where. What am I supposed to do?"

Claradon looked stricken. He reached out and put a hand on his brother's shoulder.

"What would your father tell you to do, boy?" said Ob.

Ector shook his head slightly and sunk back into the leather chair. "He would tell me to do my duty."

"Which is what?"

"To uphold the family name and the family honor. To hold the Dor and protect it and our people against all enemies. To obey the Crown."

"Right," said Ob. "That is what you're supposed to do, and that's what you will do, boy. That's what would make your father proud. Do you understand?"

Ector nodded and stared at the floor. Tears welled in his eyes, uncertain, and afraid.

"You're not alone in this," said Claradon.

434

"Sarbek is acting Castellan. Next to Ob, he has the most experience of our any of our men. He will deal with the details."

"And Indigo is a fine knight," said Ob. "You keep him close, he will help you until we're back."

"And when will that be?" said Ector, tears streaming down his face.

"When we rescue Jude," said Claradon.

"What if it's too late?"

"It won't be," said Claradon.

"What if it is?"

"Then we will avenge him, boy," said Ob, "and then we'll come home. Either way, we'll be back as soon as we can."

"I hope that's soon enough," said Ector. "A couple of drunks and an angry sheepherder could take the Dor now."

"Ector, please."

"No, Claradon. A month ago we had more than fifty named men amongst us. No other Dor could match us man for man. And now it's just me, Sarbek, Indigo, and a few squadrons of nobodies. We're finished, Claradon. The Dor is finished. House Eotrus is finished."

"We're not at war, Ector," said Claradon. "We're not under siege."

"It seems to me that we are."

"Well, we're not. We will rebuild our forces in time. And I'll ask Lord Harringgold if he can spare any more men to escort you back and help man the Dor."

"That won't bring father back. Or any of them."

***

435

Tears streamed down Marissa Harringgold's face; her cheeks flushed red; her hands trembled. She was as beautiful as Claradon remembered— maybe more so. "If you hadn't made Jude go back to Dor Eotrus, he would be here now; but he's dead, and it's all your fault."

"He's not dead," said Lord Harringgold. "Brother Claradon will bring him back to you, daughter, never fear."

Claradon's face was pale. He was in shock. He couldn't believe what he was seeing—what he was hearing. Jude and Marissa? Jude knew better than anyone how he felt about her. How could Jude do that to him? How could he betray him? Claradon clamped his eyes on the floor and did not move them, no matter how much he wanted to. He couldn't stand to look at her—he couldn't stomach it. He hoped that he would never have to look at her again. So he kept his eyes down. Beside him, Ector did the same.

Marissa marched up to Claradon.

"First you go off and become a monk, and now Jude is dead. Dead!" She turned and her eyes bored into Ector. "And you're too young." She stamped her foot. "I'll be an old maid."

She stormed from the room, wailing. "I hate you all."

IV
BORN KILLERS

"I don't expect you to duel the devil himself.
For that we need born killers."
—Barusa of Alder

The Chancellor's office in Tammanian Hall was hot, as it always was that time of year. No windows permitted in any light, air, or prying eyes. Stuffy and close, it smelled of sweat and moldy parchment.

Cartegian, son of King Tenzivel, and crown prince of the realm of Lomion, squatted on a chair and rocked back and forth, wild-eyed, unshaven, and unkempt. Chancellor Barusa of Alder passed him a document and an elderly scribe handed the Prince a fresh quill.

"And what is this one for?" said Cartegian. "Something good or something bad?"

"Something good, of course," said Barusa. "Now sign it."

"Let me read it first." Cartegian snatched up the writ in a grubby hand, drool sliding down his whiskers and dripping onto the parchment. "Hmm. Another arrest warrant, and this one for that traitorous Lord 'Blank Space to be filled in later'. Haven't we arrested old Lord Blankety Blank over a hundred times today?" he said, pointing to the pile of signed documents atop the corner of the desk. "Can we give the old boy no rest? We'll need bigger dungeons soon, oh yes, that we will."

"And just how many inbred blueblood braggarts are we arresting tomorrow, oh great defender of the realm, oh champion of justice? Just try to say that three times fast. Every one, perchance? Off with all their heads, will it be?"

"You need not concern yourself with the details of State, my Prince. Merely sign this last writ and you are free for the remainder of the day."

"Chancellor—dear, beloved Chancellor, you're such a poopyhead."

The Chancellor rolled his eyes and clenched his fists. He winced from the effort, his right hand stiff, and his arm still in a sling from his duel with Claradon Eotrus. Barusa took a deep breath and spoke in as calm a voice as he was capable. "Sign it, or there will be no supper for you."

A fiendish smile engulfed Cartegian's face. "I'll eat my cat; how would you like that?" The Prince turned and studied the feathered quill. He rubbed it on his arm, soiling his shirt. Drool spilled down his lip.

"It's the last one for the day, Cartegian. Sign it and you can go play with your cat or your troll or whatever."

Cartegian stared at the Chancellor, his eyes now focused, his voice now slow and steady. "If I sign it, Mr. Old Fart, can I go to the dungeons and play with someone, someone bad?"

"Who?"

"Whoever. Just so long as they scream."

"Fine. Sign it and you can go to the dungeons."

"Promise?"

"Yes. Sign it."

The prince signed the scroll with an exaggerated flourish and then somersaulted forward on the table, scattering papers and knocking over inkwells. He landed on his feet before the table, and bowed to an imagined audience. The scribes dived in to save the parchment from the spilled ink.

"Enough," said Barusa. "Get the fool out of here."

Cartegian turned to him and feigned shock at Barusa's words. "Yes, send me to the dungeons. To the dungeons with the great hero of Lomion. Bring forth my lizard!"

Blain of Alder burst into the room and nearly crashed into Cartegian.

"What ho," said the Prince. "The dashing brother of Mr. Farty Pants. Little Poop, himself."

Blain stepped around the Prince, ignoring him. "I have news."

"You found me a flying monkey at last?" said the Prince.

The Chancellor studied Blain for a moment, then put down the scroll he held and dismissed his aides who ushered Cartegian out with them. Only when the chamber was empty and door secured did Blain continue.

"Eotrus knows about his brother's ambush, and he knows it was the League."

"This was expected, but not so soon."

"It's worse. They know about Korrgonn's passage on *The White Rose*. Harringgold's men are at Dylan Slaayde's ship. They must plan on following *The Rose*."

"Curse that Harringgold. Does nothing pass

him by?"

"He's got many agents—Rangers, the Orphan's Guild, and more."

"We have agents too, brother, including on *The Black Falcon*."

"But Fizdar is dead."

Barusa shot him an angry look.

"But you know that, of course. You've got another man aboard?"

Barusa returned no reaction.

"Of course, you do. Do we move against Eotrus now?"

"Eotrus is nothing. He's but a boy handy with a sword. He can be killed at any time; I have only to give the command. It's the other that's the concern."

"He's only one man, and he can't possibly be the fallen one. It's ridiculous. The wizards are mental."

Barusa slammed his fist to the tabletop. "He killed Mortach! Mortach was more god than man and he killed him. He's the threat, a grave threat, and must be dealt with."

"We don't know it was him."

"Then who? You think Eotrus cut off Mortach's head? Or maybe his Gnome lackey or his hedge wizard?"

"Who knows?"

"It was the Harbinger, you idiot. The priests say he only looks like a man, but he's not. He's some ancient evil held over from *The Dawn Age*, some force of nature. A monster, a real monster, like in the old legends. The incarnation of all that's evil in the world. He must be stopped. We must stop him."

"You're losing it, brother," Blain said, shaking his head in disgust. "None of that can be true. It's crazy. Superstitious, fairy stories, that's all, told by old men desperate to hang on to power. But even if, somehow, you and the priests are right, then the farther he is from Lomion, the better. Let him go and good riddance."

"No! He needs killing and Eotrus along with him. Contact Captain Kleig at once. If Eotrus follows *The Rose*, we will follow Eotrus."

Blain looked surprised. "You're going?"

"Of course not. You are. And Bartol and Edwin too."

"Edwin? Barusa, I heard *The Rose* fit up for a long haul. I have a family. I can't just go off for who knows how long following these people. And my son too?"

"I need you to go. I need men that I can rely on for this. As for Edwin, leave it up to him. He owes Eotrus for that scar. Let's offer your boy a chance at revenge. If he's man enough to take it, well, that will tell us something, won't it? In any case, you will be there to look after him."

"And what do I tell Esther?"

"How about the truth? You're off on House business of great import. She will understand or not, I really don't care. But you will go, either way."

"Fine, but if the Harbinger is as dangerous as you think, how are we to stop him? I'll cross swords with most any man, but I've no interest in fighting ancient man-monsters or whatever he is."

"Don't pee yourself, brother. For all your skill,

I don't expect you to duel the devil himself. For that we need born killers."

"Who could possibly—"

"The Duelist of Dyvers and the Knights of Kalathen"

Blain's face brightened. "That's an idea at that. DeBoors is supposed to be the best there is, and I hear he's in the city."

"He is."

Blain paused for a moment. "You planned this? DeBoors isn't in Lomion just by chance, is he?"

"Of course I planned it. I plan everything. Have Kleig ready his ship to sail by morning while I pay DeBoors a visit."

Three cloaked men, faces concealed under hoods, made their way up the grand stair of the Roaring Lion Inn. DeBoors and his men had rooms on the second floor—some of the best accommodations in all of Lomion City, courtesy of the Chancellor, or rather, of House Alder's treasury.

"Why do we need this mercenary, uncle?" said Edwin quietly. "I can deal with Eotrus, and Uncle Bartol and my father can handle that foreign knight."

"I admire your confidence," said Barusa, "but I would rather not see my brothers and nephew dead."

"It's unseemly for us to be walking around in hiding, as if we're criminals," said Edwin.

"It would be more unseemly for the chancellor of the realm to be seen consorting with hired killers."

Bartol put his hand on Edwin's shoulder. "Keep your tongue in check while we're in there. DeBoors isn't a man to be fooled with."

"Neither am I," Edwin said.

Four armored men, Knights of Kalathen, stood on guard in the second floor hall. These were no ordinary soldiers. They were large and solid, with chiseled features, the finest armor and weapons that coin could buy, and the dead eyes of cold-blooded killers. Bartol pulled back his hood and showed them the Chancellor's seal of office.

The knights soon ushered them through a set of ornate double doors into a grand suite. A large living area with rich couches and chairs and a large fireplace dominated the room. Four doors led to bedrooms.

Beside the fireplace stood a tall, rangy, shirtless Pict of golden brown skin and ponytail. Around his waist, a sword belt; in his right hand, a spear, the haft resting on the floor. A worn bedroll lay open and disheveled at his feet; clearly, he had been lying on it before the three arrived. A man accustomed to a hard life outdoors sometimes had no interest in a soft bed.

The Chancellor and Edwin pulled back their hoods as the Pict studied them. The left side of Edwin's face was swollen and red, an ugly scar, not long old, extended from the corner of his lip to his left ear.

One of the bedroom doors opened. A chiseled hulk of gleam and gristle stood in the portal. He studied the room for some moments, then nodded to the Kalathens. Two left the room, the remaining stood guard by the door.

"I am DeBoors," he said.

"I am Barusa," said the Chancellor. He gestured toward each of his kinsmen, in turn. "My brother, Bartol, of the Myrdonians. My nephew, Edwin."

DeBoors approached and shook hands with each. He and Barusa exchanged polite smiles. Bartol tightly gripped DeBoors' hand to take his measure. At six foot four and two hundred eighty pounds of mostly muscle, Bartol stood eye to eye with DeBoors, but still looked small beside him. DeBoors was solid, and massive of arm, chest, and shoulder. His golden cuirass, articulated and fitted, made him all the more imposing.

Edwin barely contained his disdain for the whole affair.

The men took seats on couch and chairs. A servant appeared, dispensing wine, brandy, and cigars from parts foreign. Barusa and DeBoors engaged in pleasant conversation about the weather, DeBoors' journey from Dyvers, and other miscellany. All the while, Bartol said little and sat patiently. Edwin squirmed in his seat, having no interest in small talk and no use for mercenaries. The Pict stood silent, and near motionless, save for his eyes, which shifted from Barusa, to Bartol, to Edwin, and back again, no doubt imagining novel ways to kill and torture them each, such was his savage nature.

After a time, DeBoors placed his tumbler on the table. "On to business?"

The Chancellor nodded. "All that we say here tonight will remain here."

"Of course," said DeBoors.

"I will have your word on that."

"You just did."

The Chancellor nodded. "Within some hours, a ship called *The Black Falcon* will leave the harbor in pursuit of a vessel called *The White Rose*. Aboard *The Rose* are some that are friends of mine. Aboard *The Falcon* are some that are not. You will follow *The Falcon* aboard another ship called *The Grey Talon*. With you and your men will go Bartol, Edwin, my brother Blain, and a company of soldiers from my House. In addition, *The Grey Talon* is well stocked of marines and fighting seamen."

DeBoors nodded his understanding.

"Aboard *The Falcon* are two men that I would see dead."

"News of your duel has reached me, Chancellor. The young Lord Eotrus is one of the two, I have no doubt. The mercenary that travels with him is the other."

Barusa smiled a thin smile. "Indeed. I am glad to see that you are well informed."

"It's essential in my business."

Barusa nodded. "When you are well away from Lomion City, at a time of your choosing, you will do away with these two. I don't want them returning to Lomion City under any circumstances."

"What support do they have on *The Falcon*?"

"Eotrus has his House Wizard with him," said Bartol.

"Their true House Wizard fell in a skirmish alongside Aradon Eotrus in the Northlands," said

445

Barusa. "By all accounts, his replacement is no more than a hedge wizard and a coward at that. But Eotrus does have troops with him, perhaps one, or even two squadrons of knights and men-at-arms. *The Falcon*'s crew may stand with them as well, but I doubt it."

"I've heard tell of Dylan Slaayde and his reavers," DeBoors said. "They can be dealt with, if need be."

"Your price?" Barusa said.

"Your offer?" responded DeBoors.

"Twenty thousand silver stars," said Barusa.

DeBoors' face darkened. "A kingly price for the head of a merchant or a minor noble. A pittance for a Dor Lord well-guarded, and a river voyage to boot."

They stared each other down for some moments.

"Fifty thousand, and no more," said Barusa, as he stood, the negotiation over. The others followed him up.

"Thirty thousand in advance, the rest on proof," said DeBoors.

"Done," said Barusa.

V
OLD SAINT PIP

"Trust no wizards, my Lord, not one."
—Pipkorn to Angle Theta

The southern Lomerian docks stretched for over two miles. The western reaches nestled within the fringes of the High District and were filled with noblemen's yachts and pleasure vessels, elements of the royal fleet, church vessels, and ambassadorial galleons. The heart of the docks, populated with merchant craft of all manner and type, burst with warehouses and fisheries and bustled with activity from pre-dawn to late eve. Those central docks served as home to the Lomerian Navy: cutters, longships, and cruisers, swift and strong.

The eastern reaches of the docks touched a seedy section of the city called The Heights for a short stretch and ended in Southeast, which was by far the foulest district in the fair city of Lomion. The walls betwixt the city proper and Southeast continued to the water's edge and well beyond. Long and tall stone jetties extended more than three hundred feet into the harbor on each side of Southeast. Guard posts lived at the watersides, manned continuously with sturdy watchmen. Watch stations and barracks stood against the wall near the water's edge at the land sides of the jetties, and brimmed with watchmen—duty posts for the young and the out of favor.

The Black Falcon berthed in The Heights, not far from Southeast, no doubt due to its dubious reputation and alleged dirty dealings. To supplement its crew and Claradon's men, Lord Harringgold assigned a squadron of soldiers of his house. Young men mostly, fresh-faced but well trained and disciplined. They wore the livery of House Harringgold on their tabards—a silver, gauntleted fist upraised that looked to be a mighty stone tower when viewed from certain angles. These men-at-arms were girded with swords and shields; several bore crossbows, and a number brought aboard wicked-looking pikes. They wore chainmail coats, leggings, coif, and steel half-helms. Commanding them was Lord Harringgold's nephew, Sir Seran Harringgold, a muscular, fair-haired youth of ready smile and gleaming plate armor. Seran was a member of the Odion Knights, an aristocratic order both powerful and secretive.

Theta supervised the provisioning of the ship, which proceeded concurrently with the offloading of marble slabs from *The Falcon*'s hold. He had the Duke's men acquire and bring aboard foodstuffs and drink, independent of those hauled aboard by Dylan Slaayde's crew. At Theta's direction, the Duke's men acquired various additional armaments and several trunks of a type designed to float, even fully laden in rough seas. While the loading and unloading operations proceeded, Theta inspected every inch of the three-masted vessel—its extents, structure, and cargo.

Claradon's small retinue of soldiers stood watch on the pier during the loading process. They and Tanch made a game of counting how many people on the bustling dockyards skulked and loitered about, watching every move on and around *The Falcon*.

"That man on the corner—perhaps, one of the Alders?" said Tanch.

"A Black Hand," said Artol. "He's called Dirgo the Mark. A real killer." Artol took a puff of the cigar that dangled from his mouth. "He'll cut your eyes out and eat them raw, if you give him the chance."

Tanch shuddered.

"I believe I see a Myrdonian knight in the high window across the way," said Tanch. "See the insignia on his tabard? I'm quite sure I'm right, this time. And that stooped old woman by the barrels has a beard beneath her cowl. How disgusting."

"So does your grandmother, but good eyes anyway, wizard," said Artol. "Did you notice that that lady of the evening down the corner has turned away three buyers in favor of watching us?"

"Oh! There's one of the Vizier's apprentices," said Tanch, "peaking from the doorway of the fishmonger's."

"If we had sold tickets," said Artol, "we could've bought this darn ship."

***

Slaayde's crew was a company of seasoned sailors and hardened sell-swords from around the globe. They held no love for the Duke's well-coifed and uniformed guardsmen or for the knights of Dor Eotrus, who looked down upon them as the scum of the earth, which in truth, rose more than a few above their station.

N'Paag, the newly hired first mate, a dark-hued man of the free city of Piper's Hold, stood on the forecastle and surveyed the loading and unloading work, but said little.

Slaayde's second mate and chief bullyboy was a near seven-foot-tall, black-bearded behemoth called Little Tug. Though expert at working the pulleys and small gantries used to haul the slabs of marble out of the hold, Tug could lift near as much with his bare hands. His half-Lugron blood accounted for his muscle and his girth, but not his height, since Lugron typically stood inches shorter than the average Volsung.

Affronts to nature and decency are the half-Lugron, or so they say, since the coupling of Volsung woman and Lugron male almost always occurred without consent. Rarely was it that such a union bore fruit, and when it did, the pitiable result usually died in childhood, deformed and outcast. Despite his rather ill-favored looks, Tug was one of the lucky ones, as he had his share of wits, if just.

All the work and the ever-present bantering was performed under the watchful eye of the ship's quartermaster, the ill-named Bertha Smallbutt, who was near as wide as she was tall and no doubt trained the banshee in its screaming techniques. At one point, Ob found himself upended bodily and tossed over the rail into the water when he ran afoul of her during a disagreement about whose provisions were to go where.

In the final hour of loading, a stooped man of hooded brown robes and crooked cane made his way across the pier to *The Falcon*'s berth carrying a large, grimy sack over his shoulder.

"A bite of bread?" pleaded the man as he approached Theta who stood at the foot of the gangway. "A crumb, a crumb of cheese for a poor old man?"

"Greetings, Rascatlan," said Theta. "Has your larder gone empty or your head?"

The old man let out a small growl of frustration and looked up at Theta. It was the wizard Pipkorn, Sorcerer Supreme of all Midgaard, in disguise. He furtively looked around to see if anyone could overhear them. "I could never fool you, Lord Theta. I have come with council and what aid I can provide, if you will have it."

"Gladly."

Pipkorn stepped close and spoke quietly. "You know that Korrgonn is bent on opening another gateway. He won't rest until it's done. That is where he's going, to find another place of power where the veil between Midgaard and Nifleheim is thin. Only there can the door be opened. Only there can his armies come through."

"I suspected as much."

"He must not succeed or all will be lost. Everything. The whole world."

"Don't those fools helping him know?"

"Most of them are wizards. Ginalli has gathered dark wizards from across Midgaard to his cause. Worse, he has corrupted many who were never dark. When that gateway opens, magic will come storming back in the world, magic of a kind and a power not seen in an age. That's what they want, that is what they lust for. Their power will grow tenfold. They're blinded by this, they can't see past it. Dreams of such power can corrupt most anyone. Trust no wizards, my lord, not one."

"Even you?"

"Even me," said Pipkorn sadly.

"I don't trust anyone."

"That has its advantages, I suppose. If you will, my lord, gather young Eotrus, Par Tanch, your Elf, your Gnome, and young Harringgold, and let's speak in private. I have some trifles for you."

Not until they were secure within the Captain's Den, the door barred, did Pipkorn straighten and pull back his hood, his voice returning to its normal pitch.

Sixtyish and balding gray, Pipkorn had a full gray moustache and a strange boil amidst his forehead. "I come with what aid I can offer for your quest," said Pipkorn. "And to wish you well on your journey. I appreciate its true import, even if your good benefactor the Duke does not. There's much to speak of, but not near enough time. You must be away as soon as you are supplied. I've brought you what tokens an old wizard has collected over his long years." Pipkorn opened his sack and rummaged about. "One and all are precious to me, but if they're not put to good use now, then when?"

From within the sack he pulled a deerskin

quiver filled with arrows of black stony heads and shafts of exotic wood fletched with green feathers. "For you," he said, handing the quiver to Dolan. "Made by the Vanyar Elves of legend. You will find that they fly truer and farther than any others. The tips are made of ranal, a metal with the look of obsidian, but hard as steel and near half again as light. They're imbued with some queer magic of the Vanyar; use them against the minions of Nifleheim when common arrows fail you."

"Thank you, Mr. Wizard, sir," said Dolan, bowing low.

Pipkorn reached back into the tall sack and pulled out a short sword, gleaming silver and inscribed with runes. "For you, Sir Seran. This is a Dyvers blade, but no common one. This beauty was forged four hundred years ago by Lord Dyvers himself, one of his last and greatest works. Use it well."

Pipkorn handed Seran the ancient blade. "Thank you, Master Pipkorn; I'm in your debt."

"Yes of course, as is everyone. And where is young Malvegil?"

"Glimador left for Dor Malvegil some days ago," said Claradon.

"Of course," said Pipkorn. Pipkorn pulled another stylish short sword from his sack. "Sir Seran, I trust that you'll not mind holding your blade's twin until Glimador rejoins this merry band?"

"I would be honored," said Seran.

"No doubt, no doubt," said Pipkorn.

Next, Pipkorn pulled a short-hafted battle-axe from the sack, and handed it to Ob. "For you, sir."

The axe had a dull silver color to its head, and a stout oaken haft carved with curious runes.

"Mighty pretty axe there, Pip," said Ob, as he grasped the handle. "It almost looks like it were made of—"

"Mithril?" said Pipkorn. "Indeed it is. I know of no other like it."

"An axe of mithril? Even in legend I've only heard of one."

"Yes, only one," said Pipkorn, a wry smile on his face. "And this is she. The axe of Bigby the Bold, late Prince of the great Gnomish city of Shandelon, and last of his line."

Ob's eyes near popped from his head. "It cannot be. How could you ever come across this?"

"One of many tales for which we have no time, I fear. Suffice that it will serve you well, as it served the Gnomish lords and kings of Shandelon for a thousand years and more."

Pipkorn patted himself down searching for something. "Ah, here it is." From a pocket, he pulled a bronze ring. "For you, Tanch Trinagal of the Blue Tower, son of Sinch" said Pipkorn as he handed over the ring. "You hold in your hand the fabled Ring of the Magi, one of twenty born in the forge of the Wizard Talidousen, Sorcerer Supreme during the reign of King Zeltlin II, more than seven thousand years ago. The skills that ensorcelled it and its brothers are long lost to the world and likely as not, will not be found again. Keep it close, and keep it secret, for there is many a mage and hedge wizard that would gladly kill to possess one of these."

Tanch stared at it in wonder. "Legend tells that

these rings can amplify a wizard's power, increasing the strength and duration of his magics."

"It does that and more, as you'll come to know in time."

"Now, young Lord Eotrus, for you, I have something truly special." He reached under his cloak and pulled out a gold chain hung round his neck. He lifted it off over his head. From the chain hung a bejeweled amulet of fiery red and gold stones, set in a seven-sided gold base. The center stone was red with streaks of yellow, having the appearance of a great cat's eye, and giving off a soft glow. "Brother Claradon Eotrus, Lord of Dor Eotrus, son of Aradon, and first of your name, I present to you the fabled Amulet of Escandell. Its stones were forged in the heart of a falling star that fell to Midgaard in the second age of our world, the *Age of Heroes*. Lord Escandell, first wizard of the Tower of the Arcane found the fallen star, plucked these very stones from its maw, and weaved them into the golden base with eldritch spells and mighty words of power from bygone days. When worn around your neck, no enemy can take you unawares and no beast can surprise you. Wear it beneath your outer garments, close to your heart forevermore and fail you it will not. Even now it glows a bit—as there is danger here, but it's not immediate, so the glow is soft and dim. As the glow and heat increases, so does your peril."

"There are no words, Master Pipkorn, for such generosity. I am in your debt, sir. I thank you," he said, bowing before the archmage.

Pipkorn turned toward Theta. "I have not forgotten you, my Lord. For the Great Dragon I have this." Pipkorn reached into his robe and pulled out a leather sheath housing a bejeweled dagger. The handle was long, and black and silver, perhaps metal or even stone.

"That looks like Gabe's dagger, Dargus Dal, though even fancier," said Ob. "One of those old Asgardian blades."

"A good eye, sir," said Pipkorn. "An Asgardian blade it is, but no common one—if any of them could be called common." Pipkorn pulled it from its worn leather sheath.

"Lord Theta, I present to you—"

"Wotan Dal," said Theta as Pipkorn handed it to him handle first. Theta held the blade up before his eyes and studied it.

"Yes," said Pipkorn, smiling. "Wotan Dal, which means "god's blade" in the old tongue. This my friends was the blade of Lord Odin himself, the, ruler of the gods, king of the mighty Aesir. Forged before time itself in the first age of our world, in the days of myth and legend. Its blade cannot be dulled and no armor can turn it."

Theta beamed as he gazed at the blade and its ornate handle. "This is a wonder I never thought to see again."

"Bet that's worth a pretty penny," said Ob as he looked back and forth between it and his new axe.

"It's worth the good half of the king's treasury," said Tanch.

"More," said Theta. "A king's cache of gold can be replaced, this cannot." Theta placed Wotan Dal in a sheath at his belt, replacing the blade that was there. "Thank you, wizard. Truly. I will make good use of it."

"I know, my Lord. That's why it is rightly yours, and no other's."

"I have one more gift, this one made by my own hand." He pulled a small wooden box from a deep pocket and held it out to Claradon. "I call this, the Ghost Ship box. Open its lid while on deck and a duplicate of your vessel, crew and all, will appear out of nowhere and sit the water some hundred yards from your vessel, in whichever direction you point the open lid. Angle the lid higher to the sky and the ship will appear farther out, angle it down closer to the water, and the ship will appear closer. Make no mistake, this is no parlor trick. This duplicate will not only look as your ship, but will make the same noises and have the same scent. If the ghost ship is hit with catapult, ballistae, or fire it will take damage, its men will go down, and if the damage is bad enough, the ship will sink, ending the illusion. Use it wisely. It carries within it enough mystical energy to hold its illusion no more than one hour—whether that be in one use only, two half hours, or ten uses of six minutes or any other combination. One hour only. Do not forget."

"Thank you, Master Pipkorn," said Claradon. "We will use your gifts wisely."

Pipkorn nodded. "Men, I must also tell you that your enemies on this quest aren't just those sailing with Korrgonn on *The White Rose;* there will be some just as deadly behind as well. Someone, though I know not who, has hired The

457

Black Hand to slay you. I don't know if their target is Lord Theta or Lord Eotrus or both, but the Hand will follow you, however far you go. And that's not the worst of it. The Alders bear you a weighty grudge, Claradon, because you bested Barusa in that duel. They've hired mercenaries to see to you. There's talk of Kaledon of the Gray Waste—a Pict and foul sword master of mystical power. Beware him, he is a deadly foe. Worse still, the winds say that the Duelist of Dyvers was given a warrant on your life as well. With him come the Knights of Kalathen, as formidable a group of tin cans as any."

"Just kill us now," said Tanch. "The Duelist of Dyvers. The Knights of Kalathen. The Black Hand. The Shadow League. Cultists, and Nifleheim Lords too. How many of these madmen can we withstand? My back just can't take this stress," he said groaning and wincing as he slowly sunk down to his seat. "It's all too much, too much," he said, holding his brow. "It's the end of the world. The end times are here."

"Whatever happens, Claradon, do not face the duelist in battle," said Pipkorn. "Mark these words well. Heed them better than you have ever heeded any words before. The duelist is a foe you cannot match. If he stands in your path, forget your pride, forget your good name, forget your honor, forget your friends, and forget anything else that would give you pause and just flee. Just run, boy, and keep running until you're well away and then run a good ways more and pray you've lost him. Flee and live to fight another day. Don't forget these words or the duelist will be the death of you." Pipkorn turned toward Theta. "I believe you knew the duelist, my lord, in days gone by. His name is Milton DeBoors."

Theta furrowed his brow. "That's a name I haven't heard in long years. The man I knew was a soldier, a leader of men, not a hired killer."

"Times change, and so do men. But you know that, my Lord, better than any. Let not these mercenaries stop you or distract you from your goal. You must succeed in your mission. You must kill Gallis Korrgonn, whatever the cost. You must not allow him to open another gateway."

"Another gateway?" said Claradon.

"That can't be his mind," said Tanch.

"Make no mistake, my friends," said Pipkorn, "That is Korrgonn's goal, I'm certain of it." Pipkorn looked over at Theta. "You agree, my Lord?"

"That is his plan, there can be little doubt," said Theta.

"So all Midgaard is still at risk?" said Ob.

"That's the danger," said Pipkorn. "That's why your mission is so important. That's why you must not fail."

"Master Pipkorn," said Claradon. "If this is true, then why are The Shadow Leaguers aiding Korrgonn? There are powerful wizards and learned men among their number. It can't all just be religious zealotry. Do they truly want to destroy the world? It doesn't make sense."

"Why do you think powerful wizards would help Korrgonn?" asked Pipkorn.

"They're nuts, plain and simple," said Ob. "Crazed religious wackos."

"They must think they stand to gain

somehow," said Claradon.

"And what gain do wizards seek?" said Pipkorn.

"They want mystical power above all things. Somehow, they must believe that they will acquire it by opening another gateway. They must think that they'll be spared in the madness that follows, or else they plan to close the gateway after something or someone comes through, before the world can be overrun."

Pipkorn smiled a thin smile. "Good theories, Lord Eotrus. No matter what their reasons though, they must be stopped. That task falls to you. The fate of us all depends on your success."

"Now, my friends, I must be gone before too many eyes fall upon me. More spies are watching this ship than an old man can count. I'll be lucky to make it back to that hovel in Southeast unaccosted."

Pipkorn walked to the door and unlatched it, and then turned back. He looked at each man in the room. "There's a storm coming to Lomion, my friends. If your journey is long, you may find that on your return, the Lomion you knew is no longer. Be swift, but most importantly, be successful."

Pipkorn put up his cowl, stooped over, and opened the door. "Farewell," he said, closing the portal behind him.

Furnished in dark wood, the Captain's Den held a big cherrywood table and chairs, a mariner's globe, fine leather couches, shelves of books, maps, and more. Theta's floatable trunks were stacked in one corner. A spacious back room held all manner of foodstuffs, provisions, gear, and a water closet. A second room housed a dozen stacked bunks.

"We'll make our base here," said Theta. "It's defensible and more comfortable than we could ask for on a ship."

"The rooms below deck assigned to you and Claradon are spacious, Lord Theta," said Tanch. "Wouldn't they serve better?"

"If it were our ship, perhaps they would, but it's not. Better that we stay together in a secure location."

"Captain Slaayde will never agree," said Claradon.

The Den's door swung open, Captain Slaayde in its breach. He looked about at each of them. Tall and barrel built, Slaayde's hair, a straight golden blond, his age perhaps forty, eyes blue and shifty. Clad in a white doublet, loose fitting blue pantaloons, a black bandoleer, black belt, black gloves and boots, all patent leather and shiny, and girded with a cutlass and dagger of wide cage guards, he looked every bit the swashbuckler of his reputation. "Good afternoon, gentlemen," said Slaayde quietly, a nervous smile across his round face. Have you lost your way? This is a private chamber. Your cabins are below deck."

"And goodly cabins they be, Captain old boy," said Ob. "The thing is, them's just for sleeping. This here place is better suited to meeting and plotting and drinking and such, as you well know. Since we do a good deal of all that, we've pitched our tent here and here we'll stay," he said, puffing out his little chest.

"Sir, this is my office and personal store. You—"

"Now it's ours, laddie," said Ob. "And that's the end of that."

Slaayde's smile widened on his mouth, but not his eyes. Still quietly he said, "Harringgold bought you passage; he didn't buy my ship. I'll not have this."

"Captain Slaayde, sir," said Tanch. "We meant no offense, none at all, but Lord Eotrus required a room to meet with his staff and Lord Theta. We didn't think you would object to a member of the Council of Lords and a visiting dignitary," indicating Theta, "making use of your fine chamber during this voyage."

"Well sir, I do."

"And well you should, of course, of course. I'm sure some appropriate additional compensation can be arranged with Lord Harringgold for your trouble and inconvenience. We must make this right."

"Hmm, well—perhaps. We can discuss it."

"Of course, this whole business is entirely my fault," said Tanch. "I bear full responsibility and stand properly and appropriately chastised."

"Harringgold's men didn't tell me where we're headed?" Slaayde paused, waiting for some response. "He left that to you men. So? To where do we sail?"

"Just set sail downriver, laddie," said Ob. "Give her as much speed as you can muster, and shout if you see any ships ahead. We've business with *The White Rose*."

"A fast ship, and a dangerous one," said Slaayde. "Cutthroats and scalawags crew her, and her Captain's reputation is more foul than fair. Harringgold should've told me of this. There's a different price."

"You will be paid—well paid, laddie," said Ob.

At this, Theta stood and walked toward Slaayde who took a cautious step back, now just outside the threshold. Staring the Captain direct in the eye, Theta, expressionless, closed the door in Slaayde's face. A few moments later, Slaayde could be heard walking across the deck, cursing.

"Well that's that," said Ob. "Theta, what do you make of the good captain? That fellow in the temple said he was Slaayde's first mate and made no secret of it."

"I haven't seen enough yet to take his measure. It may be he knew naught of his mate's dealing with the League."

"We should've told the Duke about this," said Claradon.

"We needed a fast and sturdy ship with an experienced crew to catch *The White Rose*," said Theta. "Harringgold and Fischer made clear that *The Falcon* suited those needs best and with *The Falcon* comes Slaayde. If Harringgold suspected Slaayde might be aligned with the League he wouldn't have arranged our passage and we would be burdened with a lesser ship."

"And what if he is a Leaguer?" said Ob.

"Then he will soon be dead," said Theta.

"And what if he knows that we suspect him because of that Fizdar character?" said Tanch. "He could be laying a trap for us right now or planning to slit our throats in our sleep. Oh my, this is all too much. Too much."

"No one knows Slaayde's man spoke to us in the temple—and if he's dead, as likely he is, no one need ever know, so don't speak of it again. We'll tread carefully around Slaayde."

"Too bad the bad guys don't all wear black or red so that we could tell them apart," said Dolan.

***

With the ship ready to sail, Ob gathered all the men on the main deck, and Claradon, now clad in his priestly vestments, led them in a traditional prayer. Less than sixteen hours after meeting with Lord Harringgold in his chambers in Dor Lomion, *The Black Falcon* was off, sailing from its berth in Lomion Harbor into the heart of the Hudsar River. From the bridge deck, Claradon watched the grand skyline of Lomion, capital city of the Kingdom of Lomion, recede into the distance. Atop the tall deck, he gazed on many of the great buildings of Lomion and wondered if he would ever see them again.

Claradon admired the stalwart fortress of Dor Lomion, with its tall, gray, stone walls and high tower, home of House Harringgold. He wondered at the majestic, multi-spired, and multi-hued Tower of the Arcane, central seat of wizardom in all Midgaard and far and away the tallest edifice in the city. He could just glimpse the Royal Palace of the Tenzivels and its neighbor Tammanian Hall, bastion of government, home of the High Council and the Council of Lords. The massive Auditorium, center of spectacles, entertainment, and the arts, stood in the western reaches of Lomion. The Odinhome, grandest of all the temples, churches, and cathedrals, and central house of worship of Lord Odin, the All-Father, the king of the gods, was located amidst the High Quarter not far from the Auditorium. The peaks of these and many other buildings both common and high all slowly vanished from sight as the ship exited the harbor and plied its way down the river proper.

VI
DOR MALVEGIL

"They're really good, just misunderstood."
—Torbin Malvegil

*T*he *Black Falcon* glided into a berth in the deep cove that served as Dor Malvegil's port. Scores of buildings, stone and shingle, wood and nail, clustered around the cove, nestled between the water's edge and the base of a sheer cliff, a massive flat-topped crag that rose high above the river and the surrounding woodlands. Atop the rocky promontory, the grand old fortress of stone, ruled by House Malvegil for the previous three hundred years, boasted commanding views in all directions.

Several merchant ships of various sizes lay in port loading and unloading cargos, both pedestrian and exotic, though of *The White Rose* there was no sign. As *The Falcon* tied off to a well-kept pier, the harbormaster approached.

"Ahoy there, *Black Falcon*," said the harbormaster, a burly graybeard.

"Ahoy yourself," said Slaayde as crewmen lowered the gangway.

"I'll brook no troubles from you and yours this time, Slaayde. I warned you the last, and I will not warn you again."

"Dear Hogart, you wound me with your words," said Slaayde sardonically. "I who love thee like a son."

466

"If you were my son, I would have sold you to the Gnomes." Hogart's face reddened when he spied Ob scowling at him from the rail.

"**W**e shouldn't linger here," said Theta to Claradon. "Ask after *The White Rose* and let's be on our way."

"I have to pay my respects to my uncle," said Claradon. "He's the lord of this fortress, and a good man, but he would take offense if I passed here without calling on him. Besides, Glimador should be here long since, and we could use his help on this voyage."

"We shouldn't stay the night," said Theta. "Every moment we delay, Korrgonn gets farther away."

Tanch stared up at the fortress, which loomed high above the harbor. "Oh my, it seems a frightful walk up to the castle. It must be two, perhaps three hundred feet up the rock face."

"Three hundred fifty I'd mark it," said Ob.

"The road must be terribly steep."

"There's no road, laddie. Far too steep for one. That's why the Malvegil's built here—it's almost impossible to assault. To get up, you have to take a hoist or climb the stairs," said Ob, pointing to a wide stair built into the rock face.

The stair was steep but looked solid and safe, equipped with a sturdy wood outer railing and toe boards. The stair switched back multiple times as it scaled the cliff's face.

"There's a second stair around the other side."

"Oh my, look at that," said Tanch. "What a

climb. My back cannot abide that. No, no, I'm afraid that I would never make it. My apologies Brother Claradon, but I'll have to await your return here on the ship."

"No need," said Claradon. "We'll take the hoist."

"Hoist? What are we, bales of hay?"

"Around the bend a ways there's a series of big hoists that are used to haul up supplies and people," said Ob. "A good deal easier and a fair bit quicker than the stairs."

The largest of the hoists comfortably held nearly a score of armored men. Theta, Claradon, Ob, Tanch, Dolan, Artol, Slaayde, Seran, and the other knights of Dor Eotrus: Sirs Paldor, Kelbor, Ganton 'the Bull', and Trelman loaded onto the large cabin, all dressed in their finest. Duke Harringgold's soldiers, save Seran, remained with the ship, as did the balance of Claradon's men and Slaayde's crew.

The hoist's rectangular cabin was almost eight feet tall and built of heavy planks and timbers. A dozen thick ropes with looped ends hung one to two feet down from the ceiling beams. The hoist operator stepped in last. He swung closed the cabin door, or rather, the half-door, since it was but three feet tall. "Grab the ropes and hold on," he said.

Claradon gripped one of the looped ropes; several of the others followed suit. Ob looked up at the rope above him, far beyond his reach, and grabbed Claradon's sword belt instead.

The operator tugged on a chain, which rang a loud bell mounted atop the hoist cabin. Seconds later, the cabin lurched, sending the men reeling to one side.

"Ha! I told you to hold on."

After it moved a ways, the cabin steadied, swinging just a bit to the side as it ascended. Some of the men stared at their feet, some closed their eyes, and the rest stared bug-eyed out the door. The operator ignored the view outside, choosing instead to stare at his passengers, an amused expression on his face.

When the hoist reached the top, the group unloaded onto a wide stone terrace outside the massive outer walls of the fortress. An elaborate array of ropes and pulleys, levers and great geared wheels powered by teams of oxen pulled some hoists up and lowered others down, all supervised by more than a dozen men clad in the livery of House Malvegil.

A large staging area, currently brimming with sparring troops, dominated most of the terrace. Squadrons of soldiers dueled with wooden swords and blunted spears, weapons masters barking orders and taunts all the while. A massive barn for the oxen and horses was situated off in one corner.

The walls of the fortress hugged the edge of the cliff around its whole perimeter, save for the hoist terrace, the Dor's loading dock. Here, the walls rose up some sixty feet. Crenellated battlements loomed over the terrace, its defenders ready to lay waste to any enemy that somehow reached the crag's summit.

Majestic towers and turrets climbed to lofty heights here and there about the fortress. The flags of Lomion and House Malvegil flew atop the walls and towers, fluttering proudly in the wind.

The group was greeted by the Dor's Castellan, one Hubert Gravemare, an elderly man of lanky build and crackly voice, supported by a group of frazzled servants. Claradon explained that they couldn't stay long, and Gravemare countered that Lord Malvegil would insist they remain for a meal at the least. He escorted them to the great hall to await his lord.

Dor Malvegil's great hall was arrayed with rows of oaken trestle tables and benches, polished and spotless, together large enough to feast several hundred at a time. The floor was constructed of large stone tiles, well-cleaned and in good repair. Huge carved wood trusses supported the roof some forty feet above, spanning from one side of the hall to the other, creating a wide space free of columns or piers.

The Lord's Table sat at the head on a raised platform two steps higher than the rest of the hall. On Gravemare's orders servants scurried about it, setting plates and silverware and goblets. There would be no more debating about dinner.

Glimador Malvegil marched into the hall dressed in a blue silken shirt and black breaches, a sword belt strapped around his waist. He warmly greeted his comrades but went speechless when Seran presented him with the shining Dyvers sword from Pipkorn. Moments later, Lord Malvegil and his Lady, Landolyn, arrived.

Torbin Malvegil was a tall, burly man of bushy

470

black beard, booming voice, and pearl white teeth. He entered the hall wearing his ancestral armor, all-polished to a blazing sheen, though at that moment he was all but invisible, for every man's eyes locked on his lady. Her rare curves marked her of half-elven blood at least. Like most of her ancestry, she was narrow of waist, extra wide of hip and much more than very large of chest. Few Volsung women ever had such proportions, but unlike a pureblood Elf, her allure was natural, not enhanced by whatever strange magic surrounded the elves. Her face was at once beautiful and haunting, with sharp, almost ageless features, black eyes, and silver hair, straight and silky that fell to below her waist.

"Claradon! Welcome, my dear nephew," said Lord Malvegil as he approached the group. "Too long have these halls not seen your face." At his arm, Landolyn smiled politely.

Ob gave Claradon a bit of a push on the back, and he stepped forward, hand outstretched. "Greetings, Uncle Torbin. Good to see you, it's been far too long."

They clasped forearms. Malvegil leaned in and spoke quietly now, squeezing Claradon's forearm and shoulder. "I'm so sorry, dear boy. Your father was a fine man, and my good friend of long years. I can't believe that he and Gabriel are gone."

"Nor can I."

"There's much that we must discuss," said Malvegil.

"Ob," boomed Malvegil as he looked past Claradon. "You stinking Gnome bastard. Come here," he said, arms outstretched.

"Lord Ob to you, you stinking scum," Ob said. Ob hopped up on a chair and they embraced like brothers, smacking each other warmly on the back. Lady Landolyn looked mortified at the whole exchange.

"Do my eyes deceive me?" said Malvegil as he looked to Artol who stood nearby smiling. "Artol the Destroyer, The Hammer of Lomion, the Scourge of the North!"

"Those names are old and worn, Torbin, I'm due for a new one."

"You will have to earn it, just as the others." The two men firmly embraced; the requisite three manly pats on the back each.

"But I've forgotten my manners," said Malvegil. "This vision of loveliness," grasping his lady by the arm, "for those who haven't had the pleasure, is my consort, the Lady Landolyn."

"Welcome, gentlemen," she said, bowing her head politely, though her voice was less than welcoming.

When the greetings and introductions were completed, Gravemere offered to lead the group on a tour of Dor Malvegil's sights while dinner was being prepared. He boasted of Dor Malvegil's extensive library, well-appointed gallery, and the impressive views from the eastern terrace.

Theta gave Claradon a withering stare that commanded him to speak up. Instead, he suddenly took great interest in Lord Malvegil's shoes.

"Lord Malvegil," said Theta. "We're on a mission of great urgency. No doubt, we would all enjoy the hospitality of your fine house, but we must be off this night. Much is at stake."

Malvegil studied Theta, looking him up and down. "I will speak of this with Lord Eotrus, in private. In the meantime, you men may enjoy the hospitality of House Malvegil." Malvegil grasped Claradon by the arm and led him from the hall, the public discussion over. Ob followed on their heels.

"**W**ho is he?" said Malvegil, as he, Ob, and Claradon climbed the castle stairs.

Claradon hesitated. "Well—

"He is trouble, is what he is," said Ob. "He's a foreigner what calls himself Angle Theta—Lord Angle Theta, actually. Some folks call him by other names."

"Never heard of him. Some upstart, no doubt, who doesn't yet know his place. I can't place his accent. Where is he from?"

"Some place far to the west, or so he says," said Ob. "All very mysterious, if you ask me."

"Uncle, Lord Harringgold sent a raven—"

"I've had no ravens from Dor Lomion in weeks," said Malvegil. "If he sent one, that proves the system is compromised, as I've long suspected. What was the message?"

"Jude was kidnapped."

Malvegil stopped dead on the stairs. "What?"

"Ambushed on the north road," said Ob. "A dozen men with him found dead, including some of our best."

"Jude was taken captive," said Claradon.

"Captive! On Eotrus lands? Who did this?"

"The stinking Leaguers," said Ob. "Heard of them, I trust?"

Malvegil growled, his jaw set, but said nothing more until they reached the third floor. "Ransom?"

"They haven't asked for any, and it doesn't look like they're going to," said Claradon. "That's why we're here. Those who took Jude are aboard a ship called *The White Rose*. They would've passed here within the last day or so. As far as we know, Jude is alive and on board."

"Darned raven," said Malvegil. "If it had arrived, I could've stopped them. Jude would be free now and them that took him, in irons."

Malvegil led them toward his private den. "To attack a squad of soldiers like that—the League is moving faster than I anticipated." Malvegil grabbed a passing servant and commanded him to fetch the Harbormaster and his aides at once, though when they arrived, they reported only that *The Rose* had been seen the previous day, but did not put to port.

Malvegil settled into a wide leather chair in the Lord's Den, a grave look on his face. Claradon and Ob sat across from him. Servants poured the men wine, but fled the room at a gesture from Malvegil.

"We can do no more for Jude than what you've planned. Track that ship, bring it to heel, and get Jude back one way or another. I will aid you in any way I can. I would give you another ship or two, but nothing I have is fast enough to keep up with you. Anything else I have that you need is yours."

"Thank you," said Claradon.

"No need to thank me, boy—we're family; I

474

can do no less. Your father was more than my sister's husband, he was my best friend for all my life. From when Aradon and I were small children our families visited each other, for a week or more, several times each year. Those were some of the best times in my life, which is why we continued the tradition after you kids were born. I will always regret that we didn't keep up those trips over the last few years, but with Eleanor gone, and you boys always off in training—it just wasn't the same. I can't believe that it has been two years since I've seen your father, and now, never again. There just never seems enough time."

"Aye," said Ob. "Never enough."

"Our family visits were some of the best times of my life as well," said Claradon. "I know Glimador feels the same, and so do my brothers."

"I'm glad of that," said Malvegil. "We did that much right, at least. We could talk for hours of the happy times, and we should, but tonight, we've graver matters to discuss. I've heard Glimador's tale about your father. Mountain trolls, my ass. You swore him to secrecy, I'm sure, though he won't even admit that much. Tell me what really happened to Aradon and the others."

"The stinking Shadow League happened," said Ob.

Malvegil winced at the remark, and then took a gulp of wine. "Are you telling me that the League killed them?"

"In a manner of speaking," said Claradon.

Malvegil closed his eyes. "There's no stopping it then. This puts Lomion on the road to ruin. It can only end one way." Malvegil downed the rest of his wine. "Now tell me everything. Leave nothing out."

Claradon and Ob related the events of the Vermion, a dark tale of death, demon lords, and mad cultists. Malvegil listened intently and asked many questions.

"A hard story to swallow whole or in pieces," said Malvegil. "You did well not to tell this tale to the Council. It could only have made things worse, and they would certainly never accept the truth of it."

"If I wasn't there, I wouldn't believe it," said Ob, "but I was."

"I've seen many strange things in my days," said Malvegil, "and more often than not, Gabriel was around when I saw them. He seemed to attract the weird or mayhaps it attracted him. I've never seen a demon though, and never even believed in them. Fairy tales and ghost stories for the fireside, nothing more, I'd say."

Malvegil stared at the fireplace for a moment, considering his words before continuing. "I wasn't with you that night, but I accept your story as honest told however wild it sounds." Malvegil refilled his goblet from a glass decanter. "They died heroes, Aradon, Gabriel, Talbon, Stern, Donnelin, and the rest, defending our kingdom. Few better ways for old soldiers to pass, I suppose."

"I'd prefer old age," said Ob.

"You passed old age a hundred years ago."

"Of course, he moves slow. I've left him behind, and he can't catch me," Ob said chuckling.

"Did Korrgonn sail with *The White Rose*?" said Malvegil.

"He did," said Claradon.

Malvegil nodded. "You'll want to leave at once. I would feel the same if I were you, but still, I strongly advise you to remain here the night. The Dead Fens, as Ob knows too well, lie just to the south of Malvegil lands. It's an evil place and always has been. A fog that never lifts makes passage perilous even in full daylight. But of late, things have grown fouler—fouler than they've been in twenty-five years," he said, with a glance to Ob. "Dark shapes are seen by passing ships. Strange sounds are heard even in the day."

"Over the last year, several small boats have gone missing never to be found. In recent months, guardsmen and sailors have disappeared without sound or trace from the decks of even the largest vessels. If you leave tonight, you will find yourselves in the heart of the fens before dawn. That is somewhere you don't want to be. Get a good night's rest here, in comfortable beds and safe surroundings, leave in the morning, and with any luck at all you'll be past the fens hours before dark."

Claradon stared into his goblet.

"Aye, it might be best," said Ob, "all things considered."

"Sound advice," said Claradon.

"It's settled then," said Malvegil, "and that's good, for we've much more to discuss. Glimador tells me you gave Barusa quite a thrashing."

"You should've seen it," said Ob. "He had Mr. High-and-Mighty on his knees."

477

Malvegil broke into a wide smile. "Well, you are your father's son, I'll give you that."

Claradon's face reddened and he looked down.

"I'm sorry," said Malvegil. "The pain is still fresh, I know. It will lessen in time, but it will always be with you." Malvegil took a drink from his goblet. "Find strength and what comfort you can in the good memories of your father, of which I know you have many."

"After that duel, you're lucky to have gotten out of Lomion City alive. The Shadow League has a warrant out on your life, I'm certain."

"Religious nuts, every one," said Ob. "They've bought off half the High Council, maybe more."

"Religion isn't their aim or their purpose, old friend; it's merely their tool. This is about revolution—a revolution from within."

"The League wants to take over—to seize power over Lomion City and the whole of the kingdom, and rule it as they will. Their religious trappings are nothing more than that, a way to delude the commoners and the fools and mask their true goals. Our way of life is being destroyed before our eyes. The monarchy has already fallen, the republic, which has wielded the real power for the last thousand years, is near collapse. Once the Vizier or the Chancellor or some other gains enough power to take control of all the League's forces, they will kill the Tenzivels and the Harringgolds, they'll dissolve the High Council and the Council of Lords, and Lomion City will be lost. From there, they'll move on Kern, Dover, Sarnack, Dyvers, and all the Dors. Nowhere will be safe for us. Not here, not anywhere."

Malvegil stood and began to pace as he spoke. "They have agents everywhere; they've been infiltrating for years, right under our noses. They've been recruiting our own citizens into the cults and brainwashing them in the temples, making them hate their own land, their own government, their own way of life. They even have spies in my own House, so mind your words when we're not in private. While we've been focused on threats from without, they've been slowly eating away at us from within."

"Can't we raise the Council of Lords into action?" said Claradon. "The combined might of the Lords must still far outstrip whatever forces are loyal to the League."

"I tried to do just that when I was in Lomion three months ago. All I got was a dagger in my back."

"What?" said Ob.

"They tried to kill you?" said Claradon.

"They did, but luckily, I had on a vest of chain beneath my shirt for just such an occasion. When I had him, the assassin cut his own throat rather than be taken. That one was in it for religion, as are many of the League's agents and soldiers. It makes it easier for the League's leaders to control their troops, for religious zealotry can take hold of a man and make him do things beyond his imagining."

"Glenfinnen went into hiding after the attempt on my life. Baron Morfin wasn't so lucky. They killed him and his son. A murder-suicide declared the good Chancellor. Hogwash and horsefeathers. They think us fools enough to believe that?"

479

"So what do we do? How do we stand against them?" said Claradon.

Malvegil halted, narrowed his eyes, and stared directly at Claradon. "We go to war. Either that, or they will destroy us."

"You're not talking war," said Ob. "You're talking civil war. Not all the scum are foreigners; many are our own, like the Alders, Marshal Balfor, and Guildmaster Slyman."

"Many of the noble houses have allied with them, perhaps more than we know," said Malvegil. "Many in the Tower of the Arcane have gone over, and they've infiltrated the Heralds Guild too. The heralds praise the cults and curse the King. Only the Chancellor can save us, sing the Heralds, only the Vizier, shout the mages."

"Why would the wizards and the heralds support them?" said Claradon.

"Who knows what madness has beguiled those fools. But history teaches us that when a society grows old enough, and secure enough, some of its citizens get bored and learn to hate their country. It's some sickness of the mind that all too many seem susceptible to. They see evil only in their own, though not in themselves, and grow blind to all evil from without. They go so far as to blame their own people or their own government for the evils of foreign tyrants and the crimes of common brigands, and even for bad weather. 'We made them that way', they say. 'They're really good, just misunderstood'. It's an old pattern, my friends. It has happened before and it will happen again."

Malvegil topped off his glass and offered the bottle to Ob, who took it eagerly. "A defect in the brain. Perhaps some worm picked up from undercooked pork drills its way in and eats them between the ears. I don't know, men. But the mages and the heralds are with them, and they're against us. That's the way it is."

"When they finally understand what the League is really about, they will want to stop them," said Claradon. "These people are Lomerians—patriots— whatever our disagreements with them."

"You're right, those of good intent will come around, but by then it will be too late. Some will continue to side with the League, even then, to save themselves."

"It'll be a bloody mess," said Ob.

"And if it's bad enough, it will leave us vulnerable to attacks from without. Our foreign enemies will gather at the gates." Malvegil paused, letting that sink in for a moment. "We need Dor Eotrus to stand with us, and we need House Eotrus to be strong."

"Uncle," said Claradon. "You must know that you have my full support, but I'm not sure how much we can do."

"Our forces are broken," said Ob. "Most of our best fell with Aradon and Gabriel and Jude. We don't have enough men to deploy to the field—not for any major battle; maybe not enough even to even hold the Dor, if we're hard pressed."

"Grim news, worse than I thought. Dor Eotrus must stand. The trade route between Lomion and Kern must remain secure."

"You said we need Dor Eotrus to stand with us?" said Claradon. "Which 'us' are you talking

481

about? Who are our allies? House Harringgold, of course. Who else can we count on?"

"A fair question for any Dor Lord to ask," said Malvegil, "but I'll not tell you, not when you're about to go off after some of the League's leaders. If you're captured, under duress you might give us away. I can't chance that. All things considered, it's better that you don't know, not now, anyway. Must you go on this mission, Claradon?"

Claradon hesitated some moments before responding. "Maybe that's why they took Jude; to torture him for information."

Malvegil and Ob exchanged worried glances.

"Hold on, boy," said Ob. "There could be many reasons they want him. Maybe they will ransom him back after all, and that'll be the end of it. In any case, best not to dwell on it."

"Could be they're torturing him even now, to find out what he knows. But he doesn't know anything, does he?"

Ob shook his head.

"So then they'll kill him," said Claradon. "Theta was right, we can't linger here. We need to sail at the crack of dawn, before then, even."

"I know that you want to save Jude yourself," said Malvegil, "but sometimes a leader needs to make difficult choices, to serve the greater good. You and Ob should go back and take command of your Dor. I can spare a squadron of men to help you. Let Theta and the others go after Korrgonn and Jude. It doesn't need to be you, Claradon."

"Torbin," said Ob, "we can't lose sight that what's happening is bigger than us, bigger than

Lomion even. These Leaguers called up some kind of beasties from another world and they will do it again. It don't matter what those things really were, or where they really came from—all that matters is that they mean to kill us dead, and they're more than capable of it. Had we been a day later, who knows how many of them would've come through. Then we'd be swimming in blood. Korrgonn and the men with him are the ones what know how to open these gateways. They need to be stopped. They need to be dead. That's why we have to go. That's why we can't leave it to anybody else. Stinking Harringgold only half believed us."

"If I didn't know you for so long, I'd not believe you at all," said Malvegil. "But I agree, these men need stopping. Let's put them down."

***

Gravemare assigned Ob to a fancy room—large with big furniture, four-poster bed, a couch, and coffee table, all in dark wood, tapestries and paintings on the walls, even a private water closet and bath with running water, clean and tiled.

Ob was glad that Theta didn't make an issue of staying the night when Claradon announced the decision at dinner. That would've made Claradon look weak and would've ruined a good meal too. Maybe Mr. Know-it-All is finally learning who's the boss.

Ob washed his face in a marble basin. He'd

have a bath later, if he didn't get too drunk, since this might be his last chance in a goodly while. At the moment, though, he felt stuffed to bursting with roast meats and boiled vegetables, honeyed beer and hot wassail. Malvegil's chef had served up a meal worthy of the best eateries in Lomion City. Despite his indulgence, Ob managed two thick slices of wastelbread and made off with a plate of cookies.

After dessert, Torbin invited the group to join him later in his den for some drinking, cigars, and storytelling.

"I hope Slaayde doesn't show up," muttered Ob as he looked himself over in the mirror before leaving his room. "I don't trust that bugger. At least Torbin has a couple of guards shadowing him."

Theta's room was just down the hall and Ob decided to pick him up on the way. Ob figured that Theta would enjoy the tale of the Dead Fens. Torbin was sure to tell that one, what with Ob and Artol both there, Gabe's passing, and the group heading past the Fens on the morrow. He wasn't certain that Claradon was ready to hear that tale. How many shocks could the boy take?

As Ob exited his room, he saw Lady Landolyn step through the doorway into Theta's room. The door closed behind her.

"What's this?" Ob whispered. Ob padded silently down the hallway as quickly as he could and pressed his ear to the door.

"You are the Thetan of old?" said Lady Landolyn sharply.

That name again, Thetan, just as Mortach had

called him. If Theta made any reply, Ob didn't hear it.

"I am of the House of Adonael," said the Lady.

After a short pause she continued. "Your fell deeds are not forgotten by my House, or by many others." With each word, her voice grew louder and more shrill. "You led us astray and for this we have suffered much. Your crimes are beyond compare and beyond forgiveness."

Slap!

"Zounds!" muttered Ob, though he couldn't tell if she slapped him or if he caught her hand in his.

"You know not of what you speak," said Theta in a slow, measured, and cold voice. "The anger you harbor is misplaced."

"I think not, traitor. It's well placed as will be the dagger that pierces your black heart if you dare to remain here past this night or ever return again. Do not soil this good house with your lies and your schemes. I warn you, should any harm befall my Glimador on this quest of yours, I will hunt you to the ends of Midgaard and slay you myself."

She moved for the door and Ob dashed for cover. He skulked behind a tapestry until she left the hall and was well down the stair before he dared move.

After that, Ob thought, *I need to get stinking drunk. Theta has enemies everywhere and they all name him traitor and liar. What are we doing with this man amongst us?*

***

485

A light haze of smoke wafted about the Lord's Den, illumed by lanterns of stained glass and polished mica that cast a pleasant amber hue. Cherrywood beams and planks supported and coffered the ceiling some twelve feet above the granite-tiled floor. Exquisitely detailed maps of various sizes and styles adorned the spaces between and above the ornate mahogany bookshelves of wood and glass doors that lined the walls.

The gathered men reclined near the fireplace on leather chairs and couches, rich and dark in color and almost silky soft to the touch. The whole group was there. They smoked cigars from Dyvers and Portland Vale and sipped a fine Kernian brandy called Amber as Torbin Malvegil boomed his tales of past glories. Servants stood as statues in this corner and that, ever ready to fill any tumbler gone dry or to light the next cigar.

"First there were reports of strange sounds and stranger sights on the river," said Malvegil. "But then, men began disappearing from ships, mostly the small ones, some the larger. Whole ships started going missing too—a couple of small fishing vessels, and then a merchant ship, a caravel called *The Barking Beagle*, out of Minoc, I believe—

It was The Bellowing Banshee out of Kern, recalled Ob, though he kept his thoughts to himself.

"...went missing with all hands save the first mate."

The cook

486

"...who floated downriver clinging for his life to a broken board."

In a dinghy.

"He was found two days later, about twenty leagues downriver, slashed and torn as if by ragged blades or claws. But that wasn't the worst of it. His mind was shattered. He was utterly mad and couldn't even tell his tale. His wounds had festered and he died the next day. So afraid of disease were they, they doused him with oil while he still lived and set him aflame the moment he breathed his last.

"*The Beagle* was carrying more than just trinkets and tea—three members of a noble house were aboard: a Lady fair of Lomion, her young Lord, and their infant son. Their fate, unknown.

"Of course, I couldn't abide such crimes just beyond my borders, so I called upon and gathered my most intrepid comrades. A wrecking crew we were, the bravest, the strongest, and the best darn fighters in all of Lomion. The best of the best we were. In those days, far and wide they called us, The Sons of Lomion."

Only you call us that in your stories, my friend.

"So we set out to the Fens to see what there was to see," said Ob, no longer able to hold back. "Not to be doing any crazy hero stuff, but just to size up the issue, so we could set a plan to make things right."

"Exactly," said Malvegil. "Sir Gabriel Garn was with me, so was Ob, and The Hammer of Lomion—you know him as Artol. This all happened over twenty years ago, I should say. Artol here," pointing to the big warrior, "was just as tall in those days, but a far sight thinner, and so young he could barely grow a wisp of a beard. Ob was Ob and Gabe was Gabe, those two never did seem to change. Of course with Ob—he's a Gnome and they're known to be long-lived. With Gabe it was a bit of a mystery. Came from some old bloodline, I expect, and looked half his years, if that. Anyways, our ship put to anchor off the Dead Fens, near the west bank of the Hudsar—a mere ten leagues south of where we sit. We launched in a longboat and rowed across to the east bank and up a tributary into the Fens. By turns, we rowed and levered our way with long poles deeper into that accursed swamp."

Malvegil stood and looked at each man in turn, his expression serious.

Here it comes, the part he's got down word for word. Let's see what he's added since the last.

"The whole of the Dead Fens stretched out before us. A vast landscape of wanton degradation. A morass so putrid, so miasmic as to cloud the mind and rend the soul. It has been avoided for countless generations by all who know its reputation. In that time, it has taken only those lost wanderers who knew not whence they strayed, and a few would-be adventurers chasing fairy gold or glory. But the Dead Fens is no mere swamp or bog or marsh. There is a presence to that place. A palpable persona to it—an ancient evil from a bygone age."

That last line is new. Can't argue with it, though.

"Those that enter or even skirt its borders are besought with all manner of misfortunes, great and small. From accidents, to illness, from rotting food to rancid water, where hours before there was freshness. That place is decay, ancient and unforgiving. A slimy putrescence, a decrepit miasma likened to the grave. Such are the Dead Fens."

Gets better with each telling. He should write it down, preserve it for posterity.

Gravemare stormed into the room. "My Lord, there's trouble on our guests' ship."

***

The ship was in chaos; men ran to and fro. Captain Slaayde and his officers shouted orders to bring all pumps to the forward hold. Two burly sailors dragged a third man, limp, lifeless, and drenched in water from below deck. Seran Harringgold followed on their heels.

"What happened?" asked Claradon as he and Ob walked toward Seran.

"I caught this one drilling a hole in the hull," said Seran as he pointed to the drenched man on the deck. Seran bent down and turned the man onto his back. A dagger was buried in his chest. "I cornered him and when he saw there was no escape, he stabbed himself. What kind of man would do that?"

"Is the stinking bugger one of Slaayde's crew?" asked Ob.

"I've seen him aboard," said Seran.

Ob bent down and examined the corpse.

"How bad is the damage to the ship?" asked Claradon.

"There's lots of water down there. He must've drilled at least a couple of holes before I discovered him."

"He's a Leaguer," said Ob after exposing a tattoo on the dead man's shoulder. "He's got the mark of Mortach."

Hours later, long after they had planned to leave, Slaayde's crew had finished patching the holes in the hull and pumping the water from the hold. Much of the ship's supplies were ruined.

"You now face the same problem that you did yesterday," said Malvegil. "You will not make it past the Fens before dark. Can I convince you to remain another night?"

"I appreciate your concern, Uncle, but we can remain here no longer," said Claradon. "Too much depends on our speed."

Glimador and a dozen Malvegil soldiers carrying bows marched up to the two Dor Lords as they stood on the pier.

"These are some of my most skilled bowman," said Malvegil. "Please accept their service on your quest, nephew."

"I'll make good use of them, Uncle. Thank you."

"May Odin's favor shine on you, my boy. Come back safe and Jude with you."

Lord Malvegil and his Lady watched *The Black Falcon* depart from the eastern terrace.

"I forbade Glim to go," said Landolyn, tears

welling in her eyes; eyes not accustomed to tears.

Malvegil spun toward her, jaw clenched. "What? You forbade him? You had no business doing that. We agreed that it was his decision to make."

"You agreed, husband. I just gave up arguing."

"You shouldn't have interfered."

"Interfered? He's my only son—our only son. The only one we'll ever have, and I will not lose him to some madman's quest."

"Glimador's not a boy anymore; he's a man— a fine strong man. More than that, he's a knight, and pledged to serve the Eotrus. Where his Lord goes, he goes. Duty and honor, Landolyn; it's what makes a man a man."

"This mission and that man will be the death of him, I know it."

"What? Don't say that. Claradon loves Glimador like a brother."

"Not Claradon. Theta!"

"The foreigner?"

"Torbin, you're an old fool."

Malvegil stood there for a time, looking at her, open-mouthed and disbelieving. Then he turned back toward the river and watched *The Black Falcon* sail away to meet its fate.

"Ten years ago—no—five, and I would've went with them. Claradon is too young to lead them in this.

Landolyn shook her head. "Dead gods, you're blind."

"What? What's come over you?"

"Your nephew leads nothing. He follows."

Malvegil's shocked expression followed her as

she stormed off.

VII
EINHERIAR

"To sate my hunger, I will burn thy body and devour thy soul."
—Einheriar

Theta stood alone at the rail of the sturdy vessel, gazing into the darkness from whence they came, while *The Black Falcon* sailed down the Grand Hudsar River. A storm was gathering and it grew dark early. Soon, a mist formed, cloaking the surface of the water.

Claradon stepped up to the rail beside Theta. "Dor Malvegil is the farthest south I've ever been before today."

Theta made no reply; he didn't even acknowledge the young lord's presence.

"It's a big world, I suppose it's time that I see more of it. I just wish the reasons were better." Claradon breathed deep the clean, crisp air of the river lands and listened to the flow of the water about the ship. "I would've marked you a man to stand at the prow looking at what lies ahead, rather than looking back."

"We're being followed and not by friendly sail."

"What?" Claradon raised his brows. "A ship? The lookout reports nothing."

"I see better than most."

"He's atop the mast; he has a far better view."

"Perhaps he has his own agenda or perhaps the captain chooses to keep secrets. Or maybe he

493

just doesn't see very well."

Claradon looked hard into the growing darkness. "I can't see anything but the mist."

"It comes into view every hour or so. It flies a black sail. A large ship."

"*The Raven* out of Southeast flies a black sail and a red and black flag," said Ob as he skulked out of the shadows. "So does *The Grey Talon,* and both their reputations are as black as their sails. It could be one of them two ships, or else it could be a ship from Dyvers—a bunch of them fly the black. There is also an order of Church Knights, don't remember which one, what flies black sail too."

"Should we advise the captain to speed up?" said Claradon. "Maybe we can lose her. We've enough trouble ahead of us; we don't need more from behind."

"If we were out to sea, I would try it," said Ob, "but on the river, it's futile. Close as she is, if she's a fast ship and has a mind to, she'll catch us. Besides, the way this fog is thickening, if we speed up, we'd risk running aground. We can't chance that. If this ship gets disabled, we'll never catch *The Rose*."

"We must keep our guard up and meet those that trail us at a time of our choosing," said Theta.

"The Fens, dead ahead," called the lookout from the crow's nest.

Ob turned toward the east. "I only see dark waters and mist. Stinking mist."

In mere moments, the air grew chill and strangely pungent. A light rain began to fall. Flashes of lightning appeared in the sky followed by angry peals of thunder.

"What's that smell?" said Claradon.

Ob wrinkled his prodigious nose, and rubbed his right forearm with his left hand, as if it were sore. "I've been down this river more than a few times and there is always a stink from the Fens, rotting plants and such, but this is different. It's too strong and came on too sudden. Something is not right."

Captain Slaayde stood at the forward end of the bridge deck beside his first mate. N'Paag's hands gripped the ship's wheel like vises; sweat dripped down his cheeks. "Captain, we should drop anchor before we run aground. I can barely see; the current may run us into the rocks."

Slaayde peered into the mist for some moments. "No, stay on course as best you can. I have a bad feeling about this storm and this stench. You've heard the stories about the Fens. I will not have *The Falcon* be her next victim. We keep moving."

Slaayde yelled up at the lookout, ordering him to help keep the ship well away from the banks and clear of any rocks.

Pain flared in Ob's arm—centered around the scar from the wound he suffered in the Vermion Forest. He clutched at it and winced.

The river went silent, the air went still but for the rain that continued to fall.

Theta drew his sword, spun around, and scanned all about them.

"What is it?" said Claradon, moving his hand to his sword hilt.

"Your amulet," said Ob, fumbling to pull his axe from his belt. "It's glowing. There's danger afoot."

The air grew more chill. Steam rose from Ob's breath.

Strange bubbling and plopping sounds came from the water. Ob leaned between the rail posts and looked straight down. "That's not good."

"What?" said Claradon.

"The river," said Ob, wide-eyed. "It's boiling, and it's red. Red like blood." Ob bounced up and turned back toward the deck. "Did you hear that?

Theta raised his hand for silence. No one moved or spoke for some moments. "Something is happening," he said, his hand now gripping the ankh that hung about his neck.

A horrid scream erupted from somewhere down on the main deck, lost in the mist. It lasted but a moment before it abruptly cut off. Men yelled in the darkness, their words muffled. Then came another scream.

Claradon dashed toward the ladder that led down to the main deck, Ob at his heels.

"Claradon," boomed Theta. He stopped in his tracks.

"Don't move until we know what's happening. Gnome—keep a lookout behind us and to the sky, we know not yet what we face."

"To the sky? Look for what? Pigeons? There's nothing to see but mist."

"Just look and listen," said Theta. Theta moved to the head of the ladder and peered below into the mist that clung to the deck.

A crewman ran toward the bridge deck, shouting. "Captain, some thing came out of the mist. We can't stop it."

"What thing?" yelled Slaayde as he moved up beside Theta. "What is it?"

The crewman scrambled up the ladder. Theta stepped aside and the sailor collapsed to the deck, panting. "I couldn't see it clearly, Captain. Some kind of creature. A monster."

"What?" said Slaayde. "Are you drunk?"

More crewmen and soldiers came into sight, racing across the main deck. A strange luminescent figure stalked their heels. Shaped much as a man, but it was shimmering, translucent, and indistinct. The creature moved at a slow walk, with knees deeply bent, plodding as if it bore a great weight. A scent of brimstone and burning wood polluted the air at its approach. Steam sputtered and rose from its feet with each step it took, as if the water on the wet deck boiled away at its very touch.

Men poured onto the main deck from the lower levels, weapons at the ready. They surrounded the creature but gave it wide berth, reluctant to attack the unnatural thing.

"Stand aside," said Slaayde, pushing past Theta. Slaayde leaped from the top of the ladder and plunged to the main deck. He landed lightly on his feet despite his bulk. N'Paag remained at the wheel.

Slaayde pushed past the crewmen and soldiers, charged forward, and swung his sword— a two-handed overhand strike, aimed for the monster's neck. The vicious blow passed clear through the creature, but met no resistance, no impact at all.

Overbalanced, Slaayde stumbled to his knees directly before the thing.

The creature's claws raked down.

The captain ducked, evading the blow that would have killed him instantly. The creature's claws no more than brushed across the blonde hair atop Slaayde's head. Such was the thing's unholy power, that merest touch did damage enough. Slaayde's head rolled to the side; his limbs went limp, his eyes closed.

The creature stepped forward to finish him off. A massive figure appeared behind Slaayde, grabbed him about the collar, and flung him clear just as the creature's claws raked down again. "Take it down," shouted Tug.

A crewman swung down from the mast on a rope and crashed feet first into the creature from behind while Tug dragged Slaayde clear of the battle. Just as Slaayde's sword, the man sailed clear through the thing, as if it were completely insubstantial, some mere apparition or shadow of what once was. The crewman howled when he passed through the thing and let go the rope. When he hit the deck, his body exploded into a cloud of dust and rotted clothing.

Men rushed in to strike the creature, but each blade passed through it, just as ineffective as the last. The creature lashed out and struck one man and then another. Both exploded into heaps of dust at the hellspawn's touch, their screams echoing through the souls of all aboard.

"Devil's work," yelled one man.

"Demon," cried another.

The creature moved ever forward, toward the bridge. Men scattered and fled before it, falling over one another to get out of its path. Glimador appeared with his bowmen. They sent a flight of arrows at the thing. Each hit its mark, but just as all the other weapons, they passed through, doing the creature no harm. An unlucky seaman across the deck fell with an arrow in his arm, another took one in his belly.

"Torches," yelled Ob through the bridge deck's rail. "Burn the stinking thing."

Several men grabbed burning brands from sconces at the ship's rails and moved toward the creature.

"Shouldn't we do something?" said Claradon to Theta.

"Not until we know how to slay it. Let's see how the torches fare."

The glow of Claradon's amulet brightened sharply. Claradon started, grabbed at the amulet's chain and pulled it away from his chest. He winced in pain, for the amulet had grown fiery hot and electric to the touch, even as a blast of icy cold air washed over him, and the rain turned instantly to sleet and hail.

Beside him, Theta spun around and raised his sword just in time to block the blow of another creature that had appeared behind them. Like the one below, it was luminescent, translucent and blurry, more spectre than man. The creature's clawed hand thundered into Theta's falchion, but did not pass through. The impact slammed Theta into the rail. A loud popping sound rang out as the rail cracked and splintered and nearly gave way.

The creature held fast Theta's falchion in a grip stronger than any mortal's. The tips of the thing's deadly claws were just inches from his flesh; only the ancient sword and Theta's muscle held it at bay. But since Theta dared not touch the thing except with the sword, he had no leverage and could not push it back.

Nature turned to chaos. The rain became frost and ice in Theta's hair, mustache, and on his cloak. Brimstone burned his nose and the air grew thin and frigid, and sapped his strength. Theta's face contorted as he strained to push the creature back, but then, where the creature's claws enveloped it, his sword's blade began to warp and melt and threatened to collapse.

Claradon stepped behind the creature. Two-handed, he slammed the ancestral sword of House Eotrus into the creature's back with all his might. The blade passed through it, meeting no resistance, and sliced into Theta's chest. Sparks erupted as the sword's tip cleaved through Theta's cloak and into his breastplate.

"Zounds!" said Claradon. He stepped back, shock, confusion, and fear filled his face.

Unfazed by Claradon's blow, Theta rolled against the rail and sidestepped, desperate to evade the thing's deadly touch, even as his sword folded over in ruin and dropped from his grasp. The ship's rail iced over, gave way, and slammed into several men when it collapsed to the deck below.

"What do we do, Theta?" shouted Ob.

Theta never took his eyes from the creature.

"Stay clear, you fools."

"I will have thy soul, traitor," spat the creature in a deep gravelly voice. "Ye wilt not escape this time."

Theta backpedaled. The creature pursued him and raked the air with its claws.

"You fight on the wrong side, Einheriar," said Theta. "You've lost your way."

The creature paused for a moment. "I be on god's side, as always, deceiver. I be sworn to destroy all evil and destroy ye, I will."

The creature bounded forward and was on Theta in an instant, but the knight had bought just enough time to slide the Asgardian daggers from his belt sheaths. A thin smile formed on Theta's face, and his steely eyes remained locked on the creature's torso.

The Einheriar launched a hail of murderous blows that belied its plodding footwork. Theta dodged or parried each thunderous strike with one of his long daggers; his iron-like arms shuddered with each impact; ice flew off the blades, shattered off Theta's arms, and refroze just as quickly. Theta feinted to one side, then sidestepped to the other. Now partially behind the creature, he plunged Dargus Dal into its lower back. With a sound of rending metal, the Asgardian blade sank deep, deep into where a man's kidney would be.

The Einheriar howled—a high-pitched, piercing wail that no mortal's throat could emit. So loud was it, it brought Ob, Claradon, and N'Paag to their knees, though Theta seemed unaffected. The creature spun toward Theta, bile oozing from its lips. It convulsed, and a blast of flaming green ichor erupted from its mouth and sprayed across the deck. Theta dodged, and turned his face away, but some of the vile spray lashed across his torso, shoulder, and back, and set his cloak afire, despite the ice that clung to it. Where the ichor struck the deck, it hissed and sputtered, turned the water and ice to billowing, hissing steam, and seared the deck planks. Wisps of fire caught here and there on the deck, though the rain held them in check.

Theta barely pulled off the flaming cloak before the creature was at him again, ignoring its wound, from which flowed a thick green slime that was its lifeblood. It lashed its claws at Theta's face. He ducked below the strike and dived into a roll that brought him up behind the creature. Theta thrust Wotan Dal to the hilt in the left side of the creature's back, the blow so powerful it lifted the Einheriar from the deck. It wailed in agony as Theta held it suspended in the air.

"Aargh! You will never be safe, Thetan," it said, fiery ichor dribbling from its mouth. "My brothers will slay thee. They will send thy black soul to hell at last."

"Not today," said Theta.

Holding the creature aloft, Theta grabbed Dargus Dal's hilt, and pitched the Einheriar over the rail into the fog. The thing wailed anew all the way to the water.

Theta had dislodged both daggers but dropped them to the deck as the acidic ichor reached his gauntlets. The polished steel smoked and began to melt on contact with the vile fluid. Everything the creature's blood or ichor had touched, smoked, crackled, and burned.

Theta strode directly at Claradon, stepping carefully due to the ice and the warped and melted decking. Claradon's eyes widened in fear at his approach, though he did not move, in truth, he could not. He half expected Theta to kill him then and there for his errant slash. Ob stood frozen, bug-eyed, by his side.

"Your Asgardian dagger, quickly, give it to me."

Claradon pulled Worfin Dal from its sheath and handed it to Theta, his hand trembling.

Theta moved to the ladder, dagger in hand, and looked down onto the scene below.

***

Dolan pulled a small object from his pocket and flung it at the Einheriar on the main deck. The object hit the wood decking and exploded in a blinding flash of light. The creature let loose an anguished wail that pierced the hearts of every man on board as the bright light washed over it. The flash of Dolan's magic quickly dimmed but didn't go out. Bathed in the bright light the creature took on an altogether different aspect.

Its form was still strangely blurred, but much more distinct than in the darkened mist. The light revealed the Einheriar's true shape—that of a man, a warrior, though corrupted and distorted. Grayish white in color from head to toe, save for its eyes, which glowed a bright gold; its features,

503

chiseled and stony. It wore armor of chain and leather. Strapped to its hands were strange gauntlets, each with four wicked claw-like blades. It raised an arm to shield its eyes from the light but seemed disoriented and halted its advance.

Men moved in with torches on all sides. The Einheriar careened from side to side avoiding the fiery light. The light revealed that the deck planks along the Einheriar's trail were smoking and warped as if melted by its very touch. Even now, steam and smoke rose from the wood about the thing's feet, which seemed to be sinking into the deck, hampering its movement.

"By the Shards of Pythagorus, *gek paipcm ficcg*," emoted Tanch. Nine balls of blue flame erupted in succession from Tanch's outstretched hand and sped toward the Einheriar. One, then a second, and then a third, struck it in the back and exploded—each shredded its armor and tore gory chunks from its body.

Dolan stepped forward and fired one of Pipkorn's Vanyar arrows into the Einheriar's shoulder. It did not pass through, but sunk into the warrior's shoulder just as any arrow should, and sent green ichor streaming down its torso. Tanch's other missiles hit the Einheriar and blasted it to its knees. Dolan stepped closer, his jaw set, and put three more arrows into the thing in rapid succession. The third entered the Einheriar's forehead at point blank range. It slumped to the side, and then dropped to the deck, unmoving. The Einheriar's body collapsed and dissolved into a putrid ooze. In moments, it was naught but a bubbly, smoking stain upon the deck.

Theta peered down from the bridge deck, dagger in hand.

The battle over, the deck was quiet again for a few moments.

"Wizardry," yelled N'Paag from the wheel, pointing down at Tanch. "And why did his arrows work," pointing at Dolan, "and not the others?"

"Foul magic," shouted a crewman.

"Devil's work," shouted another.

The crewmen backed away from Tanch and Dolan both. Accusing and fearful stares accosted them from all sides. Even the soldiers of Malvegil, Lomion, and Eotrus, looked shocked and stared.

"You all know that I'm a wizard of the Tower of the Arcane," said Tanch. "Did you fools think tower mages have no power? Did you think all we could do was card tricks?"

"We'll suffer no dark magic on this ship," shouted N'Paag.

Ob moved behind N'Paag, a dagger ready for use.

"Should I have stood by and let them kill you, one by one?" shouted Tanch, his voice filled with anger. "Fools."

"Put them off," yelled one sailor.

"Let's throw them over the side," barked Little Tug. "Let the Fens have them."

"They just saved your behinds with their magic," said Bertha Smallbutt, who knelt beside her wounded captain. "Show some gratitude, not stupidity."

"Maybe so, but they waited until men were dead and the captain was grievous hurt," said

N'Paag.

Ob placed the tip of his dagger against N'Paag's back. "Not another word or you're dead," he said quietly.

"No good comes from magic," said Little Tug. He grabbed Dolan about the collar, effortlessly lifted him into the air with but one arm, and strode toward the rail.

Artol's iron grip locked on Tug's shoulder and spun all five hundred pounds of him around. "Perhaps you'd like to try that with me," he spat, meeting the giant's sneer, eye to eye.

Bertha rose from Slaayde's side. "The Captain says, leave them be. Any man that don't, will answer to him, and to me."

There was some grumbling and cursing, but soon the men began to disperse.

"Another time, tin can," said Tug, dropping Dolan to the deck. Dolan landed lightly on his feet and looked not the least bit flustered.

"Any time, Little Bug," said Artol with a big, fake smile.

"Keep your mouth shut from now on," said Ob to N'Paag. "You'll live longer." Ob stepped back and put his dagger away. He turned to Theta and Claradon. "Too bad Slaayde stopped it so soon. Would've been interesting to see Artol tangle with that giant."

"Why didn't Dolan try to break free?" said Claradon. "He just hung there, limp."

"The boy was scared senseless," said Ob. "Nothing more than that."

"No," said Theta. "He was deciding whether and when to kill the giant. He just hadn't made up his mind yet."

"Right," said Ob, with a nervous laugh. He took a swig from his flask before speaking again. "I wanted to help with the creature, you know, but I didn't expect me axe could touch it."

"You could've helped by watching our backs like I told you, Gnome. If you had, it wouldn't have gotten behind me."

Ob paled. "You're right. I never even saw where it came from. A rookie mistake and I'm no rookie."

"Next time, do as I say."

Ob bristled and puffed out his chest. "Alright, Mr. Fancy Pants, I admitted I screwed up. But you're not the one in command here. Claradon is in charge of this mission, not you, and don't be forgetting it. It's his orders I follow, not yours, you stinking tin can." The Gnome didn't wait for any response. He stormed down the ladder to the main deck, cursing under his breath.

Theta sat down on the deck, his feet over the edge, still holding Worfin Dal in his left hand. He took several deep breaths, and pulled ice from his mustache with his right hand. The ice in his hair was melting. Water dripped down his face, which was pale.

"Ob's a good man," said Claradon. "I appreciate your tolerating his words. I need him with us in this."

Theta nodded, looking down at the main deck. "Even an old dog barks to defend its master," said Theta. "That's its nature. To kick it, and expect it to stop, does as much good as kicking the wind."

Claradon chuckled and sat down beside Theta.

"Impressive work against that creature," said Claradon. "I wouldn't have believed a man your size, in full plate, could move that fast. It never even touched you."

"That was the point. One touch from those things turns a man to dust, as we've just seen. I've no interest in that. It reminds me of stone trolls—they can dissolve a man's bones. Terrible way to die."

"Stone trolls? Are such things real?"

"Most of the creatures of myth and legend are real, or at least, were real. Not many left. Magic is leaving the world, it wanes more every year, and that's a good thing."

"Are you saying that as magic leaves the world, the creatures die out?"

"The other way around," said Theta. "If I were to ask an average man in Lomion City about magic, about wizards, what would he tell me?"

"He would say that it's not real, just trickery, sleight of hand and such for entertainment's sake. Just old superstitions, kept alive to keep children in line or just out of ignorance. Nothing more to it than that, he'd say."

"Yet every fortress and city in Lomion has at least one real wizard, isn't that what you told me? Each one can cast spells and perform magics, though all in secret, except for extreme cases like with Tanch today."

"What you're telling me is that just because I haven't seen monsters, trolls, dragons, and such in my life, doesn't mean they don't exist."

Theta nodded. "There is more to the world than you know. On this trip, I expect you will see more of the weird than you ever dreamed existed."

"I already have. By the way, I'm sorry about that blow; I should never have struck it. I'm just glad your armor held. I don't know what I was thinking. I saw the other weapons pass through; I should've known mine would do the same. I guess I did know, but just didn't think."

"You went on instinct, not thought. That sometimes serves a man well when fighting other men, but not against magic or creatures such as these. With them, you must use your brain, more than your sword, or you'll not last long."

"As for the armor, don't worry about it." Theta pulled his tabard open where it was slashed through, and showed Claradon the shining steel breastplate beneath. "Not a scratch from your sword. The flaming splatter from whatever it coughed up did some damage, though," he said, pointing to some burns and gouges scattered along the breastplate and shoulder piece. "You owe me a new tabard."

"I will gladly buy you one of the best in Lomion."

"Your sword didn't fare as well as my armor."

Claradon looked to the tip of his blade. The edge was chipped and bent, as if he had slammed it into a stone wall.

Theta took a closer look. "Don't worry, it's still serviceable, and not beyond repair."

Claradon stared at the sword in surprise and then looked again at Theta's breastplate. "How can this be?"

"Some steels are stronger than others, simple as that."

They sat quietly for a time, watching the men on the deck below.

"That's your edge isn't it?" said Claradon. "Back during the miniatures game in Dor Lomion, you told us to use every edge that we had in battle. Your weapons and your armor, they are your edge, aren't they?"

"You're learning, boy," said Theta. "Better arms do give a warrior an edge, and it's often enough to keep him alive, if his courage holds. Training, knowledge, magic, loyalty, and especially luck—all these can give you an edge too. And you can never have too many edges, this battle proved that. We owe a debt to Pipkorn, for his arrows, and for Wotan Dal. The battle would have gone harder without them."

"But you would have found a way to bring those creatures down, even without them, wouldn't you?"

"There's always a way, Eotrus, if a man has the will, and the courage, and never gives up."

"Another lesson, Lord Theta?" said Claradon.

"Another lesson, Lord Eotrus."

***

Theta pulled Wotan Dal and Dargus Dal from a bucket of water, inspected them each in turn, dried and buffed them with a cloth before replacing them in their sheaths.

Ob and Dolan descended from the bridge deck and approached Theta. Dolan held Theta's gauntlets and Ob carried his ruined falchion.

"I cleaned them up as best I could," said Dolan. He handed the gauntlets to Theta who inspected them. The metal was slightly warped and gouged where the Einheriar's ichor had touched them, but both were intact and serviceable.

Ob offered Theta the falchion. "This one is done for."

Theta reached out and took hold of the blade. He held it up and studied the surface, melted, twisted, and bent almost completely in half. The fine engravings that covered both sides of the blade from hilt to tip, geometric symbols and a strange script, were ruined over much of the sword's length.

"A shame," said Ob. "A fine blade it was. How do you figure your sword and daggers stopped the creature's blows where every other blade did not? Are they magicked up or something?"

"They're made of a special alloy, similar to the arrows that Pipkorn gave to Dolan. The sword didn't have enough of the right materials, so it was damaged where the daggers were not."

"You had that sword a long time, didn't you?" said Ob.

"A very long time."

"Are you gonna keep it, for remembrance?"

"Dolan and I will repair it. We need only find a forge with the right tools and material and we can restore it."

Ob looked skeptical. "You'd need as much skill with a hammer as you have with the blade to fix that ruin."

"We can do it," said Dolan.

"What of the engravings?"

"If we had enough time," said Dolan. "Fix them, we could."

"What did it say?" said Ob. "The writings on the sword."

"That's a story for another time." Theta looked over at the remains of the Einheriar some feet away.

Dolan squatted down and fished through the ashy remains. His arrowheads survived, but the creature's ichor had dissolved the shafts.

"What were these things?" said Dolan.

"Your boss named them," said Ob. "Something familiar. What did you call them?"

"They were Einheriar."

"I know that name from the old legends," said Ob. "Aren't they Odin's chosen warriors? Those ones what will stand with him at the end of days."

"That battle has long come and gone," said Theta.

"What? Anyway, they're supposed to be the good guys," said Ob. "Heroes, every one."

"Once they were. Then Azathoth corrupted them."

"Where did they come from? The Fens? You think there's an army of them in there?"

"If there were an army of them, Lomion would be in dire trouble. No, those two were brought from Nifleheim, of that I'm certain. Conjured up by some fool wizard, probably the same ones that opened the gateway in your forest."

"If that's right," said Ob, "that means they know we're following, and they left those creatures to slow us down or stop us dead. Which they would only bother doing if—"

"They were afraid of us," said Dolan.

"Not us, boy," said Ob. "They're afraid of Theta."

Done examining the remains, Theta stood and surveyed the deck. Guards stood all about the rail. Others patrolled up and down the deck. The scent of brimstone nearly gone, the ice melted. If not for the warped and scarred floorboards, the deck looked almost normal.

"How many dead?" said Theta.

"Five of Slaayde's crew got turned to dust and one of the Seran's men too," said Ob. "Two others of Slaayde's are missing."

"How many injured?" said Theta.

"By the creatures, only Slaayde himself. Every man what was touched was dusted, except Slaayde. He's a sight—his hair all turned white, root to tip, and his strength is sapped. His mates stand vigil, though they say he will live. Besides him, one of the crewmen was gutshot with an arrow; he will not live a day. A few others were hurt when the railing came down on them, but not serious."

"Luck was with us then," said Theta. "It could've been much worse."

Artol climbed down the ladder from the bridge deck and joined the others. "No trace of dust up there."

Theta nodded. "That means Slaayde's missing

men are not missing. They turned into the Einheriar."

"What? How could that be?" said Ob.

"Perhaps they wore the guise of men only, and last night revealed their true nature. Or perhaps they were taken over somehow. The one that called the alarm and ran up the ladder past us. His was the dust Artol searched for. As I suspected, there was none. He became that Einheriar. That's how it got behind us."

"That makes four of Slaayde's crew that was Leaguers or worse," said Ob.

"How many more?" said Theta. "We can't have traitors waiting to strike us down at every turn."

"Maybe they're all Leaguers," said Dolan.

"They're not," said Artol. "At least three of the crew died fighting the monsters. These were brave men. Had their weapons worked against them, the whole crew would've been at them. Not many seamen would do that, especially not with soldiers and knights aboard. Most would hide behind us, but not these, they're made of sturdy stuff."

"I agree," said Ob. "They might be scum, but they've got heart and they're not Leaguers—at least not most of them."

"But some were," said Theta. "And some more may be. We need to root them out. I want no daggers in my back."

***

Par Tanch Trinagal turned fitfully in his sleep. His hands stung from the sorcery he had called upon in the recent battle; recurrent nightmares burned his brain. Nightmares of one hellish night deep in the Vermion Forest when he and his comrades faced outré horrors from beyond the world of man.

Through a deep, bone-chilling fog, Tanch saw a demon of nightmare come alive, a thing more reptilian than animal. A thing that had no place or right to exist on Midgaard. A creature that should be naught but myth and legend. The thing pounced on Ob, already wounded and bleeding.

Tanch called up words of power known only to true wizards, "By the Shards of Pythagorus, *gek paipcm ficcg.*" Spheres of blue fire erupted from Tanch's fingers and sped toward the demon. On impact they detonated, blasted huge chunks from it, and killed it where it stood. Several knights moved protectively around Ob.

Tanch turned and saw the big foreign knight, Lord Angle Theta, surrounded by many fiends akin to but different from the one he had just felled. The fiends stopped for a moment and looks of fear etched their inhuman faces. One even fell to its knees.

Tanch had been plagued by this dream on many a night. Each time, one and then another of the fiends opened their mouths as if to speak, but through the din of battle, Tanch could not hope to hear their words, if words they were at all.

But this night, unlike all the others, the dream was different. This time, the sounds of the battle grew dim and his vision narrowed upon the scene before him. This time, he heard the demons' words.

"No," cried one fiend. "It be the ancient enemy, the traitor. The Harbinger of Doom."

A second demon dropped to its knees. "Spare us Lord and we shall serve thee, forevermore."

Theta's sword slashed by faster than Tanch's eyes could follow, and cut the fiends to shreds.

Tanch awoke with a start, nightshirt soaked, head pounding. The demon's words, "Harbinger of Doom. Harbinger of Doom," echoed in his head. The morning sun shone in through the porthole and anchored the wizard back to reality.

They knew him. They knew him. They feared him. They named him Lord and traitor. What could that mean? Dead gods, was that naught but a nightmare, or something more?

***

Theta, Claradon, and Ob stood in Slaayde's private chambers, at the foot of his sickbed. Tug and two burly seamen stood guard by the door. Slaayde was sitting up, though he looked half dead. His cheeks were sunken and of ghostly pallor, his hair white, his eyes dim and unfocused.

Claradon had spent several minutes explaining that the missing crewmen turned into the Nifleheim warriors and that other crewmen could be suspect. Slaayde remained unconvinced. Raised voices caused a number of crewmen to gather in the hallway outside, to listen.

"Slaayde," said Theta, speaking for the first time since entering the room, "I need you to order your men to assemble for questioning."

Slaayde pulled himself up straighter. "My men," said Slaayde in an even tone, but loud enough for his men in the hallway to hear, "fought bravely." He paused to catch his breath before continuing. "Not a man amongst the crew of *The Falcon* was ever in league with those Fen creatures. *The Black Falcon* has the bravest and best crew that sails these ways, and let no man say any different. If any do, I will cut their damn heads off myself. I will not have my crew's loyalties questioned by my passengers or any other."

Nods and grunts of agreement came from the lurking crewmen.

"Laddie, one of your men was right behind me and Theta, and then he turned into that thing what Theta fought and killed on the bridge."

"Did you see this transformation? Did you see it happen with your own eyes?"

Ob narrowed his eyes.

"Did you see it, Eotrus? Or you?" he said, looking to Theta.

"No," said Claradon.

Theta didn't respond or react in any way save to stare at Slaayde.

"I say that those two Fen creatures swam to *The Falcon* from the bog and climbed up the side onto my deck. One skulked up behind my man while he was distracted by the battle below and killed him, turning him to dust, and then came for you."

"There's no dust up there," said Ob.

"So? It scattered in the breeze or in the battle or was knocked overboard, or was washed away by the rain. That's what happened and I will hear no more of it. My men—one and all—are loyal and true to me and to Lomion. We will speak no more of this. And we will see no more of those creatures—they're things of the Fens and travel not beyond its borders. We've left them well behind."

Claradon made to protest further, but Ob grabbed his arm. "Let's drop it, boy," he said quietly.

***

"**I** don't understand what went on in there," said Claradon as he sat on the couch in the Captain's Den. "Is Slaayde an idiot? Even if he doesn't believe his missing men transformed into the Einheriar, he must see the value in questioning the crew. If there are other spies or traitors aboard, next time we may not get off so easy. We need to rout them out."

Ob lounged back in a big leather chair, ale mug in hand. "Old White Hair knows all that as good as we do. Slaayde is hurt bad and that makes him afraid. Afraid his men will turn on him, and that he'll lose his pretty little ship. That's why he won't back us, least not until he's up and about and can stand up for himself."

"So, to not take a chance on jeopardizing his command, he's willing to risk his ship and all our lives?"

"Yep, that's about the size of it. Most men would do the same. I suppose he figures the odds of another turncoat or doppelganger is small, so he'll take his chances."

"So what do we do?" said Claradon, looking toward Theta. The big knight sat silently in another leather chair, an inscrutable expression on his face.

"What do you think we should do, boy?" said Ob.

Claradon looked uncertain, and paused, thinking. "I think we should take a friendly and unannounced tour of the ship. Inspect for damage, shake some hands, see how everyone is holding up after that battle, and all the while I'll keep the Amulet of Escandell close, looking for any sign that it reacts when I pass any crewman. If I get a hit, we will know who to watch."

"A good plan, Lord Eotrus," said Ob.

Claradon smiled. "Thank you, Castellan."

"Careful to whom you extend your hand, Eotrus," said Theta, "or it might not come back."

"What do you mean?" said Claradon.

"Have you forgotten that last night, half the crew, led by the First Mate, wanted to throw Dolan and the wizard in the river? If they had, things wouldn't have ended there, and they knew it. Leaguers or not, we've enemies amongst us and we need to be wary."

"The big guy has got a point," said Ob. "That First Mate, Na-poo-poo, or whatever his name is, needs close watching."

✱✱✱

"**O**b and I talked to each man in the crew," said Claradon as he leaned against the ship's rail. Theta stood beside him. "You were right. It seems a lot of them don't care for us. The amulet went warm around any number of them. I was starting to think that they're all Leaguers."

"They're afraid of you—of us," said Theta. "That's what you were picking up. Or—maybe they are all Leaguers."

Claradon perked up. "You're kidding, right?"

"Let's just watch our steps," said Theta. "I suggest you go nowhere alone on this ship. Keep at least one of your own knights at your side at all times."

VIII
DOVER

"A man makes his own fate."
—Angle Theta

South of the Fens, the river returned to its normal aspect, its waters wide, deep, and greenish blue. A place of quiet and calm, jumping fish, buzzing dragonflies, healthy breezes, and clear cool water. For some time, *The Black Falcon* made its way south, untroubled, with as much speed as Slaayde's crew could muster, oar, sail, and rudder.

They sailed past the Dalassian Hills, named for the Dwarven clan that abided deep within its rolling, rocky expanse. Then came a land of green fields and light woodland dotted with sleepy villages of white roofs, sturdy walls, and stone palisades, scattered along the western riverbank. The eastern bank remained bleak and barren, as if the Fens' fell influence extended even there. They passed the idyllic Linden Forest, and the gray fortress of Dor Linden, ruled by House Mirtise.

Along the way, the crew implemented repairs as best they could, on the move and with limited supplies. Sturdy pine deck-boards hauled up from the hold replaced those damaged by the Einheriar. The crew cobbled together a serviceable temporary rail up on the bridge deck for safety, and they reinforced the repairs below the waterline where the saboteur had drilled his holes.

After some days, Slaayde appeared on deck, looking weak, and leaning on a cane. He grew stronger though each day; the color returned to his cheeks and the spark to his step, but his hair remained ghost white, root to end, until the end of his days.

During the journey south, *The Falcon* passed a number of ships headed upriver, and asked each of *The White Rose*. Always a day behind were they, sometimes two. They could gain nothing on their quarry.

Farther south, they passed the Tornwood, a vast, foreboding woodland that ruled both banks of the Hudsar for untold miles. Trees tall and old, the Tornwood long rumored to house a secret Elven enclave—though no man in living memory had seen its sights.

***

The City of Dover lived at a fork in the river that marked the southeastern border of the Kingdom of Lomion. The Hudsar's main course continued due south for many days to the City of Tragoss Mor on the shores of the Azure Sea. The smaller, eastern fork became the Emerald River and flowed southeast to Minoc-by-the-Sea, also on the Azure, but many miles east of Tragoss Mor.

Dover, home to untold thousands, was the largest city in the kingdom south of Lomion City, and was located on the Hudsar's western bank. Its place at the borderlands of Lomion and the wilds beyond created its militant aspect. Walls sixty feet tall surrounded the inner city and a second wall of forty feet in height encircled the outer. Guard towers dotted the wall.

Dover kept a standing army of size to defend the border. A fleet of vessels, merchant and military, filled its port. Most of the knightly orders kept Chapterhouses there, and some held great power and influence.

The fortress of Dor Valadon stood on a small island that separated the two great rivers. Massive walls of stone, forty feet tall, and many feet thick, joined stone towers of twice that height, and ruled the river's fork. Men-at-arms and knights stalked the battlements.

Connecting Dor Valadon and Dover was one of the great wonders of the known world—a bridge, a stone arch, massive and strong, rose high above the river, and spanned clear across the Hudsar at its narrowest point. The masts of even the tallest ships could pass easily under the magnificent arch, even in high tide. Ages ago, the Dalassian Dwarves, renowned masons and craftsman, were engaged by the King of Lomion to construct the bridge. Legend says seven hundred Dwarves labored night and day for seven years to build the wondrous structure, which stood defiantly against wind and storm, time and troubles, down through the long years.

The Village of Yord on the river's eastern bank, opposite Dover, surrounded by a tall stone palisade, stood at the headwaters of the Emerald River. Private homes and longhouses of carved logs, skillfully crafted, dominated Yord, a sleepy town separated from the bustle of Dover by the river which was its lifeblood. A ferry system carried passengers and goods between Yord, Dor Valadon, and Dover proper.

The Black Falcon put to port at Dover's longest and tallest pier, for Slaayde needed to procure timber and other repair materials for the ship, and Theta wanted to visit a smithy, to affect repairs to his sword.

As soon as *The Falcon*'s gangway was down, Theta, Dolan, Artol, Tanch, and Ob disembarked. Uncharacteristically, Theta wore no armor save his cuirass, though his sword belt held his scimitar, and he carried his shield over his shoulder. Dolan, also unarmored, carried Theta's ruined falchion. Artol, however, was armed and armored to the teeth. The harbormaster gave them directions to what he claimed was the best smithy in town.

A burly young man pounded at a sword while a youth worked the bellows. They stopped their work as the five approached and exchanged greetings.

"We've a sword that's broke," said Dolan.

An older man, lean, lined, and solid muscle emerged from within the smithy. He looked the group up and down.

"Come in on a ship?"

"Aye," said Dolan. "*The Black Falcon* out of Lomion."

"Not a ship known for carrying passengers."

"We're—"

"It's a fast ship and we had no time to waste,"

said Theta. "We need the use of your forge to repair a sword."

"Nobody uses my forge but me and my sons. Let's see this sword of yours."

Dolan placed the blade on a table and unwrapped it.

"Dead gods, what a ruin." He picked the blade up and studied it. "Thor's hammer, this is like no steel I've ever seen." His sons looked on, gawking. The smith slowly passed his calloused fingers over the symbols etched along the blade. "Not even the Dwarves could make this. Where did you find her?"

"It's been in my family for generations."

"A shame. I've never seen damage like this before. Does this steel have a low melting point? Was it in a fire?"

Theta looked pointedly at Dolan, who removed a money purse from his belt and counted out ten silver stars. "We need your forge, Mr. Smith. We've no time for talk."

"I'm as good as any smith south of Lomion City, save for the Dwarves, but I couldn't do this blade justice. In a few days maybe I could make it serviceable, but I would never be able to fully restore it."

"We'll fix it ourselves," said Dolan. He handed the smith the coins, and then walked to the forge and put on a pair of heavy gloves.

"Do you know what you're doing?"

"Just watch." Dolan took out the arrowheads that he had recovered from the remains of the Einheriar and placed them beside the forge.

"You're gonna add their metal to your sword?"

said Ob quietly to Theta. "Smart move."

"They're almost pure ranal. They will make the sword invulnerable to the touch of Nifleheim." Theta unlatched his cuirass, laid it and his shield beside the forge, and prepared to assist Dolan in his labors.

"How long will this take?" said Ob. "Every minute we're here, Korrgonn gets farther away. If we're to save Jude—"

"There's no use catching them if we don't have the right tools to deal with them when we do. I need this sword. We'll be swift. Dolan is a master at this."

"I don't know half what you do, boss," said Dolan.

"Fine, forge away," said Ob. "Tanch and I are gonna poke around for a bit. No sense all of us watching you two sweat."

Tanch and Ob watched for some minutes as men, women, even families with children, filed into a large stone building.

"The sign of Bhaal lies over the doorway," said Tanch. "And there are other marks of Nifleheim there, and there," he said, pointing. "It's a temple. A temple to the Nifleheim lords, right here in the open."

"In Dover?" said Ob. "That can't be. This is a civilized city. A good place—always has been. We need to go in and see what's what."

"I just hope we can get out again," said Tanch.

They crossed the street and entered along with several others. The entry chamber held racks of hooded robes of red and black to be donned by worshippers before entering. Tanch and Ob hastily garbed themselves, Ob drawing from the children's section, and then proceeded in. Beyond was a large worship room lined with benches, all facing an expansive podium featuring an immense stone altar. Well behind the altar sat a group of robed men, mostly young, a few wizened and old.

The service about to start, guards noisily closed and barred the chamber's mammoth double doors. Other guards positioned about the room made a show of slamming and barring every other exit as well, one after another in practiced pattern. No one was leaving this room until the service was over, that much was clear.

Ob turned to the wrinkled old woman of blue hair and huge hat that sat to his right. "What do I do," he said, pleadingly, almost in desperation, "if I have to pee?"

The woman smiled and nodded, clearly having no idea what Ob had said.

An elderly priest stepped up behind the altar, and faced the congregation. He gripped a bejeweled staff of iron and wood, long and stately. The staff glowed when he thanked the faithful for their devotion and led them in prayers and blessings praising Bhaal and other Nifleheim lords, whom he called Holy Arkons and the blessed Lords of Light.

The formal ritual complete, the priest launched into a fiery sermon, railing against the rich, and denouncing the government. He spoke of the Crown's oppression of the common people, the corruption of the nobles, and their foul conspiracies to suppress the truth and keep good people down. He appealed to the congregation's sense of worth and entitlement. They all deserved the same success, the same wealth, the same opportunity as others. Too long had they been denied their god-given rights and privileges by those who thought themselves their betters. He urged them to stand together not as one people, but as one family, united against the forces of evil and oppression. Only then would they achieve all that they deserved, only then would their worldly happiness be assured, and only then would their honored place be reserved in paradise. The people nodded and shouted their agreement, applauding briefly here and there.

Ob and Tanch tensed when the priest produced a large chalice from behind the altar and gazed out over the gathered faithful. Hands went up amongst the congregation and the priest pointed to one man, seated near the front. Balding and middle-aged, the man kissed his wife and child before he stood up and walked to the altar, a long, wicked dagger gripped in his hand.

"Oh, boy," said Ob. "I had hoped not to see this again."

Other priests crept up behind him and held him fast about the shoulders. The high priest blessed the man, declaring that his sacrifice proved his devotion to the lord and assured his passage to Vaeden, the blessed afterlife. The man passed the priest the dagger and willingly held out his hand, wrist up. Swift and sure, the priest sliced the man's wrist, though he exhibited no pain and did not call out. One of the priests held the man's arm still while the high priest poured a decanter of wine over the wound and into the awaiting chalice.

When the decanter was empty, the high priest selected a second man from the audience, and repeated the ritual, though this time, the dagger sliced across the man's neck. It soon became clear that this was naught but ceremony, the men were not harmed at all, and no true blood was spilled. Only wine filled the chalices passed to the faithful, each devotee, young or old, man, woman, or child, all obliged to drink.

Both Ob and Tanch pretended to take a sip, though neither did. Soon the service ended, the great doors opened, and everyone left in peace.

Ob and Tanch wandered out in a daze. They didn't speak until they were well away from the crowd.

"The prayers, the sermon, it was all so similar," said Ob. "Except the sacrifices were just an act; the blood, just wine."

"Without the bloodshed," said Tanch, "their ritual was not the vile thing I remembered. Not to say I agree with their lessons, but some of them at least made sense. I can see why people attend, why they're drawn in." Tanch hesitated before continuing. "You did see the blood, real blood in the ceremony in Southeast, right?"

"I saw it," said Ob, though he seemed less certain than he should.

The crew hauled aboard bundles of wood planks, buckets of nails, cords of rope, casks of local spring water, baskets of fresh bread, and crates of salted meats and hard cheeses, in workmanlike manner.

Slaayde completed his dealings with a rotund merchant of pointy beard, colorful garb, and pasty face, trading him a goodly number of boxes marked linens, tobacco, and Gnome mead for a number of unmarked crates of dubious origin and unspoken contents. Soon after their transaction was complete, Theta and the others returned. Theta and Dolan were grimy and sweaty, and Theta's falchion was back in its sheath at this waist. His breastplate looked shiny and renewed, as did his shield.

"We've asked after *The Rose* as best we could," said Claradon, "but no one can say which way she headed. There's just too much traffic here. No one pays attention to what ships pass, and the harbormaster has no record. We need to decide which way to go—continue down the Hudsar or take the Emerald?"

"Are there any other rivers or tributaries that *The Rose* could take, off either river?" asked Theta.

"None what could handle a ship near her size," said Ob. "But they have dinghies aboard. There's a score or more small rivers and streams that flow into the Hudsar and the Emerald that you could send a dinghy up, and there's a thousand places you could make shore at."

"So how do we decide?" said Claradon.

"We know they were well-stocked at Lomion City for a long voyage," said Theta. "How long to Tragoss from here, and to Minoc?"

"Both are a week to ten days away, depending on the current and the wind," said the Gnome.

"What welcome would they receive in each port?" said Theta.

"Tragoss is ruled by monks who worship Thoth. They're religious wackos, a lot like the Leaguers, but I don't think they would abide them. Like as not, they and the League would be at each other."

"And Minoc?"

"A large trading city, ruled by a merchant's guild. One of the best of the independent cities. Korrgonn would get no welcome there."

"But in a free city, he could hide," said Claradon.

"Hiding is not his plan," said Theta.

Claradon looked to Theta, shaking his head. "If he's got no reason we know of to go to Tragoss or Minoc, he could be just passing through on his way to anywhere. We might as well flip a coin."

"Leave it to fate, then," said Ob, a pensive look on his face.

"What do you think, Lord Theta?" said Claradon.

"A man makes his own fate."

Ob pulled a silver star from his pocket. "Kings for Tragoss, castles for Minoc. Choose."

Claradon considered for a moment. "Kings," he said.

Ob tossed the coin high into the air and let it fall to the deck. "Kings."

***

South of Dover abided the Crags, a long expanse of enormous jutting rocks that comprised the river's western bank. The river's relentless flow had carved the Crags from the very stone of the earth, leaving naught but a tall stony palisade. Curiously, no similar formation existed on the opposite shore. Instead, the Mistwood—a vast, dark forest, nigh impassable and exuding a palpable dread, ruled the eastern bank.

Several hours after sunset, as *The Black Falcon* sailed through the narrowest portion of the river in the Crags region, the men spotted a score or more figures, male and female, amidst the lowest of the stony palisades, not much higher than the mast of the ship. Each stood on some rocky promontory or narrow precipice; locations where none but eagles were wont to go. Illumed only by moonlight, silent, still, and tall they looked down on the ship, their faces cloaked in shadow and mystery.

Theta, Claradon, and Ob stood on the Bridge Deck, and watched the figures watch them. As the stern of the ship passed them, one raised his arm as if in greeting or salute and then bowed low toward the men on the deck.

"Some friend of yours, Theta?" said Ob. "Another pal from the old days?"

"I know them not," said Theta.

"They're no friends of ours," said Claradon, pointing to his amulet, glowing brightly.

"Since they've no bows, unless they can fly, they're of little matter," said Ob.

The figure who bowed lofted some small

object toward them; a powerful and accurate throw. It landed on the deck.

Ob dashed over to examine it. The others kept their attention on the figures on the cliff. "It's got a rune on it, embedded in a circle and a square."

"Bring it here," said Theta. He studied it closely after they were well past the strange figures. "Azrael," said Theta, turning back toward the figures, now lost in the night. Theta gripped his Ankh in his right hand. "We shall meet them again."

IX
TRAGOSS MOR

"They have to spread our wealth around to the poor.
That gives them power. That's what this here is all about."

"Theta, any sign of our shadow?" said Ob.

"It follows us still, though it has fallen farther back."

"All the way from Lomion to the shore of the Azure Sea and not a sign of *The White Rose*," said Claradon, his hand on the ship's rail. "We must've hailed three score ships this past week and not one could say if they had seen her."

"That don't mean nothing," said Ob. "The Hudsar is wide and busy down this way, so captains rarely pay heed to what ships they pass."

"We should've taken the eastern fork to the Emerald River. I've failed my brother. We'll never find him now."

"We trusted to fate, and we will soon know if that was sound or sorry. Either way, we will catch up to them. Don't you worry, boy. We will get Jude back."

Tanch stepped up to the others, a wet cloth held over his mouth, his face pale and drawn. "What is that atrocious smell? It's been getting worse all day."

"It's Tragoss Mor, Magic Boy. It's the city that you're smelling."

"But we haven't even entered the harbor yet."

"Open sewers and such," said Ob. "You get used to it after a while. Just keep breathing through your nose, not your mouth. Smells worse, but less chance of disease, I'm told."

"Open Sewers? Disease? Someone, please put me out of my misery. What kind of a place is this anyway?"

"It's an old port city," said Ob. "Most sea trade between Lomion and parts foreign passes through here. It's bigger even than Lomion City, but the buildings are smaller. Mostly one or two stories, some are three; few are more than that. Nice cobblestone streets, as long as you watch your footing. Here's the harbor now."

Tanch turned to look. "Dead gods, it's huge."

"Biggest in the civilized world," said Ob. "More than one hundred piers, and berths for a thousand or more ships this size, and several times that many small ones. There's no other port like it."

"How will we ever find Sir Jude in all this?" said Tanch. "*The White Rose* could be anywhere."

Captain Slaayde climbed the ladder to the Bridge Deck, accompanied by Tug. "I plan to pull into a slip in the center of the harbor," he said, his usual wide grin on his face. "I assume you've no objection to that."

"Why not pull off to the very end?" said Tanch. "Wouldn't there be less chance we'd be spotted by the wrong sort?"

"And more chance *The Grey Talon* would come aside and risk boarding us. I want my ship in plain sight; there will be no safer place."

"Why would this *Grey Talon* accost us?" said

Tanch.

"She's been shadowing us all the way from Lomion City. I've no argument with her captain or her owners, but I believe you people do. I will not risk my ship unnecessarily."

"Who commands *The Talon*?" said Claradon.

"Captain Kleig is her master, but he's a lap dog of House Alder, which, I assume, is why they've been following. They want your head, Eotrus, for what you did to the Chancellor."

Claradon paled and looked as if he had just been slapped across the face.

"How many men does she carry?" said Theta.

"Her crew is half again larger than mine. I expect the Alders have loaded her up with their house guard, maybe even some Myrdonians. Probably one or more of the Alders will be leading them. I've no interest or plan to take her on, so don't go getting any ideas." Slaayde turned toward Tanch who was about to speak. "Harringgold's coin does me no good if I'm dead." Slaayde put a hand to his whited hair. "This trip has already cost me more than his gold is worth."

***

Dozens of seamen and longshoremen loaded cargo off a ship docked across the wide pier from where *The Falcon* had just tied off. *The Falcon*'s crew secured the gangway and Slaayde immediately disembarked with his bodyguards to converse with Borman, the Harbormaster, a burly man of weathered face and bushy brow. They joked and traded quips for a time, as old friends. Ob and Tanch joined them on the pier.

"What mischief brings you here this time?" said Borman.

"The usual mischief," said Slaayde.

Borman smiled and looked as if he didn't expect any more of a response than that, and he got none.

"Harbormaster," said Ob. "*The White Rose*, out of Lomion, came down ahead of us. Where is she berthed?"

Borman looked down at Ob, furrowed his brow, and turned back to Slaayde. "His kind aren't welcome in Tragoss any longer."

Ob's face darkened. He made to move toward Borman, but Par Tanch grabbed him by the collar and pushed him to the side. The stone at the apex of Tanch's staff glowed blue as he thumped the shaft on the pier's deck. "My servant asked after *The White Rose*."

Borman's eyes widened at the staff's glow, and he looked nervously about as if to see if any were looking. "I haven't seen her, your wizardship, sir," he said quickly.

"I owe her boatswain a gold crown from a game of Spottle gone bad, and promised I would settle up with him here in Tragoss. Have you heard no word of *The Rose*?"

"I couldn't say. I couldn't say. Many ships come and go through here. If they brook no trouble, I pay them little heed." He glanced over his shoulder again. "The Thothians tolerate no magic, your wizardship, no magic at all. Keep your staff dark hereabouts or you will find yourself in the deep stuff. They will be here in a moment."

Borman's deeply lined face took on a serious expression and he then spoke loudly and boldly. "The port fee is four silver stars per day, up from three last year. As is custom, you pay now for today and for tomorrow, or just for today if you plan to leave before sunset. And cause no trouble in Tragoss Mor, or the swift arm of justice will smite you."

He winked at Slaayde, turned, and walked swiftly away, leaving his aide to collect the fees. He halted after a few paces to bow to four strange men that approached.

Four Thothian monks, shirtless, bald of pate, beardless, but heavily mustached as was their custom, walked up to the group, ignoring Borman as they passed. Each wore baggy pantaloons adorned only with a wide sword belt.

"Welcome to Tragoss Mor, gentlemen," said one of the monks. "I am Finch, Prior of almighty Thoth, may he watch over us always. How fares *The Black Falcon*?"

"She fares well," said Slaayde.

"You are her captain?"

"Dylan Slaayde, at your service."

"Good, very good," said the monk with a smile. "What is your business in Tragoss Mor?"

"To purchase some fine wares and supplies for my ship."

"Good, very good," said Prior Finch, the same smile etched on his face. "You will find many treasures in Tragoss and we welcome your business." The smile then dropped from his face.

"I trust you're aware that the slave markets are long since closed." He paused, waiting for a response.

"And good riddance to them," said Slaayde.

"Good," said the monk. "Then you also know that no spirits are allowed here—not of grapes, wheat, honey, or any other. You will find no bars here, nor brothels. Seek not these things in Tragoss Mor and bring them not with you and your stay will be pleasant."

"We'll be on our best behavior," said Slaayde with a smile.

"See that you are. Good day to you." As Prior Finch began to turn away, one of his fellows placed a hand on his shoulder.

"Prior," he said, pointing at Ob, "they have an imp."

Prior Finch's eyes widened. He stepped up before Ob. "What have we here, Captain? Surely not a passenger?"

Before Slaayde could respond, Tanch spoke up. "The Gnome is but a common laborer, bound to the ship's service for the rest of his days."

Prior Finch's smile returned, and he visibly relaxed. "Good, very good. We are a civilized people, its kind are not free to roam our fair city. See that it stays on your ship or travels only with an escort."

Ob's face went beet red. He clenched both fists tightly and bit his tongue to stay it.

"Your imp is not properly trained, Captain." Prior Finch's hand darted out and slapped Ob, hard across the face, knocking his head to the side.

Ob slowly turned his face back toward the Prior, expressionless, his eyes locked on the monk's, boring through him. The monk's hand went up to strike Ob again.

"Stop!" said Tanch, placing his fist against the monk's chest to stay him. Prior Finch looked down at Tanch's hand in disgust and then met him eye to eye.

"He's no use to us if he's damaged," said Tanch.

"Discipline, not damage," said the monk. "Captain, your ship would be the better for it." He pushed Tanch's arm aside and backed away. "Your crew will show the proper respect to all Thothians and citizens, Captain, or you will be held accountable."

"I'm sure that they'll behave," said Slaayde, with his widest grin. "Good day to you."

Ob took a long drink from his rather large goblet. "I'm gonna kill that one," said Ob, his face still red from the monk's blow and perhaps the ale.

"A slap is not worth killing over," said Tanch, a serious look on his face. "Perhaps, a bit of torture, though."

All looked at Tanch in shock. He smiled and the Captain's Den briefly filled with laughter. Even Ob chuckled. The tension gone from the room, the men settled into their seats.

"The harbormaster lied," said Theta.

"He's hiding something," said Ob.

"Do you think *The Rose* is here?" said Claradon.

"Here, and gone most likely," said Ob.

"I agree, but we must check and find out what we can."

Theta directed Seran to take six men and walk the eastern docks to look for *The Rose*. Artol was to do the same at southern docks. Theta warned both to steer clear of the monks.

"It may be that Korrgonn and dear Sir Jude have disembarked and the ship has moved on without them," said Tanch.

"Unlikely," said Ob. "If they were letting off Korrgonn here, they would've stayed in port for at least a couple of days to rest and resupply. With the time we made, they couldn't be much more than a day, at most two, ahead of us."

"Slaayde," said Theta. "Resupply as fast as you can. Assume a long journey and fill your hold accordingly."

Slaayde looked surprised. "What? We've come all the way to the sea. How much farther are we to go? And who is to pay for this?" said Slaayde.

"You are," said Theta.

"I'm sure that Duke Harringgold will reimburse all your expenses," said Tanch. "And reward you generously for your service."

Slaayde didn't look entirely convinced.

After a few hours, Artol and Seran returned and the group gathered again in the Captain's Den. On deck, Slaayde's crew hauled aboard and stowed kegs of fresh water, dried fruit, and all manner of supplies.

"Gather round you scum," said Artol, displaying his characteristic toothy grin, "for our mission was a success." The big soldier casually twirled a long knife in his right hand, a thick cigar smoked in his left. Seran stood at attention, his armor shining even in the poor light of the cabin.

"My pal here Mr. Spit-and-Polish," resting his hand on Seran's shoulder, "despite his pretty face and wily ways, came up empty on the eastern docks. You might say that he's an incompetent fool not worth the gruel we feed him, but I prefer to think *The White Rose* docked to the south, so the scum of the east side knew nothing to tell."

Seran paled and looked mortified. The others who knew Artol far better than Seran looked amused.

"So what did you find?" said Ob.

"Three men I plied with a bit of silver and a bit more persuasion, if you get my meaning, told the same tale. *The Rose* sailed at dawn yesterday, stocked for a long haul, many weeks or more. To where, none of three knew."

"Perhaps more silver would loosen their tongues?" said Claradon.

Artol smiled a wicked, toothy smile. "Trust me, they told me all they knew." The long knife spun between his fingers.

"Who were the men you questioned?" said Theta.

"A petty merchant and two common sailors. Each was from parts foreign, and set to sail today or tomorrow."

"The locals?"

"Had nothing to say, despite my gentle urgings. I could be more persuasive, but then things would get messy. That wouldn't be neighborly, and probably just a waste of time.

Someone off *The Rose* made threats and spread some coin to keep their passage secret; that much is clear. Of course, there's no quicker way to gather attention than to pay people to say they didn't see you, which is the only reason those three even heard of *The Rose*. It's doubtful they told anyone where they were going, so we can bash as many heads as we want and we'll get nowhere. That's how I see it anyway."

Artol turned to Theta. "Thanks for the warning about the monks. They're everywhere and the people are scared snotless by them. We had to dodge them more than once. I thought slavers and pirates ran this city, not monks?"

"They did until a few years ago," said Ob. "Then the Thothians took over. They wiped out the slave trade and the corsairs but what they put in place is even worse. Look at them wrong and they'll stone you, I hear. Insult their religion or whatever and they will kill you dead on the street, and go after your family too. Hell, that stinking monk hit me just for being a Gnome. What's that about? Same kind of nuts like The Shadow Leaguers. Who knows, maybe they're even in with them.

"Had I known all that, I would have been a bit more subtle," said Artol, his expression and tone now serious. He sheathed his knife.

"Sorry," said Ob. "Sometimes I forget not everyone is as up on these things as me."

"Just what we need," said Tanch. "Now you've drawn attention to us. More crazies will be after us. I just can't take this, it's all too much." Tanch walked stiffly over to a couch and laid down, wincing, as if his back plagued him.

"Did you ask if any men from *The Rose* stayed behind here?" said Theta.

"They didn't know," said Artol.

Theta turned to Ob. "To what ports and what direction could they have been headed?"

"Minoc," said Ob. "Though it's less than a week's journey northeast along the coast. But if they wanted to go there, they should've taken the Emerald River, which leads straight there." Ob walked over to the mariner's globe, spun it to the right angle, and pointed to each place he named. "Boreundin is farther to the north; farther still is Vinland. Along the coast to the southwest is Piper's Hold, then comes Thoros-Gar, and other towns and cities beyond that. South, the lands stretch endlessly as far as any have gone, far beyond any semblance of civilization. There are islands too, far to the south off the coast. Bardin's Rock, Treeskull, Tekla, Radu-Mal, Tardin-Gar, Revit, and many, many more."

"They could be headed anywhere," said Claradon. "We have to find out what direction they went at least. If not, we'll never catch them. I will not abandon my brother to those maniacs."

Ob looked over at Theta. "Any ideas?"

"We've only one ship and not enough men to split our force. Given that, we must find someone who saw the ship leave. We must discover what direction they went."

"Or take our chances by choosing east or south," said Ob. "Another coin toss?"

"If we choose wrong, all could be lost," said Theta. "We must find another way."

Par Tanch sat up on the couch. "There's a seer," he said. "Azura the Seer, she's called. Exiled hereabouts years ago, or so I've heard. Trained in the Tower of the Arcane and gifted with far sight and prescience. She may be able to point the way for us."

"I put little stock in so-called seers," said Theta.

"Her powers are real enough, my lord," said Tanch, "or the tower wouldn't have passed her through."

"Hogwash and horsefeathers," said Ob. "They're nothing but charlatans and mummers."

"Let's try it," said Claradon. "If she knows nothing, we will have lost little but a bit of time."

"Where do we find her?" said Theta.

Tanch shook his head. "I've heard her tower resides in the western district, but I don't know where."

"Western district, you say?" said Ob. "Near the Raging Giant Inn, there's a tall tower. Could be that's it."

"Perhaps," said Tanch, nodding.

"Let's try it," said Claradon.

"Why don't we just ask someone for directions?" said Dolan.

"You start asking folks and the entire city will know within the hour," said Ob, "unless the harbormaster has already told them. We don't need any more attention."

***

"Slaayde—keep your men close, no shore leave," said Theta. "We may need to leave with speed on our return."

Slaayde smiled a wide smile with his mouth but not his eyes. "Bertha and her men are still out collecting supplies."

"Have them back before we return." Theta turned to Seran and Glimador who stood nearby. "Keep a watchful eye for *The Grey Talon*. She could be here any time. Keep our men on the ship. See that Slaayde's men don't stray either. Post a strong guard on deck. Be ready for trouble."

"What trouble are you expecting?" said Slaayde.

"The troubling kind. Just keep your men close."

The group set off and made their way down the long pier past Tragoss trawlers and heavy Minoc merchantmen, a trireme out of Kern and exotic sailing vessels from the southern islands. At the pier's end, a broad avenue stood before them, stretching as far as one could see in each direction along the water's edge, filled with wagons and carts, seamen and citizens, in transit in all directions. Though the way was wide, the group could walk no more than two abreast due to the throngs of dockworkers and teamsters. Claradon and Theta walked side by side at the vanguard of the group, Ob and Tanch behind them, and then Dolan and Artol.

Despite the crowds, nearly half the storefronts they passed were closed—abandoned and boarded up. Many lots were piled high with debris, stone and brick, wood and tile, the remnants of demolished buildings, long past their time.

"Last I was here," said Ob, "Tragoss had more brothels than bricks and more pubs than peddlers. Next to trading or slaving, those have always been their biggest businesses. All these abandoned storefronts were pubs. There on the corner was a place called The Great Mug. They'd been in business a couple centuries at least and sold more than a hundred kinds of beer from across Midgaard. Best tavern south of Lomion City. I will miss it. Stinking Thothians."

"What of the buildings torn down?" said Claradon.

"Gambling halls and brothels mostly. Guess even the buildings offended the monks. Reminds me of one time when me, McDuff, and Red Tybor were down here and—"

"Not now, Gnome," said Theta over his shoulder.

Ob replied only to Theta's back with a crude gesture.

Despite the changes, the streets still burst with inns and eateries, tackle and bait shops, food stands and fruit carts, and souvenir shops beyond count.

Sprawling warehouses of stone and brick and wood also thrived here, some of good repute, others ramshackle and abandoned—husks of past glories and finer days. Nearly all the buildings, save for the warehouses, were two stories, mostly built of tan-colored brick and mortar. They had flat roofs and wood-railed parapets. The citizenry were far more varied. There were tall Lomerians, dusky sailors from Minoc, short, yellow-skinned men from Tragoss Gar, colorful traders from Piper's Hold, and many more.

The women all wore long gloves extending from fingertip to elbow on both hands. The gloves, some in cloth, others in leather, varied in color, style, and pattern, and were universally worn by all women, even young girls. "In the inner city, the local women only wear white or black gloves," said Ob. "Last I was here, foreigners didn't need to wear the gloves at all. Guess that has changed."

"Need to?" said Claradon.

"The Thothians consider it improper for women to go out without gloves. "If you do, they will stone you."

"To death? For not wearing gloves?"

"Yup. And they call us northerners barbarians. They say ungloved women are unclean whores, or some such nonsense."

Everywhere were the Thothian monks, in groups of two or four and sometimes more. Stationed here and there and everywhere, watching every move, marking every word and glance. Besides the monks, and some of the merchants, few Tragoss Morians moved about the harbor district. It was a land of sightseers and seamen, tourists, traders, and foreign laborers.

It took almost an hour for the group to make their way on foot to the thirty-foot-tall wall that separated the Harbor District from the Western District. Iron portcullises barred passage from the wide gravel-filled avenues of the Harbor to the narrow cobblestoned lanes of the West. A guard post stood behind the iron, manned by a group of city watchmen.

"The Harbor District is all most visitors see," said Ob. "Once we pass this checkpoint, you will see the real Tragoss Mor. She's a beauty, except for the sewers. I expect we will have to pay to get through."

Ob stepped up to the gate and banged on it with his axe handle. "Open up."

Two uniformed guards stepped out of their shelter and approached the gate. One was middle-aged and tall, with bright eyes. The second was average height, lanky, and vacant.

"Who seeks to enter the Western District?" said the first guard.

"We do, bucko. Open up."

The guard looked down at Ob and wrinkled his nose. He looked up at the others. "Is this imp yours?"

"My servant," said Tanch. "Kindly pass us through."

"Your names and business?"

"I'm—Par Sinch of Kern," said Tanch. "I am on a pilgrimage to visit the great shrines of the Thothians. These others are but my servants and bodyguards."

The captain looked surprised, even taken aback. He looked around, as if to see if anyone was listening before he spoke. "Did you say, Par Sinch?"

Now Tanch looked surprised. "Yes," he said, uncertainly.

The captain studied the group for several moments. "If I didn't know better, I might mistake you for a wizard of the Tower of the Arcane and these bodyguards for church knights. But since any fool knows that months ago the Thothians issued an edict ordering the arrest of wizards and church knights on sight, you must, of course, be joking."

The second guard nodded knowingly, but gripped the hilt of his sword.

"Well said, sir," said Tanch without missing a beat. "A joke, it was. A bad one at that. I trust you will forgive me my foolishness. I am but a simple spice merchant seeking new markets for my wares. I hoped that if people thought me a wizard, I would garner more respect and more customers. I had no idea that magic users had come to disfavor in this fine land. What a fool you must think me."

The captain looked relieved. "Don't let it trouble you. A man must feed his family after all. Note well that the guardsmen of the 4th Gate," he said, looking at his comrade, "could not be fooled by your charade. We knew at once that you were a fraud."

The lanky guardsman nodded. "That's right, you can't fool us. We're no dummies," he said, and then hacked up a wad of phlegm and spit most of it on the ground by the gate, the balance dribbled down his beard.

"The toll for foreigners to pass this gate is one silver piece or ten bronze rings," said the guard captain. "I trust you will be heading straight to the spice market on Brick Street."

"Where else?" Tanch turned to Dolan. "Pay the good Captain."

Dolan pulled out a Lomerian silver star from his pocket and handed it to the guard through the bars.

Theta stepped forward. "Where on Brick Street might we find the best spice dealer?"

The captain smiled and nodded ever so slightly. "There are many spice dealers there and I know little of them." He glanced at his comrade who was busy stomping an ant. "I heard once though of a good one on the ground floor of the building just past the red awning about midblock. But I could be mistaken."

The captain turned to his comrade. "Open the gate. Let them pass." As the guard pulled out the keys for the gate, the captain stepped closer to Tanch and lowered his voice. "Keep your staff quiet in Tragoss, Par. The Thothians do arrest wizards on sight. Go carefully."

Tanch nodded. "Thanks."

The group filed through, and proceeded down the narrow alley. At its end, it seemed as if they had entered a different city entirely. Here, the sprawling warehouses and wide lanes gave way to narrow alleys winding betwixt one and two-story brick or stone residential buildings, some more hovel than home.

Beggars lined the streets. They extended cups or bowls as the men passed, entreating them for spare coin or scraps of food, though they kept themselves at arm's length from the armed men. Each side of the street held gutters that served as open sewers that flowed with filth and foulness. Rats, some small, some as large as cats scurried fearless along the gutters and swarmed over the occasional corpse, fallen and forgotten amongst the muck. Along each street, some men and women lay unmoving. They seemed dead, save for when a passing rodent took a nip at them—then they would curse and stir and sometimes strike out. The people ignored those sorry creatures. Only that they stepped around them, told they even saw them at all.

"Dead gods, what has become of this place?" said Ob through the cloth he held to his face to keep down the stench. "When I've been here before, much of the inner city was poor, but nothing like this. I heard that the Thothians promised that if the people followed their god and obeyed their edicts there would be an end to poverty. They said they would restore dignity to the downtrodden and fairness for all." Ob stumbled over a body fallen in the street, and barely kept his feet. "They seem to have mucked that up a bit."

"They've destroyed these people, and their culture," said Claradon.

"The price of stupidity," said Theta.

Tanch looked down in horror at the bodies and the beggars they passed. "Is it a plague? What ails these people?"

"Hopelessness and despair," said Ob. "And with that came smoking of strange plants and eating foul powders of foreign make. All stuff that muddles the mind and sours the spirit. That much had started when I was last here."

"No one seems to care," said Claradon. "They just walk past the fallen."

"Can the authorities do nothing?" said Tanch.

"They are doing something," said Ob. "They're letting them die. Some say the Thothians are the source of these poisons. That they brought them in to keep the people docile."

"Will we pass Brick Street on the way to the tower?" said Theta.

"I don't know," said Ob. "You think there are more than spice merchants there?"

Theta nodded. "Dolan, buy some fruit, and ask that merchant."

Dolan was back in a few moments with a small bag of apples. "Six blocks north, and two or three east."

"Not on our way," said Ob.

"The tower first, and then Brick Street," said Theta.

***

People crowded along the low stone wall that surrounded a well-appointed house of brick and stone, watching a group of monks drag an elderly man from the house. Other monks and guardsmen threw his paintings, books, and other belongings from the windows.

"You've no right, no right," shouted the man. "I've done nothing."

"Nothing?" said a monk. He grabbed the man and pushed him to his knees. "Yes, fool, you have done nothing. There are people starving in the streets and yet you live in a rich house. Do you care nothing for your fellow citizens?"

The man stared up at him, confused.

"You're a greedy, evil, pathetic blasphemer," said the monk, slapping the man across the face after each accusation. He grabbed the man by the hair and pulled back his head, forcing the old man to look at him. "What portion of your income do you give to the church, to the poor? Speak quick and true, or I will cut off your evil head."

Tears streamed down the man's face. "I pay my taxes, and I pay the tithe of Thoth. You can check, I always pay."

"A pittance," said the monk.

"What more do you want from me?"

"It's not what I want, fool. It's what justice demands. You give no more than the minimum and begrudge even that. By what right do you live in this decadent place when others sleep in the gutter? You think you're better than everyone, don't you, you bastard?"

"I've earned everything I own. I've worked fifty years, selling silks and linens, an honest living. I've hurt no one my whole life. You've no right to do this."

The monk grabbed the man by the chin and punched him in the face, breaking his nose. Blood poured down the deeply lined face, eyes filled with tears.

"You've earned nothing, blasphemer. You've hoarded wealth, stealing from those more deserving. No longer. Now we will take back all that you've stolen. You will pay your fair share at last, merchant.

The monk kicked the man in the ribs, a sickening crunching sound. Other monks joined in, kicking and stomping. "Kill the evil bastard," they spat. "Praise Thoth," they yelled. "Praise Thoth."

"Look," shouted the monk at the gathered crowd. "Behold Thoth's justice, citizens. All those like this evildoer will pay. All the enemies of god will be brought to justice and they will pay with their blood."

Some in the crowd looked shocked and disgusted. Others cheered each blow, each kick, each whimper.

The monks gathered the old man's books and artwork into large piles on the lawn and set them ablaze.

Other monks dragged several people out of the merchant's house. By their dress, servants all. They lined them up against the manor's wall.

The lead monk plucked a pretty young girl from the line. "What does that old bastard do to you?"

The girl looked confused; tears ran down her face. She cringed away, terror in her eyes.

"Are you his whore? Tell us, what does he do with you?"

"Nothing," she said. "Nothing. He's a good man. I'm just a maid. I clean, I just clean."

The monk slapped her hard in the face. "A good man? Good men don't hoard wealth and insult the one true god. There is nothing good about him. That you defend him proves your guilt too. You are a whore and a witch and will suffer Thoth's justice."

"No, please, I've done nothing." The girl sank to the ground, overcome with fear, pulling at the monk's leg like a pleading child. He kicked her away.

Soldiers with bows assembled in front of the servants. The monks moved aside.

"Do Thoth's bidding," commanded the lead monk.

The soldiers raised their bows. The servants pleaded for their lives. The soldiers fired. All but two of the servants fell, pierced, dying. Two ran, one shot in the arm, the other unscathed. Before they reached the stone wall, a second volley of arrows cut them down. The monks cheered and roared, jumping up and down, praising Thoth and celebrating. Many of the townsfolk joined in the cheering, even the children.

Claradon, Theta, and the group turned onto the street that passed before the manor.

"Trouble," said Ob, gesturing toward the crowd and the fire beyond. "A different street?" he said, turning toward Theta.

"Let's see what this is about."

They entered the crowd, now numbering some two hundred citizens.

"What happened here?" said Ob to a young man, bald of head, dressed as a tinker.

The man turned and looked carefully over Ob and Claradon beside him before responding. "The monks killed old Portman and all his people, the entire household."

"What was his crime?"

The man turned back toward the fiery scene. "He was rich."

"Now, they kill you for being rich," said Ob.

"Course he wasn't richer than any other smart

556

merchant what worked his whole life. Suppose they will come for us all, eventually. They have to. Without our coin, they wouldn't have enough to give away to the poor and still keep their own palaces and temples and such. Mayhap, I'll be next, I suppose. They'll be coming for me and mine. They need to. They have to spread our wealth around to the poor. That gives them power. That's what this here is about. They don't much care for Gnomes either, so you'd better get gone while you can."

X
THE ORB OF WISDOM

"From dust they came, and to dust they returned."
—The Keeper

Par Sevare grabbed Frem Sorlons's massive shoulder. "Hold up, they've stopped."

"Not again." Frem spun around sending embers from his torch flying; frustration filled his face. Frem paid the embers no heed as they washed over his steel plate armor, but Par Sevare dodged to the side and pressed tight against the tunnel's stony wall to avoid being burned.

"Watch it with the torch," Sevare said, his cheek puffed out from his ever-present wad of chewing tobacco. "I'm no tin-can. That stuff will burn through my clothes."

"Sorry," said Frem as he gazed over the heads of the mage and the two Sithian Knights behind to see what Lord Korrgonn was up to.

Some yards back, the son of Azathoth stood at a three-way intersection. Father Ginalli, High Priest of Azathoth, stood beside him, lantern in hand, though the dark of the tunnel hardly fled before it.

Korrgonn held Sir Gabriel's ankh, studying it, a look of deep concentration on his face. The ancient token was charred along its lower half, gouged in several spots across its face, and chipped at one corner. A ragged crack ran through the loop at its top, threatening to break the relic asunder.

"The boss is playing with that weird thingy again," said Frem. "If he keeps stopping, we'll never get anywhere."

"That thingy is an ancient holy symbol," said Sevare. "That's what is guiding him, helping him choose the right path for us to take, so that we can find what we're looking for."

"The main path is straight ahead and we're on it. He's gonna make us go down one of those small holes, isn't he? I don't like small places, and the main tunnel is already too small for me. What does he need guidance for, anyway? Ain't he supposed to be the lord's son? Doesn't he have powers? Isn't he supposed to know stuff?"

"That's the most you've said in one stretch since I've known you," said Sevare.

"I've been saving up."

Sevare stroked his goatee and spit some tobacco juice onto the tunnel floor. "I guess he needs a little help."

"How can it do that, it don't talk?" said Frem. "It's just a piece of carved wood—just an old piece of junk."

"Looks can be deceiving. That ankh has got a magic to it, an old magic."

"I didn't even believe in magic until I threw in with you lot. Older than what?"

Sevare considered for a moment. "Older than anything that I can think of."

"Older than Azathoth?"

"Can't be that old, since he created most everything. But it's older than Lomion, and probably even older than these darn tunnels." Sevare looked about the tunnel, which varied in height and width, from here to there. Six feet wide at its narrowest, it widened out to ten feet in most places, as much as fifteen in some. The ceiling above was no less than seven feet high, most places ten or more, and in some spots it was lost in the darkness far above. The tunnel's walls, floor and ceiling were of stone and earth, damp and dreary, dark as pitch, the air heavy and stagnant, silent and cold. Side passages led off, now and again, some narrow and short, others as large as the main tunnel, and each had a feeling of age, of antiquity. If not for their lanterns and torches, they would be hopelessly lost.

"Maybe if he got a new one, it would work better."

"Maybe so," said Sevare, grinning, his teeth stained from tobacco juice.

"How much farther do you think? We've walked for an hour at least."

"Can't be too far now, we're very deep. I didn't think anything went this deep."

Korrgonn looked up and lifted the ankh's cord over his head. He held it in his hand and passed it over a nondescript section of the tunnel's stony wall. That section of the wall began to glow with an eerie light. Just as quickly, it faded away—not just the glow, but the wall as well. A rectangular opening loomed before Korrgonn, where a moment before there was a solid wall. Behind the opening, a hidden passage. "That way," said Korrgonn, pointing down the narrow tunnel.

"Guess it works after all," said Frem. "He's

sending us down a stinking rabbit hole."

"Quiet," said Sevare.

Frem, Par Sevare, and their knights walked back to the others. A fake smile filled Frem's face as he approached Korrgonn, but the Nifleheim Lord didn't bother to look at the huge warrior as he passed.

They proceeded into the small tunnel, Frem again at the van, a rock of mass and muscle to blaze their trail. This tunnel was narrower and lower than the main course. The ceiling dipped below seven feet, and the top of Frem's helmet scraped it here and there, sending sparks flying. He had to hold his torch in front and low, grumbling under his breath all the while, since his shoulders, widened by his thick plate armor, were near as wide as the tunnel and jostled against the walls again and again as the tunnel curved and meandered in the dark.

Behind Frem's pointmen went four burly Lugron, then Korrgonn and Ginalli. Behind them were four of The Shadow League's archmages, Par Hablock, Par Brackta, Par Morsmun, and Par Ot. After them went the better part of a squadron of Sithian Knights, then Lord Ezerhauten and Mort Zag. Another group of Lugron guarded the rear.

While the main tunnel was an uneven natural passage with a gradual slope, this one was hewn through the living rock in bygone days. What arms wielded the picks and shovels that birthed her, no man could say.

The tunnel, slick with water and slime, descended steeply—a difficult passage even for the sure of foot. Mort Zag had the most trouble navigating the narrow tunnel. Where Frem could at least walk upright, Mort Zag had to proceed stooped over nearly the whole way. Every now and then, he cursed and spat when his head bumped the ceiling, or when he had to twist and turn to squeeze through some narrow portion of the tunnel. At one point, he took a hammer to a stony outcropping and smashed it away in order to squeeze past.

Deep, deep beneath the bowels of Midgaard were they now. Three cities of man stood there. The current city, Tragoss Mor, ancient itself, built atop the remnants of an older city whose name was seldom remembered. That city was constructed atop the ruins of an ancient metropolis, long lost to the passing eons. The stony tunnel took them far below even the deepest pit of that antediluvian city.

At last, upon a door of stone they came. Carved from the living rock, its seams smooth and crisp, its handle metal, but free of rust, scale, or stain. The passage widened near the door and the ceiling rose to a stately height.

The pointmen turned to Korrgonn for direction. "Open it," he commanded.

The two Sithians, large men both, pulled and pushed, and strained against the portal, but it would not yield. Frem shouldered one knight aside and took a turn. His massive hand clamped down on the handle and he pulled with all his power. His arms bulged and strained, veins pulsed at his corded neck, his face reddened and dripped with sweat. But the door would not yield, not at all, not even the slightest movement.

"I'd have better luck pushing on a mountain," said Frem as he turned back to the others.

Par Sevare examined the cold stone of the door. "No magic binds it," he said. "Barred from the far side, I would say."

"Break it down," Korrgonn said.

"Pass me up a hammer, biggest one we got," said Frem. "Swords are no good on stone."

"Kick it down," yelled Mort Zag from the rear.

Frem looked from the door to his boot and back again, and then moved carefully into a good kicking position. He blasted the door with his armored boot, a blow what could snap a man's spine in half, but the door did not yield. It shuddered ever so slightly, but barely a scuff marred its surface to mark the blow. Frem kicked again, and again, a half dozen strikes, all to no effect. "Dead gods, it's too thick. I need a sledge."

Mort Zag pushed forward from the rear, grunting; a mockery of a smile on his demonic face. "Step aside," he said as he barreled through. The others parted to let him pass. Had not the passage widened near the door, he could never have squeezed his bulk past them.

As huge as Frem was, past four hundred pounds and far beyond six foot, Mort Zag dwarfed him in both height and bulk. The red-skinned giant waved Frem aside and slammed his bare foot into the door at mid-height; it shook and shuddered but held fast. Again he kicked, harder this time. A cracking sound rang out. Two more times he kicked before the stone, which proved some eight inches thick, broke clear through, the upper half crashing to the tunnel floor.

"Ha! What do you think of that, puny man?" said Mort Zag, slapping Frem across the back.

Frem narrowed his eyes and only offered Mort Zag an icy stare.

"Well done," said Ginalli. "Sevare—check it out."

Frem and Sevare squeezed past the debris. Behind the door, a landing of polished granite overlooked granite steps that descended into darkness.

"Looks clear," said Frem quietly to Sevare. "The big red fellow called me puny. He said it like an insult. What does it mean?"

"It means small," said Sevare.

Frem looked down at his own bulk and then looked back at the others, big men most, but all much smaller than he, save for Mort Zag. "I don't get that. What is he anyway?"

"What do you mean?"

"I mean he's not a Volsung," said Frem. "He's not any kind of human. Not an Elf or anything. I've heard folks whispering dark stuff about him."

"What've you heard?"

"Some folk say he's a demon; a creature from the bad places. I don't like to hear such talk."

"Frem, buddy, he's just a giant from the deep mountains—like in the old stories."

"He's big enough, I suppose, but he's red. How do you explain that?"

Sevare paused, thinking. "Remember the time that farmer in Sarnack mashed up that basket of carrots to pulp and you drank it?"

"Sure. Wasn't bad at all, but the palms of my hands went all orange. Stayed that way a week or more."

"Exactly. Same with Mort Zag. That guy eats bushels of red apples and tomatoes. Turns his skin all red. No more mystery to it than that."

"Hmm. Never thought of that. I reckon I'm a simpleskin like Ezerhauten says."

"Simpleton," said Sevare.

"That's what I said. What does that mean, exactly?"

"Dumber than a rock."

"Thought so. I can't disagree with him, but neither he nor I are happy about what them others did to those men on the road. Killing your enemies is one thing, but cutting them up and taking away bits, that's not right, not right at all. I don't understand why Korrgonn stood for it."

"So that is what's been bothering you," said Sevare. "Frem, it's not what you think. It was a ritual cleansing. You know about those, right?"

"A what cleaning? What does that mean?"

"Zounds, Frem, no wonder you've been wound so tight these last days. You must've thought we had gone crazy, and I guess I couldn't blame you for it."

"Those Eotrus men were in with Thetan, the evil one, so they were evil too. Men like that have black souls, filled with hate. When such men die, their souls are damned and tormented for all time. But if the evil is washed away, then they can enter the afterlife, and find the lord's forgiveness in Vaeden. That is why Father Ginalli had those rituals performed. He was saving those men's souls. It was an act of mercy."

Frem visibly relaxed. "You should've told me

about of that before. I didn't know what was going on."

"Sorry, big guy. I thought you knew what was happening. You okay now?"

Frem nodded. "It's a relief to know that I am on the right side—with the good guys, I mean."

"I wouldn't be anywhere else," said Sevare.

"What do you see?" called out Ginalli.

"A stair," said Frem. "Leading down."

Four Lugron hefted the heavy debris aside, clearing the path for the main group.

Down they went in single file; a slow and treacherous descent, the steps uneven, steep and slippery, and all was pitch black save for the meager light from their torches. The air was cold there; their breath rose as mist about them.

To one side was a comforting stony wall, on the other, a black abyss of unknown depths, with no parapet or guardrail for protection. One misstep, one slip, and that would be the end. A hundred nerve-racking steps down brought them to a wide landing, a place of relative safety. They paused for a few minutes to rest and calm their nerves before continuing down, as most of them had nearly fallen more than once.

Frem first heard them when they had descended another hundred steps. Booted feet, climbing the stairs, coming up toward them. Many, many booted feet, distant, but drawing closer.

"Oh, boy," said Frem as he steadied himself against the rock face. The stair was not nearly wide enough for two men to fight side by side. "Not the best spot for a battle."

"We should move back up to the landing," said Ezerhauten. "We can't fight on this stair."

Korrgonn stood considering for a time, then ordered the men up to the landing. In their rush to ascend, one of the Lugron lost his footing and slid over the edge, wailing as he fell into the dark. Those nearest to him tried to grab him, but weren't quick enough. Most of the men peered down into the darkness, though in truth they couldn't see him at all. The rest turned away. Seconds went by, until finally, his screams faded out with the distance. They never heard him hit the bottom, if any bottom there was.

The men arrayed themselves across the landing, and planned how to switch out the lead man when he tired or became wounded. Frem stood the watch at the head of the stair.

The sounds grew louder and louder as the minutes went by.

"There must be hundreds," said Sevare.

"If they have bowmen, we won't be able to hold them off," said Frem.

Ezerhauten turned to Korrgonn. "We can't fight an entire army, my Lord, and it sounds like that is what's coming. We can't retreat up the stair, the going is too slow, and if any come down on us from above—"

"The Orb is below," said Korrgonn. "Without it, we can't restore the Lord to Midgaard. There is no turning back, not now, not ever."

Then began a mad howling. The cries of hundreds, perhaps thousands of wildmen, screaming war cries to whatever unknown gods they worshipped.

Almost as one, nearly all the Lugron dashed toward the stair going up, their courage broken. Mort Zag stepped over and barred their path. "Get back in line," he said. "Or you will follow your friend over the side."

They paused a moment, but in the end, chose to resume their places.

"We should be able to see them," said Sevare. "It sounds like they're right on us."

"Throw down a torch," said Ezerhauten.

Someone did. It landed some twenty feet down the stairs, but revealed nothing. They waited, and still nothing, only the sounds of booted feet and manic war cries.

Sevare spoke some arcane words, sharp and loud, painful to hear. The sounds of the approaching warriors abruptly stopped.

"An illusion," said Ginalli. "A trick to deter us, to make us flee."

"Let's head back down," said Korrgonn. "We've lost enough time."

Two hundred steps down, three hundred, four hundred, a landing and a switchback after each hundred. Five hundred steps and still the stair had no end. Just beyond the fifth landing, another man lost his footing and plunged silently into the darkness. The group paused for a few moments in respect, then continued down. Down and down they went, and somewhere, very deep, they lost count of the steps.

Eventually they reached the bottom, dripping with sweat and breathing heavily from the stress of the harrowing descent, though the air was chill and their pace had been slow and cautious.

At the base of the stair, their torchlight revealed a narrow hall of marble tile, polished smooth. The tile continued some three or four feet up the walls. Above that, a gruesome row of stone carvings, the heads and arms of demons and monsters, fiendish and foreboding, loomed out from the walls with eyes that glowed red in the fluttering torchlight. Above the gargoyles, the stone walls were inlaid with murals and pictograms, some colorful, others faded, but all of ancient times. Azathoth, in all his magnificent glory, was featured in many. Beside him, his Arkons, tall and powerful, but the faces of many were defaced and vandalized; their names forevermore stricken from the toll of history.

"I smell blood," said Mort Zag.

Ezerhauten held a torch low to the marble floor beside the base of the stair. A narrow, empty passage led back into the darkness, parallel to the stair. In the distance, they could see what remained of the two fallen Lugron splattered across the flooring—a gruesome sight even for hardened men to see.

"The tiles are smashed and gouged, here, and here, and there," Ezerhauten said pointing. "They were not the first to fall here. Many preceded them down, but I see no other corpses, no bones, no equipment. Nothing."

With no danger in sight, most of the men collapsed to the floor, taking however brief an opportunity to catch their breath.

"Someone or some thing must have carried away the fallen," said Ginalli. "There are more than just old wards at work here. Be on your guard."

Mort Zag looked up and down the hall and back again, tensed, ready to spring.

"You sense something?" said Ezerhauten.

"A feeling," said Mort Zag. "Something is not right. Be ready. Be wary."

"I sense something as well," said Korrgonn. "There is magic at work here. Old magic."

Ezerhauten spied something—some flicker of movement, some shadow of something along the walls, above the men's heads, where they reclined against the passageway's walls.

"Well, this is the perfect place for an ambush," said Frem. "After that climb down, who has got the energy to fight?"

Ezerhauten's eyes widened in alarm. "Up," he shouted. "Get away from the walls! Up!"

Even as the words flew from his lips, the walls came alive with movement. Stony, demonic arms silently flailed out, grabbing men's heads and squeezing, crushing, with strength beyond imagining. Gargoyles stretched out and down, emerging from the very walls. Stony fangs, inches long, bit down and bore into the skulls of Lugron, knight, and wizard.

The hall descended into chaos. Screams rose up on all sides. Geysers of blood erupted as men's heads exploded within the gargoyles' stony grips. Swords blunted and shattered against stone heads and stone arms. Torches went flying and others went out; spells were thrown, weapons crashed, men roared, and swore, and died.

"We have to go," shouted Sevare.

Korrgonn's sword crashed through a stone arm

that tore at his cloak.

"My lord, we must fly," said Ginalli as he pulled on Korrgonn's arm.

"Frem, grab him," shouted Sevare.

Then they were running—running through black halls, slick and desolate, wondering if the gargoyles would or could pursue, wondering if there was any way out.

A pit opened up before them; men fell in and screamed, impaled on sharp spikes a dozen feet down. Whirling blades flew from the walls; spears shot down from the ceiling; more men screamed in the dark.

They came upon a stone door, held fast. They stopped and turned, weapons held at the ready. Not even a third of their number remained. Korrgonn, Ginalli, Frem, Sevare, Hablock, and Brackta were there, along with a handful of Lugron; that was all.

Sevare looked around at how few were left. "Bloody hell," he said. "We're in the deep stuff."

"Are you hurt, my lord?" said Ginalli to Korrgonn.

"I don't run from my enemies," said Korrgonn, his golden eyes afire with rage. "I don't leave my men behind. We should've kept fighting."

"We couldn't even see," said Sevare.

"Swords are no good against stone," said Frem.

"We had to get you out of there, my lord," said Ginalli."

"This is a madhouse," said Hablock, sinking to his knees.

"A tomb," said Sevare. "It's a tomb of horrors."

"Get some torches lit," said Korrgonn. "You men," he said to Frem and Sevare, "see to that door. You others," pointing to the Lugron, "form a line across the passage."

A few minutes later, they heard the drum of footsteps marching in the darkness behind, drawing closer.

"Get that door opened," said Ginalli. "Now."

"Frem pounded and pounded on the door, but the stone would not yield.

"I've one more trick," said Sevare. He knelt before the door and spoke some words of magic. After but a moment, a clicking sound came from the door, then it swung open of its own accord. Beyond, silence and darkness.

"We're through," said Frem. "It's open."

"Do we flee or do we stand?" said Ginalli.

"We stand," said Korrgonn, as he drew his blade. "Wizards, ready your magic."

The footsteps grew louder. In a moment, Ezerhauten came into view holding aloft a torch. With him, nearly a dozen Sithian Knights, several wounded. Behind them loomed Mort Zag carrying the stone head of a gargoyle in one of his massive hands.

"They won't be following," said Ezerhauten. "But we had best find another way out. That was a gauntlet I would rather not pass again."

"Morsmun? Ot?" said Ginalli.

"Both dead, and a dozen more with them."

The survivors greeted each other: some smiled and shook hands with their comrades; others stood alone in silence.

"We passed several passages along the way,"

said Ezerhauten. "Which way do we go? Through this door or back to some side passage?"

Korrgonn studied his ankh for a time. "Through the door," he said.

The group made their way down the wide hall, slowly, carefully, expecting something else unpleasant to happen. A thin layer of gray dust coated the floor there, only noticeable for its contrast with the sheen of the marble floor just passed. As they proceeded, the layer of gray grew thicker and thicker, their steps kicking it into the air, forming an irritating haze about them.

Upon another door they came, this one of marble cladding and gold rungs. A dead end; no farther could they go until that door was opened.

Before the group could examine the door, a voice called out from the darkness. "Who are you?" The deep sound reverberated through the hall, its direction and source unclear and unseen.

"Who are you?" said the voice again, louder.

All eyes looked to Korrgonn. "Find him."

The men spread out and thrust torches into every niche and corner of the darkened hall, high and low, but found no one.

"Who are you?" said the voice again, louder still, much louder. It seemed to come from everywhere and from nowhere. The whole hall shook; chips of stone fell from the ceiling; gray dust rose about them.

"We must respond," said Ginalli to Korrgonn. "Or they'll bring the whole cavern down on us."

Korrgonn nodded.

"I am Ginalli, high priest of Azathoth," he shouted. "Who are you?"

"I am the Keeper," said the voice. "Why are you here, Ginalli of Azathoth?"

"We seek the great Orb of Wisdom."

"Of course you do," said the Keeper, this time softly, wearily, as if he had heard the same answer untold times. "And why do you seek the Orb?"

"So that the glory of his almighty majesty might be restored to the world."

There was a pause of some moments before the Keeper spoke again. "The Orb alone will not accomplish this, however strong your faith. Have you another token?"

"We do."

"What token is that?"

Ginalli looked again to Korrgonn who nodded his permission. "We have the blood of kings."

There was a long pause.

"Most that came here sought treasures. All were disappointed. Some few sought the great Orb. Fewer still spoke of the blood of kings. From dust they came, to dust they returned. You may enter, disciples of Azathoth, but be warned, if your words be not true and you be not blessed of the one true god, if you be not his holy minions, the fires of Archeron will take you and deliver your immortal souls into everlasting torment. Go not forward unless this peril you can face."

Korrgonn signaled to open the door. It took the combined strength of Frem and two Sithians to pull the massive door open. Beyond, the passageway was lit, wall sconces afire, oil burning, its scent and smoke in the air. The passage continued for a goodly ways, and then curved out of sight.

"Form up, men," said Ginalli.

"Wait," said Sevare. "We don't know what this Keeper has in store. We can't risk you and Lord Korrgonn in this—you're too important. Someone needs to scout ahead."

"Wise words," said Korrgonn.

"Who will go?" said Ginalli. He looked about to the group. Some looked away, others took great interest in their feet or their fingernails. Mort Zag stood there grinning.

"I will go," said Par Hablock.

"That Keeper fellow sounds dangerous, Hablock," said Frem. "Maybe you shouldn't go in there alone."

"I'm an archmage of the Sixth Circle, fool, not an overstuffed half-wit." Hablock turned back toward Korrgonn and Ginalli. "I will go cloaked in every protective spell known to wizardom. Whatever traps the Keeper has laid will do me no harm."

"Cast your charms, but take two Lugron and two knights," said Korrgonn.

Ezerhauten rolled his eyes at the mention of the Sithians, no doubt concerned that two more of the crack troops that he personally trained would be lost.

Hablock stepped away from the others, and spoke some strange wizard words and tossed a handful of sparkling powder over his head. The powder ignited, and cloaked Hablock in an eerie, translucent, blue light. He waved his hands about and spoke more words, ancient words, forbidden words of power, and a golden helm appeared about his head. More gestures and strange

575

incantations turned his skin and eyes silver.

"*The Shield of Fenrir*," said Sevare. "*The Helm of Hogar*, and *Steelskin*. Rare magics all, and good choices."

"I'm surprised that you recognize spells of my Tower so easily," said Hablock.

"My studies of the art are more varied than most. I can place the *Baneshield* on you, if you wish."

"And I can give you *The Cloak of Azathoth* and *The Lord's Blessing*," said Ginalli.

"I will place *The Cloak of Life* on you," said Par Brackta.

"I will take them all and gladly.

Sevare approached Hablock and put his hands on Hablock's chest. Sevare's sorcery was altogether different than Hablock's. He spoke his magic in a bizarre guttural tongue that sounded more reptilian than human. In moments, it was done, though Hablock appeared no different for it.

Brackta stepped up and murmured before Hablock; her words too soft to be heard. "Done," she said after only a moment.

"You men," Ginalli said, pointing to two of the Lugron and two Sithians, "Stand beside Par Hablock." They did. Ginalli spoke his own words of power, sharp and crisp, followed by a short prayer to Azathoth, holy symbol in hand. "Done."

Hablock stepped up to the portal. The Lugron with him shuffled their feet and breathed heavily, nervous from the course of events. Hablock stepped through the doorway, the knights and Lugron following. They crept slowly, cautiously, down the passage, weapons bared and battle ready. Just as they moved out of sight, around the bend in the passage, the massive door began to close behind them of its own accord. Frem tried to halt it, but could not. Mort Zag appeared and grabbed the door, but even his might and Frem's combined could neither halt, nor even slow its inexorable progress. They let go at last and the door ground to a close, its grating sound echoing through the chamber, a sound of finality, a sound that said, this door will not open again.

"Last we've seen of them," said Frem.

Some minutes passed before they heard a faint crackling sound from beyond the doors. Then movement, as the door slowly opened with nary a sound. A strong burning odor washed through the chamber and wisps of smoke trailed in.

"Not good," said Ginalli.

"Hablock," yelled Sevare. No response. "Hablock!"

They waited, but no sign appeared of Hablock or his men.

"Keeper," shouted Ginalli. "What has happened? Keeper!"

No response.

"Do we go in or go back?" said Ezerhauten.

"There is no going back," said Korrgonn. "We must retrieve the Orb or die in the attempt."

Everyone froze and stared at Korrgonn.

Korrgonn studied his followers' faces. They were fearful and uncertain. His expression softened.

"Men, without the Orb, we can't open the gateway. The Lord is counting on us. We're the only ones that can do this. So I must go on, whatever the danger. I will understand if you can't stand with me in this. I will meet you back at the ship, and nothing more will be said of this."

"I'm with you," said Ginalli.

"And I," said Mort Zag.

"And I," said Brackta.

One by one, the others affirmed their resolve. Ezerhauten spoke last, but stood with the rest.

"Look for something to wedge the door open," said Ezerhauten. "We may need to make a quick retreat; we've no wish to find it closed fast behind us."

"There is nothing to wedge it with," said Sevare. "Bare marble and dust."

"Knock the marble from the walls?" said Ezerhauten.

"Marble tile won't hold that portal if it wants to close," said Sevare. "It will crush them to powder. Any weapon wedged in will snap."

"Forget it," said Ginalli. "Onward, together, without fear. The mantle of Azathoth is upon us; no harm can come to us."

"Tell that to Hablock," said Frem.

Ginalli's assertion notwithstanding, the wizards cast their wards on themselves and the others. The whole group passed through the door and proceeded down the hall, the Lugron and Sithians at the fore. Just as they anticipated, as soon as the last of them were through, the portal began to close. Mort Zag tried to hold it for a moment, but it pushed him back, sliding his bare feet across the dusty stone.

"I knew we should've taken more men," said Ezerhauten. "Can never have too many men."

"Too many makes the food run out faster," said Frem.

"No problems there," said Mort Zag. "Just eat the extra men."

Frem looked at the red giant in disgust and disbelief. Mort Zag roared with laughter.

After a ways, the hallway opened into a large chamber, circular, but with walls of strange slopes and angles, its ceiling lost in the darkness above. The floor was mounded with gray dust, two feet deep or more along the walls. An odd vibration filled the air and it was bitter cold, a cold to chill a goodly man to the bone.

At the center of the chamber, six stone steps led up to a circular dais. Atop the dais sat a sphere, six inches in diameter and black as midnight—the Orb of Wisdom itself, fabled vessel of power from times ancient and long forgotten. On the floor beside the dais, a blackened, smoking heap. Bits of cloth, blackened flesh and bones, and legs all but turned to ash. This was all that remained of Hablock.

"Zounds! Hablock!" spat Sevare. "What did this? Where is that stinking Keeper?" He spun around, gazing at the bizarre chamber, searching for sign or spoor of the Keeper. The chamber's walls crept up and out and in at weird unnatural angles. You couldn't even look at the walls for long without growing dizzy and lightheaded. Not a place meant for men, not even men such as these.

"Where are my knights?" said Ezerhauten through clenched teeth.

"Not good," said Ginalli, gazing down at the remains. "Not good at all."

"We should go back," said Frem as he began backing up the way they had come. "This place is death."

"The door is closed," said Ezerhauten. "There is no going back."

The Keeper's voice filled the chamber once again. "Your wizard was not beloved of Azathoth. He burns now in the everlasting flames."

"Skunk you, you rat turd," spat Sevare. "Show yourself." He spat out a spray of tobacco juice onto the steps of the dais.

"What of the others?" yelled Frem. "What did you do to them?"

"From dust they came, and to dust they returned," said the Keeper.

Sevare looked down at the thick gray dust that covered the floor. He squatted and sifted his hand through it, brushed something solid and plucked it from the dust. Charred and battered, but clearly a finger bone. The wizard threw it down in disgust. "Dear lord."

Ginalli grasped Korrgonn's arm. "The dust—"

"Is men," said Korrgonn. "Burned to ash."

"Hundreds must have died here."

Korrgonn squatted down and sifted through a handful of dust. "Thousands."

The group looked about and found fragments of a piece of armor here, a melted or charred weapon there.

"He burned them," said Sevare. "Burned them all to ash."

"What do we do?" said Ginalli.

"We stop wasting time," said Korrgonn. "I will get the Orb; woe to the Keeper if he tries to stop me."

"Wait, my Lord," said Ginalli. "The Orb we used in the Temple of Guymaog in the Vermion—it was enclosed in a sphere of Asgardian glass, suspended at its center by ancient sorceries, the glass itself protected by untold charms and incantations. We ever touched naught but the glass. This Orb is bare." Ginalli pointed to the Orb atop the dais. "Without the glass, its touch is death."

Korrgonn considered for a moment. "Anyone have any ancient Asgardian glass spheres on them? If you do, just pass them forward." He paused, to give the men ample time to respond. "None at all?" He looked around at the others who stood there blank-faced. "Very well then. Anyone have anything else that protects from magical death orbs? No?" He turned back to Ginalli, smiling. "If you've no more advice, priest, I suggest you step back."

Ginalli backed quickly away. As he neared the cold wall of the foreboding chamber, he tripped on a mound of ash and went down. The fine ash gave way beneath him, sprayed over his face, and more than a bit found his open mouth. He spit and hacked it out and brushed the foul stuff from his face and hair.

As Korrgonn strode boldly up the steps, two of the Lugron yowled and started to flee the hall. The others all took cautious steps backward, save for Mort Zag, who stood rooted, his customary grin plastered to his face. Atop the dais, Korrgonn reached out and grasped the Orb with his bare hand.

As Korrgonn's hand touched the Orb, sparks erupted from its depths. A monstrous bolt of lightning came down from on-high and struck the Orb, enveloping Korrgonn in burning electricity. Bolts of crackling lightning flew around Korrgonn in all directions. Bathed in the mystical light, Korrgonn's aspect shimmered and morphed. He wore the form of Sir Gabriel no longer. Now before the Arkons of The Shadow League stood the son of Azathoth in his true form, his inmost self revealed before his god and his followers. There stood a man of wondrous golden hue, form and face beautiful and perfect and noble, a being of the heavens, of paradise, divine. He glowed with strength, wisdom, and mercy, yet was terrible and awesome to behold.

At once, each man dropped to his knees, awe-struck by Korrgonn's true aspect. "Kneel before the son of Azathoth," sputtered Ginalli, still coughing from the dust that clogged his throat, though each of his companions was already prostrated. Even Mort Zag dropped to one knee and respectfully bowed his head.

The sparks about Korrgonn grew and suddenly arced outward; golden-hued bolts slammed into each man in the chamber and reached out even to those few that had fled. The men were flung backward; some were even lifted into the air, suspended by the fiery bolts. Scorching tongues of lightning crashed around them. One man's pants caught fire, another's sleeve ignited, several men's hair smoked.

As quick as it came, the lightning fled, the smoke dissipated. Korrgonn inhabited the body of

Gabriel Garn once again, and stood atop the dais, Orb in hand, wisps of smoke rising from his hand and from his clothes. The others picked themselves from the floor, some battered and bruised, and stood gaping, or patting themselves down or pulling off various garments that smoked and hissed. All of them were covered in the fine gray ash.

"Rise, my friends," said Korrgonn. "Rise."

They did.

Some moments later, a burning outline of a door appeared in the chamber's wall, where moments before there had been naught but smooth stone. The glow faded, but an ornate wood door remained.

The door opened and out stepped a wizened old man. He was an Elf, ancient, wrinkled, frail, and stooped. He wore an ancient suit of chain mail, stained and tarnished, and far too large for his shriveled frame. A broadsword hung from a sheath at his waist. Trailing behind him was a young Elf, similarly clad, hand on his sword hilt. The venerable Elf struggled under the weight of his gear, and shuffled forward in tiny flat-footed, old-man steps. His hair was long, and stringy, sparse and whited; his nose, long; ears even longer and pointed as Elven ears are wont to be.

Ezerhauten drew his blade and started to move forward, but Ginalli waved him off.

The old Elf spoke in a strong clear voice that belied his ancient aspect. "My lord," he said, bowing low before Korrgonn, and dropping to one knee with great effort. The young Elf did the same, though he kept his eyes up, cautiously surveying Korrgonn and company. "I am the Keeper," said the old Elf, "and this is my apprentice. I have awaited your coming these ten thousand years, all that time holding safe this Orb of divine wisdom and holy power, my own long years extended by every magic known and unknown, embraced and forbidden, just as were the line of Keepers before me, back unto the very dawn of the second age of Midgaard."

His eyes bright, and blue, the Elf smiled with pride. "Apprentice and I have kept out the Thothian upstarts. Before them, we kept out the slavers and the pirate lords. I fought back the Thaulusians, the Marikites, and the Scurds before them, and the Hejirs and the Kalumeers and Throng-Baz who came earlier. Mercenaries, soldiers of fortune, knight errants, mages and archmages beyond count, and monks of this order and that have tried to enter here. Sometimes, one lone man would come, most times a handful or a dozen or a score there would be. Sometimes a hundred screaming barbarians would burst down my doors. And more than once they came in the thousands, howling, murderous, gibbering hordes of primitives. All were felled by my art and my hand or by the Lord's holy fire, when all else failed."

"Not one thief that entered here ever left. Not one, though many tried. Many tried. All so that this day, upon your arrival, the Orb would be here still, and safe, and could pass rightfully to you— you who can hold it in hand and withstand the holy fire. Unfortunately, like all the others, your wizard could not withstand it. The holy fire consumed him

584

and those with him. Had I known who you were, I would have warned him off. I beg your forgiveness."

"You have it," said Korrgonn.

The Keeper looked over at the remains of Hablock. "Usually, almost nothing is left. Never so much as this. He was a powerful wizard. But unlike you he was not meant to hold the Orb. Please, my lord, give me your name."

"Korrgonn."

The old Elf beamed. "A goodly name; a name of power from the old tongue."

"Give me your name, Keeper," said Korrgonn, "so that I can have it and your long service duly honored in the scrolls of the faithful."

"Whatever name I had, my lord, I have long since forgotten. I am just the Keeper now, it is who I am, and all that I will be until I pass back into the dust."

"And your apprentice, what name does he go by?"

"Apprentice is the only name for him that I can recall, but my memory is not what it once was."

"I am Stev Keevis Arkguardt, son of Stev Terzan of the Emerald Forest," said the young Elf.

"Stev is the Elven title for an archmage," whispered Sevare in Frem's ear.

"You are young for a Stev," said Ginalli.

"Those of the blood are older than we look to you Volsungs."

"Of the blood?" whispered Frem.

"That's how elves refer to themselves," said Sevare.

"My lord, tell me truly now whether or not you

serve the great lord, the one true god, Azathoth."

"I do."

"Only one of the flesh of Azathoth could grasp the Orb in his bare hand and survive the heavenly fire. How did you this?"

"I am Azathoth's son."

The Elf's grin widened still. "The son of the lord, himself? I see in your eyes and in your heart that it be true; indeed, it must be true. Your glorious coming was foretold in the ancient scrolls of Cumbria. I know them well, I do. You are he of golden eye and lordly bearing of which Cumbria speaks, though she was rather vague on the timing of your arrival. Glory be to Azathoth that I have lived to see this day."

"Pardon my directness, but I must ask you now, will you use the Orb as it was meant to be used? Will you use it to open the holy portal to the paradise of Nifleheim? Will you beseech the lord to travel back to Midgaard with all his divine hosts, so that we might worship before him as in olden days?"

"That is my plan."

"You swear this?"

"I do."

The old Elf studied Korrgonn carefully, staring deep into his golden eyes. Then he smiled and nodded his head. "The Orb can only be used at one of the Lord's ancient temples, those consecrated in bygone days by the Lord's holy Arkons. Your journey will be long and grievous hard no matter to which temple you head. The minions of evil will haunt your every step, and seek to stop you with all their infernal power. Are you prepared to face these trials?"

"I am, and I will."

"Then the Orb is rightfully yours and yours alone. Use it well, and wisely, my lord. My labors are now complete. It's strange, but I never thought to speak those words; I never thought this day would truly come—for Apprentice maybe, or one of those that follow him, but not for me."

"You have done well, Keeper," said Korrgonn. "Your long and loyal service is at an end; you may rest now and when your time comes, take your rightful place in Nifleheim where you will be rewarded beyond imagining for your faith and loyalty."

"Thank you," he said, tears welling in his ancient eyes. "I imagine you are anxious to be off, my lord, but can I offer you and yours a meal and wine before you depart? The tunnels are long and the stairs are steep; rest here a brief while, if you will."

"We will," said Korrgonn, "but only for a short while."

The Keeper led the group beyond the hidden door and into a wondrous cavern. The high ceilings were covered with glowing lichen that lit the place half as bright as day. The Keeper proudly showed them his vast laboratory, filled with table after table cluttered with glass jars of all shapes and sizes, each filled with smoking and bubbling elixirs. There was row upon row of crystal vials filled with powders and strange colored liquids. All manner of wizard wares haunted the place, though all were labeled in some ancient Elven script unknown to any of Korrgonn's party.

The Keeper led them to his trophy room. There were displayed the remnants of many of the ill-fated thieves the Keeper spoke of. There were racks of weapons, spears and swords, axe and hammer, some ancient and archaic, others far newer. Displays of dented armor, shattered helms, and mangled shields were scattered about the hall. Here and there, a full-bodied skeleton hung from hooks, and there and there a great display of skulls, all carefully arranged, displayed not in a gory manner, but more like a macabre museum exhibit.

The cavern included a well-appointed library where Korrgonn and the wizards lingered, leafing through musty old tomes called the books of Dyzan, Eibon, Iod, and Thesselak, before joining the others for a meal of fresh vegetables grown in the cavern under the strange lichen light, and clean, pure water extracted from a well.

After their repast, the Keeper showed them a true wonder. At the far end of the cavern, the Keeper had a magnificent little stone quarry and workshop. But the wonder was not the beautiful marble and veined granite that was quarried there and cut into stone tiles and stone doors for the cavern complex, it was the stone mason himself. Besides the Keeper and his apprentice, the mason was the only creature that lived within the cavern complex, if lived could be applied to him at all.

"This is Mason," said the Keeper. "A creation of mine in my younger days." Mason looked to be living stone, shaped like a very tall, very broad man, down to the eyes, nose, and mouth, though he had no skin or hair—only hard, cold, gray stone.

"A golem of stone," said Korrgonn.

"Indeed, my lord," said the Keeper. "I learned the craft to make him from some old book, but I've forgotten which."

"Impressive," said Ginalli. "A lost art. I've only heard of such creatures in legend. Until now, I thought them no more than fancy."

"As you see, he is real enough. I made him several thousand years back, I think," said the Keeper. "Mason keeps up the place, repairing anything that needs repairing, replacing the tiles and doors when they're broken, and cleaning up the messes that need cleaning." Even now, Mason labored over a stone slab, measuring and cutting it to the size of a door, no doubt to replace the one the group had earlier broken down. "And he's handy in a fight too; his hammer is deadly, as have found more than a few intruders."

"No need, no need, Mason," said the Keeper. "Your labors are done, as are mine." Mason looked up; his stony features took on a look of surprise. "No sense replacing any doors now, as there is nothing left to guard. The lord's son has come for the holy Orb and has it now. We're quite through here, quite through." Mason put down his tools and looked confused, lost.

"Through?" he said in a deep gravelly voice.

"It talks?" said Sevare.

"Of course," said the Keeper, "any amateur wizard can make a mute golem, but one that talks, that is a rare thing that requires a bit of skill."

"Now, Apprentice, gather your things,

including the choice books from the library, for you will not be returning here. I have one last task for you."

Stev Keevis looked surprised. "What task, Keeper?"

"You shall journey with Lord Korrgonn and aid him in opening the holy portal. Mason shall go with you." He turned to Korrgonn. "With your permission, of course, my lord."

"We will gladly accept their help," said Korrgonn.

Keevis dashed off and the group made their way back to the strange chamber that had housed the Orb, a slow trek due to the snail-paced shuffling of the Keeper. By the time they stood before the dais in the orb chamber, Keevis rejoined them carrying a large pack over his shoulder, another in hand, and wearing a traveling cloak. Mason now wore a thick hooded cloak that concealed his true nature, and a large pack was slung over his shoulder, a huge hammer hung from his belt.

"Well, now, Apprentice, Mason, step up here so I need not shout," though every word of the Keeper was something of a shout. "No wizard has ever had as accomplished an apprentice as you, my boy. I am proud of you, both as a wizard and as an Elf."

"Mason, you old blockhead, you've been loyal and tireless, and not much trouble at all. I thank you for all your toils these many years."

"I expect that you both will serve Lord Korrgonn as you have served me. When your quest is completed, so too will be your obligation and you may pursue your own course thereafter. Have you the tomes of spells? The tokens and the potions?"

"Yes, Keeper," said Keevis.

"Good. Fare thee well, and remember all that I have taught you."

"That I will, Keeper," said Keevis, his voice crackling with sorrow.

"And I," said Mason.

The Keeper and Keevis shook hands and embraced. Even Mason extended his stony hand and shook the Keeper's hand, though the old Elf winced from the golem's strength.

The Keeper turned back to Korrgonn. "One last boon, my lord, before you depart. My time on Midgaard is at an end at last. Touch me upon my shoulder, so that I might feel your divine essence before I leave this life."

Korrgonn nodded his agreement.

The Keeper closed his eyes. "From dust I came, and to dust I return," he said as Korrgonn placed a hand on his shoulder. A peacefulness came over the Keeper's old face, a look of contentment and relief, and then before the eyes of all, the Keeper's flesh turned to gray and dissolved to dust from the head down, all in the merest of moments. A heap of old clothes and rusty armor was all that remained. A breeze came up out of nowhere and blew the Keeper's ashes up and away, though the piles of ash about the floor remained untouched.

XI
AZURA THE SEER

"Beware him. He's the Prince of Lies.
He will be the death of us all."
—Azura the Seer

At some sixty feet in height and more than twenty-five feet in diameter, Azura's rough-hewn stone tower dwarfed its neighbors. Painted a bright blue, it stood at the center of a cobblestone square ringed by low stone walls. A gardener tended the flowers that adorned the square's carved stone planters while a servant swept the pavement clean. Two guards flanked the tower's door.

"Good afternoon, gentlemen," said one guard at the group's approach. "How may I help you?"

"Good day," said Tanch. "We come seeking an audience with Mistress Azura.

The guard looked the group over.

"All of you?"

"These are but my bodyguards and servants. Pay them no heed."

"Of course, sir. May I please have your name and occupation?"

"I am Sinch, the spice merchant. I trust you've heard of me."

"Of course, sir, and welcome. Please remain here a moment and I will see if the seer is available to meet with you."

The second guard remained outside. He

looked uncomfortable as he sized up the large men that stood with Tanch. He kept a nervous hand on the hilt of his sword, but looked ready to run at the first sign of trouble. In a few minutes, the first guard returned.

"Merchant Sinch, the seer will see you now. I regret, the rules of the house permit no more than four visitors at a time, regardless of their station. The remainder of your party must remain in the courtyard."

"Very well," said Tanch. "You and you, remain here," pointing to Dolan and Artol. "And don't make a nuisance of yourselves."

The guard showed Tanch and the others through the outer door and into an entry hall that served as both cloakroom and guard post. The second guard joined them, and closed and barred the outer door. An inner door now opened, revealing a dimly lit chamber of incense, tapestries and hanging beads.

Azura sat at a wood table facing the group as they entered. Youthful, shapely and striking, her auburn hair fell thick and wavy about her shoulders. Beside her, stood a barbarian of the southern islands, shirtless but adorned with tattoos across his barrel chest and bulging arms. A giant—taller than Theta, dark of skin, bald of pate, and past four hundred pounds.

Azura's hands rested on the table before her. A large sphere of blue crystal sat in a carved wooden holder on the table before her. A flickering candle beside it caused light to dance within the crystal, creating strange shapes and an eerie glow. Nearby, a deck of tarot cards, careworn but ornate. Tapestries adorned all the walls and silks draped the ceiling. Candles burned here and there, but the room was intentionally dim.

***

A *wizard, a Gnome, and soldiers, finely clothed—just as Rimel said. They can pay.*

"Greetings, Mistress Azura," said Tanch as he reverently bowed. Tanch raised his staff up and thumped it down lightly on the wood floor. "Forgive my small deception to your guard. As you no doubt can discern, I am no spice merchant."

"Indeed, you are not, Par—"

Tanch smiled. "I am Par Sinch Malaban of The Blue Tower. My retainers," gesturing toward the others, "are a sordid lot of little consequence."

"And two more of your men remain in the courtyard."

Tanch nodded.

"So many bodyguards, Par Sinch. You must have many enemies." *And much coin to pay all these.*

"Alas, bodyguards are a necessity in these dark times," said Tanch. "A wizard's welcome is all too thin in some lands, Tragoss among them."

"Too true, Par Sinch. It's my good fortune that the Thothians don't look down on seers as they do on wizards. Nonetheless, as you see, I keep my own bodyguards as well, both seen and unseen." She paused, letting the last words sink in. "Please now, sit and be comfortable."

Tanch took a seat at the table. The others remained standing.

"You honor me with this audience. I regret that I had not the opportunity to forewarn you of my visit."

"No regrets are necessary. Wizards in good standing with the Tower of the Arcane are always welcome guests to my tower, if not to my city."

Tanch smiled and bowed his head slightly. "Thank you, Mistress."

A true smile? Is he one of Pipkorn's or the Vizier's or some other's?

"I understand that the Tower has undergone much upheaval in recent months."

"Indeed."

I can't read him. Where are his loyalties?

Azura peered into the depths of her crystal ball for a few moments. "You've journeyed to parts foreign to escape those that would mean you harm."

Tanch smiled. "I support what is best for the Order, as is my duty."

He won't reveal himself. Try another approach.

Azura passed her hands over the crystal sphere and gazed into it. She looked up.

"You've come seeking my wisdom, my knowledge. You seek the answer to a question of grave import."

He smiles, unimpressed. He's no fool.

"Your knowledge, wisdom, and mastery of the art of divination are known far and wide and much admired even within the Tower of the Arcane."

"Known, perhaps," said Azura. "Admired, no,

not at all. But I thank you for your flattery."

The older soldier is studying the room. Dead gods, he looks dangerous. Why are they here? Do they mean me harm? Could even Gorb protect me against them?

"Tell me now, Par Sinch of the Blue Tower, what knowledge do you seek?"

"We search for a ship," said Tanch.

"Hmm," she nodded. *I can work with that.*

Each time, before making a pronouncement Azura caressed the crystal sphere and gazed into it. She looked back up before she spoke so that she could see her guests' reactions.

"A sailing vessel, out of Lomion," said Azura.

"Yes."

"And why do you seek her?"

"There is a man on board that is a traitor to the Order. We're tasked with bringing him to justice."

Enforcers or bounty hunters. But whose? Pipkorn's or the League's, or someone else's? "I see," said Azura. *These men are dangerous.* "What name does this man go by?"

"Par Otto, of the Red Tower."

I don't know that name. A lie?

"When did this ship reach Tragoss Mor?"

"Within the last two days or so."

Azura gazed deeply into the crystal ball, caressing it over and over. *The White Rose—it must be. They're in with Pipkorn or Harringgold— enemies of the League. Good thing that I paid for that information about The Rose. Always someone willing to pay for secrets. Must be sure.*

"The ship this man sailed on is no longer in

Tragoss Mor," said Azura.

Still can't read the wizard. The young bodyguard nodded, I think.

She looked back at the sphere for a moment, and then back at Tanch.

"The man you seek is still aboard her, and no one can tell you where she has sailed." *The Gnome looks surprised. I'm right. I have them.* Azura made a show of gazing close and long into the sphere. *Now for the hook.*

"The ship you seek is called *The White Rose.*"

Tanch raised his eyebrows, despite himself.

I was right!

"Impressive."

"And you seek knowledge of where this *White Rose* is sailing?"

Tanch nodded. "Yes."

They're mine. How much should I ask for? "I believe that my powers can divine this information for you—but the task is difficult and draining. I'm afraid that the cost must be high."

Tanch furrowed his brow.

He will pay.

Azura returned her gaze to the crystal. *If I ask for too much, what will they do? Try to kill me? That would be foolish, that would gain them nothing but a battle with my guards. Gorb is at my side, so strong—and Dirkben and Rimel. But Dirkben is a useless coward. Both warriors and the Gnome are casing the room. Are they thieves? Assassins? I must tread carefully.*

"Five hundred silver stars is my price." *Fifty times what I paid for the information.*

No reaction from Sinch. He's holding back.

597

"A high price indeed for such a small piece of information," said Tanch. "A piece of information that would put the Order in your debt."

I must lower the price to appease him. "The divination is difficult. I know nothing of the ship or its crew, save what little the crystal's mists have only now revealed to me. It will take much power and concentration and I will need to expend valuable herbs and powders. For the Order though, I will do this thing for four hundred silver, no less."

Tanch glanced over at Claradon for a moment.

What was that? Is he a young lordling and the true master here? Does it matter, so long as they pay?

Sinch nodded. *He approves.*

Tanch pulled out a leathern purse from his belt. It jingled with the sounds of coins. He opened it.

"Keep your money, wizard," said Theta.

What's this?

"This one is a mummer. She'll take your money and send us on a wild goose chase. Best we be on our way."

What game is this?

Tanch squirmed in his seat and looked mortified. He turned and glared at Theta. "I hope that my guard has not offended you, my lady. He's naught but an uncouth barbarian that knows not his station. I assure you that I do not agree with his insulting remarks, and I will see that he regrets them."

I still have him.

"He does, however, bring to mind some

concerns."

Oh, smigits, where's he going with this? "And what concerns are those?"

"You will pardon me, Mistress, for saying so, but we haven't chanced to meet before today. In truth, I know not if you are truly the famed seer, Azura, or some imposter who has taken her tower and her trappings. As we both agreed, these are dark times and things are not always as they seem."

Lies. They know who I am, they just don't believe in my power.

"I knew of your *White Rose*."

"You did indeed, my Lady, and that was most insightful, but mayhaps, just a guess."

Fine. Then proof I'll give you.

"Perhaps you require a small demonstration of my skills?"

"That would be most appreciated, my lady, and would go a long way toward providing me the comfort I need to expend the monies you've requested."

Stinking wizard. "For this, my price goes back to five hundred silver stars."

"Of course, my lady," said Tanch. "If you can convince me you speak true."

"I will do a reading of one of you." She looked them each up and down. "You, doubter," she said, pointing to Theta. "I will tell you things only you would know, then you will know my power. Agreed, Par Sinch?"

Tanch looked back at Theta who offered no reaction. "Agreed."

Theta stepped forward. "Do your reading,

woman, though I warn you—if your powers be true, you may not like what you see."

Is he a raper and a killer? I've seen such things before and don't fear them. Little shocks or surprises me anymore. "Take a seat and hold out your hands."

Theta sat down, but paused before extending his hands. He grasped the cord of his ankh and lifted it off, over his head. He turned toward Claradon. "Hold this for me until we're done." Theta handed Claradon the ankh and extended his hands toward Azura, palms up.

I must get this right.

Azura grasped Theta's hands and shuddered. Her head snapped back, eyes opened wide, though they saw nothing of the now. Her eyes rolled back in her head, only the whites exposed.

A maelstrom of images, sounds, and emotions unlike any reading before flailed Azura's mind, trampled her thoughts and shattered her defenses. She saw nothing through the blur and heard nothing but the din. She felt everything and nothing, lost in a vortex of madness.

She struggled to manage the torrent, to control the flow before it destroyed her. If she didn't master it in moments all sanity would be lost, and all that which made Azura an individual would be gone, forever, reducing her to a gibbering, drooling, mindless thing.

Azura exerted all her discipline and all her will and regained some semblance of control. Gradually, the images slowed and cleared; the cacophony ebbed; the world came into focus. Azura became her subject, seeing through his eyes, hearing with his ears, and feeling his feelings. Not of the now, but of the past, long past. All her will bent on maintaining control and keeping the maelstrom that ever threatened her in check.

She looked out Theta's eyes and a feeling of power washed over her. A sense of incredible strength, and vast, unmatched knowledge. A feeling of durability, vitality, and near limitless energy. A feeling of age, a sense of eternity.

She, no Theta, stood atop a smoking snowcapped mountain, then in a boat on a roiling sea, in a desert, on a field of ice, in a forest glen—but somehow, this was all the same place, all the very same spot on Midgaard—as if the world changed, but Theta remained. As if he had walked Midgaard forever through all its epochs and geological upheavals. As if he were always here, immortal, everlasting.

The images shifted and churned, faster and faster again. Azura set her will against them and pulled them into check once more. She saw a woman that she loved grow old, sicken, and die almost within the blink of an eye, and her heart broke. All the people in all the lands began to age rapidly, so rapidly, and they grew sick, and weak, and died. They all died. But Theta remained; everlasting, ever strong, a warrior, a knight eternal.

Guilt beyond imagining assaulted her; a sorrow beyond all sorrows rended her soul, and a loneliness without end engulfed her. Worst of all, the helplessness and the anger it stirred within her. An anger that ever threatened to erupt. A simmering need for vengeance. Nothing she could do could stop the suffering and the dying. Nothing.

The images and sounds blurred and shifted again. A terrible sight came into focus. She stood now before a large portal, an unnatural gateway through which sprang and leaped and flew the very monsters of nightmare. There came dragons, black, red, winged and serpentine. Basilisks and bogart, demons and devils, hags and harpies, giants and djinn, minotaur and manticore, ghost, ghoul, and goblin, wight and warg, and countless more. All the monsters of legend, myth, and nightmare raced through that portal from Abaddon as she looked on.

The scene clouded again, and a chorus of voices began to chant. Most voices were strangers, but some were familiar, some were those of friends. Traitor, traitor, traitor they chanted. Slayer they marked him. Rebel, widowmaker, bogeyman, devil, prince of lies they called him. Great Dragon they named him. Harbinger of Doom they boomed. Harbinger of doom, harbinger of doom, harbinger of doom they chanted over and over and over again. That title of infamy echoed in her mind, no his, without end and through all time. Azura felt herself falling, falling into a bottomless abyss with no hope, no help, no friends.

Then before her, He stood. Azathoth. The ancient god himself, bathed in holy light. His arms outstretched to the sides, palms up, tears streaming down his kind and careworn face, the white of his beard lost in like-colored robes. He looked pained, wounded, suffering.

"Why?" said Azathoth, his voice unsteady. "Why hath thee betrayed me, my son? Why doth thou forsake me? You who I loved more than all others, how can thee turn to darkness, to evil?"

"Take my hand, Thetan. Take my hand and repent. Repent and all will be forgiven. All will be as it was."

Theta's hands came into view. But they were not bare. They held a sword.

Azathoth looked shocked, but then he seemed to grow and darken. His face became hard and terrible. "You have chosen the dark road, Thetan. Now your name will go down in infamy through all the ages. So must it be. Now feel my wrath and despair."

Theta bounded toward the god, so fast, faster than any man could move. But Azathoth was faster. His hand shot out and from it exploded a stream of blinding yellow fire that engulfed Theta.

Azura felt herself falling and screaming. An indescribable pain that threatened to tear her very soul from her body.

Azura's face stung. She opened her eyes and Gorb stood over her. She was lying on the floor. Did he slap me? Such things helped end the spell when things went bad.

The wizard knelt before her. He offered her something—a cup of water? She couldn't focus enough to be sure, and pushed his hand away. Her vision was blurred; her ears rang; and her thoughts raced, unfocused. Memory stormed back to her. *Harbinger of Doom!* She started and arced up into a sitting position. She began shaking uncontrollably.

It's him. Dead gods, it's him. The Harbinger of Doom. The lord of evil. Make them go away.

"Get out!" screamed Azura. "They've gone to Jutenheim. *The White Rose* has sailed to Jutenheim. Now get out. Get out."

The soldiers turned and left. The wizard bent down beside her. "I'm sorry, dear Lady, we did not mean you harm."

Azura grabbed him by the collar and pulled him close. She could feel Gorb beside her, tensed, ready to strike at her command. "He's the prince of lies, wizard."

Tanch looked confused. "What?"

"He's not what he seems. He's the bogeyman of legend. The Harbinger of Doom—it's him, your man, it's truly him."

Tanch stood up, a look of horror on his face.

"He will be the death of you, wizard. Beware him. He will be the death of us all. Go now, go. Never return here. Get out! Get out!"

Gorb stood, menacingly. Tanch fled the tower, Ob beside him.

After they were gone, Gorb lifted Azura into her chair. Her vision cleared, though a strange ringing still filled her head.

Gorb looks frightened. I've never seen him frightened before. The way he's staring at me; how odd. Dirkben and Rimel have the same look. Why?

Azura looked up and saw her reflection in the tall mirror across the room. Her long auburn locks now ran gray from root to end. She put her hands to head and grabbed at her hair in disbelief. *My*

604

hair, my face!

"No!" Azura screamed. "No, no, no!"

***

The group walked quickly through Azura's courtyard.

"What happened?" asked Artol. "We heard a woman's scream. Another minute and that door would've been splinters."

"The seer went bonkers and booted us," said Ob.

Tanch came up beside Theta as they made their way onto the street. His face was flushed and his voice harsh. "What did you do to her?"

"Nothing," said Theta.

"Tell that to her hair," said Ob. He turned to Artol. "It went white before our eyes. Mr. Fancy Pant's doing. Maybe we should introduce her to Slaayde."

Artol looked shocked. "What?"

"Nothing?" said Tanch. "It didn't look like nothing to me. She is a wizard of the Order, not an enemy. What did you do? I demand to know."

Theta ignored him, never slowing his pace.

"Answer me," said Tanch.

"Your back seems better today," said Theta. "Put your teeth together and it may stay that way."

"Enough," said Claradon. "We can discuss this back at the ship. We got what we came for and that's what's important."

XII
FREEDOM SQUARE

"Can I do any less?"
—Angle Theta

"**S**ome commotion up ahead in Freedom Square," said Ob. "That's where the main slave market was."

"Freedom Square?" said Dolan. "Why call it that if slaves were sold there?"

"Don't know," said Ob. "Never made no sense to me."

"Because evil oft denies its nature and pretends to be good," said Theta.

Tanch looked to Theta, searching his face.

"They never even called it slavery. They named it workhood or some such. Who did they think they were fooling?" said Ob.

"None but themselves," said Claradon.

"No," said Theta. "They fooled many, for many are fools."

Ob turned to Claradon. "Shall we see what's what? Just a few blocks out of our way."

"Alright," said Claradon. "But let's be quick."

The avenue opened up into a large square where many streets intersected. A noisy crowd was gathered. Men were up on the large, raised, wood platform upon which untold slaves had been exhibited and sold. For generations, the pirate lords of Tragoss Mor raided villages and cities and islands up and down the coast for hundreds, even

606

thousands of miles, taking what booty they could and capturing people for slaves. They brought them all there, for sale in Freedom Square to the highest bidder. Any land that had no trade treaty with Tragoss and that paid no tribute to them lived in fear of their attacks.

That day, dozens of Thothian monks stood on and around the slave platform. One spoke into a speaking-trumpet soon after the group entered the square.

"Come forward, citizens," said the monk. "We have rare goods for auction today." He gestured to his fellows and they opened the rear door of a large covered wagon beside the platform. The monks pulled out several people, their heads covered in hoods; their hands tied before them. Two were adults, a short male with a slight build, and a curvaceous female; the rest, mere children, little more than babes. The monks dragged the prisoners up onto the slave platform and lined them up for all to see.

Murmurings spread through the crowd.

"What's this?" shouted one man. "The freedom market was closed."

"Workhood is no more," shouted another.

"No," shouted several more citizens. Soon the whole crowd took up the chant, "No. No. No."

The lead monk, one Del Koth, a tall, thick man of bushy beard and yellowed teeth, motioned the people to silence.

"Don't be alarmed, good citizens," said Del Koth. "The freedom market is closed and will remain so. No man will ever be sold here again." He paused, took the measure of the crowd, and let them settle.

"But these creatures," gesturing toward the prisoners, "are not men." He turned to his fellows. "Remove their hoods."

The monks ripped the hoods from the two taller prisoners. Each had a strange greenish tinge to their skin and large, distinctive, pointy ears.

"Elves," shouted the crowd.

"Yes, citizens," shouted Del Koth. "Elves, wicked, wicked elves." He smiled in triumph. "The very servants of evil."

"Wood elves," said Ob quietly. "Half-blood at best; probably three-fourth's Volsung."

The monks pulled the hoods from the children, though children they were not. Each had a beard, a bulbous nose, and large ears. Adults all. Some were middle aged, some older—far from children despite their diminutive heights.

Ob's mouth dropped open in shock, then his expression turned into a snarl and his hand went to his axe.

"Imps," yelled the crowd.

"Yes, citizens, imps. Greedy, evil, imps." He surveyed the crowd; his smile grew.

Theta grabbed Ob's arm. "Stay your hand. There are too many of them."

Tanch looked in alarm at Ob and Dolan, their features all too resembled the prisoners. "We must be off."

"Far too long have we suffered these sub-human creatures amongst us," boomed Del Koth. "Imps hoard their wealth and share with none. Too long have they cheated us, and plotted and schemed against us. Too long have they held what should belong to us, what is rightfully ours. Too long have they acted as if they are our betters. They're not. They're little more than animals. They are creatures of evil and darkness and dirt. Enemies of our dear lord, Thoth, source of all good and light. We will suffer them in our midst no longer. No longer. No longer," he boomed, his fist upraised.

"No longer," came a shout from the crowd. Then another and another and still more. "They're all no good," shouted one woman.

"Kill the scum," shouted one man.

"And these," boomed the monk, pointing to the elves. "These fell creatures of legend still skulk in the dark woodlands and the sinister places where no goodly man would ever tread. You have all heard the stories of their fell deeds. They steal our children in the night or leave them dead in their cribs. They murder innocent travelers who have lost their way. We will suffer these atrocities no longer. No longer, I say. Now they will serve us. Now they will do our bidding."

Scattered cheers went up through the crowd from many parts of the square. Others booed and shouted, "No," but the monk's supporters outnumbered and out-shouted his critics and he smiled his yellow smile.

"Who will bid ten silver stars for this imp?" said Del Koth, pointing to the smallest in the line.

"I will," shouted someone."

"No," yelled several others.

"Stop this madness," shouted a tall, red-cloaked man near the slave platform. "Workhood is outlawed. Do not do this."

Theta and the group waded through the crowd toward the nearest side street leading in the general direction of the harbor. Dolan pulled his collar up to hide his ears as best he could. Ob, jaw clenched in anger, tried to stay hidden between his comrades.

"Imp," shouted a man that they passed. He grabbed at Ob. "Imp!"

"He's my servant, you fool," said Tanch. "Unhand him or my men will cut you down."

Artol shoved the man aside. He went down cursing.

The scene in the square rapidly turned into a riot as those that supported the monks and those against yelled and cursed each other. Soon after the group turned down an alley, they heard a clash of blades from the square. A melee had broken out. Many had joined in.

Theta stopped in his tracks at the fore of the group. Ob drew his axe and turned about. Artol grabbed Ob, to hold him back.

"We can't leave them to be sold like cattle," said Ob, "or slaughtered where they stand."

"We've no time for this," said Tanch. "It's not our fight. We have a mission. We've got to get back to the ship or we'll never catch *The Rose*, and Sir Jude will be lost."

The sound of steel clashing in the square and the twang and whoosh of arrows filled the air.

"There are men fighting to free them," said Ob, his face reddened. "Can we do any less? Can we?"

Claradon looked to Theta. "What do we do?"

Theta's eyes were closed, his expression grim.

"Lord Theta," said Claradon. "What should we do?"

Theta spoke slowly, seemingly to himself. "Can I do any less?" He spun back toward the others. He drew his falchion and pulled his shield from his shoulder.

"Theta, there are too many monks, you said so yourself, and more will surely come," said Tanch. "Only a fool would interfere in this. What're you going to do?"

"I'm declaring war on the Thothians." He strode down the alley. Dolan, bow in hand, followed on his heels.

"I love this guy," said Artol grinning. He pulled his massive warhammer from its shoulder sheath and followed Theta. "Whoo-ha!"

"A madman," mumbled Tanch. "He will be the death of us all."

Theta strode from the alley into Freedom Square—Dolan, Artol, and the others followed. The square was in chaos. People ran in all directions. Screams filled the air. A small group of men battled the Thothians at the foot of the slave platform. Scattered melees flared elsewhere about the square.

Theta and Artol marched directly toward the heart of the fighting and shoved aside any that got in their way. Several disheveled citizens with swords or daggers fled the battle, some bleeding and battered. Many of the Thothians had bows. They stood atop the slave platform and indiscriminately fired down into the crowd.

As Theta neared the slave deck, an arrow crashed into the center of his chest. It bounced off

611

his breastplate leaving neither scratch nor dent; two more shafts deflected off his shield, the steel too strong, too thick for such weapons to pose a threat. Theta didn't seem to notice the impacts; he didn't pause for a moment. He didn't even flinch. Artol held his shield high and ducked and dodged as the shafts flew by him, but his luck held, and not a one struck home.

Numerous citizens and more than a dozen Thothians were down or dead. A red-cloaked man hacked at the monks with a broadsword, several dead and dying at his feet. A handful of skilled swordsmen battled at his side, coordinated, a trained unit.

Theta and Artol bounded up onto the deck. Theta swung his falchion; Artol, his hammer. Two monks died from those swings, one cleaved in half, one's head smashed to pulp. Then two more fell—one thunderous blow took each. The remaining monks scattered before them. Dolan's arrows slammed into four monks in rapid succession, each pierced through the forehead, neck, or chest.

"Kill the workhooders," yelled Del Koth. "Kill them all," he boomed.

A volley of arrows streaked toward the two Elven prisoners. The male interposed himself in front of his companion and collapsed with three arrows in his chest.

Tanch charged the Thothians at ground level, aiding the red-cloaked warrior and his men, while Claradon and Ob leaped up and scrambled onto the slave platform. Wild-eyed, Ob charged straight for Del Koth, axe bared and gleaming.

Claradon ran toward the monks that menaced the fallen elves.

An arrow deflected off Ob's axe-blade as he approached Del Koth. He ignored the arrow and raised his ancient weapon over his head, his face contorted in fury. Del Koth brought up his scimitar to block the blow that thundered down on him with all the Gnome's strength. The mithril axe sheared through the monk's iron blade, and cleaved through his chest with a sickening crunch of bones. Ob landed atop him; a spray of blood lashed his face.

Del Koth's big hands closed around Ob's throat and squeezed. Despite his mortal wound, Del Koth's grip was iron, as was his resolve to take his slayer with him to the other side. Ob tried to pry Del Koth's hands from his throat, but the big monk was too strong, too desperate. Ob grabbed Del Koth about his neck and choked him back, but Del Koth's neck was all corded muscle, more likely that Ob could choke a tree.

"My wife," said Del Koth, coughing blood, now half delirious, his eyes glazing over. "My children. Dear lord, give me strength for my children. Save me."

Ob's face turned to blue; his head swam, but he could feel Del Koth's grip loosen, blood loss sapping his great strength. Moments more and Del Koth's hands grew limp, his breathing shallow, and then he moved no more. Ob didn't loosen his grip for a while more, just to be sure. Then he rolled over, gasping and coughing, covered in Del

Koth's blood, and tried to catch his breath.

Two monks charged toward the fallen elves. "Pull him off," yelled a fat monk.

His companion grabbed the male Elf by the collar and dragged his corpse off the female. Still bound and gagged, she lay helpless, whimpering, eyes darting from side to side, searching, almost pleading for some route of escape.

One monk raised his sword, an evil leer on his face.

The Elf's leg sprang out with speed and power—a vicious kick to the monk's knee that popped it out of its socket. The monk howled, collapsed, and toppled from the platform.

Claradon's sword slammed into the second monk, tearing through his chest. The monk dropped to his knees, clutching at his wound, trying in vain to stem the flow of blood. He looked up pleadingly, his eyes begging for mercy. Claradon lowered his sword and the monk lunged, dagger in hand, pulled from parts unknown. Claradon caught the man's wrist in his right hand and swung his sword. The blow took the monk's arm off, just below the elbow. A moment later, Claradon's sword slammed into the back of the monk's neck, severing his head.

The slave deck was clear. The corpses of more than a dozen monks lay broken and bloody about the wood decking. Even more lay dead amongst the crowd, most piled about Red Cloak and his swordsmen. Those monks that still lived, and were   able,   fled   the   square.

Two of the Gnome captives lay dead on the platform. Ob and Red Cloak's swordsmen got the survivors to their feet and cut their bonds.

The female Elf stood up, a dagger clutched between her bound hands, all fear gone from her oval face, which was exotic, stunning. Her eyes darted around, but there were no more monks to fight.

Frozen, Claradon stared at her. "Let me cut your bonds," he said, after some moments. Her eyes met his and lingered. She held out her hands. Claradon cut her free using the dagger she had found. "Come with us."

"Gladly," she said with an accent that Claradon couldn't place. Claradon held out his hand. She stared at it for a moment, surprised, even taken aback, then her expression softened and she put her hand in his.

"Let's   move," shouted Red Cloak. "The Thothians will be here in force in minutes. We must fly."

"Who are you people?" said Tanch.

"Who are you?' said Red Cloak.

Neither answered.

Whistles sounded in the distance. The monks had roused the city guard.

The group fled the square at a run. The Gnomes, elders amongst them, and weak as they were from their ordeal, had trouble keeping up. Ob stayed beside them, and soon shouted to Artol and Red Cloak's men to carry some of the weakest, which they did.

They sped through deserted alleys and quiet streets for some minutes before reaching a populated street that opened into a square, similar but smaller than the one they had just fled. Here, there were no captives, just carts of fruits, vegetables, pies, and sundries.

"Hide your weapons, and act natural," said Red Cloak. "Be calm." They crossed the busy square in three groups to garner less attention. The shoppers and shopkeepers chattered and speculated about what calamity the whistles harbored, but no one paid the group any heed.

They turned down Brick Street, a busy lane of well-appointed storefronts and filled with the pungent scent of spices of all varieties. Red Cloak led them halfway down the street, just passed a spice store with a large yellow awning. There, they descended a few stone steps to a cellar door.

Red Cloak knocked.

A small wood panel swung in and a man peered out. Satisfied with what he saw, he opened the door, and the group filed in.

They found themselves in a storeroom piled with sacks, crates, and barrels of salt, spices, and foodstuffs. Several men dressed in nondescript workman clothing stood about, tensed, swords in their hands. More men with swords came from the rear.

Ignoring them, Red Cloak proceeded toward the back of the room. "Follow me," he said over his shoulder. A door led to a huge warehouse filled with crates and barrels, far larger than the small storefront above. That basement extended under and well past the buildings to either side and behind. Red Cloak led them to a door on the far side of the warehouse, hidden behind a row of large crates.

The group filed into a sparsely furnished room with two wood tables and benches, and more crates and barrels. About ten of Red Cloak's men, all armed, and several armored in chain or plate, filed in behind them.

Red Cloak stood before them. He was tall, rangy, and broad shouldered but thin of face and waist. An old scar zigzagged down his right cheek, marring an otherwise handsome, if weathered face. A man of forty-five, perhaps older, with a bearing that commanded respect, and was accustomed to receiving it. "I am du Maris. Who are you?"

One of the Gnomes stepped forward, still winded and sweating from the run, though Artol had carried him most of the way. Old and stooped, his glasses had but one lens, his shirt torn, his lip bloody. "I am Snor Slipnet of the Clan Rumbottle out of the Good Hills. Those with me are my kinsmen." He bowed low before du Maris. "I thank you and your men for rescuing me and mine, except for Bindel and Brodle who were shot dead by those scum. Good lads were they. We are in your debt."

"You're welcome, Master Slipnet," said du Maris.

"If I may ask, why did you risk yourselves to help us?"

Du Maris straightened and lifted his chin. "Because all people have the right to live free, and should be judged by their actions, not the shape of their ears or the shade of their skin. Simple concepts, but beyond the Thothians."

"Tell me," said du Maris, "Why did you come to Tragoss?"

"We sailed on a caravel out of Kern," said Slipnet, "foolishly seeking adventure, though I'm afraid we found far more than we bargained for. At my age I should've known better," said the Gnome, staring at his feet. "I hesitate to ask, but—"

"We'll get you passage on a ship up the Hudsar. It may take a few days, but we will see you safely on your way home."

"I can't thank you enough. My clan will remember your service to us, du Maris of Tragoss Mor."

Du Maris ordered rooms prepared for the Gnomes. Slipnet and Ob shook hands and wished each other well before one of the guardsmen escorted the Rumbottles out.

Looking to Theta, du Maris said, "And who are you?"

Ob firmly pushed Claradon on the back.

Claradon began to speak. "I am—"

"I am called Sinch," said Tanch stepping forward. "A spice merchant out of Lomion, and these hulking brutes are my bodyguards."

"A spice merchant?" said du Maris. "It's not many a spice merchant that would risk his life to take on a couple score Thothian monks." Du Maris eyed some crates piled nearby him. He opened one, rummaged about for a moment and then pulled out a small cloth bag. He tossed it to Tanch. "Open it."

618

Tanch did so, and pulled forth a handful of something that looked like small dried berries.

"Name them," said du Maris.

Tanch studied the berries. He knew them not.

"Any spice merchant out of Lomion City would know," said du Maris," a hand on his sword hilt.

"Show us your armor," said Claradon, as he removed his traveling cloak, revealing his gleaming plate and chain armor beneath. "Come now, you don't think us so deaf not to have heard your armor clanking as we ran through the streets."

Du Maris stared at the crest etched on Claradon's breastplate. "You're from Dor Eotrus?"

"We are."

Du Maris removed his cloak, revealing armor similar to Claradon's. His men did the same.

"Church knights," said Ob.

"Sundarians," replied Claradon, the Elf woman by his side, her face sad, but proud.

Du Maris nodded. "I am Sir Hithron du Maris, of the Sundarians, as you have surmised."

Claradon put a hand to Tanch's shoulder and moved past him. "I know your family. A du Maris sits on the Council of Lords of Lomion."

"My uncle," said du Maris.

"I am Brother Claradon Eotrus, Lord of Dor Eotrus, and Caradonian Knight. These others are with me, save for this young woman whom we rescued in the square."

Du Maris studied Claradon. "A Dor Lord in Tragoss? That's a rare thing. Show me your signet and your shield."

Claradon held out his right hand. A golden ring

with the Eotrus family crest dominated his ring finger.

Du Maris approached, studied the ring for a time, and nodded.

Claradon pulled up his right sleeve to reveal a silver bracer embossed with an image of a small shield within which was inscribed the insignia of the order of Caradonian Knights.

Du Maris studied it, and then pulled a golden chain from beneath his tunic. From it hung a golden medallion in the shape of a small shield inscribed with runes. He displayed it before Claradon.

"I'm honored to meet you, Lord Eotrus."

"And I, you, Sir Hithron."

They shook hands.

"I'm from Dor Caladrill originally, so I know well the Eotrus name. Your noble family has safeguarded Lomion's northern border with honor and courage for many generations. Be at ease, you and yours are welcome here. Tell me please, what business brings you to Tragoss Mor?"

Claradon stared at du Maris for some moments before responding. "We're following a ship called *The White Rose*. She is a day out of port at least. My brother is aboard, a prisoner."

"Who holds him?"

"The Shadow League, we believe."

Du Maris nodded. "Long have black rumors swirled about that name."

"What is this place?" said Claradon, looking about the Spartan room. "A safehouse?"

"More than that. To outsiders, it's but the warehouse of a middling merchant. In truth, it's a

Sundarian Chapterhouse, the southernmost chapterhouse in all Midgaard, and rather secret, of course. I am its preceptor."

Du Maris's voice took on a grave tone. "Were you not who you are, or someone else I could trust, you would not leave this place now that you know what and where it is."

Claradon nodded. "I understand your caution; I've heard the Thothians arrest Churchmen on sight."

"That they do. Your men can be trusted, of course?" said du Maris, with a hint of a smile.

"Have no fear there. I expect the Thothians would enjoy arresting us as much as you."

"I doubt that," said du Maris. "We've many enemies here, amongst the monks, if not the common folk.

Du Maris looked to the Elf. "Young lady, what are you called?"

"I am Kayla. Kayla Kazeran."

"And how did you come to be a prisoner of the monks?"

"They attacked our ship. My brother and I were sailing down the Hudsar from the Linden Forest to sell our silks at Dover. A longship commanded by some monks attacked us." She looked down at the floor; tears welled in her eyes.

"The monks attack ships, now?" said Ob.

"They said we had no right on the river—that it's for Volsungs only. They demanded we pay them a toll—a hundred pieces of silver. The captain wouldn't pay and they put an arrow through his chest. Before we could pull away, they swarmed aboard, killing everyone without cause or mercy. Now only I am left."

"They've done much the same at least twice in the last month," said du Maris. "They grow bolder now that they've fully taken over Tragoss. My condolences for your losses, Miss. You've been through a terrible ordeal, but it's over now. You're safe here and we will see you safely home. The Linden isn't far from the Good Hills. You can travel with Slipnet and his clansmen. I will send some of my men along to assure that have no more trouble."

"Thanks, but no. There is nothing in Lindenwood for me to return to now."

"You can't remain in Tragoss Mor. As an Elf, it's just not safe."

"I'm only one-sixth Elf, or so the Lindonaire often remind me."

"That matters little to the monks. If you've any Elven looks, they mark you an Elf and that's that."

"Believe me, I've no wish to be in this accursed city one moment more than I have to. These monks are the worst of men. Their kind is why my people live apart from you Volsungs."

"Then what do you propose to do?" said Claradon.

She considered for a moment and turned to Claradon. "I know how to sail a bit, and to hunt with a bow, and I can wield a sword as good as most men. I will join your crew, if you'll have me."

Claradon's eyebrows rose. "I—well—I don't know—but—maybe—"

"That means, yes, in dumbass," said Ob. "About time there was a woman on this adventure."

"What about Bertha Smallbutt?" said Dolan.

"She doesn't count," said Ob.

"Why not?"

"Just because."

"**G**etting you back to your ship won't be so easy," said du Maris. "At the first sounding of the whistles, the watchmen will have closed the gates between the Harbor District and the inner city. Passing the gates is no small task. Solid iron, fifteen feet high, with a dozen guards defending it, and more but a whistle away."

"So if we hadn't stopped in the square to help free the captives, our butts would've been trapped on this side anyhow?" said Ob.

"More than likely, yes," said du Maris.

"So, how do we get through?"

Du Maris and his knights led the group through a narrow tunnel, dark and dank, deep beneath the streets of Tragoss Mor, torches held high to light their way. The tunnels went on and on.

"What are these tunnels?" said Claradon. "This is no basement or sewer."

"Tragoss Mor is an ancient place," said du Maris. "City upon city has been built on this ground, one atop the other. These tunnels are from olden days. They lead to most parts of the city. I can't take you all the way to the docks, as that branch of the tunnel has collapsed, but I will get you close."

"How did you find them?" said Claradon.

"We built them."

"The Sundarians?"

"Yes. My order has served here for long years. We use these passages to travel unseen. The citadel that the Thothians defile and call their temple was once our stronghold. Now we hide behind spice sacks, but the landscape will change again with the passing years. It always does. We will outlast them."

After a time, they came upon a side passage, barred off and posted with a sign that read, "No entry—beware the beast."

"What is that about, du Maris?" said Ob, after tipping his flask.

"There is a creature somewhere down that way. A demon. Something left over from the old world. No man goes that way and lives."

"Old friend of yours, Theta?" said Ob.

Theta ignored him.

"Guess we'll have to come back, eventually," said Dolan.

They traveled a goodly distance, and then turned down a side passage that ended at a rusty metal ladder bolted to the stone wall. Du Maris proceeded up and lifted a large flat stone banded with iron that covered the opening atop the tunnel. The group ascended and found themselves in a musty basement, unused and unkempt.

"I can take you no farther," said the Sundarian. "Above is an old warehouse, now abandoned. The western docks are about ten blocks due south."

XIII
NOT LONG FOR VALHALLA

*"Don't forget these words or
the Duelist with be the death of you."*
—Pipkorn

"Lord Theta, Mr. Seran is coming," said Dolan. "Up ahead."

"Dolan, you've got the eyes of a hawk," said Artol squinting.

Seran and two of his men approached, still several blocks away. They looked from side to side, searching, as they made their way down the avenue, which was only lightly crowded with pedestrians, carts, and the ever present street hawkers cajoling passersby into entering the shops that lined both sides of the street.

"There must be trouble," said Ob. "Everyone was supposed to stay with the ship."

Seran looked relieved when he caught sight of the group some moments later and dashed the rest of the way toward them, waving them toward the mouth of a narrow alley that put them out of sight of most prying eyes along the avenue.

"Lord Eotrus, Glimador sent us to find you. *The Grey Talon* berthed not two piers away from *The Falcon*. Her marines are crawling the docks, bristling for a fight. Somehow they know you're not aboard and they've sent patrols to scour the city for you."

"Is the ship secure?" said Theta.

625

"For now," said Seran. "But they aim to move on us, I'm sure. There are a lot of them and they have Kalathen Knights with them—more than a few."

"Dolan, see if anyone followed Seran," said Theta. Dolan pulled down the cap that covered his ears a bit farther, nodded, and slipped away, silent as a panther.

"Some followed," said Seran. "We lost them in the crowd back in the dock ward. We thought it worth the risk to warn you."

"You did well," said Claradon.

"It's the Alders behind this," said Ob. "Let's cut the buggers down. Darn it boy, you should've killed that old fart Barusa when you had the chance."

"His kinsmen would still be after us," said Claradon.

"Without stinking Barusa they would be lost. We're in the deep stuff, now. They'll be at least twice our number, perhaps more."

"Three or four times our number, I would say, from those I've seen," said Seran.

"And we can't count on Slaayde's crew to stand with us," said Artol.

"We've no time to linger here," said Theta. "We push through to *The Falcon*, fighting our way if we have to and put straight to sail."

"Agreed," said Claradon.

"And if we run into the Kalathens?" said Ob.

"We power through," said Theta.

The group marched down the avenue toward the docks. They had not gone two blocks before they were spotted by a *Talon* patrol that blew their

626

whistles, calling to their brethren. The group sped toward the docks at a run, citizens scattering in a panic as the armored men barreled through.

A dozen men clad in chain mail armor and black cloaks stepped out from the shadows and barred their path. A tall man in silvered armor stood at the fore.

"A Myrdonian," said Ob. "The Chancellor's men."

Claradon turned to Kayla as he drew his sword. "Stay back from the fighting and keep your head covered."

"Fine," said she sharply from beneath her cowl, though she drew a short sword that du Maris had given her.

The two groups moved together. Theta, Artol, Seran, and Claradon leaped out in front. Theta's sword flashed by quicker than the eye could follow. Artol's huge hammer smashed through the air, two, perhaps, three times. Six men were down, including the Myrdonian, as quick as that. The others scattered, running for their lives. Neither Claradon nor Seran even had time to strike a blow. What citizens were about screamed and scattered.

The group continued at a run toward the docks.

"They're on the roofs," said Ob. "Tracking us."

"I see them," said Theta.

"They're signaling ahead, they will be waiting for us."

Two blocks later, in sight of the ship, they

came upon another group of men that stood in a line across the street, blocking any path to *The Falcon*. Eight men in heavy armor; swords, axes, and shields in hand. The corpses of several Thothian monks lined the street. But for these dead and the men from *The Talon*, the street was deserted. The group pulled up, and readied their weapons.

"Kalathens," said Ob. "The big Myrdonian out in front is one of Barusa's brothers. Bartol or Blain, I think."

"Looks like they had a dispute with the Thothians," said Artol.

"Four more knights behind us," said Dolan, bow in hand, an arrow nocked.

"Hold your ground for a parley," said Bartol. At the sound of Bartol's voice, a group of soldiers streamed out of the buildings on either side—two dozen at least, several Myrdonian Knights amongst them. The soldiers wore the livery of House Alder. A number of them held crossbows, which they leveled toward the group.

"I am Bartol, Knight Captain of the Myrdonians, here on order of the Lomerian High Council. Make no foolish moves, men, as you can see, you're far outnumbered. There is no need for a battle here."

Bartol held up a piece of parchment. "This is a warrant, signed by the Crown, lawful and true, for the arrest of Claradon Eotrus and the foreign mercenary that accompanies him. They are accused of complicity in the death of Aradon Eotrus, lawful and true Lord of Dor Eotrus."

"Lies," yelled Ob.

"That is for the High Magisters to determine. I have been ordered to bring them back to face these charges and a trial, fair and equitable. If they're innocent, they will go free. They will be well treated, you have my word. Those that wish may even return with us, provided you turn over your weapons. The rest of you are free to go."

"Eat dung," yelled Ob.

Bartol winced at the remark, no doubt bristling at having to take such insults from a Gnome. "Listen to the imp, men, and you will all end up dead or in irons. We know your reputations and your skills, but you're outnumbered four to one, that gives you no chance. This writ is legal and true. There is no honor in standing against it. If you do, you stand against your country and your king. Eotrus and his man will answer to these charges one way or another. There is no need for any of us to die today."

"Go home, Alder, and take your stinking paper with you," said Artol.

Frustration filled Bartol's face. "Last chance, men. Turn over the upstart or die where you stand."

The crossbowmen each took a step forward, bows leveled.

Claradon didn't know what to do. His instincts told him to fight, but what if the warrant was valid? What if it was signed by the king? Even now, the army could be marching on Dor Eotrus, to confiscate his lands. What of Ector and Malcolm? Would they be arrested? Would they be killed? He may never be able to return home without risking being arrested on sight. But it couldn't be true. The Alders are schemers and liars; this was nothing more than a trick to get his men to turn against him.

He had to fight. Four to one odds were poor in the best of times, and today they faced a dozen Knights of Kalathen, some of the best trained blademasters in all Midgaard. The very mention of their order was enough to put most men to flight. Not to forget the Alder crossbowmen. At this range, armor would be scant protection. What to do?

Without a word, Theta strode forward, shield held high in his right hand, falchion in his left.

"Stop him," commanded Bartol.

Crossbows fired at Theta from the front and from both sides. Theta never slowed nor made any attempt to dodge. He merely shifted his shield to intercept what bolts he could. The heavy steel tipped projectiles made a loud pinging sound as they bounced off Theta's shield. Two bolts struck his plate armor but each ricocheted harmlessly away.

The remainder of the crossbowmen fired; their bolts equally ineffective.

"Charge!" yelled Ob.

And they did.

"Dead gods, this is the end," said Tanch.

Claradon ran forward yelling a war cry to Odin, his sword and shield at the ready. Kayla ran beside him. Men raced at him from all sides. Battle engaged all around. Before he reached the line of Kalathens, Alder men intercepted him from his right flank.

A sword crashed into his shield, numbing his arm for an instant. He struck back blindly and felt his sword strike a man's armor and bite into his flesh. He pulled his blade free, and blood splattered his face and tabard. He heard the man scream, but never did see his face.

An older man with a scarred face came at him, a sergeant in House Alder's guard by his uniform. Half Claradon's size was he, but wiry and quick as a cobra with his sword. Claradon fought on instinct, his sword slashing and stabbing, employing all the maneuvers that Sir Gabriel and Ob had drilled into him hour after hour in Dor Eotrus' battle square. Scar-face lunged in close with a thrust. Claradon dodged the blow and pummeled the man's face with his shield. Scar-face staggered back, his face crushed, his ruin of a nose spouting blood. Claradon didn't know where Kayla was, but he had to look out for her, to keep her safe.

Claradon saw Ob fighting not far away, his mithril axe chopped and slashed and then shattered his opponent's sword. Then he saw Kayla. She lunged in beside Ob and stabbed the man he was fighting through the gut. Apparently, she needed no protection.

Claradon saw Tanch club a man with his staff. The man's skull shattered with the impact; bits of blood and chunks of brain went flying.

The battle had taken Claradon into the mouth of an alley, just off the main avenue. Two soldiers of House Alder appeared before him, swords blazing, the wild in their eyes. They pressed him hard, coordinating their strikes. If not for his large shield, Claradon would have had no chance to parry the hail of blows. A lucky slash nicked one man's neck and he dropped back. Claradon took advantage of the momentary reprieve and hacked at the remaining man with all his strength. He beat the man back, raining overhand blows down at his head. When the man lifted his guard too high, Claradon's sword bit deep into his chest. The man grabbed at the sword, his eyes wide with disbelief as his lifeblood spurted out. Claradon kicked him in the chest and wrenched his sword free just as the second man lunged in again.

Ob crashed into number two, knocking him to the ground. As Ob moved to finish him, Claradon spun, sensing something behind him.

There stood death, gaunt, wild, and merciless. Kaledon of the Gray Waste, spear in hand, the battle lust of the barbarian burning in his black eyes.

Claradon had heard his name uttered in fear and fireside stories since he was small boy, though this man looked less than ten years his elder. The ponytail, the tattooed chest, bare and unarmored, there could be no doubt this was he. The Wild Pict they called him—a bounty hunter and professional killer. Here not to settle some score like the Alders or serve some political agenda, but simply for coin. Here to kill him for money.

Claradon took no comfort in the thought that sometimes a man's reputation is far greater than his prowess, for Pipkorn's warning echoed in his mind. Beware Kaledon—a foul sword master of mystical power.

There were no taunts or boasts, no bows or salutes. No nods of respect, no looks of regret at what now must be done. Nothing but death flared in Kaledon's eyes as he sprang like a tiger, leaping high into the air, his spear bound for Claradon's throat.

Claradon caught the blow on his shield and punched with it, hoping to break the shaft or even to smash Kaledon himself, but he hit only air. The Pict's thrust barely glanced the shield—a feint with no power behind it. Claradon felt something crash into the side of his helm. Then he was falling.

Claradon opened his eyes. He was on the ground. The battle sounds were strangely muffled. He looked up and saw Kaledon stalking toward him, spear held in both hands. Two more steps and he would drive the tip through Claradon's throat or a joint in his plate armor, and that would be the end.

Claradon yelled, "Odin," and Kaledon screamed some crazed, Pictish war cry as the barbarian raised his spear high for the deathblow. Claradon's mouth moved to form words almost of its own accord. Ancient words, words lost to all but adepts of the Caradonian Knights, words forbidden to be spoken except in dire-most need. Claradon spoke them quick, a few short words, that was all. A bolt of numinous energy, sparkling blue, sprang out from Claradon's hand and blasted into Kaledon. The Pict was flung through the air and slammed into the stout wall of a building many yards away.

Claradon's head was swimming. His helm was gone. Blood streamed down the side of his face.

More blood came from his nose; he tasted it in his mouth, gagged and spit.

The battle still raged throughout the avenue. At any moment, another enemy could enter the alley and he would be done for unless he got to his feet and cleared his head. He had to get up.

Claradon grabbed his sword and pulled himself up. He felt dizzy for a moment, but then it passed, though his head pounded. He backed up against the wall of the alley.

He saw Artol swinging his hammer and trading blows with a tall knight.

Four soldiers pressed Seran; their swords clanged against his stout armor as he desperately tried to beat them back.

Across the alley, a barrel and some crates fell over. Rising behind them was the Pict.

His chest was charred black and smoking, but still he stood, the same madness in his eyes. His spear was gone, but he drew a sword from his belt. He vaulted effortlessly over a waist-high pile of debris and advanced, seemingly unhampered and unfazed by the ugly wound to his chest.

Adrenaline pumped through Claradon; his heart pounded. I will finish this. I will not be defeated. The two warriors charged at each other, the young knight, full of honor and ideals, and the brute, savage and wild, cagey and relentless, unyielding as the sea.

Their swords clashed together: a thunderous blow that would have shattered lesser blades and numbed the arms of lesser men.

Then came the swordplay. Claradon's measured strokes were conventional, skillful, powerful, yet full of finesse. An expert was he, working sword and shield together as two halves of the same weapon, artfully wielding his shield as much for attack as for defense.

The Pict's way was altogether different. For him, swordplay had no styles or maneuvers to master; the sword was an extension of his arm, a part of his very being. He wielded it fluidly yet wildly, without thought or plan, attacking and reacting, all with the preternatural instincts of the barbarian, the primitive. His thrusts were cobra strikes; his slashes, lightning; his cuts, the swipe of a bear's claws. So fast was the Pict, that Claradon, for all his skill, could parry at best two of each three strokes. Ten seconds into their melee, Claradon would have been dead three times over, if not for his steel plate and shield. These and his art were his edge and he would use them unto the last.

The Pict's sword chopped off a third of Claradon's shield, nearly taking part his hand with it. His stabs and thrusts had bit into Claradon's armor at several joints, cutting his chainmail. Claradon felt blood flowing from several wounds, though none seemed bad. He couldn't match the Pict in speed or strength or skill and his armor was failing him.

Claradon roared and hacked and as the Pict dodged back, he gained just enough time to voice more words of power—his one chance to survive.

His words spoken, a bolt of translucent blue flame launched from the tip of his sword and arced into the Pict's chest. The Pict's whole body vibrated; all his muscles seemed to lock up for a moment, and then he staggered backward; the smell of burning flesh filled the air. Claradon plowed forward and slashed the Pict across the chest, biting deep into his flesh.

The Pict roared in pain and returned Claradon's strike as he fell, horribly wounded. The warblade slashed across Claradon's breastplate, cleaving through at the center. Claradon stumbled backward. Blood seeped through his armor soaking his tabard. How bad the wound was, Claradon could not yet tell. Dead gods, he thought, has he killed me?

Claradon felt afire as his amulet brightened and seared his chest.

"Eotrus!" boomed a powerful voice.

Claradon turned, dazed, his shield down, his sword hanging loose from its wrist strap.

But an arm's length away stood Milton DeBoors, the duelist of Dyvers.

Claradon saw the thrust, but had no time or strength to move. He watched the blade enter near the center of his chest, precisely where the Pict had shredded his breastplate.

Everything now moved in slow motion.

The sword sank halfway to the hilt, stopping only when it exited Claradon's back and slammed into the inside face of the plate armor protecting his rear.

Claradon stared down at the sword in disbelief, his mouth hanging open. Strangely, it didn't hurt, not until DeBoors slid the blade out again—then, there was nothing but the pain.

"Valhalla," he said.

Then Claradon Eotrus fell.

END OF VOLUME 3

####

EXPERIENCE MIDGAARD LIKE NEVER BEFORE

Are you ready to take up your sword and stand beside Theta, Ob, Claradon, Tanch, and the rest? If so, pick up your copy of the Audiobook for *Gateway to Nifleheim* or *Harbinger of Doom* – Volumes 1 through 3 today and begin your epic journey. Grammy award-winning narrator Stefan Rudnicki's magnificent performance will transport you to Midgaard and drop you straight into the fray! You'll feel like you're shoulder to shoulder with the heroes. Your heart will race when the fiends of the Nether Realms accost you. But never forget, in Midgaard, nothing is as it seems.

Get the Audiobook here:
http://smarturl.it/Nifleheim_Audio (US Link)

http://smarturl.it/Nifle_Audio_Foreign (Non US Link)

Thanks for reading *Harbinger of Doom*, Volumes 1 through 3. I hope that you enjoyed it, and that you will consider taking a few moments to return to where you purchased it to leave a brief review.

GLOSSARY

PLACES

<u>The Realms</u>
Asgard: legendary home of the gods
Lomion: a great kingdom of Midgaard
Midgaard: the world of man
Nifleheim: the realm of the Lords of Nifleheim. The very hell of myth and legend.
Vaeden: paradise, lost

<u>Places Within The Kingdom Of Lomion</u>
Dor Eotrus: fortress and lands ruled by House Eotrus, north of Lomion City
Dor Linden: fortress in the Linden Forest, ruled by House Mirtise
Dor Lomion: fortress within Lomion City, ruled by House Harringgold
Dor Malvegil: fortress and lands ruled by House Malvegil, southeast of Lomion City on the west bank of the Grand Hudsar River
Dor Valadon: fortress outside Dover
Dover: large city at Lomion's southeastern border
Dyvers: Lomerian city known for its quality metalworking
Lomion City (aka Lomion): capital city of the Kingdom of Lomion
Riker's Crossroads: village at the southern

border of Eotrus lands

Tammanian Hall: high seat of government in Lomion; home of the High Council and the Council of Lords

Temple of Guymaog: where the gateway was opened in the Vermion Forest

Tower of the Arcane: high seat of wizardom; in Lomion City

Vermion Forest: foreboding wood west of Dor Eotrus

Parts Foreign

Dead Fens, The: mix of fen, bog, and swampland on the east bank of the Hudsar River, south of Dor Malvegil

Grand Hudsar River: South of Lomion City it marks the eastern border of the kingdom

Emerald River: large river that branches off from the Hudsar at Dover

Minoc-by-the-Sea: coastal city

Tragoss Mor: large city far to the south of Lomion, at the mouth of the Hudsar River, where it meets the Azure Sea

PEOPLE

<u>High Council of Lomion</u>
Selrach Rothtonn Tenzilvel III: His Royal Majesty: King of Lomion
Aramere, Lady: Councilor for the City of Dyvers
Balfor, Field Marshal: Commander of the Lomerian army
Barusa of Alder, Lord: Chancellor of Lomion
Cartegian Tenzilvel, Prince: Selrach's son, insane
Dahlia, Lady: Councilor for the City of Kern
Glenfinnen, Lord: Councilor for the City of Dover
Harper Harringgold, Lord: Archduke of Lomion City
Jhensezil, Lord: Preceptor of the Odion Knights
Morfin, Baron: (reportedly dead)
Slyman, Councilor: Master of Guilds
Tobin Carthigast, Bishop: Representative of the Churchmen
Vizier, The (Rabrack Philistine): Representative of the Tower of the Arcane

<u>House Alder</u> (Pronounced All-der)
Bartol Alder: younger brother of Barusa, Myrdonian Knight
Barusa Alder, Lord: Chancellor of Lomion, eldest son of the House
Blain Alder: younger brother of Barusa
Edwin Alder: son of Blain

<u>House Eotrus</u>
The Eotrus rule the fortress of Dor Eotrus, the

Outer Dor (a town outside the fortress walls) and the surrounding lands for many leagues.

Aradon Eotrus, Lord: (pronounced Eee-oh-tro`-sss) – Patriarch of the House (presumed dead)

Claradon Eotrus, Brother: (Clara-don) Eldest son of Aradon, Caradonian Knight

Ector Eotrus, Sir: Third son of Aradon

Eleanor Eotrus: wife of Aradon

Gabriel Garn, Sir: House Weapons Master (presumed dead, body taken over by Korrgonn)

Jude Eotrus, Sir: Second son of Aradon

Knights & Soldiers of the House: Artol 'The Destroyer', Sir Paldor, Sir Glimador Malvegil, Sir Indigo, Sir Kelbor, Sir Ganton 'the bull', Sir Trelman, Sir Marzdan, Sir Sarbek, Harsnip, Baret, Graham, Sergeant Balfin

Malcolm Eotrus: Fourth son of Aradon

Ob A. Faz III: (Ahb A. Fahzz) Castellan and Master Scout of Dor Eotrus, a Gnome

Tanch Trinagal, Par: (Trin-ah-ghaal) of the Blue Tower; Son of Sinch; House Wizard for the Eotrus

House Harringgold

Harper Harringgold, Lord: Arch-Duke of Lomion City; Patriarch of the House; Lord of Dor Lomion

Grim Fischer: agent of Harper, a Gnome

Marissa Harringgold: daughter of Harper

Seran Harringgold, Sir: nephew of Harper

House Malvegil

Torbin Malvegil, Lord: Patriarch of the House;

Lord of Dor Malvegil.

Landolyn, Lady: of House Adonael; Torbin's consort. Half-elven.

Glimador Malvegil, Sir: first son and heir of Torbin, working under the service of House Eotrus.

Gravemare, Hubert: Castellan

Hogart: harbormaster

The Lords of Nifleheim

Azathoth: god worshipped by the Nifleheim Lords and The Shadow League

Arioch; Bhaal; Hecate

Korrgonn, Lord Gallis: son of Azathoth

Mortach: (aka Mikel) – killed by Angle Theta

The Crew Of *The Black Falcon*

Slaayde, Dylan: Captain of *The Black Falcon*

Bertha Smallbutt: ship's quartermaster

Fizdar Firstbar 'the corsair': former first mate, presumed dead

N'Paag: First Mate

Tug, Little: Near 7-foot tall half-Lugron seaman

The Crew/Passengers of *The Grey Talon*

DeBoors, Milton: 'The Duelist of Dyvers'. A mercenary

Kaledon of the Gray Waste: a Pict, mercenary

Kleig: Captain of *The Grey Talon*

Knights of Kalathen: mercenaries, work for DeBoors.

The Crew/Passengers of *The White Rose*

Rastinfan Rascelon: Captain of *The White Rose*

Ginalli, Father: High Priest of Azathoth, Arkon of The Shadow League.

Ezerhauten, Lord: Commander of the Sithian Mercenary Company

Finbal, Brackta: archmage

Frem Sorlons: hulking warrior, simpleton; Captain of the Pointmen

Hablock, Par: archmage

Lugron: hulking brutish humanoids

Morsmun, Par: archmage

Mort Zag: red-skinned giant

Ot, Par: archmage

Sevare Zendrack, Par: wizard

Sithians: sect of knights and soldiers, trained by Ezerhauten

Others Of Note

Angle Theta, Lord: (Thay`-tah) (aka Thetan) knight errant and nobleman from a far-off land beyond the sea.

Azura the Seer: Seer based in Tragoss Mor

Caradonian Knights: priestly order of knights

Dolan Silk: (Doe`-lin) Theta's manservant

Du Maris, Sir Hithron: Preceptor of the Sundarian Chapterhouse in Tragoss Mor; from Dor Caladrill

Einheriar: supernatural warriors

Kayla Kazeran: Part elvish woman from the Linden Forest

Myrdonians: Royal Lomerian Knights

Picts: a barbarian people from the Gray Waste

Pipkorn: (aka Rascatlan) former Grand Master of the Tower of the Arcane. A wizard.

Snor Slipnet: Patriarch of Clan Rumbottle; a

Gnome

Talidousen: Former Grand Master of the Tower of the Arcane; created the rings of the magi.

Thothian monks: monks that rule Tragoss Mor and worship Thoth

Vanyar Elves: legendary Elven people

Volsungs: men/humans

THINGS

Miscellany

Amulet of Escandell: detects presence of danger; Pipkorn's gift to Claradon.

Asgardian Daggers: legendary weapons created in the first age of Midgaard. They can harm creatures of Nifleheim.

Dargus Dal: Asgardian dagger, previously Gabriel's, now Theta's

Worfin Dal: "Lord's Dagger," Claradon's Asgardian dagger

Wotan Dal: "Odin's Dagger". Pipkorn's gift to Theta.

Axe of Bigby the Bold: Made of Mithril; given to Ob by Pipkorn

Dor: a generic name for a Lomerian fortress

Dyvers Blades: finely crafted steel swords

Ghost Ship Box: calls forth an illusory ship; created by Pipkorn.

Mages and Monsters: a tactical wargame using miniatures

Mithril: precious metal of great strength and relative lightness

Ranal: a black metal, hard as steel and half as heavy, weapons made of it can affect creatures of Nifleheim

Ring of the Magi: amplifies a wizard's power; one of twenty created by Talidousen

ABOUT GLENN G. THATER

For more than twenty-five years, Glenn G. Thater has written works of fiction and historical fiction that focus on the genres of epic fantasy and sword and sorcery. His published works of fiction include the first eleven volumes of the *Harbinger of Doom* saga: *Gateway to Nifleheim*; *The Fallen Angle*; *Knight Eternal*; *Dwellers of the Deep*; *Blood, Fire, and Thorn*; *Gods of the Sword*; *The Shambling Dead*; *Master of the Dead*; *Shadow of Doom*; *Wizard's Toll*; *Drums of Doom*; the novella, *The Gateway*; and the novelette, *The Hero and the Fiend*.

Mr. Thater holds a Bachelor of Science degree in Physics with concentrations in Astronomy and Religious Studies, and a Master of Science degree in Civil Engineering, specializing in Structural Engineering. He has undertaken advanced graduate study in Classical Physics, Quantum Mechanics, Statistical Mechanics, and Astrophysics, and is a practicing licensed professional engineer specializing in the multidisciplinary alteration and remediation of buildings, and the forensic investigation of building failures and other disasters.

Mr. Thater has investigated failures and collapses of numerous structures around the

United States and internationally. Since 1998, he has served as a member of the American Society of Civil Engineers' Forensic Engineering Division (FED) (formerly called the Technical Council on Forensic Engineering), is a Past Chairman of that Division's Executive Committee and FED's Committee on Practices to Reduce Failures. Mr. Thater is a LEED (Leadership in Energy and Environmental Design) Accredited Professional and has testified as an expert witness in the field of structural engineering before the Supreme Court of the State of New York.

Mr. Thater is an author of numerous scientific papers, magazine articles, engineering textbook chapters, and countless engineering reports. He has lectured across the United States and internationally on such topics as the World Trade Center collapses, bridge collapses, and on the construction and analysis of the dome of the United States Capitol in Washington D.C.

CONNECT WITH GLENN ONLINE

My Website:
http://www.glenngthater.com

To be notified about my new book releases and any special offers or discounts regarding

my books, please join my mailing list here:
http://eepurl.com/vwubH

My Twitter Page:
http://twitter.com/GlennGThater

BOOKS BY GLENN G. THATER

THE HARBINGER OF DOOM SAGA

GATEWAY TO NIFLEHEIM
THE FALLEN ANGLE
KNIGHT ETERNAL
DWELLERS OF THE DEEP
BLOOD, FIRE, AND THORN
GODS OF THE SWORD
THE SHAMBLING DEAD
MASTER OF THE DEAD
SHADOW OF DOOM
WIZARD'S TOLL
DRUMS OF DOOM
VOLUME 12+ (forthcoming)

HARBINGER OF DOOM
(Combines *Gateway to Nifleheim* and *The Fallen Angle* into a single volume)

THE HERO AND THE FIEND
(A novelette set in the Harbinger of Doom universe)

THE GATEWAY
(A novella length version of *Gateway to Nifleheim*)

THE DEMON KING OF BERGHER
(A short story set in the Harbinger of Doom universe)

THE KEBLEAR HORROR
(A short story set in the Harbinger of Doom universe)

#

Printed in Poland
by Amazon Fulfillment
Poland Sp. z o.o., Wrocław